THE ACADEMY

Making of a Ruler

C.C. Monö

Black Chair Publishing

STOCKHOLM, SWEDEN

Black Chair Publishing
Pilotgatan 42
Stockholm, Sweden

Publisher's Note: This is a work of fiction. Names, characters, places, and incidents are a product of the author's imagination. Locales and public names are sometimes used for atmospheric purposes. Any resemblance to actual people, living or dead, or to businesses, companies, events, institutions, or locales is completely coincidental.

THE ACADEMY/ C.C. Monö. – 2nd ed.
ISBN 978-91-983963-4-8

To Cindy, Zoey, and Emmy, who, despite all my hours at the computer, still seem to remember who I am.

"Everything in my own immediate experience supports my deep belief that I am the absolute centre of the universe; the realest, most vivid and important person in existence."

David Foster Wallace –
2005 Kenyon College Commencement Address

PROLOGUE

FOURTEEN MONTHS EARLIER

The young man sat in the dark, staring out the window across the room into the starless night. He'd been sitting there for hours, listening to the old grandfather clock as it ticked depressingly behind him. Outside, dense fog had swept in over the garden, and it swirled above the ground. He watched its graceful movements, using it as a distraction from the dark thoughts gnawing at the back of his mind.

At last, the phone rang.

"Yes?"

"It's been decided," a tired voice affirmed.

"And?"

"Listen, son, the others agree; it's an enormous risk."

"I know the risks, Father," the man said, wiping his clammy hands on his trousers. "We *all* know the risks, but what choice do we have?"

"It's the timing I'm worried about. We need to get a little stronger. Maybe we should wait another three years. Perhaps then..."

"Three years is a long time," the young man interrupted, his voice soft and respectful so as not to increase tension. "And while we may grow a little stronger, our enemy's strength will increase tenfold. We need to do this now before it's too late."

"Well, the decision has been made," the old man muttered. "I don't like it, mind you. No one does, but we'll go ahead as planned."

In the dark, the young man exhaled. He did it as much out of fear as out of relief. He was no fool, the task ahead wouldn't be easy, but it had to be done.

Standing up, he walked over to the window. "And the plan?"

"There's a plan. A brilliant, but complicated, one. I'll tell you about it tomorrow."

"All right, and when do we begin?"

"Begin? Son, it has already begun."

CHAPTER 1

Axel sat up in drowsy confusion. He threw a glance at the clock on his bedside table. 5a.m., on the dot! He sat without moving for a few seconds, straining to catch a sound in the darkness. At first, there was nothing. Then the doorbell let out an aggressive ringing that shredded the serenity.

"Mother of…!"

Axel threw the covers aside. It was Friday morning, a week in on the new year, and spring term wasn't starting for another two weeks. Most of his friends were still out of town on holiday, and those still in the capital were no early risers.

This can't be good, he thought, snatching a pair of sweatpants from a nearby chair. While wrestling them on, he impressed himself with feats of extraordinary imagination, coming up with various reasons for this early visit. Most of them weren't good. Maybe someone was ill or had died. Perhaps the house was on fire.

He kept fretting until he reached the door and peered through the peephole. Baffled, he furrowed his brow and grabbed his jacket from the coat stand to pull on before opening the door.

There was a brief moment of silence as he and the visitor regarded one another.

"Uh…" Axel blinked and glanced down the empty corridor behind the stranger. What the hell was going on? "Yes?"

The woman gave him a wide, dimpled smile and took a step forward, her green eyes locked on his. "Good morning, Mr Hallman. It is a great pleasure to finally meet you, sir." She had a tantalizing voice with a typical highborn-British accent. "I apologise for this rude intrusion, but we have a long day ahead of us."

Axel considered the woman. She was dressed in a black, tailored, business suit that did nothing to hide her well-shaped figure. Her blonde hair was pulled back in a French twist and when she extended her hand to shake his, a pair of diamond earrings glimmered in the cold, fluorescent light from the stairwell.

"My name is Nicole Swan. May I come in?"

Two conflicting thoughts collided in Axel's head as he shook her firm grip. The reasonable one argued that he couldn't let a stranger into his apartment. The less reasonable one, which was just as sensible from a twenty-two-year-old man's perspective, concluded that Nicole was drop dead beautiful and didn't look like a mass murderer.

"So, may I?" she probed, nodding towards his apartment.

Axel stepped aside as if commanded. Nicole strode into his apartment; a sweet, sensual scent wafting in behind her. The whiff of her perfume tickled his hormones, and Axel became terribly aware of his own appearance.

"Eh…" he began and ran a hand through his messy hair.

Nicole stepped into his small living room and gave him a charming smile. "So, would you prefer to get dressed *before* we talk, or vice versa? Either way is fine with me, sir."

Axel looked down at his open jacket.

"Oh…eh…before?"

"Splendid."

After pulling on a T-shirt and a sweater, Axel dashed into the bathroom. Seeing himself in the mirror, he let out a quiet moan. His grey eyes were red and puffy, and his hair a wild mess. It took half a bottle of gel to get it in to some kind of presentable state. After rinsing his face in cold water and dabbing his cheeks with too much aftershave, he hurried back into the living room.

Nicole had moved in to the kitchen and was leaning over the counter, pouring boiling water into a cup. She laughed when he entered. "That was fast, Mr Hallman. I hope you don't mind, but I've made us some tea. It'll be good for you, considering the weather." Returning the kettle to its base, she pointed at the second drawer by the door. "Could you please hand me a spoon?"

Axel frowned and considered the narrow drawer. Had that just been a lucky guess or did she know his cutlery was in the second drawer?

"Thank you." She accepted the teaspoon with a warm twinkle in her eye and fished out the teabags. Then, without hesitation, she opened the left cabinet under the sink and threw them in the dustbin.

Axel swallowed. This was beyond creepy. How did she know which side of the cabinet he kept the garbage can?

"There you go," she said a second later, handing him one of the steaming cups. "Black and strong with a little bit of milk and no sugar." Axel peered down at his cup with growing unease. Another lucky guess or did she know his tea habits? "It's Kericho Gold," Nicole continued, inhaling the sweet aroma rising from her cups. "Your favourite brand."

Axel frowned. Okay, no one could be *that* good at guessing. He took a tentative step forward, unable to decide whether he should be impressed or frightened by this strange woman's knowledge of him.

His confusion must have been evident, for Nicole let out a soft laugh. "Oh, I know a great deal about you, Mr Hallman. I know you study economics at Stockholm University, although I'm not sure you actually enjoy it. You go to the gym five days a week. You don't drink alcohol because you hate the taste of it and because it contains too many calories. Your father worked as a diplomat for many years, so you grew up abroad. You co-started the successful Talk Thirteen organisation in South Africa nine years ago. Six and a half years have passed since you returned to Sweden. You find turtlenecks itchy, and your favourite colour is blue. When it comes to literature, you prefer fiction, especially suspense novels and thrillers. You listen to most kinds of music, but prefer rap and hip-hop."

An overwhelming sense of dread gripped Axel by the throat and in the back of his mind, a tiny thought began clamouring for attention. What if this woman was a psychopath? A beautiful, British psychopath.

"I could go on," Nicole continued, glancing at her watch, "but we better get started. Our flight leaves at nine-thirty."

"Hold on." Axel felt his frustration bubble up to the surface. "I'm sorry, but what's going on here? Who *are* you and what do you want?"

Nicole laughed and gave him a polite bow without spilling a drop of tea from her cup. "Mr Hallman, I'm happy to inform you that you've been accepted to the Eagle King's Academy. It is my great pleasure to be the first to congratulate you."

Axel gaped at the woman. "B-b-but…" he stammered, shaking his head in disbelief, "that's not possible!"

CHAPTER 2

EIGHT MONTHS EARLIER

Axel was standing on the depressing underground platform at Stockholm University. It was a dreadful place to be on a day like this. Above ground the sky was a vast blue. The trees seemed to glow in the sun, their spring-green coats rustling in the wind.

It was one of the first sunny days of summer, and those who could were quick to embrace it. In the city, the streets and downtown docks were bustling with life. Around campus, pale students emerged with their computers and books, squinting at the bright light as they made their way to the nearby fields. There, where the bumblebees hummed and the smell of freshly cut grass lingered, they gathered in small groups to study, converse, and flirt with one another.

Yes, summer had arrived, but down here, deep underground, the air was still cold, damp, and raw. As was Axel's mood. He stared at his best friend in disbelief. Had the man lost his mind?

"You can't be serious."

"Of course I'm serious," Mikael replied. "Why would I make that up?" He glanced at his phone before pocketing it. "Anyway, it's just an application."

A group of students ambled by, engaged in a loud debate. They were so engrossed in their own conversation that they seemed oblivious to the world around them. One of them bumped into Axel, knocking his backpack off his shoulder.

"Hey, watch it," the woman growled and marched off before Axel had a chance to reply.

He gritted his teeth. The world was full of them; egocentric idiots who thought they were the centre of the universe. "It's not *just* an application," he said, readjusting his backpack. "You know that. If you're accepted, then you can't back out. They'll own you!"

Mikael pulled at his thin moustache and made a face. "Geez, Axel! Why'd I want to back out? It's the freaking Academy we're talking about!"

"My point exactly! People don't apply to the Academy unless they dream of becoming a tyrant. It's revolting." Axel paused, knowing he sounded angry beyond reason. "You don't want to become another Napoleon-wannabe, do you?" he asked, nodding towards the student who had bumped into him a few seconds earlier. "Aren't there enough tyrants in the world already?"

Mikael grinned while his eyes followed the departing woman. "Compared to many others, I think I'd be a rather good tyrant, don't you?"

"That's not funny. The people who study at the EKA are power-hungry narcissists trained to dominate others. Shit, we're supposed to fight that kind of behaviour, not encourage it."

"Oh, come on!" Mikael laughed. "Don't you ever get tired of being such a righteous do-gooder? You started Talk Thirteen and made it successful. How many hours have you spent on fundraising and securing donors? You're a hero, my friend. Isn't that enough?"

"Are you deliberately trying to piss me off?"

Mikael held out his hands in a sign of peace. "I'm sorry, I don't mean to piss you off. All I'm saying is that by being an Academy leader I will be able to make a real difference. And yes, I know there are tyrants in the world, but that's just bad leadership. Good leadership is what saves mankind from these tyrants."

Axel rolled his eyes in frustration and began drumming his fingers against the strap of his backpack. "God, you sound like one of their bloody commercials."

He regarded the large underground billboard that had started their discussion a few minutes earlier. "The Eagle King's Academy", it announced, in large, gold letters on a dark background. Below was the Academy Logo: an eagle with its wings spread wide, a golden crown on its head. "Apply before the 30th of June," it read at the bottom.

There was no need for any additional information. Everyone knew what the Eagle King's Academy was.

The EKA, or the Academy as most people called it, had been established eighteen years ago. Its objective was to turn ordinary students, between the ages of twenty-two and twenty-five, into powerful, global leaders.

Axel glared at the eagle on the poster, who glared back. Everyone seemed to agree that the Academy was the world's number one leadership-training institution. Experts said it had revolutionised the entire industry, and *no one* disagreed. Axel might just be the only person on the planet who *didn't* like the Academy. In fact, it represented everything he hated: dominance; superiority; control and power. Why would Mikael be attracted to such things? He was a kind, warm-hearted, intelligent guy. Sure, he could be a little unconventional at times, no doubt about it, but he wasn't stupid. This made no sense at all.

Axel peered at his friend. They were an odd pair, the two of them. Axel was tall and lean, with wide shoulders and a large chest. He had golden-brown hair, a square jaw, and striking, grey eyes that he knew many women found attractive.

Mikael, on the other hand, was blond, skinny, and short. A straw with arms, Axel thought. He concluded that, even with that dead earthworm glued to his lip, his friend looked fifteen rather than twenty-two. No moustache in the world could change that.

Yet, despite their physical differences, the two of them usually had the same perspective on things. That was why Mikael's behaviour was so disturbing. It was out of character.

Axel peered into the tunnel. Where was that damn train?

* * *

With all the technology in the world, nothing could beat the traditional form of eavesdropping; being there, watching, listening, and observing. It was an art form and some were better at it than others.

The inconspicuous man pulled his cap down a little lower, hiding the tiny scar above his right eye. It'd been years since he'd done this kind of work, but he felt confident, excited even. He knew he could melt into a crowd like a drop of water in a pond. It came natural to him, which was why they'd asked him to do this. The Box needed him. This was a delicate assignment, and they needed someone who spoke the language.

The observer took a casual step towards Axel and his friend. The platform was filling up with loud students and he was struggling to hear what the two men were saying.

"Aren't you the least bit tempted to apply?" came Mikael's voice. "We have one shot. By the next application period, we'll be too old."

While fidgeting with the strap of his backpack, Axel shifted his weight from one foot to the other and back again.

He's genuinely not interested in the Academy, the observer thought in amazement, moving a little to the side so the camera in his shirt button could catch the young Swede's facial expression. Maybe the others are right. Maybe he's our best choice.

"I'm so bloody tired of constant talk about leadership," Axel muttered, shoving his hands in his jeans pockets with force. "Everyone wants to be a leader, an EKA leader in particular. It's just selfish. All they want is power."

Mikael continued with his ridiculous habit of pulling at his moustache. "I disagree. If I am accepted, I'll have the chance to make this world a better place. Anything I'd say would be valued. Anything I'd do would get attention. I would be able to influence the entire world. How can that be bad?"

"Are you serious?"

"Yeah."

"Because no one should have that kind of power," Axel barked. Then, as if someone had just pierced his bubble of fury, his shoulders slumped a little and his eyes fell upon his feet. "It's just plain wrong."

Mikael shook his head.

"People need someone to lead them. It's human nature."

"Christ," Axel moaned. "You've lost it, haven't you?"

"On the contrary, but I'm beginning to question *your* sanity. EKA graduates are already running key global organisations. They've built the most successful companies in the world. They'll solve our environmental problems, end wars, and improve living standards for millions of people. They're our future and people love them. They're good leaders."

"They're powerful, that's what they are! What happens if the Academy trains the wrong kind of person?"

The observer smiled. Good question, he thought to himself, but Mikael showed no appreciation for the question. He just laughed.

"The wrong person? Are you aware that more than a hundred thousand people entered the application process last time? This year they expect twice as many. Out of all these people they choose twelve students. So, no, Axel, the Academy won't accept anyone who can't handle power." For the first time since they began their discussion, Mikael let his frustration show. "Why are you so upset, anyway? I'm the one applying, not you."

Axel shuffled his feet in silence for a while. His demeanour began to change. For a moment, all he did was stare at the ground, poking at a dark spot with his shoe. Then he began to mumble something.

Damn it. The observer hesitated, then took a small step towards the men. Any closer and they would notice him.

"...and for the past three months, my dad has been pressuring me to apply," he heard Axel whisper. "It's driving me crazy. We can't have a single conversation without him bringing it up. His argument is always the same; I can't make any difference in the world without power, and the only way to get any real power is by becoming an EKA leader."

"Maybe he's right, Axel?"

"Or maybe he's a bloody moron."

CHAPTER 3

PRESENT DAY

Axel felt empty inside, as if someone had sucked his brain out of his head. It was an awful feeling. At one point, he almost expected to hear an echo between his ears every time he took a breath.

I need to think, not panic, he reminded himself, although there were parts of him that found this strategy difficult to accept. If there was ever a moment to panic, it was now.

"You look pale, Mr Hallman," Nicole said, sounding more amused than concerned.

Why me, Axel pondered with despair. There must be thousands of people who are better qualified than I am; people who *want* to become leaders.

"Are you sure about this?" he asked with a whisper.

"Most definitely, sir." Nicole said, laughing, before tilting her head. "Do you want a glass of water?"

"Yes, please." Axel watched with unease while Nicole picked the right cupboard without hesitation, taking a glass from the lower shelf. She knows everything about me, he thought with dread. They must have studied me for months, even broken into my home, so how in the world did they miss my true feelings about leadership? "I don't understand," he croaked. "I thought I just did the first four steps of the application process."

"No, sir," Nicole replied and walked over to the sink. "You did them all."

"I thought I'd failed."

"Well, you didn't," Nicole affirmed with a merry voice, handing him a glass of cold water. "You're one of the twelve, and we're all waiting for you at the Academy."

Axel emptied his glass in one go. The cold liquid washed through his system, and his mind began to clear. There was but one person in the world who could help him right now. "I need to call someone," he said, bolting out of the chair, still holding his glass.

With surprising speed and strength, Nicole's hand shot out and grabbed him by the wrist. Her smile had vanished.

"Mr Hallman, your parents and sister are being informed as we speak. You can call them later."

"I'm not calling my parents."

"Should I remind you, sir, that you've signed form AG14, stating that, if accepted, you'll refrain from contacting or communicating with any form of media until after graduation?"

Axel shook his head to the point where he began to resemble an aspen leaf in a storm. "No, no, no. I'm not calling the media! I'm calling Mikael!"

Nicole released her grip. "Ah, your friend," she said, taking his empty glass from his hand. "Well, you can rest assured that anyone who needs to know about this change of yours will be informed, and this includes your friend. He's busy filling out the relevant forms at the moment, so you can call him from the airport."

"He's filling out forms?"

"Yes, regarding confidentiality. He's your closest friend, is he not?"

"Yes, but…"

"And you don't have any other friends, do you?"

"What do you mean? Of course I have other friends!"

"Hmm, let me rephrase, sir. Other than Mr Mikael Andersson, do you have any *close* friends?"

"Not as close as Mikael, but I *do* have other friends," Axel said, feeling a strange need to defend himself.

"Then you have nothing to fear, Mr Hallman. With the exception of your immediate family and Mr Andersson, no one will know the truth until you graduate. In a few hours, we'll spread the news that you have taken on a job abroad as a volunteer for a small NGO. You can trust us, Mr Hallman. We've done this for years and have never failed." Nicole took a sip of her tea, watching him over the rim of her cup. "Providing you follow our rules, you and your family will be protected."

Axel stood by the kitchen door, his arms hanging loosely by his side. The tiny boost of energy he'd felt a minute ago escaped him, leaving nothing but a sense of resignation. And so it begins, he thought. My life is over.

From a pocket inside her suit jacket, Nicole pulled out a few papers. "Speaking of rules, I need a signature here." She held out the bottom page along with a pen.

"What is it?"

"Oh, this is just a formality. We need a signed consent stating that, from now on, you'll tell no one, not even your friends and family, about what you see or do at the Eagle King's Academy." Nicole pointed at a dotted line. "You just sign there."

"Shouldn't I read it first?"

Nicole laughed. "You should, sir, but I'm afraid we don't have the time. We've wasted it on small talk."

"But I think I should read the document first."

"Why? You read all the security documents when you applied, didn't you?"

"Yes."

Okay, so that wasn't true. Axel had just read a couple of documents in the beginning of the application process. There had been so many, and since he couldn't imagine the Academy accepting him, it had seemed like such a waste of time to read them all.

"Then you must know we demand a signed contract," Nicole continued, her face now grave. "Really sir, we don't have time for this."

Frustrated, Axel grabbed the document. What choice do I have, he thought, signing the damn thing. He handed it all back to her, and she accepted it with a nod.

"Thank you, Mr Hallman. Now I should inform you that if you break this contract, whether by intention or not, you *will* be kicked out of the Academy and taken to court."

"What?"

"There we will do our very best to ensure that you are jailed as well as economically ruined for the rest of your life."

Axel began to sweat. Was she serious? Could they even do that?

"The Academy does not take lightly on breached agreements," Nicole continued, putting her cup in the sink. "Perhaps next time, you'll be a little more persistent when someone hands you a contract."

Axel felt his cheeks begin to blush. He should have known better. His father always said that a smart man "checks his receipts and never signs a document he hasn't read".

"You said there was no time," he protested.

"Never let anyone pressure you into making bad decisions, Mr Hallman. As a global leader, *you* decide if there's time or not. There can be no excuses. You are the one who'll face the consequences of your actions." She paused, giving him a tiny smile before leaning forward and placing a hand on his shoulder. "I want you to remember something, Mr Hallman," she whispered. "At the Academy you're *always* evaluated. Even when you least expect it."

CHAPTER 4

Nicole wore an expression of sly amusement. "Any questions?"

"Yes," Axel said, "I have about a million of them." But where would he begin?

"Anything about confidentiality?"

"What about my family?"

"They're being informed at this very moment. All you need to focus on right now is packing your bag. I've a packing list. You'll be wise to follow it."

Nicole retrieved a small envelope from her pocket and handed it to him. It was a black envelope with the well-known Academy logo on the front; a golden eagle with its wings spread and a crown on its head. It contained a handwritten gold card.

Dear Mr Axel Hallman,

Congratulations! We are delighted to have you join us as a student at the Eagle King's Academy. You are advised to bring the following:
- Personal items such as photos or jewellery
- Passport
We look forward to meeting you soon.

Yours sincerely,
Mr Henry Milton, Concierge Manager

Axel read the note twice.

"Is this a joke?"

"No, sir. Why would you think that?"

"Well... It says I should bring 'personal items'."

"That's an option, sir. The passport, however, *is* a requirement."

Axel glanced around the room. He couldn't think of anything to bring except the book he was reading and his favourite sneakers, if you could call them "personal". He read the note again.

"No toothbrush?"

"No need, sir."

"What about trousers? Shoes? Sweatshirts?"

"No."

He grinned. "Underwear?"

Nicole smiled and turned for the door.

"No, sir."

"Then where in the world are we going?"

"You'll know soon enough."

Axel shook his head. "It better be a warm place if we're going to be walking around butt naked," he mumbled.

Nicole laughed but chose not to answer.

"Wait, are we coming back here?" Axel asked, hurrying after her.

"No."

"So who's going to water my plants and feed my fish?"

"No need to worry about it, sir. We have it all organised. We'll take care of your apartment, including your plants, fish and any expenses until you decide what you want to do with it all. There's no rush. Your only focus should be on graduating from the Academy. As I'm sure you already know, failure is not an option."

* * *

Large snowflakes fell from the dark sky, heading aimlessly for the car park below. At the edge of the parking lot, hidden among shadows and shrubs, stood a weathered-face man in his late-thirties. His piercing blue eyes scanned the surroundings like an eagle searching for prey. The tiny scar above his right eye itched under the black knitted hat. He ignored it, just as he ignored the fact that his shoulder-length hair, light brown with streaks of grey in it, clung wet to his neck.

The man rubbed his frozen hands together while keeping a trained eye on the black Volvo parked outside the entrance of the building. He tried to relax, embracing the cold as if it was a friend rather than an enemy. Many years ago, during his training, he had a sergeant who would argue that the idea of being cold was a very human concept. "Animals just accept the world as it is," he had said, "cold or hot, comfortable or not, they accept it. A true soldier must learn this skill; to embrace the environment he works in. You don't want two enemies, do you?"

For almost an hour the observer stood motionless, letting the heavy snowflakes settle on his head and shoulders. When Nicole finally exited the building, Axel was at her side, a backpack over his shoulder. She whispered something to him and he nodded. The observer knew what she was saying, "Don't mention the Academy or anything connected to it while we travel."

The driver of the black vehicle opened the rear door and Nicole slid in. Axel placed his backpack in the trunk and joined her.

A smile found its way to the observer's lips. He waited until the car began to move, then pulled out his phone and dialled a secret number.

It rang twice, then:

"Yes."

Thor stepped out onto the parking lot.

"We've got him, sir," he said in his calm, husky voice, forming a tiny cloud with his warm breath. "Everything went as planned. Phase one is now complete."

CHAPTER 5

They rode in silence. Nicole kept herself busy with her smartphone, leaving Axel to himself. He gazed out the window, feeling oddly calm as he watched the snow-covered city pass by. He suspected it was the warmth of the car and the humming of the engine that lulled him into this false sense of serenity.

His right pocket began to vibrate. He pulled out his buzzing phone, only to see it was his father, the last person on earth he wanted to talk to right now. No doubt excited at the prospect of having an EKA leader for a son, he was probably calling to offer some last-minute advice. "Don't embarrass me, Son", or "make sure you graduate!"

Damn you, Axel thought, and turned back to the window. This is *your* fault. He let the call go to voicemail, knowing it would annoy his father. That gave him a bit of pleasure.

It didn't take long before the phone began to buzz again, but this time it was Mikael.

"…rue?" came his friend's excited voice.

"Excuse me?"

"I said, is it true? Have you been accepted?"

"So it seems."

"I can't believe it! You're one of the twelve!" Mikael let out a roaring laugh, which Axel imagined left his little moustache bouncing up and down like a cowboy on a bucking horse. "Shit!" he cried. "You're going to be famous!"

"I guess." Axel cringed.

"This guy knocked on my door about an hour ago," Mikael continued, "all polite and formal. He said the Academy had accepted you. *You!* I couldn't believe it. I thought he was lying until he pulled out a big pile of security documents that I had to sign." He laughed again. "Man, this is surreal! Do you know where you're going?"

"No, not yet."

It was one of the Academy's many well-known eccentricities: to move their operation from one location to another every third year. That way they could keep their students anonymous and protected during their studies.

Mikael paused, as if just now realising his friend's predicament. "I know this isn't what you wanted, Axel, but it *is* an amazing opportunity. You understand that, don't you? There are people who would kill to be in your shoes. You're incredibly lucky."

Axel didn't feel lucky. Not at all! "Listen, Micke," he said, feeling a great urge to end the call, "I need to go."

"Really?"

"Yeah. I'll call you when I get a chance."

There was a momentary but uncomfortable silence.

"Man, this is so unfair." Micke sighed with genuine envy. "And worst of all, you don't even realise it."

The car came to a stop outside the Royal Dramatic Theatre in central Stockholm. Axel looked out the window and then turned to Nicole. He hadn't expected this.

"Have you set up the Academy here?" he asked, perplexed.

"Of course not, Mr Hallman." She laughed. "I just want to show you something." She grabbed her coat and glanced at her gold Rolex. "Wait here," Nicole said to the driver, "we'll be back in thirty minutes."

Without expecting a reply, she opened her door and, in one fluid motion, slid out. A cold, whirling wind blew into the car, bringing with it an army of wet snowflakes. Axel winced and was quick to pull on his jacket. With hunched-up shoulders, and a far less graceful exit, he followed Nicole out into the early morning darkness.

"I did a little research before picking you up," she explained with a cheerful manner while they trudged up the snowy staircase towards the main entrance. "This is an art nouveau building, designed by Fredrik Liljekvist, and opened to the public in 1908. I love the exterior design, the statues, the gold…"

Nicole continued to give him facts about the building as they ascended, but Axel wasn't listening. While the snow spun around them, Axel's mind wandered to more pressing matters.

He knew he had many good qualities. He was well-educated, well-travelled, and a good conversationalist when he wanted to be. As the child of a diplomat, he knew how to behave among people of all ages, cultures, and classes, and his mother had always said he had integrity.

Of course, none of this was enough to get him into the Academy; not by a long shot. To become an EKA student, you had to be *special*, and the only thing special that Axel had done was Talk Thirteen. But somehow that didn't seem enough.

Nicole dusted the snow off her coat. They had come to a stop in front of a large wooden door with glass windows. She leaned forward and rubbed some of the frost off the glass. "All right, Mr Hallman," she said and gave him a little wink, "let's see if anyone's home."

CHAPTER 6

Nicole peeked in and knocked. It took a few seconds before a man, bent by age and hard labour, came shuffling out of the dark with a flashlight in his hand. He pressed his wrinkled face against the glass door and gave Nicole a suspicious look. Then, with a visible sigh, he opened the door and waved them into a large, marble-cladded room with gold embellishments.

The old man scuffled past his visitors, muttering as he went. After a few steps he beckoned them to follow with a sloppy hand gesture. Nicole pursed her lips but didn't say anything. They began a sluggish procession up some broad stairs and through dark corridors until they reached an old, wooden door.

"Here," the old man said, puffing and panting as he raised a finger and waved it at Nicole. With narrow eyes and a stern expression, he spat out a few sentences in Swedish. When he was done, he turned and slouched off into the darkness.

Nicole frowned and turned to Axel. "Would you mind translating that for me?"

Despite the situation, Axel smiled.

"He said we have thirty minutes at our disposal. After that he'll throw us out."

"A feisty old fellow, is he?"

"You could say that. He also told us not to do anything…dirty in there."

"Dirty?"

"Yes, you know, 'dirty'."

"Oh…" For a couple of seconds Nicole seemed stunned. Then she filled the hallway with warm laughter. "What a charming, well-mannered, and perverted old gentleman," she said. "I'm sure he's a favourite among the ladies." She shook her head and opened the door with a grin. "I guess we better hurry then, Mr Hallman. We have twenty-nine minutes left, which is short, even if we skip the sexual bits." She laughed. "After you."

They entered a dimly lit room, which turned out to be one of the top balconies of the theatre. From there, they had a good view of the large stage below. Axel scanned the great open space. He had been here before, many years ago. His grandmother had taken him to see a performance he no longer remembered the name of.

"This is the main stage," Nicole explained, as they reached the balcony railing. "It's not very big, I'm afraid. A meagre seven hundred and seventy people can fit here."

Axel eyed the empty seats below.

"You find that small?"

"So will you in a few years' time. Nevertheless, it's a perfect size for our purpose."

Axel clutched the railing.

"Which is?" he asked with dread.

"Two and a half years from now, on June fifteenth, you'll step up on that stage to deliver your graduation speech. The audience will consist of the Swedish royal family, top Scandinavian politicians, and the most influential businessmen and women in this region. Everyone else will have to view the speech on TV."

Axel stood dumbfounded, staring at the stage as her words sunk in. The graduation speech; he hadn't even thought about that. Seven hundred of the most important people from the region would be there, all of them keen to hear him speak.

I can't do it, he thought, squeezing the railing until his knuckles whitened. He dropped into the chair behind him. My father will kill me, but I'll have to tell her the truth. I have to tell her now, before we reach the Academy. After that, it'll be too late.

Leaning against the railing, Nicole watched him with interest.

"You shouldn't worry, sir," she said in a kind attempt to calm him. "You are entering the Academy. By the time you walk out on that stage, giving speeches will be as natural to you as drinking a glass of water." She left the railing and took a seat next to him. "I know this because the Academy *never* fails. We will turn you into one of the most important individuals on the planet. People won't only know you, they'll glorify and respect you. They'll turn to you for guidance and strength. Yes, people will expect many great things of you, Mr Hallman. And you *will* deliver."

If Nicole intended to comfort Axel, she had failed miserably.

"That's great," he wheezed and clasped his hands together in front of him. "I know you're good at what you do."

"Indeed we are," Nicole replied and turned as the door behind them opened. A man stepped in from the darkness, carrying a coat over his left arm as he moved towards them with confidence in his strides. Nicole stood up and straightened her suit.

"As mentioned, Mr Hallman, people will expect great things from you in the future. I'd like you to meet one of those individuals."

She strode over to the approaching man. Axel's jaw dropped.

"Good morning, Mr Prime Minister," said Nicole. She gave the man a formal embrace. "It's nice to see you again."

"Likewise, Ms Swan. I take it this is our nation's hero-to-be, Mr Axel Hallman." Axel stood dumbstruck as the tall, round-faced prime minister offered his hand. "It's a pleasure to meet you, Axel."

Nicole excused herself, claiming she needed to make a few calls, leaving Axel alone with a man he'd seen hundreds of times on television but had never met in person. Now what? Axel watched the door close behind Nicole. What does one say to a prime minister? It had to be something unusual, something befitting a person who was about to enter the world's most prominent academy.

The seconds ticked away and Axel began to sweat. He could feel the awkwardness grow.

"So," he began, wiping his sweaty palms against his trousers in a quick and discreet motion. It was time to say something. *Anything.* "I see you don't have any bodyguards with you," he blurted.

For a second, the prime minister appeared confused. He stared at Axel before letting out a wholesome and hearty laughter.

Axel closed his eyes. Bodyguards? Really? Was that the best he could do?

"I meant…your safety," he stammered, knowing he was coming across as a complete idiot.

"It's very kind of you to prioritise my safety," the prime minister said, patting Axel on the shoulder, "but don't worry, I'm well protected." With an amused expression on his face, he nodded towards the seats in the front row of the balcony. "Shall we?"

CHAPTER 7

The prime minister sniffled and pulled out a handkerchief. "I blame the Minister for Finance," he said before blowing his nose. "She had a terrible cold last week when she came to my office."

Axel tried to smile, but he was so nervous it probably came out as a sneer. After his pathetic attempt to say something clever, he had decided to remain quiet until spoken to.

The prime minister tucked his handkerchief into his pocket.

"Anyway, let me start by congratulating you. You are the first candidate from Scandinavia that the Eagle King's Academy has ever admitted. What an achievement."

"Thank you," Axel managed.

"No, it is *I* who should thank *you*. Sweden is a small country. We do well in global terms, yet we're not recognised as being a country of importance. It seems size still matters." The prime minister chuckled at his little joke. "It's a shame, though. I believe we have a lot to offer this world," he continued. "But to do so, we need to get more of our citizens into key international positions. Now, here you are, just about to embark on a journey that will take you to the very top of global power and hierarchy. That means you'll also represent Sweden, and we're very proud of that."

Axel felt his cheeks begin to redden. "It's kind of you to say that," he mumbled.

"No, young man, I'm being honest. And I want you to know that if there's anything I can do to help you along the way, just let me know." The prime minister handed Axel a card with nothing more than a telephone number on it. "You can reach me on that number." He sniffled. "Who knows when you might need a friend outside the Academy?"

Axel accepted the card as if it was the most delicate thing in the world. Had the prime minister just offered him his friendship? The thought was mind-numbing.

He studied the card and its shiny, thick paper. Hmm, it was almost as thick as a credit card. Was that normal for a business card?

"It's very special," the prime minister whispered and leaned in, his eyes darting between Axel and the stage below. "It gives you access to me any time, any day, no questions asked."

Axel looked up and met the eyes of the man who ruled his country.

"I'm honoured," he admitted, "but...you don't know me."

"The Academy chose you, Axel," the prime minister replied, his voice dark and solemn. "That means you're a person worth befriending. However, I must ask you to never let anyone else get their hands on this card. Do you understand?"

"Okay."

"I mean *no one,* not even Ms Swan or any of the professors at the Academy."

"But..." Axel thought better of it and fell silent, wondering why the prime minister would want him to hide the card from EKA professors.

"I know what you're thinking," the prime minister said and gave Axel a little smile, "but I'm not giving this to you because you'll be an EKA leader. I'm giving it to you because you're going to be a *Swedish* E.K.A leader. The Academy will make you powerful, but your nationality will make you loyal to our country. You and I share the same interests because we both want what's best for our nation, don't we?"

"Uh...of course."

"And that's why that card is yours and yours alone. The two of us will do great things together once you've graduated, but until then you have to keep that card hidden. No one must know you have it, or they can abuse it."

Axel flipped the card in his hand. He wasn't sure he understood what the prime minister was getting at, but he nodded nonetheless.

"All right, I'll keep it hidden, I promise."

The prime minister let out a quiet sigh. "Good." He sat silently, admiring the elegant stage below. After a moment he began fumbling with one of his coat pockets and pulled out a handkerchief. "Do you mind if I ask you a question?" he inquired while dabbing his nose.

"No, of course not."

"Was the application process as hard as people say it is?"

Axel swallowed. To him, the entire process had been pure agony. Not because he feared he would fail the application, but because he feared he wouldn't. Even so, applying to the EKA had been no walk in the park.

The application process was made up of seven phases. During the pre-application phase the applicant had to fill out a number of forms, answering hundreds of questions regarding his/her background and personality. Axel had found the questions not only time-consuming but, to his surprise, difficult to answer. Even if the topic was straightforward, the instructions and questions were so vague and confusing that it was easy to make a mistake.

Axel had read somewhere that forty-five per cent of all applicants failed the pre-application phase. An automated email reply informed those who passed that they could now proceed to the next step.

Phase two consisted of a number of advanced stress tests, as well as IQ and EQ tests. The few who passed continued to phase three. Here they had to write several complex essays, and by the time phase four began, only five per cent of the initial applicants remained.

"Yes, it's tough," Axel admitted. "Very tough."

"But you passed, which is sensational." The prime minister scraped the edge of the armrest with his finger. "I have a son who's a few years younger than you. He's already preparing for his own application, three years from now." The prime minister stopped fidgeting and gave Axel an inquisitive stare. "He told me something I didn't know. Apparently the first three phases of the application are well defined on the EKA website. In fact, it's even possible to buy old questionnaires. I believe my son bought three of them, and Lord knows they're not cheap, but according to my son, the last four steps remain undisclosed. The Academy refuses to reveal any information about them whatsoever."

Axel nodded. "That's true." He knew this because his strategy had been to fail phase four, which, it turned out, hadn't worked very well. The prime minister shook his head and laughed.

"That's amazing. How do they keep it all a secret, one wonders? Of course, it's a little unreasonable, if you ask me," he continued, his face turning grim. "Keeping it a secret, I mean. My son is a wreck at home because he can't prepare for the final phases. It's a shame. He's smart, determined, and a hard-working young man." The prime minister lowered his voice and leaned in. Axel caught a faint whiff of cologne and coffee. "He's desperate to get in, and, as his father, I want to help him."

It took a few seconds before Axel realised what the prime minister was asking for.

"Information," Axel mumbled before he could stop himself.

"Just a little advice would be helpful," the prime minister confirmed, scratching a spot under his double chin.

Axel looked away. This was absurd! How could he say no to the Swedish prime minister? The man ruled his country!

"I'm not allowed to reveal anything," Axel said, sounding just as pitiable and weak as he felt.

"Oh, but it would just be a little information between friends. No one would know about it."

"What about your son?"

The older man gave a little shrug. "Well, I'd have to share the information with him, of course, but he'll never tell anyone. He won't even know who gave me the information."

Axel intertwined his fingers in a forceful grip and began rubbing his palms against each other. The prime minister's words echoed in his mind. "Just a little information between friends…" Axel sighed. "Believe me, I wish I could help you and your son, but I've signed confidentiality contracts that I can't break."

If I do, I'm sure all hell will break loose.

"Ah. Yes, of course. I shouldn't have asked." The prime minister stood up. "Well, it was nice meeting you, Axel. I really *do* hope this is the beginning of a long, fruitful friendship."

Axel exhaled, feeling as if an entire mountain had been lifted off his shoulders.

"I hope so too." He smiled.

"Good...because friendship is important. Certainly among people with power, wouldn't you agree?"

"Uh...yes."

"Indeed. It doesn't take much for a mistreated friend to become an enemy, and we don't want powerful enemies, do we? It makes life *very* problematic, if you know what I mean."

CHAPTER 8

TWELVE YEARS EARLIER

Sarah stepped off the old bus onto the muddy road. The wonderful smell of wet soil was almost overwhelming. She straightened out her uniform and smiled. It felt good to be back. Behind her, the bus coughed and moaned with the same passion as a grumbling old man. A cloud of black smoke trolled behind it as it began to roll down the street, picking up speed as it went.

Sarah viewed the open savannah. It was so green. God had begun the new year by blessing Tanzania with rain. In fact, the entire East-African region was experiencing heavy showers. Although the effects were visible in a large city such as Dar es Salaam, it was more noticeable out here, where roads were unpaved, and no bulky buildings destroyed the view.

"It's beautiful, isn't it?"

Sarah spun around. Her friends considered her a courageous woman but the unfamiliar voice had startled her. Next to the village road, leaning against the yellow stem of a large acacia tree, stood an old, thin man. He was dressed in an expensive, grey suit that seemed inappropriate on the African savannah, and wore a small hat on his white-haired scalp.

"How was your trip," he asked, nodding in the direction of the bus.

He was a Brit; she could hear it in his voice. She gripped her handbag a little tighter. The man wasn't dressed like a thief, but then again she knew thieves came in all shapes and sizes.

"It was a pleasant ride, sir," she replied with caution.

"I'm glad." He gestured towards the village road. "I assume you're on your way to your orphanage? Would you mind if I join you? I believe I have some information that will interest you."

Sarah's heart skipped a beat. He knew about her orphanage. Could he be here to offer her a little funding? He exuded both wealth and wisdom; similar to that of an old, rich grandfather wishing you nothing but the best. She nodded. The orphanage was in desperate need of finance.

"Thank you," the man said with a bow, as if she'd done him a great service.

Together they started down the muddy road. Sarah glanced at the man's polished shoes. There was no mud on them. How was that possible? Then her eyes moved up and she caught a glimpse of his gold watch and gold cufflinks. Yes, this was a wealthy man, but what was he doing here, alone in the most rural parts of Tanzania?

"My name is David Garner," the man began, "and I must say, it's an honour to meet you at last, Ms Wangai. You see, I know a lot about you. I know you're twenty-three years old. You grew up in an orphanage outside Dar es Salaam. Although you never knew your parents, you considered yourself lucky. It was a good place to grow up and you were given an education."

Sarah froze. Fear slithered through her body and she found herself struggling to breathe.

"How do you know these things about me?"

"I suppose that's information anyone could uncover." The man smiled. "But I know more than that. I know that when you were nine, you began to dream of one day building your own orphanage. I must say, that's quite a remarkable dream for a nine-year-old. At the age of fifteen, you heard of an orphanage in financial difficulty." Mr Garner nodded in the direction of the village. "You came here and found a small bungalow with twenty children and an old lady with no money. Through sheer determination, you managed to keep the orphanage afloat until you turned eighteen. After that, you got a job as a maid for a wealthy family in Dar es Salaam. Since then, you've spent all your money on your little orphanage. You come here every Saturday afternoon after work and help out until Sunday afternoon when you have to return to the city."

The wrinkled old man locked his hands behind his back. Sarah gawked at him, unable to speak. Who was this peculiar man, with his peculiar clothes and peculiar behaviour? How did he know so much about her, and *what did he want*?

"You've got a big heart, Ms Wangai, and a very determined mind. When you want something, you get it. It may take you years, but you'll get it in the end."

Hearing someone speak so highly of her made Sarah uncomfortable.

"I believe you exaggerate, Mr Garner."

The man seemed amused. "I doubt it, Ms Wangai. You're willing to take risks in order to get what you want. I know, for example, that when the family you work for leave their house in the morning, you spend about two hours on their computer. First you read the news for an hour, then you spend the second hour searching for funding and assistance to help sustain your orphanage."

Sarah thought her heart had stopped beating. How did he know this? She'd been so cautious!

"Oh, don't worry, Ms Wangai. Your employer remains clueless as to your activities, and I'm not here to scold you. Desperate times call for desperate measures. What you've done takes courage, and that's important when becoming a leader."

Sarah blinked and then gasped as the pieces fell into place. "What do you mean?" she asked, clasping her worn little bag with force.

Behind Mr Garner, a black jeep came into sight, bouncing down the pothole-infested road.

"Ah, now that's a good question," he said with a grin. "Let me see; about six months ago, you used your employer's computer. This time, you applied to the Eagle King's Academy. You impress us, Ms Wangai, and so I am happy to inform you, that you have been accepted as one of the twelve."

CHAPTER 9

PRESENT DAY

The business card felt heavy in his hand. Maybe he should just apologise. What harm would a little information do? After all, there wasn't much to say. Axel had received an email, instructing him to log on to a specific EKA webpage on the 14th of October, at 7.45p.m. sharp. At the given date and time, he'd followed the instructions and found three questions on his screen: What makes someone a leader? Why do we need leaders? What would make you a good leader?

There had been no other instructions; nothing stating how long the answers should to be or how much time an applicant should spend on each question. To make matters worse, three minutes after the questions appeared, they had faded away, leaving just two options: "Cancel Application" or "Attach file".

Axel had spent over an hour contemplating what to write, trying to find an angle that would guarantee his failure without making it obvious. In the end, he'd written a single essay instead of three, hoping the Academy would regard this as laziness. He'd also made a silly analogy about good leaders being the roots on a large tree, holding the entire structure in place. He'd been certain it was ridiculous enough to make him fail the application. And as the months passed without a word from the Academy, he thought he had made it. He thought he'd found the perfect way out of his dilemma.

Axel was still staring at the business card when the door opened and Nicole entered.

"Thank you, Mr Prime Minister! That will do." With haste, Axel slid the card into his pocket, earning him a tiny nod from the man beside him. Nicole didn't seem to notice. "And congratulations to you, Mr Hallman. You have just passed phase eight of the application process. *Now* you're officially part of the Eagle King's Academy."

Axel stood dumbfounded, trying to understand what was happening.

"I hope you accept my apologies," the prime minister said, pulling out a small remote from his coat pocket and handing it to Nicole. "When the Academy asks you to help, you help." He fished out a small microphone from the breast pocket of his suit jacket and placed it in Nicole's open hand. He gave her an apologetic smile. "I'm sorry, Ms Swan. I didn't turn it on in time."

"So I noticed, sir," Nicole replied, placing the microphone and remote in her pocket. "You had me a little worried for a moment."

"Yes, well, my only excuse is that I got a call from the Minister of Defence just as I was about to enter. The topic we discussed..." He shrugged. "Anyway, I got the important bit, didn't I?"

Nicole's dimples reappeared. "You did, sir."

"Good." The prime minister pulled out his handkerchief and turned to Axel as he dabbed his nose. "I was afraid you'd suspect something when I couldn't find the remote in my pocket."

"I can see you're confused, Mr Hallman." Nicole laughed giving him a flash of her white teeth. "You've just passed the last phase of the application, which is a confidentiality test," she explained. "It's a final assessment to ensure that we indeed picked the right candidates." She paused and held up her buzzing phone with a puzzled expression. "Oh, excuse me. I need to take this."

As soon as she was out of ears' reach, the prime minister turned to Axel with a grim expression. "Remember what I said about the business card," he whispered. "That card is yours and I want you to keep it safe and hidden."

Axel fingered the card in his pocket. He didn't believe for a second that the prime minister had "forgotten" to turn on the microphone. *I better start paying more attention,* he thought, with a sour feeling in his gut. After all, he was entering a world where power ruled.

He took on his turbulent emotions with determination and managed to give the prime minister a little nod. "I promise. I'll keep it hidden."

"Good." Satisfied with his answer, the prime minister began putting on his coat. "It'll be our little secret." Glancing at his wristwatch, he continued, "Now, I have to go. I have a meeting with the president of Latvia in forty-five minutes." He turned to Nicole who was approaching with long, elegant strides. "Well, Ms Swan, don't forget to tell Principal Cunningham that I'm expecting a dinner with him next time he's in Scandinavia."

Nicole positioned herself next to Axel, her shoulder touching his arm. "The principal is a man of his words, sir. I'll contact you soon and arrange something."

"Very good." The prime minister pulled out a pair of leather gloves from his coat. "Axel, it's been a true pleasure! I look forward to meeting you again." They shook hands before the man hurried off towards the door.

"He hated the idea of deceiving you," Nicole said as the door closed behind the man. "I think he was afraid you might hold it against him some day. But we needed someone influential enough to test your integrity."

"I thought there were only seven steps in the application process."

"No, there are eight, but the last one is more of a quality control on our side. Oh, I see you're surprised, Mr Hallman, but I told you, you'll never know when the Academy is testing you. Besides, I knew you'd pass. I've done this for quite a while and not once have I met a student who passed all seven steps but failed the eighth." She took him by the arm and nodded towards the door. "Come, we must go."

"So what would have happened if I had told the prime minister about the fourth phase," Axel asked as they walked down the wide stairs. Nicole gave him a playful look.

"I would have given you some money for a taxi and you would have gone back to your old life."

"Just like that?"

"Yes, just like that."

In his mind, Axel cursed himself and his righteousness.

"Of course, you would have been prosecuted and jailed for having breached the confidentiality contract."

"Oh." Axel fell silent for a moment. "The prime minister; he was a little...strange."

Nicole seemed amused. "What makes you say that?"

Axel could feel the business card in his pocket, pressing against his leg. "I don't know. He just was. Anyway, so what happens now?"

Nicole laughed and squeezed his arm. "Now, Mr Hallman," she said, her eyes twinkling, "we head for Brussels."

CHAPTER 10

Dark, menacing clouds engulfed the Belgian capital. The sapphire black BMW pushed on as cold rain pounded the busy streets. Somewhere in the distance lightning struck, followed by the deep roar of thunder.

Nicole took her eyes off her phone and wrinkled her nose at the raging weather outside.

"My God, perhaps Julien should have picked us up in a boat instead of a car." Julien, the EKA driver, threw her a fleeting glance, visibly unimpressed by her humour. "He's the silent type," Nicole continued with a whisper and a wink. She then nodded towards the window and pocketed her phone. "Anyway, we're almost there."

Axel peered out. It was hard to see anything in the pouring rain. From what he could gather, they were entering an exclusive part of town, lined with impressive buildings, fashionable shops, and small restaurants.

"Where are we?"

"This is Avenue Louise. And over there..." she waited until a stunning white building with great exterior detail came into sight "...is where we've set up the Academy for the next three years. That, Mr Hallman, is your new home."

Axel cringed at the thought as Julien pulled off the main road, stopping outside a large, double-door entrance. This was it. There was no turning back.

Grabbing an umbrella from underneath the seat in front of her, Nicole gave him a questioning look. "Are you ready?"

A wave of nervousness swept over Axel. He dug his fingernails into his palms. Whatever happens, I'll deal with it, he thought, in an attempt to boost his confidence. I'm doing it for Talk Thirteen.

"Yeah, I am."

"Good, then let's get you settled in."

Rough winds and cold rain struck them with force as they stepped out into the storm. The massive wooden doors were already opening, exposing nothing but darkness. A lightning bolt forked across the menacing sky, joined by a hellish rumble. To Axel it had the sound of a warning: a warning not to enter.

"Oh, my," Nicole exclaimed and gazed at the heavens above. "Such weather." She took him by the arm and they ran across the broad sidewalk, entering a short dark corridor, guarded by two large men in black suits. "This is the main entrance security checkpoint," Nicole explained while shaking off her umbrella. She nodded towards the guard closest to them and laughed. "That's why these men have such serious faces."

The man gave her an impassive nod and turned to Axel. "May I have your bag, sir?"

"Afraid I might be smuggling drugs?" Axel said in a nervous attempt to make a joke.

"It's policy, sir," the guard replied, with a stony expression, and began to dig around in the small backpack.

"It can be a little annoying sometimes," Nicole explained, "but it's for our own safety. It's stated in our Physical Defence Policy that security must search any bag brought into the premises. They look for all kinds of threats, including drugs, weapons, and explosives. It doesn't matter who you are, it's the same for everyone; staff, students, and professors. Even Principal Cunningham is searched." She pointed at a number of panels, embedded in the dark-wooded walls. "And do you see those black plates?"

"Yes."

"The first row is a body-scanner, combing you for weapons. The second searches for technology that can be used to record or transmit data, for example phones, cameras, hand recorders, etc."

The guard zipped up Axel's backpack and handed it over. "You may proceed," he declared.

Axel took the bag and, together with Nicole, he made his way down the short distance towards the second guard.

Passing the black metal plates, an aggressive red light began flashing, accompanied by a pulsating, buzzing sound. Nicole laughed as Axel stared at her with startled confusion. "Don't worry, sir. It's your phone. It's not recognised as part of our internal communication system." She held out her hand. "Here, I'll hold it for you while you clear the checkpoint." She motioned Axel to repeat the process. When he was done, she returned his phone and beamed like the sun. "You'll be given a new one today, one adapted to our security system." Behind her, the second guard shifted his weight, which caught her attention. "Well, Mr Linch. We're all clear to enter."

The guard eyed Axel with a wolfish grin. "Mr Hallman…" he said with a stark, reverberating voice and gave the large inner doors a firm push. "Welcome to the Academy."

Like a lover's embrace, warm light spilled into the little entryway, trailed by the sweetest scent of flowers. In an instance, Axel forgot his apprehension. He could hear birdsong and the soft murmur of running water, begging him to enter.

His mouth ajar, Axel walked into an enormous foyer with marbled floor and sand-coloured walls. High above, vast chandeliers hung from an arched ceiling, glimmering in gold. "Wow," he gasped.

Nicole turned. "It's unique, isn't it?"

"It's amazing!" he managed, staring at huge trees and thick bushes that stood clustered on each side of the room. "It's…wow."

Nicole laughed. "Shall we?" She pointed towards the end of the room. "The reception desk is over there." They began to stroll down the centre of the foyer while Axel gaped at everything he saw. There were birdcages among the greenery; massive things made of gold, in which colourful birds sang as they passed. Huge pillars stood here and there, covered with great climbers reaching for the ceiling. "You can't see it from here," Nicole said, nodding to the right in the direction of a wide waterfall, "but there's a pond over there, filled with water lilies, turtles, and fish. It's a fabulous place for a quiet cup of tea. There is also a newspaper stand with all the necessary papers at hand. Oh, that reminds me, you're expected to keep yourself updated with current world events, meaning everything from sports and entertainment to business and politics."

"Uhu…" Axel mumbled.

They were now halfway to the reception desk. There were plenty of men and women moving about in the foyer, and they all greeted him with respectful bows. He felt like a king returning from a long trip abroad. It made him uncomfortable. He was just about to point this out when he saw something that made him stop dead in his tracks. In the middle of the great hall was an enormous gold statue of a crowned eagle with its wings spread wide. It was mind-boggling.

"You got to be kidding me." He laughed. "It's the size of a van!"

"Yes. It's one of the few things that gets shipped to each new EKA location." Nicole snickered. "The employees call it Jackson, after Professor Jackson. I think it's because of the eyes, but don't tell anyone I said that."

Axel considered the eagle with its unyielding eyes.

"And who's Professor Jackson?" he wondered out loud.

"You'll meet him soon enough." Nicole picked up her speed. "Come, let's get you registered."

"Was that thing made out of real gold?" Axel asked as he hurried after her.

"But of course."

"Through-and-through?"

"I wouldn't know, sir."

"It doesn't matter." Axel smirked. "There's still more gold here than I've ever seen in my entire life."

Nicole led him to the reception desk, manned by a young woman and a short, stout man in his mid-thirties. Both appeared busy behind their computers until Nicole and Axel approached.

"Ah! Mr Axel Hallman," the man exclaimed with a bright smile. "At last!" He bowed his head. "It's an honour, sir; a true honour. We've been preparing for your arrival for so long it feels as if I've known you my whole life."

He spoke with a near-perfect American accent. In fact, everything about him was perfect; from his white shirt, red tie, and grey suit, to the inky black hair, pedantically combed to one side. Despite his meticulous appearance, there was something about him that made Axel think of a grinning opossum.

"My name is Mr Henry Milton," the man continued. "I'm the concierge manager here at the Eagle King's Academy." He pushed up the seemingly expensive glasses on his nose and nodded towards a young woman next to him. "And this is Miss Davis, one of my assistants."

The woman blushed and reached for the gold scarf around her neck but, after a discrete ahem from Mr Milton, she dropped her hand as if burnt.

"It's an honour to meet you, sir," she said with a curtsy.

"Likewise," Axel replied, feeling a little uncomfortable with the formalities.

"I'm running a little late, Mr Milton," said Nicole while checking her watch. "I'm off to Paris in an hour to pick up Ms Baton. Professor Jackson also wanted to see me before I go. Would you mind showing Axel to his new home?"

"It would be my pleasure, Ms Swan."

"I appreciate it. And do you know if Principal Cunningham is back yet?"

"No, ma'am. According to Mr Hennigan he'll arrive around five-thirty tonight." There was obvious awe in Mr Milton's demeanour as he spoke about the principal. "Everything has been prepared in detail for his arrival. As always."

"Excellent." Nicole turned to Axel with her warm smile. "You and I will meet later tonight at the introduction dinner, Mr Hallman. Now, if you'll please excuse me, I must see what Professor Jackson wants of me."

She left with her signature long, confident strides. Axel watched her go, feeling both abandoned and empty inside. When she swept across the floor towards the two elevators behind the reception, Axel's eyes widened. They were the most bizarre-looking elevators he'd ever seen, with the doors shaped like colossal eagle wings, glimmering with gold. The detailed feathers interlocked in a zigzag pattern at the front, creating doors with a slight curved shape.

"What's the 'introduction dinner'?" Axel asked, still staring as a pair of wings closed around Nicole.

Mr Milton frowned.

"Haven't you heard of the EKA introduction dinner before?"

Axel gave the stout man a little shrug. "I must have missed it."

Mr Milton pushed a pile of papers aside and grinned. "That's odd since it's a well-known sadistic EKA ritual in which all new students are whipped."

Behind Mr Milton, Miss Davis covered her mouth and tittered.

"Funny," Axel replied, shaking his head at the poor humour.

"My apologies, Mr Hallman," the concierge manager chuckled. "It's just a little joke. As the name implies, the dinner is a welcoming feast for all students. No whipping included. Now, shall I show you your apartment?"

Axel was stunned.

"Did you say *apartment*?"

"Yes, sir!"

"I'm getting my own apartment?"

"But of course! Now come with me. We'll take the elevator."

A few minutes later Axel stepped out into a narrow, windowless space on the ninth floor, to a large extent occupied by a huge marble statue. He regarded the thing with both scepticism and amusement. It showed a great lion bowing to the King of Eagles that was resting its wings on the hilt of a long sword. "Our Future; Our Hope" was inscribed in gold letters on its base.

"Your neighbour, Mr Reed, is an American," Mr Milton explained pointing at a white door to the left. "He'll arrive around four this afternoon. And this…" Mr Milton nodded to the door on the right "… is *your* apartment. All you need to do is press your thumb against the scanner."

Axel studied the thin, metal plate attached next to the door handle. It didn't look like much, but placing his thumb against its cool, black surface resulted in a faint click.

"There you go," Mr Milton said as the large door swung open.

CHAPTER 11

TWELVE YEARS EARLIER

With eyes filled with wonder, Sarah watched the large city pass by from the back seat of the most luxurious car she'd ever seen. There was plenty of time to take in the view. Traffic here was slow and noisy; similar to the streets back home, only there were fewer cars and a lot more scooters. There was another difference. While the streets in Dar es Salaam reminded her of a slow-moving hoard of elephants, the boulevards here in Da Nang had a certain organised frenzy to them. Like ants around a nest. It made her all giddy. There were people everywhere, yet somehow they all managed to avoid each other.

Sarah had never been outside Tanzania, let alone Africa. Now all of a sudden, she was in a new city, in a new country, on a new continent. The thought was mind-numbing. She'd read about Vietnam before, both in school and in the newspaper, but never had she imagined her feet would touch its soil.

"You're awfully quiet, miss," Mr Garner said. "Is something troubling you?"

"Oh, no sir. It's just a lot to see."

"And a lot for you to take in, I imagine."

He said it without arrogance or abasement. It was a simple fact, and Sarah knew he was right. There was much she hadn't seen or experienced in her life; so much she had to learn. Some might regard that as a disadvantage, but to Sarah it was only a temporary setback. She would learn. Ever since she was a little girl, she'd understood that knowledge was the fastest way out of poverty. That's why she wanted all her children, every single one of her orphans, to learn how to read and write. With those two skills, they could learn anything.

"Ms Wangai, I must warn you that most of the students you'll meet tonight come from upper-class families. They'll expect you to behave in a certain...manner."

The man tugged at the cufflink on his right sleeve, and Sarah smiled. How sweet of Mr Garner to worry for her, she thought, as she folded her hands in her lap.

"I know there are people who believe that being poor is the same as being stupid. I'm sure the other students are wiser than most people."

The corner of Mr Garner's lips twitched. "Of course," he said with a soft voice. "Still, when we arrive you have an appointment with Mr Bell. He's one of our teachers and specialises in culture and etiquette. He'll help you get organised before the introduction dinner tonight. That's when you'll meet the other students."

Sarah beamed.

"Oh, that's very kind of you, Mr Garner. I'll make you proud."

Mr Garner bowed his head a little.

"You have a good heart, Ms Wangai," he said and turned back to his window.

CHAPTER 12

PRESENT DAY

"Welcome Mr Hallman," said a recorded voice. "Your entertainment and communication system is now activated."

Puzzled, Axel stepped into an airy hallway and drew a deep breath.

"Wow, what's that wonderful smell?"

Mr Milton whiffed the air with a frisky expression.

"I'm not sure, sir. We have a brilliant fragrance expert. She'll create new, personal fragrances for your apartment on a regular basis."

"You have a person who just works with smells?"

Mr Milton scrunched his face in distaste. "We use the words *fragrances* or *scents*, sir, not smells. And yes, we have such a person employed with us. You'll be amazed at the extent to which different scents affect our moods. She is very important to us." Mr Milton shut the door behind them. "Anyway, before I show you around, would you care for something from the kitchen?"

"That would be great! I'm starving."

"Then what would you like, sir? Perhaps Vietnamese Pho Ga soup or a Brazilian feijoada? Maybe something vegetarian, for example an Indian Baingan bharta?" Seeing Axel's blank expression, Mr Milton laughed. "Perhaps something more familiar then; sushi or a roasted chicken with lemon garlic butter?"

"Well, chicken would be nice."

"Chicken it is."

While Mr Milton called the kitchen, Axel pulled off his jacket and shoes, before entering his new home. The living room was about twice the size of his entire apartment in Stockholm. Warm light, thick rugs, and a wide bookshelf created a sense of intimacy and personality. A chessboard stood set up on a coffee table, along with a guidebook on Brussels. Someone had also gone to the trouble of creating beautiful flower arrangements, which, along with a number of potted trees, gave the room both colour and life. In one corner there was a massive fireplace, but the true centrepiece was, without a doubt, a gigantic aquarium built into one of the walls.

A shark, the length of Axel's leg, swam back and forth along the sandy bottom. Colourful schools of fish fled its path in panic. Like a bully on the playground, Axel thought to himself, and decided he didn't appreciate the shark. But the aquarium was remarkable.

"This is amazing! It's like a window under the sea."

"Thank you, sir. I'll pass on your compliments to the EKA interior designer."

Next in line was the kitchen.

"I know it's not very big," Mr Milton apologised, "but I'm sure you'll eat most of your meals in the restaurant with the other students. Or order up food. However, should you want to eat here you'll find anything you need, whether it's for cooking or dining."

Opposite the kitchen was a home movie theatre room with all kinds of technological gadgets. It would have been nice to explore it all, but unfortunately, Mr Milton seemed eager to move on.

Next stop was Axel's new study. It was a beautiful room – well organised and stylishly furnished – but in one corner stood a hideous object. It was a vast thing, looking like a black, oversized refrigerator with a curved wall.

"What in the world is that?"

"Why don't you have a closer look, sir?" Mr Milton asked and opened a door on the side of the box.

Axel peered in and raised his brows. "A podium?"

"Yes. Please step in and I'll show you how it works."

Axel felt a fair bit of apprehension as he stepped up behind the podium. There was a twinkle in Mr Milton's eyes that worried him. "Okay, now what?"

"How does it feel, sir?"

"I'm standing behind a podium in a small box, so kind of silly right now."

"Ah, but what if you *weren't* standing in a small box." Mr Milton laughed, grabbing a remote control from the podium table. "Do you see the glasses over there?"

Axel bent over and pulled out a pair of spectacles from a shelf under the table. "These?"

"Yes. They're special 3D glasses developed by the Academy. Put them on, please."

While Axel did so, Mr Milton pressed another button on the remote. The box came alive. The entire inside of the machine lit up. In the far distance, snow-covered mountains pointed their sharp peaks towards a blue sky, and straight ahead, a black dot materialised. As it grew in size, Axel identified it as a proud and graceful eagle. It flew right over his head, wearing a golden crown, glimmering in warm afternoon light. Axel could even feel the wind from its wings as it passed. It felt so real he ducked.

The eagle made an elegant turn and came flying in from the left. It landed in front of Axel, giving him a deep bow with one wing tucked under its chest, before fading out. The whole thing took no more than a few seconds. Axel found himself gawking at a crowd of about a hundred people, all clapping their hands in polite anticipation.

"My God!" Axel exclaimed.

"It's fantastic, isn't it?"

"It's so real!"

"We call it the Speechomat. It's for training your communication skills. Let me show you how it works. He pressed one of the buttons. "Now say something."

"Such as?" Axel asked, before throwing his hands over his ears. "Ouch!" he cried as his words came back in amplified strength.

Mr Milton was quick to adjust the volume.

"Sorry about that, sir. It appears Greg tested your Speechomat."

"Greg?"

"He's one of our computer engineers. Has hearing like a ninety year old with earplugs, but he's the most competent engineer we have. If *he* built this Speechomat, then you can rest assured it works. Anyway, you can control the volume here." Mr Milton pointed at two buttons on the remote. "Now, do you want to give it a try?"

Axel regarded the crowd and felt his excitement blossom.

"Sure."

"Excellent, sir. As soon as I've closed the door, all you have to do is press the green button. If you want to, you can change the size of the crowd and the level of difficulty with these two buttons." Mr Milton showed him on the remote. "Just remember that the Speechomat is soundproof, so if you want to speak to me, you'll have to press that yellow button in the corner of the podium. Yes, that one." Mr Milton paused. "I think that's it. Are you ready?"

"I guess."

Mr Milton smiled and closed the door. The light in the Speechomat dimmed, leaving Axel alone with the virtual audience. He was about to press start when a thought struck him.

"Mr Milton," he asked, pressing down the yellow button. "Can you hear me?"

"Yes, sir."

"What shall I talk about?"

"It doesn't matter, sir. The audience reacts to *how* you deliver your speech, not what you say. Talk about your favourite colour, the political situation in the Middle East, or the production of wine glasses. It's up to you. My only advice is that you pick a topic and then stick to it. Don't talk nonsense. The crowd reacts to your entire speech, not just word for word or sentence for sentence. If you talk gibberish, the crowd will pick up on it and react."

"Okay, thank you."

Axel pressed the "start" button.

"Eh…hello."

The audience began to applaud at once. Axel was amazed. It felt so real it was frightening.

"I hope you're all doing well," he continued. The crowd clapped a little harder. "I've just arrived here at the EKA and Mr Milton is showing me around the apartment. I must say it's fantastic."

As he spoke with increasing confidence, the audience remained silent, but as soon as he stopped, they all rose from their seats and began to clap as if mad. The overwhelming enthusiasm wasn't natural. Axel pressed a red "stop" button on the remote. In an instance, the audience were sitting down again, their faces neutral. So this was an easy audience. How would a hard one behave?

He flipped through different options and settled for a crowd of one hundred thousand protesters. He chose a difficulty level of nineteen out of twenty-two. Then with butterflies in his stomach, he pressed start.

Once more the screen flickered and before he knew it, he was standing outside with the sun beaming down on him. It was amazing. The light in the Speechomat had increased, and so had the temperature. A few trees behind the crowd were swaying in the wind, and a light breeze within the Speechomat followed the movement of the trees. Just as in real life, the wind would sometimes increase or decrease in strength and as soon as Axel felt the change, he could see it in the movement of the trees.

A hundred thousand people were standing below him, glaring at him with angry eyes. Some held large placards with text too small to read. A long line of police officers kept the protesters away from the podium. Axel cleared his throat.

"Dear ladies and gentlemen," he began. At once, the crowd began to hoot. Baffled, he lost his focus. This didn't sit well with the crowd, leading to more hoots and shout. The crowd began to push forward while the police did their best to hold them back.

"Eh…I'm thrilled to be here at the EKA," Axel tried, but fell silent as more and more people began to shout at him. The crowd kept pushing forward. "I…no!"

A police officer struck a man in the crowd with a baton. The man fell to his knees. The people closest to the injured man reacted in pure anger. They began to strike at the officer with their bare hands. The police, protected by their large shields, struck back. Things were getting out of control.

"Please step back," Axel yelled. He was now completely absorbed in what was going on. "Stop!" Neither the crowd nor the police were listening. "I'm ordering you to stop!"

Now the crowd reacted but not as Axel had hoped. A few of the police officers turned with startled expressions on their faces. That moment of distraction allowed a young woman to pass through the police line. Before Axel had time to react she ran up to the podium threw something at him: a tomato.

What the…

Something whistled past his head and struck the wall behind him. You've got to be kidding me. Two more objects flew past and then, with a large splash, something wet and slimy hit him right under the eye.

"Ouch!" he shouted before yet another slimy tomato struck him, this time on the forehead. "Shit!" He blinked. Several people were now pushing through the police line while tomatoes whooshed past his head. "Mr Milton!"

Desperate to escape, Axel jumped back and slammed right into the wall behind him, making the entire machine shake. Another tomato struck him on the chin. "Stop!"

CHAPTER 13

The tomatoes struck him like slimy tennis balls. One hit him so hard his 3D glasses fell off his face and he tumbled against the Speechomat.

"Ouch!" Axel yelled.

He was beginning to panic when the door opened and Mr Milton leaned in with a chuckle. He grabbed the remote and pressed "Stop".

"Sorry about that, sir. I should have warned you not to pick a difficult crowd."

"Why...they were throwing tomatoes at me." Axel wiped his face with the back of his hand. "You have a machine that throws tomatoes?"

Mr Milton's thin lips pulled back into his opossum-like grin.

"They're not real tomatoes, sir. They're made of a harmless substance, invented by our engineers. In fact, I believe Greg had something to do with it." Mr Milton picked something up from the floor. "See. It feels wet and cold when you touch it, but it's dry and it won't leave a stain. The sensation will fade in a minute or so."

He handed Axel a soft, red ball of slime, about the size of a tennis ball. It had the same feeling as a wet towel. Axel placed it on the podium table, but even after he'd dropped it, the wet sensation remained on his fingers.

"How did you know when to come in," Axel wondered. "I thought you said you couldn't hear me."

"I didn't, but when the Speechomat began to wobble, I suspected you needed help.

"Sorry about that."

Mr Milton's eyebrows dipped, forming the shape of a V.

"You mustn't apologise, sir. Your reaction is normal. One of our previous students punched a hole in the screen on his first attempt. He was trying to protect himself from an angry mob. Shall we move on?"

Axel placed his glasses under the podium table and looked at the mess around him.

"What about these...tomatoes?"

"Just leave them there, sir. The maid will deal with them."

Axel stepped out of the Speechomat and rubbed his face. The wet sensation was already beginning to fade, but he still felt dazed by the whole experience.

"It feels real in there, doesn't it, sir," Mr Milton continued.

"Yeah, for a moment I thought the crowd would climb onto the stage."

"Believe me, sir. In a year or so, you'll be able to control a crowd that size without even thinking about it. Oh," he said, pulling out a silk handkerchief and removing some red goo from Axel's back. "Just a little tomato-slime," he said and grimaced.

"Thanks. So how does it work? The Speechomat, I mean."

"You mean the technical aspect of it? I'm not sure, sir. I only know how it works in practice. Now, before I forget –" Mr Milton pointed at a small laptop sitting on a height-adjustable desk "– all the necessary passwords for your computer can be found in the introduction manual. You'll find it in your bedroom, sir. Let me show you."

The bedroom, situated at the end of the apartment, was, like the rest of the apartment, spacious and light. On a king-size bed, which held a ridiculous number of fluffy pillows, lay parcels in various colours and sizes. Curious, Axel made his way over to have a closer look.

"Oh, that's some clothes and other necessities you might need," Mr Milton explained, waving his hand in a dismissive gesture. "Some are given by the Academy, but most are donated by our sponsors and partners. You can go through them later."

"Is that a welcoming mint on the pillow?"

"Yes, sir," Mr Milton replied without throwing the bed a second glance. He made his way to a narrow desk by the window. Ignoring the packages and paper bags that lay there, he picked up a thin, leather folder and handed it to Axel.

"This is your introduction manual. You'll find a lot of important information in it. We ask all our students to go through it in detail. You're expected to read it before dinner tonight." Turning, he pointed at a door by the other end of the room. "The main bathroom is in there. The maid will replace your towel every day, and the toothbrush twice a week."

"A new toothbrush twice a week?"

"Yes. Now one last piece of important information." Mr Milton picked up a package. "Here's your new phone; the most advanced available, of course. Our IT department has installed everything you need on it, including a new SIM card with all relevant phone numbers. Your old phone needs to be handed in for safety reasons."

"What? Now?"

"Yes, please. Your new phone won't trigger the security alarm at the entrance."

"Can I keep the old phone case? I use it as a wallet."

"Yes, sir, although I believe there's a new wallet among your gifts."

Axel pulled his phone out of its case and, with a sense of loss, handed it to Mr Milton.

"What about photos and my music etc."

"Not a problem, sir. I'll ask IT to transfer them onto your new phone at once. That said, I must also inform you that you won't have access to any of your social media accounts from now on. It's far too risky."

"But...I can't just stop posting things on the net. My friends will get suspicious!"

"*You'll* stop posting, but Axel Hallman won't."

Axel stared at the small man. It struck him that despite the smiles and tiny bows there was a hint of sarcasm bubbling behind Mr Milton's polished surface.

"What I mean, sir," the concierge manager continued, "is that our communication's officer will post small messages in your name.

Nothing much, just enough to keep people thinking you're online. The same goes for your private email account."

"You can't read my emails," Axel objected. "They're private!"

Mr Milton raised a brow.

"You agreed to it when you applied, sir."

Damn it! Axel looked away in shame and exasperation, wishing he'd read those stupid application documents with a little more care.

"Mr Hallman," Mr Milton said with a silver-tongued voice. "You *are* aware of the fact that as an EKA leader you won't have much of a personal life to speak of, aren't you?"

CHAPTER 14

On a hillside, a few hours north of the Norwegian capital, stood a simple cabin, half buried in snow and well out of sight from the winding road below. White smoke puffed from its brick chimney, rising slowly at first before gathering speed as it climbed towards the darkening sky. Warm light poured out of the small windows, giving life to shadows that lurked around the massive snowdrifts.

The young man turned away from the window and considered his company. This was the very core of the network; the instigators of the grand plan. It was rare to see them all gathered like this. It was too complicated, time-consuming, and dangerous to congregate on a regular basis. But now, with phase two initiated, the little group needed to meet. They all had roles to play and information to share. Some had teams to manoeuvre or members to protect. These were things that required a face-to-face discussion.

He gazed at the crackling fire, watching the flames flicker peacefully around the dry wood. A faint smell of smoke hovered around the room, mingling with the more enjoyable scents of coffee, whiskey, and cinnamon.

"It's time, sir." Thor's husky voice cut through the silence, snapping everyone out of their thoughts. "We've got to go. It's started to snow again."

He stood in faint light by the door, like a statue peering out through the small window. Waiting. How can he stand like that for hours on end, the young man wondered, his eyes falling on the gun at the back of Thor's waistband. My feet would kill me.

At the round table in the centre of the room, an elderly gentleman, the one they all called Smooth, emptied his whiskey glass and nodded. "All right." The wooden chair scraped against the floor as he pushed it back and got to his feet. "Duty calls."

"May I ask something?" the young man inquired in a hushed voice. "I need to know; do you think we can pull this off? Will we succeed?"

Smooth gave him a little smile.

"But of course! We wouldn't do this if we thought we'd fail, would we?"

The young man had his doubts. So did his father. The old man caressed his grey beard with pensive strokes and let out a heavy sigh.

"It's a dangerous game we're playing," he said. "There are too many things that can go wrong."

"I agree," Smooth replied, "but who said starting a revolution was easy?"

"Come on, you guys." Smooth's daughter, a young copper-blonde woman in her mid-twenties, picked up her coffee cup. "We've been over this a hundred times. Let's stay positive. We're prepared, and the odds are in our favour. After all, we got Mr Hallman into the Academy, didn't we?"

In an old armchair at the other end of the room, a wiry young man with intelligent eyes and a head shaved like a Buddhist monk turned his gaze from the fire. "It all comes down to Hallman," he said with a silky voice. "He's our tool. If he fails, we fail."

"I know," said the young man. "And I know we've talked about this a hundred times but part of me still believes we should have told him something; at least enough to let him know what we expect of him."

"And then send him into the Academy?" The Box agent coordinator, Pixie Young, shook her head. "They'd read him like an open book. At this point in time, Mr Hallman's not skilled enough to handle such emotional pressure. Hell, he might not be able to handle it six months from now."

Over by the door, Thor was pulling on his suit jacket, still without taking his eyes from the window. "Sir. We *have* to leave."

"Yes, yes. I'm coming." The wooden planks creaked under Smooth's steps as he made his way over to Thor. "We've been over this before, and the others are right. Let's stick to the plan and ensure that Mr Hallman plays his part well. If not, we'll have to intervene. For now, Mr Hallman is on his own. It's essential that he settle in, but when the time is right we'll make our move." He let Thor help him on with his coat, and then wrapped a black scarf around his thick neck. "There are no certainties in life, young man; only hope, dreams, and determination. But one thing is undeniable, we can't change anything without trying." There was a murmur of agreement among the others. "Now, I must go." Smooth walked over to his daughter and kissed her on the forehead. "I'll call you."

Cat nodded.

"Be careful."

"Always, my dear. Always."

He patted her cheek with affection and left. Cat gave the young man a little smile, and he returned it with a playful wink. Then he turned back to his window. Staring into the darkness, he thought about the future, about all it promised and everything that could go wrong.

Then he thought about Axel Hallman.

CHAPTER 15

The afternoon rain smattered against the bedroom windows. Once in a while, thunder roared. Leaning against a mountain of cushions, Axel sat on his new soft bed, flipping the prime minister's business card between his fingers. He was in the process of emptying his old phone case, moving everything to his new black leather wallet.

Staring out into the room, his mind reeled back to that wretched day when it all began.

"You have so much potential," his father had bellowed, his face red from anger. "How can you throw it all away?"

"Wait a minute!" Axel had yelled back. "*You* were the one who made me study economics to begin with, remember? I hate it!"

"Bah! You keep saying that you want to make a difference in the world. Well, you can't do it without money and leadership. You need those two components. Without them, you can't change anything."

"There are other ways to make a difference," Axel had said, doing his best to remain calm, "by exposing injustice or misuse of power, for example." His father had waved his hands as if this was the dumbest thing he'd ever heard. Still Axel pushed on. "You're not going to like this, Dad, but I've decided to become a journalist. I'll complete my studies as agreed, but after that I'll apply for a course in journalism. I've already talked to the Department of Media Studies. They say I have a greater chance getting in with a degree in National Economics…"

Eyes bulging with fury, and lips pulled back in pure revulsion, his father had practically jumped off of the sofa.

"A journalist!" he'd spat, his voice a loud shrill. "That's not making use of your potential! That's not making a difference in the world! It's just an excuse to get out of a job and an education."

"But…"

"No! You hear me? You are meant for great things. You started Talk Thirteen, for heaven's sake."

"Peter and I did it together," Axel had pointed out, tired of having this conversation again.

"Still, it was *your* idea, and it shows you've got potential to become a great leader one day. You're good with people; they listen to you. And God knows you're stubborn, which most executives are." He paused and pointed at his son. "Don't give me that face! You know I'm right. You're not afraid to speak your mind and growing up abroad has taught you how to socialise with people of many nations and social backgrounds. You have your mother's good looks, and if you apply to the Academy, I'm confident you'll be accepted!"

"It doesn't change how I feel, Dad," Axel had muttered. "Don't you get it? I'm not applying!"

Even now he could remember the expression on his father's face: the anger and the disappointment. Behind his eyes had been a wrath that Axel had never seen before.

"My parents had nothing. They were simple country folks with no dreams. I pulled myself out of that gutter. I made myself a very good life. I'm now a respected man, and I won't let you shame me by being lazy and arrogant."

"You see!" Axel had retorted. "You say you're doing this for me, but it's not true. You want me to gain power and fame so *you* can brag about it to your friends."

To Axel's great surprise, his father had lowered his head like a dispirited pastor. "You're my son. I know I don't say it very often, but I love you. I want you to be happy and I'm trying to help." He'd raised his head, eyeing Axel who'd sat there in stunned silence. "You have a good heart, and Talk Thirteen is a great example of that. I believe you when you say you want to make a difference in the world, I do. But if that's the case, then you *have* to become a leader."

"Sorry, Dad. I'm not doing it."

His father had given his head a slow shake. "Very well." He'd walked over to the window, run his finger along the windowsill, and puffed up his chest. "You think you'll be happier doing things your way?"

"Yes."

"Fine, have it your way. You're an adult; your mother and I can't force you to listen to our advice. If you want me to back off, then I'll back off." Axel had watched his father with growing suspicion, and the man had given him a small nod before walking back to the sofa to pick up his coat. "Of course, I should add that if you want your mother and me to back off, then we'll back off in every sense. It means you're on your own. We'll sell your apartment and cut any financial support you're getting today."

Axel had felt his anger beginning to rise beyond his control.

"You can't do that! You promised me this apartment. You said that if I got my masters, it'd be mine!"

"As a matter of fact, we never specified which subject you had to graduate in. Apply to the Academy and get your EKA diploma. If not..."

It was at that moment that Axel realised how much he hated his father. The man was a freaking dictator.

"Then sell the damn apartment!" he'd yelled, overwhelmed by fury. "I don't care!"

"Fine, if that's your choice." The man had walked over to the front door and pulled on his coat. "You know, Talk Thirteen has come a long way because of me. You and Peter have done a great job, I don't want to take that away from you, but you wouldn't have succeeded without me." His father had smirked. "I can see you don't believe me, which doesn't surprise me. Despite all my effort to teach you, you still don't understand how the world works. How many of Talk Thirteen's largest donors have you secured through my contacts?"

"Around forty per cent," Axel had growled.

"And should you explore the backgrounds of other donors, you'll see that about seventy-five per cent can be connected to me in one way or the other. All of them, whether you've talked to them or not, have been encouraged by me or my employees to support your cause." A smug smile had spread across his father's face. "You see? That's how success is built; through influence and power, and you don't get that by being a journalist." He'd reached for the door. "I wonder what would happen to Talk Thirteen if seventy-five per cent of its biggest donors pulled out?"

Axel had felt as if the world had collapsed around him. All the work that he and Peter had put into their organisation – all the people they'd helped and would help – would crumble if their donors pulled out.

"The Academy only accepts twelve students," he'd whispered. "I'll never get in."

"No one cares for a pessimist, son. Apply, and you'll have your apartment and an organisation that will continue to thrive."

The doorbell rang and Axel was jolted out of his depressing memory. He placed the business card in his new wallet, which he then threw into the drawer of his bedside table.

Screw the old man, he thought, as he rolled out of bed. His father wasn't half as smart as he thought he was. On the contrary, he was an idiot. Once Axel had the power his father wanted him to have, he'd use that power to get even with the old man. Anyone with half a brain could figure that out.

The thought gave him some comfort as he jogged through the long corridor, past the spacious living room and over to the front door. Mr Milton was waiting for him at the door with a gleeful expression and the new phone.

"I see you've opened the packages from our sponsors," Mr Milton observed. Axel glanced at his new Rolex and smiled. At least now he knew why Nicole told him not to bring anything. "If there's anything you're missing, just let us know and we'll provide it for you."

Axel laughed. The heaps of gifts on his bed had contained everything from high-class clothes and accessories, to a gold tablet with his name inscribed.

"I doubt you've missed anything," he said.

"I'm glad to hear that, sir," Mr Milton replied. "Dinner is at seven-thirty, would you care for a tour around the premises before that?"

"Thank you, but I think I'm going to take a shower and maybe rest a little before the evening's event."

"As you wish, sir."

Mr Milton bowed again and left.

For a little while, Axel played around with his new phone. After managing to connect it to a series of wireless speakers, he turned on some music to lighten his mood. Then he wandered around the apartment, marvelling at all the furniture and exclusive art that filled his apartment.

It's strange, he thought to himself, as he peeked out of one of the living-room windows, it's *so* different, yet somehow they've managed to make it feel like home.

CHAPTER 16

His mouth was dry and his pulse raced. The new clothes and shoes, which had fitted him perfectly an hour ago, were now either too tight, too stiff, or too itchy. He caught a glimpse of his reflection in the mirror. He looked fine, didn't he? Suitable for an introduction dinner?

Somewhere in the back of his mind, a scornful voice laughed at him. Since when are you worried about your appearance? Ignoring the voice, Axel shoved his hands in his pockets to stop them from trembling. In a few seconds, the elevator doors would open and he would step out on the fourth floor to meet the other eleven students for the first time.

What if he didn't like them? What if they didn't like *him*? It was easy to assume that they were all ambitious and arrogant individuals who thought themselves better than everyone else. How would he be able to socialise with such people, let alone respect them?

The elevator came to a stop. Axel took another deep breath, rolled his shoulders twice, and exhaled as the doors began to open. This was it.

A wonderful aromatic smell forced its way into the elevator, followed by the soft tunes of a well-known love song. Axel pulled his hands out of his pockets. They were still shaking. He tugged at the bottom of his suit jacket and stepped out.

Spellbound, he stared at a huge hall with oak floor, sand-coloured walls, and massive trees that reached for a vaulted ceiling. Way up there hung great chandeliers, casting their warm light over him in a welcoming embrace. He couldn't help but smile. It *was* amazing.

Mesmerized by the atmosphere, he almost forgot how nervous he was. For a moment he just took in the sight, wishing Mikael could have been there to experience it. His friend would've loved it.

A group of servants gave him a quick bow before scurrying off past a great marble statue. Curious, Axel walked over and found it to be a statue of Hayato Sano, the most famous EKA student to have graduated from the Academy. Axel turned and realised that spread out along the walls were more statues, all of them of former students. *Will they have one of me?* He laughed at the thought. It was crazy.

Axel had just spotted a gigantic ice sculpture of the Academy logo when someone called his name.

"Welcome, sir." A waitress in black uniform and a sunny expression approached from a nearby bar carrying a champagne glass on a tray. "May I offer you a drink?"

"Uh…"

"Don't worry, sir. We are aware that you don't care for alcohol. This is a White Jasmine Sparkling Tea." The waitress gestured towards the tables. "Let me show you to your seat, sir."

"That won't be necessary, Miss Russo. I'll show Mr Hallman to his table."

Axel turned to find Nicole approaching with long, elegant strides. She'd visited two countries in one day, three if you included Brussels, and Axel guessed she'd been up since at least half past three that morning. Even so, she looked stunning in a beautiful dark-blue gown. Her blonde hair was pulled back in an elaborate up-do, and around her long neck hung a pearl necklace.

"Ms Swan!"

"Oh, please, you can call me Nicole."

Axel smiled. "As long as you call me Axel."

Nicole laughed. "That's kind of you, but I don't think the management would approve. There are rules about these things, you know." She waved off the waitress and took Axel by the arm. "Come, I'll show you to your table."

Making their way across the floor, Axel took in the surroundings. They were approaching the five dining tables. One long square table was placed along a windowless wall. The remaining tables were smaller and round, placed in the middle of the room. They were all elegantly set, with white, linen tablecloths, candles, and wide but short bouquets of red roses. The most spectacular feature, however, were 3D holograms of eagles, flying in circles at the centre of each table. Most of the other students had already arrived. Axel could hear their hushed conversations and feel their eyes upon him as he passed.

"So how are you finding your apartment, Mr Hallman?" Nicole had an inquisitive smile on her lips, one that suggested she knew things Axel didn't. "Is it to your liking?"

"It's perfect."

"I'm pleased to hear that, sir. Well, here we are." Nicole stopped at one of the small tables. There were four chairs, three of them were already occupied. "Everyone, this is Axel Hallman from Sweden." Nicole pulled out the empty chair and turned to Axel. "And Mr Hallman, this is your study group." She let go of his arm.

"Thank you, Nicole."

"My pleasure, Mr Hallman." She turned to the other students. "Now I hope you all enjoy your evening."

CHAPTER 17

TWELVE YEARS EARLIER

Maybe there's a limit to how much excitement a human being can handle in a single day, Sarah pondered, as she took in the sight of the great hall. She'd never felt this way before. The thrill and anticipation that filled her was almost painful.

From the moment she'd arrived at the Academy, she'd been awestruck. The school resided in a grand, Asian-inspired palace outside the small historical town of Hoi An, situated along Vietnam's central coast. Protected behind a thick stonewall, the palace sat proudly on a little hill surrounded by the most magnificent garden Sarah had ever seen. The palace itself was no exception to the grandeur. The gold, the marble, the statues and the art…the luxury was endless, and everywhere she turned there was something to admire.

"So you're from Tanzania?"

Sarah snapped out of her thoughts and turned to Lorena De Paz, the Spanish student who had arrived at the table a few minutes earlier.

"I've been to the Serengeti once on safari," Lorena continued. "It's a nice country."

Sarah lit up. "Thank you," she replied while her fingers fidgeted with her dress under the table. Mr Bell had picked out a beautiful apricot-coloured gown for her, along with a pair of gold earrings. She'd never worn gold jewellery before, and now she owned *several* pieces.

"So what do you do for a living," Lorena asked. "If you don't mind me asking, of course."

Sarah hesitated and snuck a peek at the well-dressed man on her right, the one who had introduced himself as Kostay Aristov from Russia. Already she thought of him as "the man who never smiled".

He had a handsome face but unnerving eyes that revealed nothing of his emotions. It made her feel uneasy.

"I work as a maid," she replied, turning back to Lorena. "Or I did before coming here."

Lorena's eyes widened and, for a moment, there was a crack in her confident façade.

"A maid? You mean like a servant?"

"I mean like a housemaid."

"But…" Lorena and Kostay exchanged looks. "A *housemaid*?

Sarah gave a defiant little shrug. Under no circumstances would she be ashamed of who she was or where she came from. She had done her best with the hand she'd been dealt, which was more than one could say for many people born into wealthy families. As Ruth always used to say, "it's not how we start our life that matters but how we end it."

In front of her, Lorena leaned back in her chair with her glass of champagne in a steady grip. "I'm confused. You've got an orphanage?"

"Yes, together with Ruth."

"Oh." There was a brief moment of silence. "And who is Ruth?"

The question triggered a flood of warm memories and Sarah almost closed her eyes as they washed over her. "Ruth is the kindest person I know. She and her husband started the orphanage many years ago, but when he died she couldn't afford to feed the children anymore. She was desperate so I decided to help her. Now she takes care of the orphans while I make sure they have a roof over their head and food in their bellies."

"I'll be damned." Lorena laughed. "What about your parents? Are they also servants?"

"I never knew my parents. My mother left me at an orphanage when I was a baby."

"You're kidding me? You're an orphan with an orphanage?"

"Yes."

Lorena considered Sarah while toying with her glass. Then it was her turn to shrug.

"Cool. And now you're here to rule the world. That's a remarkable achievement."

"I'm not here to rule the world," Sarah objected. "I'm here to make it a better place."

"Same thing, isn't it? Anyway, I'm impressed. It takes a lot of courage and determination to get anywhere in this world. Believe me, I know. I'm a twenty-three-year-old woman who just attained the rank of lieutenant colonel in the Spanish armed forces. It wasn't easy. Even my family thought I was nuts, but I did it and no one can take that away from me." She raised her glass with a grin. "So what do you say? To strong, independent women?" She looked over at Kostay, who didn't touch his glass, and she laughed. "Cheers!"

CHAPTER 18

PRESENT DAY

Confident and intelligent. That was Axel's first impression when Izabella Martins introduced herself. The young Brazilian had chosen a sleeveless silk dress of the deepest red, daring enough to make her stand out in a crowd without coming across as provocative or distasteful. It was a brilliant choice if you were a woman who liked getting attention, Axel concluded.

"It's a pleasure to meet you," Izabella said with a silvery voice and extended her hand.

"Likewise," Axel replied, and then surprised himself by adding a little bow. He had no idea why he did it and was feeling like a complete idiot when he looked up and found Izabella watching him with a mixture of curiosity and amusement.

Great, he thought, how can I pretend to be a leader when I'm already copying the servants?

To evade further embarrassment, he turned to the man on his right, a proud-looking fellow, with a back straight as a ramrod.

"Hello Axel. My name is Thabo Zulu," the man declared with a calm, almost noble expression on his face. "I am from South Africa."

"He's a prince, you know." The third man at the table stood up and offered his hand with a wide sunshine smile. "Nice to meet you. I'm Paul Harris, born and raised in Sydney, Australia."

Paul was a little shorter than Axel but a great deal wider around the waist. He made a sweeping motion towards Thabo. "His father is the king of the Zulus."

Having lived in South Africa for several years, Axel knew a fair bit about the Zulus. They were a proud people, with a rich and fascinating history.

"Really? I lived in South Africa when I was younger."

"Are you serious, mate?" Paul let out a rumbling laugh. "That's fantastic! You guys must have a lot to talk about."

"I'm sure we will," Thabo concurred with a wry smile.

It was interesting, Axel thought, as he took his seat; Izabella, Paul, and Thabo were confident but in very different ways. Izabella had a touch of aggressiveness to the way she spoke and behaved, reminding him of a commander giving orders. Thabo showed a more composed confidence, an inner strength that suggested a fearless character. Paul was socially gifted and completely at ease as he conversed with the others. He had a certain wit to him that made him likable from the moment you met him.

"So Izabella," Paul said with a cheerful voice after having taken a deep draught of his champagne, "why were you accepted to the Academy?"

Izabella reached up and touched a small ring of gold that glimmered in her right ear.

"When I was fifteen I launched *Velvet Media,* a web marketing and advertisement company. I sold it three years later for two and a half million dollars. I believe another factor is that my father was a successful business owner and my oldest brother is the mayor of João Pessoa. I guess you could say that leadership is in my genes."

In the soft candlelight, Paul raised his glass in a cheer.

"Two and a half million dollars in three years; that's impressive."

"Thank you. What about you?"

"I run a very successful golf academy just outside Sydney."

"Is that a profitable business?" Izabella asked with a frown.

"Sure is, but I make most of my money as a sports agent. I represent seven of the ten top junior golfers in Australia. I was also studying management when I got accepted, and did pretty well there too." He grinned and turned to Thabo. "And you're a prince."

Thabo offered him a slight nod.

"Yes, a Zulu prince. I've also studied diplomacy and foreign policy in London."

Izabella leaned forward, her eyes sparkling.

"Will you become a king one day?"

"No; the oldest son will inherit the throne, and I have many older brothers."

"Ah." Izabella picked up her crystal glass and leaned back while surveying the surroundings. "I see."

Thabo watched her for a second before turning to Axel. "What about you, Axel? How is it you were chosen for the Eagle King's Academy?"

Axel felt as if his racing heart stumbled in his chest. He was no royal or successful businessman. He had neither money nor power; all he had was Talk Thirteen, and that, he now knew, was thanks to his father. The bastard.

"To tell you the truth, I don't know. When I was thirteen, a friend and I started a network in South Africa called Talk Thirteen. The idea was to get kids our own age to stand up for children's rights."

"I've heard of Talk Thirteen," Thabo said with his strong, African accent. "They have a slogan, right? 'We are all the same and equal'?"

"Actually, it's 'Let's change the game, we're all the same'." Axel let out a nervous laugh. "Not the greatest of slogans but we were thirteen years old. We wanted people to realise that all humans are equal and should be treated as such."

"Oh, that's cute." Izabella laughed. "So you started this…network?"

"Yes, together with a friend, but it was a long time ago. I don't work there anymore." A silence fell over the table. Axel cleared his throat. "And my father is a successful businessman."

"I thought he was a diplomat," Thabo said, his face impassive.

"He was. Now he owns a couple of companies."

"But what do *you* do?" Izabella asked.

"I studied economy." Again there was a reaction from the others. Axel drank some water, hoping his nervousness wouldn't show. "That's it, I'm afraid."

The silence remained another second or so.

"I think I'll have to look up that organisation of yours," Paul declared. "It sounds interesting." He took a moment to drink and then gave them all a smug smile. "Now, if you don't mind me changing the subject, you'll never guess who I saw earlier today," he said. "Principal Cunningham."

Izabella gawked.

"You're joking?"

"No, I met him by the elevators on the fourteenth floor. I was trying to find the virtual golf simulator. Mr Milton said it was up there, next to the bowling alley."

Axel furrowed his brows. "There's a bowling alley?"

"Sure, mate. And a gym, pool, a squash court…"

"What about Principal Cunningham," Izabella interrupted.

"He'd just arrived to the premises. I asked one of the servants who said there's a helipad on the roof, which is only accessible via stairs from the fourteenth floor. The principal had just arrived when…" The candles in the hall flickered and died. The music and chatter died down. "Wow. How did they do that?" Paul breathed.

Axel raised his gaze towards the ceiling. Above them the lights had begun to fade. The hologram eagles made one last turn before they flew off towards the ceiling and vanished.

He let his eyes travel around the hall, searching for Nicole, but he couldn't see her. All the Academy employees had pulled back into the growing shadows among the large trees. The great hall became dark and quiet. To his left, Axel could hear Izabella shift in her chair.

"Oh, this is it," she whispered.

On the wall behind the long, still-empty table, came an image of the universe, lit up by millions of twinkling stars. For a few seconds, nothing else happened. Then in the distance came the sound of an electric guitar and the rapid beating of a hi-hat. An eerie, yet exuberating, sensation swept over the students as the volume began to increase, followed by a low, guttural humming.

Axel grinned. He knew this song. It was AC/DC's "Thunderstruck".

The stars on the wall began to move, creating a sense of moving through space. It was as if the music brought with it some ancient power, making the hairs on Axel's arms stand up. A bass drum let loose a heavy beat and the humming voices sang out one word – "THUNDER!" At that moment, the stars on the wall exploded into white, and the picture of a young, bearded man appeared. Under his smiling face, written in gold letters, stood his name, "Edward Reed"; Axel's new neighbour.

As the photo faded back into stars and darkness, the surrounding Academy employees began to clap. They clapped at a steady rhythm, following the music. Then came a second "THUNDER!" and Izabella's face appeared. Despite the music, he could hear her inhale in surprise.

One by one the twelve students were recognised on the wall. Federico Calvo, Julie Baston, Ava Taylor…

For each photo, the hall grew increasingly vibrant. The students, even Axel, were now clapping along with the staff members. Some, among them Paul, drove their fists into the air, shouting "THUNDER" as each new photo appeared.

It was absolute madness. The atmosphere seemed to captivate students and staff alike to such a degree it was laughable. Yet somewhere in his heart, Axel felt an extraordinary and uncomfortable desire to shout along. It was unnerving, and he tried to ignore it since he wasn't the kind of person who lost his control amongst others.

Axel was the last to be recognised. His photo faded just as AC/DC's lead singer, Brian Johnson sang, *"You've been...THUNDERSTRUCK."* At that precise moment, the room lit up. Lights flashed and danced across the tables. Around the hall, flames shot out from the floor, and as the lights faded a little, three large hologram eagles appeared under the ceiling. Stunned, Axel looked up as the birds dove towards the students; one eagle for each table. It happened so fast he barely had time to react. Instinct made him rear as the massive bird approached with increasing speed.

"Shit!" Paul cried, and a split second later the eagle exploded, turning into a glimmering, hologram rain.

"*Ladies and gentlemen*," a dark voice boomed from the speakers as the tiny light particles fell around the students, "*please give a warm welcome to your teachers!*"

CHAPTER 19

At the far end of the great hall, a spotlight lit up a massive double door. Axel craned his neck as it opened, and two muscular guards with grim faces stepped in. Dressed in tailored black suits, they positioned themselves on either side of the door, hands behind their straight backs and a grim expression on their faces.

Then the world's most renowned teachers made their dazzling entrance.

"Professor Evans," Izabella gasped as a short, stout woman emerged to the wild applause of the spectators. On the wall behind the empty table, the woman's profile photo appeared, along with beautiful animated gold letters, spelling out her name. The professor smiled and gave the students a little wave before making her way to her seat.

Behind Professor Evans came an elderly man named Professor Plouffe. One by one, the teachers entered while their photos and names appeared on the wall. Izabella knew them all, all but the one who entered last.

"Who's that?" she asked, pointing at the broad-shouldered Asian man with hard eyes and a serious face. "*Mr Nakata*? I've never heard of him before."

"Neither have I," Paul admitted.

Thabo shrugged and Axel certainly didn't know who it was.

"I guess we'll know soon enough." Izabella laughed and gave Axel a beaming smile.

There were fifteen chairs. Seven teachers had placed themselves on the right and seven on the left. The chair in the middle remained empty. It was a little bigger than the other chairs, and above it, one of the hologram eagles had returned.

"That has to be Principal Cunningham's seat," Izabella continued. "God, he's amazing! I can't believe I'm going to meet him. In person!"

Axel suppressed a moan, not so much in regards to what Izabella had said, but rather a reaction to his current feelings. He'd never understood people's obsession with the famous principal. The man was a living legend and even the media treated him like some kind of superhero or messiah. Such absolute adoration had to be questioned. No human being was perfect, which was why it annoyed him to the core that a part of him shared Izabella's excitement.

To his relief there was little time to contemplate the matter. The music died along with the lights until the room was set in complete darkness. Only the sound of nervous students shifting in their seats could be heard. A few seconds passed and stillness settled in the great hall.

Then there was an explosion. Powerful sparklers ignited along the floor, creating a burning corridor from the elevators to the head table. Axel was almost blinded by the white light.

"And now the greatest of them all…" the booming voice announced.

Geez, this was getting a little corny, wasn't it? All the same, as Axel turned and saw the golden wings of one of the elevators begin to glimmer, he felt a rush of anticipation run through his body.

"…Principal Cunningham!"

They were only twelve students, but together with the teachers and thirty or so excited servants, the great hall shook as a thunderous applause erupted. Teachers and students rose to their feet.

Axel had seen the famous principal on TV many times and always imagined him taller. Despite being in his late sixties, the man made his way between the sparklers with calm, confident strides. He was the "leaders of leaders"; top of the hierarchy, and he knew it.

When he reached his chair, he pushed the round spectacles further up on his prominent nose before motioning everyone to sit. The applause died down, and the silence that followed felt almost intrusive. Principal Cunningham beheld the audience, his pudgy hands on the backrest of his chair.

Izabella let out a little giggle. Paul picked up his champagne glass, saw that it was empty and put it back. Thabo didn't move a muscle. Axel clasped his hands under the table as the tension grew. I'm doing this for Talk Thirteen, he reminded himself a few times.

"Almost two hundred and forty thousand people applied," Principal Cunningham began with his high-born, British accent, and a voice so clear and charismatic, it was almost hypnotic. "Twelve were chosen. It was no simple task. Many people have the potential to become good leaders, yet, at the Academy, good isn't good enough. We don't even settle for 'great'. Our students must have the potential to become historical. Their presence must make those around them feel thunderstruck." He paused, considering his audience with an air of tranquil wisdom glowing around him. "After long and rigorous testing, thorough evaluations and meticulous scrutiny, twelve students were finally chosen. Twelve potentials. Twelve leaders-to-be…and these twelve …are you." He allowed another dramatic pause, then opened his arms wide. "*Welcome to Eagle King's Academy!*"

The students broke out in wild whoops and cheers. Lights flashed across the room and confetti began to rain down from the high ceiling. Axel peered around the hall feeling sceptical about the whole thing. The students behaved worse than teenagers at a rock concert, and the servants like religious fanatics worshiping a god. It was unnerving to see.

Then his eyes fell upon one of the teachers sitting next to Principal Cunningham, Professor Jackson, the man Nicole had referred to when discussing the golden eagle at the foyer. Dressed in a black suit, he sat with his hands interlocked in front of him. He was in his mid-fifties, handsome but with a grim, unyielding face and piercing blue eyes that stared at… Axel paused. Why was Professor Jackson staring at him?

Shit! The realization struck him hard and he cursed his own carelessness. While everyone else was clapping, shouting, and cheering, Axel sat there quiet and wide-eyed, taking in the spectacle around him. He must have stood out like a paralysed raven among lorikeets.

Putting on a smile he began applauding and it took over a minute before he dared another glance at the teachers' table; by then Professor Jackson had turned his attention elsewhere.

At last, Principal Cunningham raised his hands, and the room fell silent.

"*The Eagle King's Academy.* We are proud of our name. Throughout history, the eagle has symbolised power, authority, wisdom, and strength, and we live by our name. With our guidance, you will become the greatest among leaders; the king of eagles. It will not be easy. To succeed and graduate you must work harder than you ever imagined. Over the next two and a half years, you'll be pushed to your limits and discover sides of yourself you never dreamt of.

"I tell you this so you understand the magnitude of what you have embarked on. There will be days when you question yourself; days when you feel all alone, and moments when you wish you *were* alone. There will be times when you want to give up and go home, and days when getting out of bed seems to be the most difficult task in the world." The principal waved his index finger in the air. "And by that I am not referring to you waking up on a Sunday morning with a bad hangover."

The students laughed and Axel had to admit he was drawn to the principal's words. Not so much by what the man said but *how* he said it. The way he emphasised his words, pausing at the right time and using the right intonations unhindered.

His gaze moved to Professor Jackson, who sat rigid in his chair, scanning the room like a prison warden expecting an inmate riot. Axel was quick to turn away before their eyes could meet again.

"To be a true, successful leader is not an easy task," the principal continued. "You will continuously face new challenges, even long after you've left the Academy, and therefore I would like to tell you a little story.

"Many years ago, a student of ours faced a particularly difficult dilemma. She began doubting herself and her ability as leader. To help her make the right decisions, she came up with a few words based on some of our guiding principles. It strengthened her when she needed it the most, so when she graduated, she decided to share her words with the other students. That is how our Leadership Allegiance was born." Principal Cunningham pointed at the wall behind him. "Please stand up and let us read the sacred text illuminated behind me."

> "I'm the role model who leads the way,
> People follow, and they obey.
> I empower and foster trust,
> I can be tough, but always just.
>
> I motivate and make decisions,
> I point the way and shape our visions.
> I refuse to lose or fail,
> This is why, it's me they'll hail."

In the dim light, Axel stood at his place. He felt dreadful. He was an outsider and an imposter in a world that was unlikely to accept either. As the applause broke out around him, he closed his eyes, knowing somewhere deep in his heart that he was heading for disaster.

CHAPTER 20

Taking a deep breath, the man pulled the black mask over his face. Dressed in black sweatpants and matching hoodie, he slipped through the door, leaving the safety of the stairwell behind him. From this moment on, he wouldn't be able to move without the security cameras recording him. With any luck, the guards wouldn't pay the ninth floor any attention. If they did, this would all be over within minutes.

Checking his watch, he determined the teachers had now left the party and were three stories up, staring at large screens while analysing the students as they interacted with one another at the party. This meant the security guards were focusing on five areas; the outside premises, the entrances, the roof, the restaurant, and the twelfth floor where the teachers were. In other words, he should be safe. At least that was the theory.

With trembling hands, the man placed a key-card against the lock to open the door. He adjusted the hood over his head and entered Axel's apartment. The creepy blue light from the aquarium shimmered into the hallway creating an unsettling atmosphere. The man took a moment to collect himself; just long enough to get control of his breathing. He didn't turn on the lights as it could draw the attention of one of the patrolling night guards.

He passed through the living room and reached the dark corridor. With a bit of fumbling, he managed to turn on the night-vision function on his mask, bringing the area into full view. After allowing himself a second to scan the surroundings, he hurried down the corridor to the bedroom.

The wallet was in the drawer of the bedside table. Working as fast as he could, he pulled out the business card, replaced it with a replica, and returned the wallet where he found it.

Two minutes and seventeen seconds had passed since leaving the safety of the stairwell. At midnight, the automated back-up system would kick in. The security cameras would transfer the past twenty-four hours of recordings to a secure hard drive, impossible to breech. That was in forty-two minutes. Before then, he needed to manipulate the recordings to make himself vanish from every camera in the building. Every step had been planned in advance, but it would still take him at least twenty minutes to complete that process. It was time to get a move on.

CHAPTER 21

Axel woke early the following morning to sunlight peeking through the edges of the thick curtains and the refreshing smell of ocean and warm sand. Confused he sat up and let his eyes wander the room. Oh yes, the Academy!

He kicked off the goose down-filled duvet and headed for the bathroom. After a hot shower, he pulled on pair of black trousers, a turquoise shirt, and matching sweater. Pretty good, he decided, checking his reflection in the mirror before heading out for breakfast. To his surprise, most of the students were already in the restaurant. He received a few polite nods on the way to his table.

"Good morning," Izabella said with a sly grin. She appeared the picture of professionalism in a pair of fancy grey trousers and a pink blouse. "You're not an early riser, are you?"

"It's ten past seven!" Axel replied and sat down. "Oh, thank you."

The last comment was directed at a waitress who appeared out of nowhere with a cup of steaming tea, a jug of warm milk, and a pile of newspapers, which she handed him with a polite bow.

Izabella laughed and pushed up her glasses.

"I got up around five thirty figuring I might as well get used to it. I've a feeling that from now on we won't be sleeping much. This is the EKA, after all.

Paul looked up from behind a newspaper. "I was thinking the same." He smiled. "I got up at six."

Axel poured some milk into his cup. Considering the massive bags under Paul's blood-shot eyes, the guy could have used a few more hours in bed, he thought.

"How are your feet?"

Paul barked out a laugh.

"A little sore, mate. Too much dancing, you know."

Axel picked up his steaming cup. "What about you, Thabo? When did you get up?"

"Hmm," Thabo said, without taking his eyes off his paper. "Too early for my liking."

All right, so Thabo wasn't much of a morning-person. Of course, neither was Axel. Since the others seemed content to spend the morning in silence, he dropped the pleasantries and focused on the breakfast buffet instead.

The Academy's offerings easily rivalled that of any five-star hotel. The long table, behind which the teachers had sat the previous night, now displayed a vast array of breads, pastries, juices, fruits, cereal, sausages, eggs, baked beans, and anything else one could desire for breakfast.

Half an hour later, stuffed to the brim with pancakes and an omelette, Axel waddled down to the majestic foyer for the morning orientation. He was the first student to arrive. Nicole was waiting for them by the golden eagle, engaged in a quiet conversation with one of the guards.

A faint scent of rose hovered over the place as Axel made his way across the marble floor. He gave Miss Davis at the reception a polite nod. She bowed in return which made him feel both uncomfortable and a bit pompous. When two other staff members also lowered their heads in respect, Axel made a silent vow to never get used to the bowing. He wasn't better than these people and didn't want to be treated as such.

Soon his thoughts moved on to other matters. Even from a distance, Nicole looked stunning. Her blonde hair stood out in sharp contrast to the black coat that seemed to hug her body. Lucky coat. When she saw him, she brightened and waved off the guard.

"Good morning, Mr Hallman. How are you this beautiful morning?"

"Great! And you?"

"Oh…I'm very well, thank you." She paused and seemed to study him for a second. "How kind of you to ask. Did you enjoy the party last night? I met Ms Izzati at the restaurant this morning, and she said there was a fair bit of dancing going on."

Axel laughed. Dalilah Izzati was an intense woman from Malaysia. They hadn't spoken much as she'd spent most of her time on the dance floor.

"Well, she, Julie, and Paul were dancing as if there was no tomorrow," he confirmed. "The rest of us weren't as persistent."

Nicole let out a charming laugh, the kind that washes over you like gentle breeze on a hot summer day. It was so sweet and radiant it seemed to light up the entire foyer.

At that moment, Izabella, Paul, and two other students, Julie and Federico, stepped out of the elevators. Dressed in their new black coats, they crossed the large open space with proud faces, passing the bowing servants without as much as a glance.

"All right," Nicole said, watching the students approach. "Are you ready to explore Brussels?"

CHAPTER 22

Brussels was a charming city with narrow cobblestone streets and great architectural buildings. Known for its chocolate and beer, the city offered countless cafés and pubs, along with waffle stands and restaurants. By the time the students returned to the Academy six hours later, Axel felt as if he'd seen every corner of the city.

"I'm exhausted," Federico Calvo sighed, as they passed through the security checkpoint.

Axel had spoken to Federico the day before and found him to be an ambitious man. He'd started his career at the age of ten, selling fresh juice in his hometown of Choele Choel in Argentina. By twelve he had twenty-three friends working for him, pressing and selling the juice. By eighteen, he'd saved enough money to start his own juice bar. Now, at twenty-three, he was a millionaire, owning several bars in the country. It was crazy. He was only a year older than Axel.

Federico ran a hand through his thick, curly hair and turned to Cordelia Campbell, a charming woman from Victoria, Canada. "I'm going up to the pool for a swim. Do you want to join me?"

Cordelia, who during lunch had told Axel about the successful network she'd started for young entrepreneurs, turned to Julie Baston, a bright but serious woman from France. "Sounds fun. Will you join us?"

Izabella gave Axel a nudge. "Come on, we should go too."

Before Axel had a chance to reply, Paul stepped in and placed his big hand on Izabella's shoulder. "That's a great idea," he said. "Let's rendezvous in twenty minutes."

Axel stepped out of the elevator on the fourteenth floor. He was in a wide corridor with marbled floor and large, arched windows. Izabella, Paul and Thabo were already waiting for him on a bench under a massive, potted tree. According to a wall-mounted sign made of gold, the pool area was at the end of the passage, near the sports centre.

"That way," Paul declared and stood up.

They passed an old man in green overalls, tending to a colourful flowerbed along the wall. As soon as the servant saw them, he stood up with effort and bowed. Axel gave him a fleeting smile. The others, however, ignored the man. Instead, they admired the spectacular, curved ceiling, which functioned as a massive screen, displaying a blue sky with small tufts of clouds moving down the corridor at a slow pace.

"Fascinating," Thabo mumbled.

Right as he was, the captivating ceiling dwarfed in comparison to what they discovered a few minutes later. The pool area was nothing less than a grand indoor rainforest, and as soon as the students stepped through the doors, they came to a unified stop, eyes wide with amazement.

"Wow!" Axel managed after a moment's stunned silence. He drew a deep breath, filling his lungs with hot air that smelled of tropical fruits and coconut.

The ceiling and part of the walls were made of glass, similar to that of a greenhouse, but massive trees, creepers, and exotic plants made it hard to see the sky from the ground. Despite this, the space felt airy and full of light. A symphony of singing birds, rustling of leaves, and chirping insects welcomed them, and somewhere in the background came the muffled sound of a waterfall. For the first time since his arrival, Axel felt completely at ease.

Beside him, Paul shifted his weight.

"Crikey," he mumbled in awe.

"Look!" Thabo pointed towards the ceiling. Axel peered up just in time to see a huge eagle, proud in its appearance, fly above their heads before disappearing behind the treetops.

"Okay, boys, the changing rooms are over here," Izabella said, already moving towards a small bungalow near the entrance. "Let's get changed so we can explore this place."

Swimsuits and cover-ups on, they set off along a narrow stone path, following small wooden signs with the word "Pool" on them.

They walked underneath palm trees and between clusters of bamboo. They passed golden cages nestled among the exotic greenery, occupied by large turtles, strange lizards, and colourful birds. They even crossed a wooden bridge, stretching over a slow-moving stream.

"My god, have we found the Garden of Eden?" Izabella laughed as a butterfly flew past her head.

"Come on," Paul said, grinning, "I think I can hear Federico and the ladies."

The pool was in a clearing, and it was, as with everything else within the walls of the Academy, a spectacular sight. Along one side was a natural-looking waterfall with vines climbing up its sides. Huge trees reached out over the water. Axel was once again reminded of just how creative and eccentric the Academy was. There was even a small island in the middle of the pool. On it stood Federico, about to dive into the water.

"You've got to see this!" he shouted and dove in.

Thrilled, the four students dropped their towels and jumped into the warm water.

"You've got to be joking!" Paul yelled as his head appeared above the surface a moment later. "They've built the pool *inside* an aquarium?"

Hidden underneath the deck was a huge aquarium that enclosed all sides of the pool.

"Isn't it neat?" Cordelia laughed before disappearing under the water again.

"There are goggles by the waterfall," Julie said putting on a pair she had already grabbed. "It is fantastic."

Axel swam back and forth under the water enjoying the spectacular view of colourful fish and sea horses. If only Mikael could have seen this.

Exhausted, they crawled out of the water and collapsed into a few sun chairs around the pool. They lay there until Paul grew bored and dragged them down to the EKA restaurant for dinner and drinks at the bar.

To Axel's astonishment, he felt excited when he returned to his apartment later that night. It had been a remarkable day. The other students were smart, well-educated, and attentive. They were all ambitious and driven, and not the Napoleon wannabes he'd feared. Maybe Mikael was right. Perhaps the chosen students were here because they wanted to help the world, not rule it.

On Sunday morning, Axel called his mother. She was happy to hear his voice and kept him on the phone for half an hour, careful not to discuss anything related to the Academy.

Next, Axel called Mikael.

"I wish you were here," Axel confessed. "I'm experiencing all these amazing things and I can't share it with you. It's so frustrating."

"Tell me about it." Mikael sighed. "I'm dying to know everything there is to know. Have you met the teachers yet?"

"I'm not sure if I can tell you that."

"Really?" There was a moment of frustrated silence. "This is silly," Mikael stated with irritation. "Did you know I had to sign three different confidentiality agreements with the Academy?"

Axel smiled to himself. "My parents had to do the same."

"So in theory," Mikael continued, "should you happen to tell me things about the Academy, I wouldn't tell anyone because I'm not allowed to talk about such things."

There was a faint click followed by complete silence.

"Micke?"

No answer.

"Micke, you there?"

Nothing.

Axel waited a little longer but Mikael didn't return. With a bad feeling in his gut, Axel hung up.

A few seconds later, his phone buzzed with an incoming text.

"Security Warning: Today at 9:43, security blocked your call with Mr Mikael Andersson due to the risk of breached contract. According to Security contract

SA1.9, you may not disclose any information about the Academy to people outside the EKA. For more information, contact the EKA Security Team."

CHAPTER 23

Axel read the message for the third time. He hadn't actually said anything to Mikael that could be considered a breach of contract, had he? This text message was the Academy's way of letting him know they were keeping an eye on him. After a few minutes of wavering, he decided to give Mikael another call.

He apologised for the abrupt termination of their previous call but didn't give any explanation as to why it had happened. He then spent about half an hour talking about this and that until he felt there was nothing left to say. When Axel hung up he realised that keeping everything a secret from his family and best friend wouldn't be as easy as he'd hoped.

Later, while searching the bookshelves for something to read, his phone buzzed again.

> "Dear Mr Hallman,
> Report to Madame Garon on the 14th floor ASAP.
> Kind regards,
> The EKA reception."

Fearing it had something to do with his conversation with Mikael, he hurried up to the fourteenth floor. A man, no older than Axel, was waiting for him outside the elevators. There was something feminine about the way he held himself.

"Please come with me, Mr Hallman," the man said with a soft voice. "Madame Garon is waiting for you at the spa."

"Spa?" Axel echoed confused. "Madame Garon isn't part of the security team?"

The young man let out a sound that could have been a cough, but was most likely a muffled laugh. "No, sir. Madame Antoinette Garon is the head of our exquisite EKA Spa and Salon Centre." He threw Axel an amused glance. "She is quite famous, you know."

"Oh."

"Yes. She's related to the Monaco royal family."

"I see."

Axel's lack of enthusiasm for the topic killed the discussion and he was led the rest of the way in silence.

The E.K.A Spa and Salon Centre resided in a beautiful, Asian-inspired room with rose petals on the floor, burning candles, and a scent of incense so overwhelming it was almost hard to breath.

It turned out Madame Garon was a petit, extravagant woman in her late forties. Even with her high-heel shoes she barely reached Axel's shoulders. Fascinated, he peered at her copper-red hair, pulled back in a complex hairdo that must have taken hours to do. Who would spend hours on a hairdo?

His thought was interrupted by a loud "humph", and behind the thick layer of colourful make-up, a pair of dark eyes blinked.

"*Bonjour*, Monsieur Hallman." There was a distinct French accent in the almost childish, nasal voice. "Are you ready?"

Without waiting for a reply, she made a sloppy hand gesture resulting in five glamorous assistants rushing forward.

"*Non!*" Madame Garon barked as Axel moved back. "Stand still." He obeyed and the assistants began circling him like vultures around a carcass. Madame Garon advanced, her eyes scanning him from top to bottom. "First impression is everything, Monsieur Hallman," she explained. "You must radiate confidence like the sun in the Sahara, and glow like a full moon at night." She stopped and let out a dramatic sigh. "But to make that happen, *you must stand still.*"

"Oh, sorry." Axel snapped to attention while the peculiar woman started to make her way around him.

"Bon. There is potential," Madame Garon declared after a while. "You are not a hopeless case, but this way –" she waved her hand in front of his face "– you *are* boring. We need to do magic." She tugged his hair. "I want a lighter colour, Ileana; something that draws focus to his grey eyes. I want people to become hypnotized when they see him. Understand?"

"Yes, Madame Garon. How about ash blond?"

"*Très bien*. And Stephan, I want a more stylish haircut. This –" she grimaced and yanked Axel's hair "– is what schoolboys wear. I want something that brings out the man in him. You know what I mean. And please, trim his eyebrows. Right now they remind me of the Amazon jungle." Madame Garon paused, tapping a finger against her red lips. "Now his skin isn't too bad. I think a classic facial will do, don't you agree, Mario?"

"*Si*, Madame Garon. What about the manicure? Should we…"

"I think you look good," Izabella said later that day. "That hair colour suits you."

She, Axel, Thabo and Paul had left the Academy to explore Bois de la Cambre, a public park situated near Avenue Louise. On this particular Sunday afternoon, the large park had been full of people, from aged couples walking their dogs to groups of people out for a jog.

The students were treading along a human-made lake where geese and ducks bobbed around like feathered buoys in the cold water. Axel ran a hand through his hair. He'd barely recognised himself after returning from Madame Garon. His hair was short and blond; his skin tanned and smooth. His teeth were so white they could blind you, and the eyebrows perfectly shaped.

"Thanks," he said, and moved to the side as they passed a couple with a stroller. "You too. What happened to your glasses?"

"Madame Garon gave me contacts. She said I don't have a face for spectacles."

"What the heck does that mean?" Paul wondered out loud. His hair was now short and a little darker than before. Similar to Axel, his teeth were whiter and his skin seemed polished in the light of the winter sun.

Izabella shrugged and shoved her hands in her coat pocket. "Who knows?"

"I don't like Madame Garon," Thabo concluded with a low growl as he gazed out over the little lake. "I told her this was unacceptable. I'm a Zulu prince. We don't do make-overs."

"Still, you got your head shaved," Axel grinned.

"That's acceptable. Zulu warriors can have their heads shaved."

"Do Zulu warriors also have their nails polished?" Izabella asked with a titter.

Thabo glared down at his hands. "Madame Garon is not a nice person, but she can be *very* convincing."

CHAPTER 24

TWELVE YEARS EARLIER

"What's this?" Sarah asked, as the waiter handed her a pineapple cup drink with a straw and a tiny umbrella.

Lorena threw aside her newspaper and sat up in her sun chair.

"Ah, that's the alcohol," she said with a grin, accepting her own drink from the silent waiter. "The first step in my elaborate plan to erase that gloomy face of yours."

Sarah tittered and began stirring her drink with the straw while admiring the gigantic pool around them. It was an amazing creation with narrow canals, wide openings, and great waterfalls. Curved bridges made of dark wood connected the small islands, where beach umbrellas and comfortable sitting arrangements were nestled in among the palm trees.

Some distance away, a few of the students enjoyed themselves in the water, making a lot of noise in their attempt to impress one another. They're no different from the young men and women in her village, she reflected; richer, but the same, nonetheless.

Sarah took a sip of her drink, enjoying the sweet, cool liquid as it ran down her throat. Once in the classrooms, however, it was a different matter. Then they'd all pretended to be kings and queens. Sarah didn't appreciate people who pretended to be something they weren't.

"So? What do you think?" Lorena asked and nodded towards the drink.

"It's very refreshing, but strong."

"I bet it is. It's called a Bahama Mama, believe it or not."

Sarah found herself giggling. "You're crazy."

"Nah, on the contrary, actually, I'm pretty damn smart." Lorena paused. "I know, for example, that you mustn't let them get to you," she continued, her voice growing serious. "They don't know you and, until they do, they'll treat you as an inferior human being. You have to prove them wrong. You have to show them that you're smart and won't take any of their crap."

"That's not how it should be. We should be helping each other, not competing against one another."

Lorena threw her head back and laughed. "Are you kidding me? If that's what you expect, then you'll be mighty disappointed, my friend," she said, shaking her head. "People aren't very bright, you know. It doesn't matter if they're rich or poor, black or white, educated or illiterate; they're about as smart as a daft monkey on heroin. Do you think I became lieutenant colonel in the Spanish armed forces because people *wanted* me to succeed? Hell no! People were doing everything they could to ensure that I failed. Although we were there to learn how to fight together, they still didn't want me there."

"Why?"

"It appears male soldiers still don't like the idea of being led by a woman. For some reason they think it belittles them; as if it makes their dicks smaller or something. No, I had to fight my way up, every bit of the way, until they realised they couldn't break me. That's when I gained their respect."

Sarah chewed on her straw and watched the other students goof around in the water.

"That's a depressing view of the world," she said after a while. "I don't think people are stupid, but I admit I don't understand why they work against each other instead of collaborating."

"Oh, that's simple, it's survival of the fittest. Everyone wants to be at the top."

For some reason, and Sarah had no idea why, her heart told her that Lorena was wrong.

"It just doesn't make any sense," she said while her fingers played with her straw. "It takes a lot of energy to fight and compete against others; energy that could be used for better things."

"I told you," Lorena said, grinning, "people aren't very smart."

"So isn't true leadership about helping people work together?"

"God, you're philosophical." Lorena laughed. "Of course it's about helping people, and yeah, we want people to perform together."

"Then why aren't we talking about anything but power and follower obedience? When will we study collaboration?"

"Collaboration happens when followers feel that we're in control of the situation," Lorena said, and leaned back with a yawn. "Anyway, we're getting off the subject. My point is that the others are well educated and knowledgeable in the ways of the world. If you want them to respect you, you have to prove yourself."

A warm breeze swept over the little island. Above them the palm trees swayed, allowing the sun to peek through the leaves. Sarah closed her eyes and felt the warm rays tickle her skin. Lorena and the other students were smart, but they had a very naïve perspective of the world.

"Have you lived on the streets or been disowned by your parents?" Sarah asked, keeping her voice as gentle as possible, in order not to come across as provocative.

"No."

"Have you held a child whose mother just died of AIDS?"

Lorena shook her head.

"Have you seen the sorrow in the eyes of a teenage mother who abandons her child because she knows there's no way she can support that child?"

"No."

"Ah, but I have. So have *many* other people. The world *they* live in is very different from yours, and they could argue that it is *you* who is not knowledgeable in the ways of the world. There are more poor people in the world than rich."

"You know," Lorena said, after a long silence, "I think I finally know why the Academy chose you."

CHAPTER 25

PRESENT DAY

She saw the kick coming and ducked. Using her momentum, Nicole swept her right foot along the floor in a wide circle towards his leg. Wú jumped, looking like a raven at flight in his black Kung Fu uniform and outstretched arms. He cleared her leg without difficulty.

Nicole was up in an instant as Wú advanced, his hands a blur of fury. Nicole blocked, ducked, and defended herself the best she could. Then she saw an opening, and quick as a striking cobra, she moved in, aiming for his ribs. To her frustration, the sinewy man slipped out of reach.

"Too obvious," he said and fell back into a cat stance. "Try again."

Nicole crouched before bolting forward. She did her best to hit him, but Wú was moving like the wind. No matter what she did, he seemed to know what was coming.

"Too sloppy," he concluded after blocking one of her wrist strikes. "You can do better."

Nicole grimaced and attacked again. Without a word, they fought. Wú was quick to change the game from defence to attack. Soon he was forcing her back, making her retreat towards one of the stone walls. Desperate to get away, Nicole ducked to the left and tried a round kick. Wú caught her leg mid-air.

"Too slow, Ms Swan. Focus!"

He pushed her leg away from him, spinning her into a dragon stance. With a growl, Nicole advanced again. This time she did better, forcing Wú to retreat a few steps until she tried to get him with a sidekick. She missed, thereby exposing her chest. With a smooth motion, Wú stepped in and snapped the back of his fist against her shoulder.

"Throat," he informed, thereby indicating where he would have hit her, had they been in a real fight. "Too slow, too obvious, and too sloppy. You are better than this."

"Yes, Master Wú," Nicole replied, panting heavily while rolling her aching shoulder. Tomorrow, it would be black and blue. Not that she'd complain. Master Lì Wú was a phenomenal teacher. For the past eight years, they'd trained together, either early in the morning or late at night. Of course, Nicole was neither a guard nor a Watcher, and she didn't report to Mr Nakata. In fact, there was no reason for her to train, other than that of personal enjoyment. Moreover, there was no reason for Master Wú to train her. He did it out of kindness, and, for this, she adored the man.

"You're not focusing," Wú continued and nodded towards the corner of the dojo where she'd left her things on a wooden bench. "You have too much on your mind; things that bother you."

How does he do that, Nicole wondered as the two of them left the training mat. How can he learn so much from watching me fight?

"I've been working a lot," she said, wiping her face with the towel she'd grabbed from the bench. "And I haven't slept much the last couple of days."

Wú smiled.

"You always work hard, Ms Swan, and lack of sleep has never bothered you before."

Nicole laughed.

"Maybe I'm growing old."

Wú snorted.

"You'll never improve if you try to find excuses for your failure." He sat down on the bench, his hands resting in his lap. "How are the new students?" he asked.

Nicole eyed him before taking a seat beside him. Unlike the rest of the EKA building, the guards training facilities were simple, just large open spaces with training gear and equipment. The dojo was no exception, a small windowless room with black walls and wooden floor. There was a large training mat in the middle of the room and along the walls stood simple wooden benches, like the one they were sitting on. It was this simplicity that she appreciated. Even luxury becomes routine after a while.

"You've never asked me about the students before, Master Wú."

"There has never been any reason to," her trainer replied, his Chinese accent evident in every word. "Your mind is distracted. It was not distracted four days ago, so I assume it's connected to the new students."

"I wouldn't say…"

Wú raised his arm, cutting her off.

"It doesn't matter, Ms Swan, but if you want to improve, you must learn to empty your mind before we train. You cannot demand that your mind learns Kung Fu while it worries about other things. You have to focus."

He fell silent, allowing Nicole to consider his words. It was Axel, or rather her feelings for him, that occupied her mind. She'd read his profile so many times she knew most of it by heart. He'd started Talk Thirteen out of kindness, not with the intent of making money or becoming famous. Nor had he studied any leadership prior to EKA, which indicated he wasn't interested in power. Nicole had always found kind and grounded men attractive, and Axel had it all; a kind heart, handsome face, and a dry humour that she loved. He was, quite frankly, a *unique* student.

Nicole frowned. God, she was doing it again, thinking about Axel when she should be focusing on more pressing matters.

"Ah-ha," Master Wú said with amusement playing on his lips. "Are you thinking about Kung Fu or could it be that your mind is elsewhere again?"

Nicole laughed to cover up her embarrassment.

"I guess you'll have to find out, Master Wú." She stood up. "Shall we continue our training?

CHAPTER 26

On the surface, Axel remained calm, but inside a storm raged.

It was Monday morning. They were in room "A", a bright classroom on the twelfth floor. Outside, the citizens of Brussels were waking up to a cold, but beautiful, winter's morning.

Axel squeezed his hands together, staring at the wall in front of him. The sun fell through the large windows, warming his cheek and lighting up the tiny particles suspended in the air. Around him, the other students sat behind spacious desks, in black chairs that had to be among the most comfortable in the world. Axel could probably get a good night's sleep in one if he had to.

Above each desk was a 3D hologram of the EKA logo. They were difficult to see in the sunny room, but still they hovered in mid-air, rotating at a slow speed around their own axis.

"Did you see the morning news?" Thabo whispered, handing Axel a newspaper. "All they talk about is the Academy."

Axel nodded. He'd seen the news. The day before, Principal Cunningham held a press conference in Toronto, Canada, informing the world that the Academy had chosen twelve new students. The news had broken the hearts and hopes of many applicants; there were even reports of a suicide.

"Everyone wants to know who we are," Thabo continued, and, despite his calm surface, Axel could see the excitement in his eyes. "Did you read about the man in Portugal who has to be force-fed because he refuses to eat until our names are revealed?"

It was the same after each application period. People, especially journalists, were doing all they could to find out *any* information about the Academy's new location and novel students. It had turned into a game. An American radio station offered a hundred and fifty thousand dollar reward to anyone who could find out where the Academy was located. A French newspaper had hired two private detectives to identify the name of at least one student.

Gambling sites were offering bets on anything related to the Academy. It was one big festival and Axel couldn't believe he was in the centre of it all.

"Surely there must be more important things to write about," he said.

Thabo's brows dipped in confusion.

"More important than us?"

The door to the classroom flung opened and a tall man in his mid-fifties entered. "Good morning!" he snapped in an unmistakeable Irish accent and threw a pile of papers on his desk. The room fell silent while he glared out at the students.

"My name is Professor Jackson and I'm the assistant principal. As such, I'm in charge of your training. If you want to graduate, then I'm the one you need to impress." He spoke with a sort of brusque efficiency that suggested he had no patience for slow learners. "So how do you impress me, you wonder? By proving that you're willing to sacrifice everything you hold dear to become a leader. *Great leadership demands great sacrifices*. Never forget that."

A profound silence filled the room. The professor's expression remained rigid, almost aggressive. He was a good-looking man in his impeccable black suit and shoes so polished they could function as mirrors. Clearly, this was a man who valued perfection, and by the way he considered his students, he seemed to expect everyone else to be just as perfect.

The silence seemed to last forever, and when the assistant principal spoke at last, his voice came out in a near roar.

"Very well. I shall be your teacher in the field of Business Leadership. We begin our first official lesson tomorrow. Today I'm merely giving you some general information. But before we do anything else, we must pledge allegiance to the Academy and our roles as EKA leaders. Stand up!"

He waited, tapping his foot against the floor until all the students stood to attention behind their chairs.

"This is something you'll do at the beginning of every lesson." He began walking down the rows of desks, inspecting each student. "So I hope you've all memorised the words."

No one replied and, a moment later, it was clear why. Most of the students got as far as "I'm the role model who leads the way", before they fell silent, leaving Professor Jackson to read the rest of the Leadership Allegiance on his own.

In their defence, no one had told them to learn the allegiance during the weekend. Not that it seemed to matter. Their poor performance left the assistant principal in a foul mood, and by the time they were done, he was glaring at them.

"Unacceptable!" he snarled. "If you can't memorise a few words, then you don't belong here." He stopped and gave Axel a long, unyielding look. Then he snorted and moved on. "Tomorrow, I expect you to know it by heart! Understood?"

"Yes," a few students replied.

"Yes, *sir!*" Professor Jackson said with an icy voice. "You shall address me and the other teachers by our role and surname, or by 'sir' or 'ms', is that clear?"

There was a moment's confusion when all the students called out either "yes, sir" or "yes, Professor Jackson" at the same time.

"Oh, lord," the professor moaned, leaning his head back until his perfect nose pointed at the ceiling. "Just say 'yes, sir', will you?"

"YES, SIR," the students replied, sounding more like soldiers during a military training than students in a classroom.

"Ah. At least I can take comfort in the fact that you seem to be fast learners," said Professor Jackson, and his lips pulled back into a cold smirk. "That gives us a little hope."

CHAPTER 27

"As I've already mentioned, you won't become a leader without sacrifices," Professor Jackson declared as he passed Axel and Thabo's desk with long, proud strides. "Freedom is one of them. As of today, you are to minimise the time you spend outside the premises. If you want to leave for more than two hours, you must get approval from one of the teachers or the concierge. Mr Nakata, your Security and Defence teacher, will give you further instructions concerning your personal security. Make sure you pay attention to what he says."

"Security and defence?" Axel mumbled to Thabo. "Why would we need such a class?"

Professor Jackson stopped, his back against his students.

"Do you have a question, Mr Hallman?" he asked with a low, menacing voice.

Around Axel, the other students began fidgeting, making darn sure they looked busy.

"Well, sir...I was wondering why we're going to study security and defence."

"Is that so?"

"Yes, sir. I don't understand why such a topic would be important."

Professor Jackson turned to the other students, his blond hair glowing in the morning light.

"Let me make myself clear. We tolerate nothing less than one hundred per cent effort from all of you. Our sponsors and partners are spending a lot of money on you greenhorns, and they expect a great deal in return. You had better not fail them. You better not fail *me!*"

"YES, SIR," the rest of the class answered in chorus.

Axel regarded Professor Jackson with growing dismay. Why was the man not answering his question?

"Sir, I..."

He fell silent as Professor Jackson, looking like the devil in bad mood, turned and leaned forward until his mouth was close to Axel's ear.

"I'm going to give you some advice," he whispered. "I'm not a man you want to disappoint."

"I don't want to disappoint you, sir. I was just wondering..."

"Don't."

"But I—"

"No."

"But—"

"Shhh."

The Professor's warm breath wormed itself into Axel's ear and the young Swede froze. He tried not to breath, for the professor's cologne was so strong, it could raise the dead. Instead he stared at a spot on his desk and waited.

After what seemed an eternity, Professor Jackson straightened his back. He glowered at his students with his cold, cold eyes.

"You're students of the Eagle King's Academy, and you won't have a snowball's chance in hell of graduating unless you get your act together. We will assess everything you say and do. Therefore, don't take your studies lightly, don't disrespect your teachers, and *don't* ask stupid questions that annoy me. Is that clear?"

"YES, SIR."

The professor growled, turned on his heels, and marched up to the teacher's desk, his blond hair glowing in the sunlight.

Axel realised his hands were still clasping the wide armrests with force. He drew a shallow breath and relaxed his grip before daring a quick glance at Thabo. Their eyes met and the young African raised his brows.

I'm doing it for Talk Thirteen, Axel thought, while trying to ignore the chill that swept through his body.

"We have classes from Monday to Saturday," Professor Jackson continued as he walked up to one of the windows and looked out. "Sundays are yours to do with as you please, although previous students have used this time to catch up with their studies. I suggest you do the same. You'll be given individualised schedules. And do you know why that is, Mr Hallman?"

Professor Jackson turned and gave Axel a cold and contemptuous smile, a smile so perfectly malicious, it must have taken him years to master it.

Axel was lost for words. Why did the man pick on him? As the seconds ticked on, his cheeks reddened until he knew had to say something; anything at all.

"I don't know, sir," he admitted.

Professor Jackson snorted.

"You don't know." He shook his head. "Mr Calvo! Leaders refrain from using the words 'I don't know'. Do you have any idea why that is the case?"

Federico froze, his lips pressed so hard together they seemed to vanish.

"Because a leader must never show insecurity?" he tried.

"For crying out loud," the professor groaned. "Is that a question or a statement?"

"A statement, sir!"

"Then why did you make it sound like a question?" He shook his head. "Lesson number two; think like a ruler, not like an idiot. Mr Reed!"

"Yes, sir."

"Why do you get individualised schedules?"

Edward Reed adjusted his glasses and ran a hand over his trimmed beard. "Because our trainings will differ, sir," he said with such confidence it almost sounded arrogant.

Professor Jackson held out his hands to his sides, palms towards the ceiling.

"Now that's embarrassing, isn't it, Mr Hallman? So easy and you couldn't figure it out."

"Yes, sir," Axel mumbled as he pushed down the anger that was seething within him.

"Every one of you have been chosen with a specific task in mind. By that I mean there are specific problems, threats and challenges in the world that require, or will require, great leaders.

Our analysts chose you because they believe *you'll* be able to solve these problems. They believe *you* will make the world a better place."

At last some good news, Axel thought, still tasting the bitterness of having humiliated himself in front of the class. If all this madness and absurdity led him to do something good in the world, then maybe he could find ways to motivate himself. Too bad Professor Jackson was such an arrogant and loathsome jerk. Of course, what else could one expect? This was the Academy. He glared at the professor who in turn scowled at his students.

"Six months from now, you'll be assigned a mentor. He or she will prepare you for your intended field. What it is, you won't know until right before your graduation. *If* you graduate, that is. Nothing will please me more than to kick you out if I have to. In fact, I'll take any opportunity I can to do so." He paused, letting his students reflect on what he'd said. Seeing their worried faces, he added, "And if you think that's unfair, let me remind you; we only accept the best of the best. If it turns out you can't deliver what we expect, then you don't belong here. It's that simple. Understood?"

"YES, SIR!"

Professor Jackson nodded to himself. Maybe he was pleased with their answer or perhaps it was nothing more than his way of affirming his own words. Either way he decided to move on.

"A year from now, you'll face what we call 'The Challenge'. It is part of your final exam where we look for practical evidence that you know how to lead. Well, that sums it up. Any questions?" The twelve stunned faces in front of him remained quiet. No one moved. "Good. At the moment, you're a sorry-looking bunch, but don't worry. We'll transform every one of you from an ordinary bore, to men and women with power. It will be tough, so prepare yourselves for a lot of blood, sweat, and tears."

The door opened and a woman in her late fifties entered with a small cardboard box in her arms. Professor Jackson eyed the woman as she crossed the room with confidence. She placed the box on the teacher's desk with a cheerful expression, giving the assistant principal a tiny nod, and he turned back to his class.

"Starting at two o'clock this afternoon, our tailor will be taking your measurements for your new suits. Once you get them, you shall wear them to class unless instructed otherwise."

Thabo couldn't hide his surprise.

"They're giving us a uniform?"

"So it seems," Axel whispered.

"You'll find the time for your individual appointments posted on your personal e-calendar. There you'll also find your schedule, which is updated every hour." He paused. "Unless there are any other questions, I'll leave you with Professor Evans."

Professor Jackson looked around the room and when no one said anything, he turned, nodded to Professor Evans and left the room.

"I have come to the conclusion that I don't like the man," Thabo said in a low voice.

"You're not alone, mate," Paul answered from behind. "You're definitely not alone."

CHAPTER 28

Professor Evans had a wonderful laugh; warm, honest, and rich.

"You might as well get used to it," she said, pulling at the bright orange scarf that stood out against her pale face and dark hair. "I know Professor Jackson comes across as rough, but his intentions are well meant. You may not believe it, but by the end of their studies, all our previous students have come to adore the man."

"She's right," Axel whispered, "I find that hard to believe."

Thabo gave him a quick smile.

"I'm your communications teacher," Professor Evans continued. "A topic I've been engaged in for forty years. I've written several books and trained some of the world's greatest speakers. It's a fascinating subject, and do you know why? Because a single word can give you more power than any army in the world." She paused, giving them a moment to consider her words. "Of course, a single word can also destroy you in an instance. It can strip you of your powers and leave you without followers and a future. So learn how to communicate well and the world is yours."

Axel watched Professor Evans with curiosity. There was such passion in her eyes it was contagious.

She motioned them to stand up.

"Before we continue, let's pledge the EKA Leadership Allegiance together."

Axel got up and placed his right hand over his heart for the second time in under an hour. This is ridiculous, he thought, as he began to mumble the words. At least Professor Evans was better than the sourpuss, Professor Jackson, and her subject seemed interesting.

"How do you perceive a person who uses foul language, slang, and incorrect grammar?" Professor Evans asked, when Axel and his fellow students had taken their seats again.

Edward raised his hand.

"Yes, Mr Reed?"

"He or she would come across as being of lower class, less educated, and not of importance."

"I'd be careful and not use the words 'not of importance'," Professor Evans said with a grave expression on her face, "but other than that I agree. What we say, and how we say it, will define how others perceive us. The same goes for what we wear or how we act. For example, why do you think we want you to wear tailored suits and expensive accessories? Because they signal power and sophistication." The Professor clasped her hands in front of her. "The Academy will perfect your communication skills. We shall examine the way you talk, what words to use and when to use them. Of course, communication isn't only about words; in fact, about seventy per cent or more of all communication is non-verbal. Great leaders are great communicators, so a large part of your training will focus on reading and mastering non-verbal messages." She turned and walked over to her desk. "Most people dread speaking in public. Some studies indicate that, as one comedian put it, 'at a funeral, the average person would rather be in the casket than giving the eulogy'."

The students all laughed and Professor Evans pulled out twelve copies of a book she'd written called *Introduction to Communication*.

"This book will be our starting point," she explained, while handing out the books. "We will begin by focusing on body language, micro expressions, and the power of intonation. We will also work on your public-speaking skills. It won't be easy, but by the time we're done, you'll be able to talk a blind man into seeing."

CHAPTER 29

Talk Thirteen is an international youth empowerment organisation with its headquarter in South Africa. It started off as a social network, initiated by two thirteen-year-old boys, Axel Hallman from Sweden and Peter Kruger from Cape Town. Their dream was to create a network that would help young South Africans get involved and collaborate for the benefit of other children in the country. The network grew at a remarkable speed, gaining both national and international attention. Mr Hallman and Mr Kruger were both honoured with a number of awards.

Three years after launching the network, Mr Hallman and his family moved back to Sweden, leaving Mr Kruger to run the network. With the support of various donors, Talk Thirteen grew into a world-wide organisation of which Mr Kruger remains the president. Today the organisation has mobilized more than five million children around the globe, working on a large number of issues. It remains one of the most influential youth organisations…

Professor Jackson took off his reading glasses and threw the article on the table. He leaned back in his chair, staring at the glass of scotch in his hand while his mind worked. He sat like this for a very long time, attacking the problem from various angles. He was missing something, something important, but what?

He let out a frustrated sigh and pressed a button on the intercom.

"Yes, sir?" came Nicole's cheerful voice through the speakers.

"I want you to print everything we have on Mr Hallman," Professor Jackson demanded. "I want it before my meeting with Mr Nakata. Understood?"

"Everything?"

"That's what I said, didn't I?"

"Yes, sir. Anything else?"

Professor Jackson took a sip of his scotch and felt the strong liquid burn its way down his throat.

"No, except I trust you won't tell anyone about my request."

"Wouldn't dream of it, sir," Nicole said. "I should inform you that Ms Sokolova has requested a meeting with you or Principal Cunningham next Wednesday. She would very much appreciate it if one of you could attend her next management meeting. According to the principal's schedule, he's in South Korea at that time. Will you be able to go?"

Professor Jackson sighed. Twice a year, Ms Sokolova, head of staff, invited Principal Cunningham or Professor Jackson to one of her staff management meetings. She believed their presence was good for morale. She was right, of course, but it would be damn nice if Principal Cunningham could attend one of these bloody meetings for once. All he did was travel, give some speeches, and get his arse kissed by presidents and business owners. Everyone loved the old gaffer and praised him for the Academy's success, but it was Professor Jackson who ran the EKA. He was the one who did all the hard work.

"See if I'm available," he muttered. "If so, I'll go."

He let go of the intercom button and leaned back in his chair once more. One day he'd run it all. It was just a matter of time. Until then...

Professor Jackson tapped his glass and inhaled its comforting smell.

Axel Hallman. The wild-card. The youngster concerned him, which was annoying. Powerful men shouldn't be concerned. They should be in control. Professor Jackson grinned. Of course, one didn't become the assistant principal of the world's finest academy by sitting idly by. Hell no, Professor Jackson knew how to get things done. He knew how to be in control.

He stood up and walked over to the window, his glass still in his hand. It was time to act.

CHAPTER 30

"From kings to beggars; that's the secret!" Mr Christopher Bell, teacher in Leadership Etiquette, stood grounded in the middle of the classroom. "It's not very hard to attract followers from *one* social class," he said with a charming smile. "All you have to do is praise their significance and degrade everyone else. People are rather gullible that way, but if you want to achieve greatness, you must attract followers from *all* classes. From kings to beggars."

Mr Bell had an impressive, aristocratic face that fitted perfectly with his immaculate dark suit. He was a man who, in every sense of the word, personified a true gentleman.

"To start off, I would like Mr Reed, Mr Zulu, Ms Martins, Ms Neferet, and Mr Kamala to position themselves over there!" He pointed at the wall behind the teacher's desk, and the named individuals hurried to obey. "Perfect. Ms Taylor, Ms Baton, Ms Campbell, and Mr Hallman; will you stand to my left, please." Axel and the others got to their feet. Mr Bell gave them a polite nod. "Excellent. The rest of you, stand at the back."

Paul, Dalilah, and Federico walked across the room to position themselves at the rear. Mr Bell inspected his class and nodded.

"Good, now Mr Reed, would you be so kind and give us a short presentation of yourself?"

"It will be my pleasure," Edward replied and puffed up his chest. "I'm twenty-four years old from Beverly Hills, California. I was born to be a great leader. I started my first company when I was eleven. Together with my father, I run several international businesses. We have nine different estates around the world, eighty-seven cars, two planes…"

Mr Bell held up his hand.

"That's enough, Mr Reed. I didn't ask for a full inventory." Edward glared at Mr Bell who raised a finger as a warning. "There's a fine line between being informative and boastful. One is appreciated; the other is not. And don't give me that look; you come across as sulking. People won't follow you if you act like a child."

The muscles around Edward's jaw hardened, but he dropped his gaze. Mr Bell turned his attention to a woman who somehow managed to exert intelligence simply by the way she held herself.

"Your turn, Ms Neferet."

Layla nodded and took a step forward, mindlessly spinning a thick, gold bracelet around her wrist.

"I am twenty-three years old. I come from Cairo, Egypt. My father is a very wealthy man and my mother is a well-known actress. I was studying leadership and law at Harvard University before being accepted to the Academy. I've known my whole life that I was destined to become a great leader. Just like Edward, I run several businesses. Among others, I started…"

Mr Bell raised his hand.

"Thank you, Ms Neferet. The same goes for you. If people want details, they'll ask." Layla nodded and stepped back. Mr Bell turned to Axel's group. "Let's see…who shall we take? How about you, Ms Baston?"

A grave-faced woman stepped forward.

"I am Julie Baston from Lyon, France," she began with a strong, French accent. "Before coming here I lived with my parents and little sister, whom I love very much. My father is the sales manager for a medium-sized retail company, and my mother is a pharmacist. I believe leaders are the key to success and I've always wanted to become one."

She fell silent and took a step back. Mr Bell tapped a finger against his lower lip as he eyed Julie.

"I assume Professor Evans has told you this already, but you come across as a little robotic; both in the way you speak and hold yourself."

Julie's cheeks reddened and she nodded.

"Yes, sir. Professor Evans has told me this."

"Good, then you'll work on that. I also want you to consider what information you reveal when introducing yourself. You have seven seconds to make a mesmerising impression; make each word count."

Mr Bell steepled his fingers and turned to Paul's group. "Mr Harris. Why don't you tell us a little bit about your background?"

Paul scratched his neck and took a step forward.

"I'm twenty-four years old. I'm a sports agent as well as the owner of a golf academy. Three years ago, I wrote a paper on leadership and its effect on economy. It was published in the *Sydney Morning Herald* and won me a scholarship at Sydney University."

"Well done, Mr Harris. Very good." Mr Bell rolled back on his heels. "And what did you do for a living before you started your businesses?"

Paul's confidence evaporated. He stared at the teacher for a second and then began cracking his knuckles quite loudly.

"Eh…is that of importance, sir?"

"Yes, and don't crack your knuckles. It gives away your nervousness."

Paul slid his hands behind his back.

"Well, if you must know, I worked at a golf club, sir."

"Doing what, Mr Harris?"

Paul drew a deep breath.

"I was a…uhm…parking valet."

From some of the students came a low snicker, and Paul's typically joyful face darkened. With an elegant flick of his hand, Mr Bell hushed his students.

"I would think twice before laughing at Mr Harris' background," he warned, keeping his voice flat. "People prefer to follow someone they can relate to. Since most people aren't born with a silver spoon in their mouth, a simple background can be an advantage when leading people."

"I just worked there so I could play golf," Paul said with a low voice.

"You mustn't defend yourself," Mr Bell observed. "You come across as either guilty or ashamed. Now, tell me about your parents. What do they do for a living?"

Paul's shoulder slumped a bit and he looked down at his feet.

"I'm sure you already know, sir."

"Of course I know."

"Then I don't see the point of this," Paul grumbled.

"Whether you see a point or not is irrelevant, young man."

"But no one else got these questions."

Mr Bell smiled.

"Instead of worrying about the injustice of the question, you should focus on giving me a brilliant answer."

Paul let out a deep sigh.

"Fine, if you must know, my father is unemployed and my mother is a waitress."

Despite Mr Bell's previous words, someone giggled. From where he stood, Axel couldn't see who it was, but it came from the direction of Izabella and Thabo's group.

"I won't tell you again," the grey-haired teacher warned. "Disrespect is not accepted in this classroom. It shows bad character and, quite frankly, I can't stand people who are rude. Do it again and I'll have you thrown out of this classroom quicker than you can say Jack Robinson. Understood?"

"YES, SIR!"

Axel leaned over to Julie.

"Who's Jack Robinson?" he whispered.

She shrugged, keeping her eyes on Mr Bell as he turned back to Paul and his group.

"Thank you, Mr Harris. That will be enough. What about you, Ms Izzati? What's your story?"

Dalilah stepped forward, her chin held high.

"I'm Dalilah Izzati. I come from Malaysia. After high school, I got a job in a small bookstore near China Town. The owner was very kind. He taught me English and German. While working there, I discovered leadership and I read many books on the subject."

"What about *your* parents, Ms Izzati?"

Unlike Paul, Dalilah didn't weaver.

"I never knew my father, and my mother was a prostitute. For a while I lived on the streets in Kuala Lumpur until I was brought to an orphanage at the age of eight."

No one said anything. Axel could feel the tension in the room. Dalilah's honesty had stunned them. Now she glared at her fellow students with her hands on her robust hips while defiance burned in her eyes.

"I don't come from a rich family," she snapped, "and I'll never inherit any money. I don't look like a Barbie doll, and I lack the finance to start my own company. But you know what? I'm smart. I've learnt three languages. I'm hard working and just as keen on learning the art of leadership as the rest of you." She paused. "Plus, I know how to survive on the streets, which means I can kick your ass if I have to."

Edward grinned. "I don't waste my time fighting. I hire people to do it for me."

This brought laughter from the others and the tension evaporated.

"And that's my point," Mr Bell said, gesturing the students back to their seats. "You're all different. This time I grouped you according to your social class, but I might as well have arranged you by culture, gender, or interests to name a few. In this class, you'll work together. I expect you to share your experiences, knowledge, and skills with each other. Is that clear?"

"YES, SIR!"

"By working together, you'll learn how to judge the quality of a cigar and the taste of the finest whiskey. You'll understand how the middle class reason when they buy a car, or what it's like for a child to grow up in poverty. You'll learn how to dine with royals and how to eat noodles on a side street in Vietnam." Mr Bell took his time, making his way back to the front of the classroom, letting silence settle. Then, leaning against his desk, he continued, "Your other teachers will show you how to rule people. *I*, on the other hand, will show you how to become a chameleon. With my training, you'll learn how to gracefully melt into any gathering you encounter. You'll be an eagle among eagles, and a shark among sharks." He beamed. "Yes, I'll teach you to be what people *expect* you to be, and this, my dear students, is how you attract followers!"

CHAPTER 31

The young man pulled aside his curtain and glanced out into the dark.

"The Watchers are out there," his father said while dipping a dry biscuit in his coffee. "You won't see them but they see you. Of that, you can be certain."

The young man let go of the curtain.

"So Smooth is away on business?"

"Yes."

"But do you know when it'll happen?"

The old man swallowed and helped himself to another biscuit.

"I don't, I'm afraid. I know our mole is exploring various alternatives."

"And Axel?"

"I believe he's doing well."

"Believe? Isn't that something we should know?"

"It's not that easy, Son. The Academy protects its students well. What we know is what little information our mole has been able to gather the past few days, and according to the reports we're getting, everything seems to be in order."

Feeling frustrated, the young man leaned against the kitchen counter.

"And the prime minister's card?"

"I assume it went well, otherwise we would have heard about it. Now all we can do is hope that no one else finds the card."

"Assume? Hope? These are all words of doubt. Tell me something we know for sure, something certain."

The old man chuckled.

"The only thing certain is that there is no such thing as certainty."

The young man sighed. He loved his father but sometimes the man drove him nuts.

"All right, what about project California?"

"I talked to Thor yesterday. He said things are moving forward according to plan. We're still trying to confirm some aspects of Jack's background but things are looking good. Of course, we have a long way to go before we're done, but we're off to a good start."

The young man sighed and leaned his head back against the cupboard above the counter.

"You know, I can't help but feel like we've thrown Axel to the wolves just to watch him be devoured. He has no idea what the Academy is capable of."

The old man patted his son on his shoulder.

"We all knew there would be sacrifices. Axel won't be the last."

CHAPTER 32

Professor Bernard Plouffe was a gentleman from France, with a belly that suggested a passion for great food. Axel guessed he was around mid-sixties, but it was hard to tell since he walked with a slight limp that made him look older. His subject was Political Leadership, and although he did a marvellous job at engaging his students, Axel found the first lesson to be dreadfully boring. All they talked about were historic rulers and their successes or failures. It was "leaders" here and "leaders" there. By the end of the session, Axel was so fed up with the word "leader" he wanted to scream.

"That was interesting," Thabo said with a broad, uncharacteristic smile as they walked down the corridor towards the elevators. "Very fascinating!"

Axel frowned.

"Mhm," he mumbled.

"What? You don't agree?"

Axel moved his laptop from his left hand to his right.

"If you want to know the truth, I thought it was kind of...dull."

"Jesus, Hallman," Edward exclaimed from behind, where he came strutting along with Ava, Aseem, and Layla, "are you for real?"

"How can you find political leadership strategies dull?" Ava asked.

"It's why we're here," Aseem added. "To learn strategies."

Axel sidestepped to allow his fellow students to pass.

"You're right," he murmured and stifled a yawn.

Aseem laughed.

"Tired, huh? You better get used to it. It'll only get worse."

Thabo and Axel watched the others leave.

"Lunch?" the young African asked.

Axel shook his head.

"No, thanks, I want to try out the gym. I'll join you later."

Axel had not done any weightlifting at all since his arrival on Friday, five days ago. He was used to working out four to five times a week and felt it was time to get back into his regular training routine.

After a quick change of clothes, he left his apartment with his gym shoes in one hand and a bottle of water in the other. As a pre warm-up, he decided to take the stairs to the fourteenth floor instead of the elevator, but when he entered the stairwell, he heard the muffled voices of a man and woman arguing above him.

"…not ethical, is it?" said the woman with a toneless voice. "Even if he's a wild-card, it isn't right."

"I don't care what you think," a familiar voice said. "You're here to do as you're told by your superiors. And *I* am your superior!"

"Of course, sir, but…it feels wrong."

Axel hesitated. He was obviously intruding on a conversation that was supposed to be private.

"It's not just a matter of him being a wild-card. There's something else. We need to know where his loyalty lies. You know what happened to Sarah Wangai." There was a moment of silence. Axel turned to sneak out when he heard something that made his heart stop. "I'm telling you," the man continued, "there's something fishy about Mr Hallman. We need to find out what it is."

Axel froze.

"I agree," the woman said, "but even so…"

"Enough!" Professor Jackson snapped, his Irish accent thicker and more aggressive than usual. "I don't trust Mr Hallman. We need to protect the Academy no matter what, which means you *will* do as I tell you!"

Perhaps he should have been upset, frightened, or maybe even angry, but, more than anything, Axel was confused. What reason did Professor Jackson have to distrust him? The two had barely spoken to each other. And what did he mean by "wild-card"?

The questions gnawed at him the entire afternoon, making it impossible for him to focus on Professor Alessia de Mare's Vision and Marketing class. Nor did he impress Professor Peter Williams who taught Economics and Leadership, a topic that, at least to some degree, should have fitted Axel well.

"What's wrong?" Izabella asked between classes. "You seem a bit distracted today."

"It's nothing," Axel muttered. "I've just got a lot on my mind."

"If you need someone to talk to, you know where to find me," she said with a hint of playfulness in her voice. Axel wasn't sure if she was teasing him or not.

For the first time since his arrival, Axel had dinner in his apartment, alone. He tried to study for a few hours, but gave up around eleven and went to bed. Lying under his thick duvet, staring at a hologram universe that rotated slowly above his bed, Axel dwelled on Professor Jackson's words: *"There's something fishy about Hallman. ... We need to protect the Academy no matter what."* Protect the Academy against what? Against Axel? In what way could Axel be a threat to the E.K.A?

An hour later, Axel exhaled his frustration and rolled over. He pressed a button by the bedside table and the universe vanished. Darkness engulfed the room.

This is madness, he thought. Why waste time on things I can't control? If Professor Jackson doesn't care for me, that's his problem, not mine. I'm doing this for Talk Thirteen, not for him.

CHAPTER 33

Three weeks had already passed since Axel first arrived at the Academy. It was Saturday evening and Izabella was curled up on his sofa with a big bowl of popcorn and a glass of wine. Her normally professional-looking hair was pulled back in a simple ponytail, and her classroom business attire was replaced with casual trousers and a T-shirt that was tight enough to show off her female curvature without exposing too much.

She'd knocked on his door an hour earlier, wondering if he wanted to watch a movie with her.

"I brought my own wine," she'd laughed, holding up a bottle. "Perhaps you want to share it with me?"

Axel admitted he couldn't stand the taste of alcohol, but he did fancy a movie. Now the two of them were watching a bizarre, dark comedy that Axel found insufferable. Izabella seemed to love it though. She was laughing out loud, making sounds like a seagull in a scuffle. It wasn't a very attractive laugh, but her company was enjoyable nonetheless.

Outside, the sun had long since set behind the city horizon. A carpet of thick, foreboding clouds began to roll in from the east, and by the time Axel turned off the TV, the rain hammered against the windowpanes.

"I wonder what the Belgians did to piss off God?" Izabella sighed. "Doesn't it ever stop raining in this damn country? I know it's supposed to be the centre of Europe but why did they have to choose *Brussels* of all places?"

Axel smiled.

"Do you want me to make you a cup of hot cocoa?"

Izabella stared at him. "Are you making fun of me?"

"No." Axel leaned against the windowsill. "Would you prefer tea?"

"Don't you have coffee?"

"Sorry. I'm not much of a coffee fan. But I can order up a cup from the restaurant, if you want."

"No alcohol or coffee? What are you, a child?" Izabella giggled.

The comment stung but Axel pretended he didn't care and shrugged. Why people considered certain beverages childish was beyond him.

"My grandmother used to make hot cocoa for my sister and me when we were small and the weather was bad. She would light a fire and we would sit on the carpet in front of it eating homemade cinnamon buns and drinking our cocoa while she read us a story. It was nice."

Izabella laughed. "You make it sound cosy and nice." She reached out and touched his arm. "Tell you what; why don't you make us a fire and I'll order us some hot cocoa and cinnamon buns?"

Making a fire wasn't very difficult. All Axel had to do was put some wood in the fireplace and then press a button. Lighter fluid drenched the wood and a spark ignited the whole thing. Within ten seconds, a warm fire crackled in the fireplace.

While they waited for the cocoa to arrive, Izabella began telling Axel about herself, a topic she seemed to enjoy more than he did. She came from a wealthy family, she explained, with great influence in politics and business. One of her brothers was a well-known politician in Brazil and another ran the family business. What kind of business was unclear, but it appeared to have something to do with transporting goods.

Axel had a feeling that Izabella was trying to impress him, so he listened despite the boredom, trying not to yawn. When, at last, a waiter arrived with their hot beverages, Axel and Izabella settled back in the armchairs, gazing at the flames while sipping their hot liquid.

"You're very different from the others," Izabella declared after a while.

Having no idea what she meant by it, Axel gave her a fleeting smile.

"Why? Because I don't drink coffee?"

"That's not what I meant, silly. And you're not different in a bad way, the opposite actually. All the others are so obsessed with themselves, but you…" She put her cup to her full lips and tasted the chocolate. "One might almost think you didn't care about becoming a leader."

Axel's smile faded. The darn woman was like a bloody mosquito. Not only did she make a lot of annoying sounds, she seemed to have a natural gift for smelling blood. Was she on to him, or what?

"Of course I care." He took a mouthful of hot cocoa and burned his lying tongue. He bit back a yelp and coughed in an attempt to cover his blunder. "I'm here to become a leader."

Technically, that was true; he *was* here to become a leader. The fact that he had no desire to become one was a different matter.

Izabella's eyes gleamed in the soft light.

"You don't sound very passionate about it. If I didn't know better, I'd think you were lying to me."

In that instance, Izabella's presence felt oppressive. Axel wanted her to leave at once, but he kept the charades going with a grin.

"And that makes me all the more mysterious, right?" he said.

Izabella laughed, placing her hand on his.

"I suppose."

Squirming under her touch, Axel threw a quick glance at the massive aquarium where the shark made its slow circle, scaring the other fish.

"Sorry," he mumbled and yawned, "but I'm exhausted. It's been a long week."

Izabella pulled back her hand.

"Oh," she said. He could see she was trying to read his face. Maybe she thought it was an invite, for she lingered a little, waiting for him to say something more. When he didn't, she ran a hand through her ponytail and got up.

"All right, I'll see you tomorrow."

Axel put on his best smile.

"Of course. Can't wait."

He woke up panic-struck. The room was pitch black and smelled of sweat and blood. Strong hands held him down while someone shoved a large piece of cloth into his mouth. Axel gagged as the rough material reached the back of his throat. He kicked and wriggled the best he could.

Years of going to the gym had made Axel both lean and strong. He felt his attackers struggle to hold him down. Without thinking, he threw a punch and both felt and heard his fist hit the target. Someone grunted and for a second the pressure around his left arm weakened.

"*Merde*," someone swore.

A strong hand grabbed Axel by the throat and held him pinned down on his back. Axel gasped for air, clawing at the hand with all his might. Then someone pulled a bag over his head.

"Hurry," a voice panted.

In an instance, Axel was on the floor, his feet tied and hands cuffed behind his back. The attackers grabbed him by the arms and began dragging him through the corridor, out of the apartment and into the elevator.

"How long before the security cameras are turned on again?" a voice whispered as the elevator began to descend.

"Three minutes and twenty seconds," someone replied with a thick, French accent.

The elevator stopped and the doors opened.

"*Se dépêcher*," someone yelled from outside.

Axel heard the sound of an engine and someone opening a car door. Pain shot through his arms as his assailants dragged him out of the elevator. They threw him onto what had to be the floor of a van. Axel could feel the rumbling of the engine beneath him.

"Don't move," a voice growled.

The door closed and the van took off.

CHAPTER 34

TWELVE YEARS EARLIER

It was clear that he didn't like her. Sarah could see it in his eyes; the disapproval. He always found reasons to scold her or to punish her with extra homework, and Sarah knew why. It had nothing to do with her ability to learn. She grasped and retained information faster than any other student. Nor did he consider her ignorant because of her background. He didn't care if a student was poor or rich. No, Professor Jackson didn't like her because of her questions.

Sarah lay on her back, staring at the hologram universe circling above her bed.

How can he hate me because I question his theories? Is he afraid I might be right? Sarah rolled over to her side and stared out into the dark room. Or am I the one who's wrong? Have I misunderstood the reasons we're here? Will the world not change without rulers?

The thoughts slashed through her head until they gave her a headache. It wasn't supposed to be this way. The Eagle King's Academy turned young men and women into heroes and sent them into the world to make a difference. So why did the teachers talk so little about helping the world and so much about gaining power? It made no sense.

Sarah had tried to discuss these questions with Lorena on a few occasions, but her friend just laughed at her.

"You don't get it, do you?" she would say. "If you want to make a difference in the world, you have to unite people, and to do that, you need them to love and obey you. Only then will they listen to you, allowing you to help them change the world. It's that simple."

Well, if it *was* that simple, maybe that would explain why Professor Jackson hated her questions. He would be of the opinion that she made everything complicated. Of course, just because Professor Jackson and Lorena thought it was simple, didn't mean they were right. And another thing: making people obey and love you seemed selfish, unethical somehow.

Sarah closed her eyes and let out a long, depressed sigh. Maybe things would make more sense to her in a few weeks' time.

CHAPTER 35

PRESENT DAY

Axel sensed someone leaning over him. The soggy cloth in his mouth seemed to swell with every passing second, making it hard not to retch. Breathing through his nose was almost impossible as the bag seemed glued to his face. He fought the approaching panic by shifting. Immediately, someone slammed his head against the floor.

"Don't try to be a hero," a dark voice whispered. "Next time you move, I'll smash your head in so many times, it'll look like a Rubik's cube when I'm done. Got it?"

Nearby, a different voice snickered.

After what seemed to be hours, the van came to a stop. There was a low murmur of people talking, and then the back door opened.

"Get him out," a new voice ordered.

Someone cut the rope around his ankles before pulling him out, scraping his chin and bruising his knees in the process. A pair of strong hands grabbed him by the arms and began leading him through what seemed to be a maze of damp and earthy-smelling corridors. He heard doors opening in front of him, before slamming shut behind him. At one point, his attackers forced him to climb stairs, and on a few occasions, they told him to duck. He couldn't see anything, so all he focused on was the intimidating sound of heavy boots echoing against the concrete floor.

"Stop," the dark voice commanded. Axel obeyed. He heard another door open and the powerful hands that had held him gave him a brutal push forward. "Kneel!"

Axel lost his balance and fell forward, hands still behind his back. Someone caught him by his lower arm and yanked him up. The pain was excruciating.

"On your knees, I said!" Axel shook as much from fright as from cold. He was still in his underwear, and the air around him was icy and damp. "Don't move!"

The cuffs were unlocked, the bag pulled from his head. Axel blinked. Behind him, the door closed and locked. He sat motionless, listening to the icy silence. When he felt confident that he was alone, he snatched the sodden cloth from his mouth and swallowed hard so as not to vomit.

He was in a tiny, windowless room. Above his head, a pale light bulb swung back and forth, ghostly, its movement giving life to the shadows around him.

Like a trapped mouse, Axel sat on his knees, too afraid to move. On some level, he realised he should be analysing the situation. Who had taken him and why? Could he escape? What would happen now? These were all questions he should be focusing on, but he didn't. Instead, he just stared at the wall in front of him and his shadow swaying back and forth with the movement of the light bulb.

He watched. He listened. He waited. Then there was movement.

Axel heard footsteps and the door opened. Still on his knees, staring forward, he heard someone enter.

"Stand up," a thick, aggressive voice ordered. A large man, dressed in black clothes and a ski mask, cuffed Axel's wrists behind his back and pointed at the door. "Let's go."

They walked through dark, concrete corridors, just wide enough for the two men to walk side by side. Axel felt like a death row prisoner, making his way to the gallows. None of them uttered a word until they reached a dark, depressing cell, no bigger than the one they'd just come from. A wooden chair stood under a naked light bulb in the middle of the room. The man removed the cuffs.

"Sit," he demanded and left.

Axel sat shivering in the dark. Still he thought of nothing. He simply waited until the room unexpectedly exploded in bright, white light. With a cry he covered his eyes. Then came a loud voice that shredded the silence to pieces.

"Your name?"

With his eyes still shut, Axel gave his name. His voice sounded small and pathetic.

"Why are you in Brussels?"

"I…I'm here to study."

"Study what?" When Axel hesitated, the voice grew agitated. "Answer me!"

"I'm studying communication, economics, and politics."

"What school are you attending?"

This time, Axel remained quiet. He kept his head down, shielding his eyes from the bright light. Professor Jackson's words echoed in his head: "I don't trust Mr Hallman, and you *will* do as I tell you."

"I asked you a question," the voice roared. "Give me the name of the school!"

"Who are you?" Axel demanded with attempted defiance in his voice. He held his breath as he waited for a reaction. None came, and after a while, he exhaled in relief.

With a loud crash, the door flung open and three masked men rushed in. The lights in the room faded. Axel wasn't a fighter but he leapt out of his chair, ready to defend himself. When the nearest attacker, a massive man, reached out for him, Axel threw a punch. He missed as the man moved his head out of reach without much effort.

The second man moved in. Axel swirled and threw himself over the attacker. Someone cursed as both he and the man fell to the ground with a loud thud. The attacker groaned as the air was pushed out of his lungs.

Axel rolled over to the side in an attempt to get up. He didn't get far. The first attacker approached from the front while a third man came in from the left. Shit! Axel was still on one knee. With a cry, he pushed off towards the first attacker, hitting him square on the jaw with his shoulder. The man tumbled back, pulling Axel with him.

There was a moment of complete chaos. Arms and legs seemed to be everywhere. Axel tried to punch the man and get up at the same time. In the confusion, he got hold of the attacker's mask and pulled. A face he recognised stared up at him.

"You!" Axel shouted, before the other men yanked him back with brutal force.

They pinned him down, once again cuffing his hands behind his back and placing a bag over his head. At least they didn't shove a cloth in his mouth. Axel was now more angry than frightened.

The brutal men hauled him out of the room, through a set of corridors.

"You better be quiet," one of the men whispered. "If you so much as breathe a sound, we'll kill you."

Axel didn't reply, but he didn't object either. They seemed to be entering yet another room. His attackers forced him to his knees once more and left without a word. Axel was still panting from the fight. His right shoulder and left arm were hurting, but, on the positive side, his mind was awakening. He had exposed Mr Linch, the EKA guard with the wolfish grin. The man had betrayed the Academy but...Axel froze. Deprived of his eyesight, he turned his ear in the direction of where he thought he'd heard a sound. Holding his breath he picked up sounds of others in the room; faint sounds of breathing and quiet snivels.

What the...?

"Remember this feeling." The sudden sound made Axel recoil. He didn't recognise the heavy, clipped Asian accent but there was something in the ominous voice that made him cringe. "Feeling of fear, confusion and panic! Remember it! As leaders, you will face it again."

In the quiet room, the voice thundered with more intensity than a roaring lion. There was movement behind Axel, and after a few seconds, someone removed the cuffs behind his back and the bag over his head.

He was in a large room. Around him the other EKA students sat, fear written all over their faces. Like him, some in their underwear; others wore pyjamas. Thabo was sitting to his right and nodded as their eyes met. Beside him was Paul, a blank expression on his face. Izabella was sitting behind him, staring at the floor in front of her.

"My name is Mr Nakata," the stranger said. He was a short man with wide shoulders and a grim face marked with scars and a nose that had obviously been broken one too many times. "I'm your Security and Defence teacher."

He stood with his hands behind his back, dressed in a black training suit and pristine white sneakers, regarding the students with attentive eyes. Axel had seen him once before, at the introduction dinner.

"Welcome to Black Sunday. This is an exercise of mind; to show how you react under pressure. People react different to stress and you must know your reaction. Today you react on instinct, but a leader who acts on instinct is weak; his actions unclear, even to himself."

Mr Nakata turned to his men, all still wearing black ski masks. Without a word, they slipped out of the room.

"We leave you now to think about your feelings. This is very important. Tomorrow we meet again."

Mr Nakata left, followed by the loud click of the door's lock sliding into place.

CHAPTER 36

On the radio, a commercial break interrupted the early breakfast show. Nicole stood back and studied her canvas with a critical eye. She would have to review it in full daylight to ensure the colouring was right, but she was pleased.

She threw a glance at the large, vintage clock on her living room wall. It was time. She rinsed off her brushes and wiped the paint off her fingers, thinking how lucky she was. Had it not been for Principal Cunningham, she'd be lying in the gutter somewhere or in a graveyard. It was a humbling thought.

Yes, Nicole owed Principal Cunningham a lot, but it wasn't her place to meddle with Academy politics. She'd heard what happened to her predecessor, and she wouldn't make the same mistake. Within the Academy, the rules were simple; obey those superior to you, no questions asked.

Steam filled the little bathroom as Nicole stepped into the shower. Indeed, only a fool would challenge Professor Jackson's decisions, and Nicole didn't consider herself a fool. The man was harsh, even brutal at times, but he was a genius when it came to turning students into rulers. He knew what he was doing.

Thoughts raced through her mind as the hot water washed over her body. Why did she feel so bad? Why did she let her emotions affect her the way they did? Axel was a student, well beyond her reach, and if Professor Jackson thought this was what Axel needed, then who was she to question it?

CHAPTER 37

Axel was awakened by a gentle touch. In the faint, cold light he found Nicole crouched beside him with a serious expression on her face. She placed a finger over her lips and gestured him to follow.

Shivering, Axel sat up. His body ached. The other students lay spread out on the floor sleeping, most of them curled up in the foetal position, trying to keep warm.

Many of them had expected Mr Nakata to return after an hour or so. They'd waited in vain until they all fell asleep, exhausted by the night's terrifying events.

Axel rubbed his tired eyes and got to his feet. Careful not to step on anyone, he followed Nicole out of the room.

Without a word, she led him through a maze of dark corridors to a thick metal door, all painted black. There was something very menacing about it.

"You have to enter on your own, I'm afraid," Nicole said and stepped back.

They were the first words she'd uttered since waking him up. Axel searched her face for clues of any kind, but came up with nothing.

"Should I worry?" he asked with forthright unease.

Nicole's face broke into a fleeting smile.

"You're studying at the EKA, Mr Hallman. You should always worry."

"Great," Axel muttered, pushing open the door.

It was a small, bright room, painted entirely white. Even the floor was white. A middle-aged woman – a doctor by the looks of it – was standing in the middle of the room reading a file. As soon as he entered, she raised her head, revealing a narrow face plastered with a stony expression.

"Good morning, Mr Hallman. Please have a seat."

She pointed at a hospital bed pushed against the end wall. There was something familiar about the woman's toneless voice, something that made Axel feel exposed and uncomfortable.

"Could I get some clothes?"

"Soon." The woman closed the file she'd been reading and tossed it on a nearby desk. She looked at him the way he imagined a zoologist would study the mating ritual of porcupines; with amused fascination. "My name is Dr Vella. I'm going to do a quick medical examination if that's okay with you?"

She pointed at the bed. Axel nodded. What choice did he have?

Dr Vella took her time, and while she was poking, pinching, and squeezing him, Axel cast his eyes around the tiny room. On the opposite wall hung a large TV, showing an appalling video of war, pollution, and famine. Geez, how uplifting. The depressing film ended and the Academy logo appeared along with a message: "The world needs you!" After that, the video went lovey-dovey, with clear-blue skies, green forests, and happy people. This was followed by yet another message: "You are our future. You are our hope."

Axel sighed and turned away, his eyes falling upon a small toilet in the corner. That was a little odd, wasn't it? Why would they have a toilet in here? At that point, Dr Vella took a seat in front of him and pulled back her thin lips into an ugly smirk.

"Tell me, Mr Hallman, how are you feeling about last night's exercise?"

"May I have some clothes?"

Dr Vella pulled back a strand of her red hair behind her ear and looked him over in a manner that made him uncomfortable.

"As soon as we're done with this examination, you'll get something to wear. But first, your feelings?"

Axel thought for a moment.

"I guess I felt many things; anger, confusion, relief."

"Can you explain that a little?"

"I'm angry for being exposed to this exercise, relieved that it wasn't a real kidnapping, upset that I didn't handle it better, confused about why you put us through it, and curious to know if this kind of behaviour is legal."

Dr Vella burst out laughing, a reaction Axel hadn't been prepared for.

"That was a superb answer. I bet Professor Evans is very pleased with your communication skills so far."

"Where are we?" Axel asked, ignoring the comment.

"In a medical examination room."

"And where exactly is this room located?"

"In a building. Tell me, when you were woken up in the middle of the night, what was the first thing that went through your mind?"

Axel studied his cold, bare feet. Dr Vella's unwillingness to answer his questions was an answer in itself. This absurd game wasn't over, which meant he was still being evaluated. The question was: what were they trying to teach him?

"I guess I was wondering what was happening, and why."

"What can you tell me about the people who took you from your room?"

Axel hesitated. "Are these questions part of your medical examination?"

"Just answer the question, Mr Hallman."

"I'm cold."

"Then you better answer my questions."

Axel glared at the woman.

"I can't remember much. I think they were two, maybe three men."

"Did they say anything?"

"I don't remember."

Dr Vella eyed her computer screen.

"What do you think the purpose of this exercise was?"

"To see how we react under pressure."

"And why would that be of interest?"

Axel ran a hand through his hair. He needed a shower.

"The subject is called Security and Defence. My guess is that the teacher…"

"Mr Nakata," Dr Vella informed.

"...that Mr Nakata wants to help us improve our reactions when faced with stressful and threatening situations."

Dr Vella closed her computer and stood up.

"Thank you for your patience, Mr Hallman. I'll have someone bring you some clothes in a few minutes."

"That's it?"

With her laptop and file under her arm, she left the room.

A silent old man entered and gave him a grey sweatsuit. After that, Axel was left to his own thoughts. This place was a bloody madhouse! What *is* wrong with these people? How *can* they drag students out of their beds, scare them half to death and expect them to just accept it?

Annoyed and frustrated, he sat on the exam table staring at the TV-screen while waiting for something to happen. After an hour or so, the door opened and the same old man appeared with a tray. He gave Axel a courteous bow. Without a word, he placed the tray on the desk and left. Axel wrinkled his nose. Porridge and a glass of water. How nice, he thought sourly. They're still playing games.

CHAPTER 38

Dr Vella reappeared with her computer in one hand and a brown paper bag in the other. Axel swung his feet over the side of the bed. He watched her without a word as she pulled out the chair and took a seat in front of him. With the laptop on her knee, she gave him a courteous nod.

"Why do we need leaders?" she asked with her obnoxious smirk.

Axel glowered at the woman. Her arrogant and patronizing aura seemed to suggest that she knew more about him than he did. It was provocative, and a part of him wanted to strangle her.

"How is this connected to me being dragged out of my room and scared senseless?" he countered.

"Just because you don't see the connection, Mr Hallman, doesn't mean there isn't one. Now, why do we need leaders?"

For Talk Thirteen, Axel thought with a loud sigh.

"To motivate and inspire people," he said, knowing that's what she wanted to hear.

"Good. And why is that important?"

"So that they'll follow."

"Follow whom?"

"The almighty boss."

Dr Vella tapped her finger against the edge of her computer and leaned forward.

"I advise you to cooperate, Mr Hallman," she warned. "This isn't a game."

"Fine. So they'll follow *me*."

Dr Vella wrote something on her computer.

"And do you think people will follow you?"

"I hope so." Dr Vella repeated her question. Axel tried again. "All right, I am *convinced* they will."

The doctor's fingers smattered against the keyboard again.

"Imagine that you walk down a dark alley," she said. "Turning a corner, you see a young woman being raped by a masked man. What would you do?"

Axel stared at Dr Vella.

"What kind of question is that?"

"What would you do, Mr Hallman?"

"Jesus. I'd help her, of course!"

Dr Vella stood up and handed him the paper bag. "I thought you might want this." Axel watched her leave and then glared into the bag. A toothbrush, toothpaste, comb, and an electric shaver. He stared at the items as concern slowly grew from the pit of his gut.

CHAPTER 39

Professor Jackson turned to Mr Nakata and grunted.

"He's not thinking as a global leader should. He's too altruistic and he's got a damn attitude."

The Security and Defence teacher stared at the large TV screen; his hands behind his back.

"Wanting to help woman being raped show bravery. Bravery is good."

Professor Jackson cracked his knuckles in a manner that would have annoyed Mr Bell and held back a moan. Mr Nakata was a smart man, brilliant within his field. He had a natural aura of authority and was, just as the professor himself, fiercely loyal to the Academy. As such, Professor Jackson liked Mr Nakata, which was astonishing, considering the fact that there were very few people Professor Jackson actually liked. The most annoying aspect of Mr Nakata was his English. It was appalling, and, to make matters worse, he refused to do anything about it.

The Academy had staff members and students from all over the world. One could hear many different accents within the premises, but the Academy expected everyone to speak English fluently. Those who didn't got orders to take private lessons at once. Why Principal Cunningham allowed Mr Nakata to refuse such lessons was a mystery. It was embarrassing to have a teacher who spoke worse English than the students. If Professor Jackson had been the principal, he'd never have tolerated such behaviour. There were many things he wouldn't tolerate.

"Bravery is as useful as tits on a bull if not combined with a little common sense," he muttered. "Mr Hallman's willingness to risk his life for an unknown girl might be brave but it sure as hell isn't wise. He's supposed to protect himself, damn it!"

"*Hai*, but he is wild-card. They think different."

"Wild-card or not, we have to make him think as a ruler."

"Then what you want to do? Shall we quit?"

Professor Jackson thought for a moment while watching Axel on the screen.

"Does he remind you of anyone?"

"Sir?"

"The questions he asks, the attitude. Does Hallman remind you of anyone?"

Mr Nakata nodded without hesitation.

"*Hai.* He reminds me of Ms Wangai."

Yes, Professor Jackson thought, staring at the screen. He does, doesn't he?

"Let's continue," he decided. "Our dear principal is still on business. I want to see where this leads us."

CHAPTER 40

Minutes, hours, and days passed. Axel lost track of time. The TV and the lights were on at all times. To sleep he had to place his sweatshirt over his eyes. Now and again, the silent man entered with a bowl of porridge and a glass of water. Sometimes he came with a fresh set of clothes, but he never uttered a single word.

With the exception of these brief visits, the Academy left Axel to his own thoughts. Most of the time, he mulled over Dr Vella's question; would people follow him? It felt both strange and egotistic to even imagine himself as a leader with power. Power was a dangerous thing. How many people had died in reckless conflicts related to control and dominance? Of course, as Mikael had pointed out, leaders could use power to do good in the world. Axel thought about this a lot. If more kind-hearted people, like himself, would rule the world, then perhaps everyone would benefit? There was certain logic to it, although Axel suspected that anyone who had authority was likely to think they deserved it.

Finding himself in a philosophical dilemma he couldn't solve, Axel turned his attention to another peculiar matter. How had the Academy overlooked his disinterest in leadership? The more he thought about it, the stranger it got. The most reasonable explanation he could come up with was that the EKA didn't think anyone would be dumb enough to apply unless they wanted to. Maybe they couldn't even imagine someone *not* wanting to study at the Academy. After all, who, except Axel, didn't dream of becoming a global leader?

All these thoughts, and many more, troubled Axel for days, until, after what seemed an eternity, the door opened and Dr Vella returned.

"When will you let me go?" Axel asked as the woman took a seat in front of him.

Dr Vella's insufferable smile lit up.

"I have a question, Mr Hallman. Do you think people will follow you?"

Axel clenched his fist as hard as he could.

"At least bring me something to eat; something other than this goddamn porridge."

Dr Vella kept smiling, and he hated her for it.

"Will people follow you?" she repeated.

Axel glanced at the TV behind the doctor. "You are our future. You are our hope."

"Of course they'll follow me," he snapped as nonchalantly as he could.

"Why?"

Bitch! Axel unclenched his fists.

"Because I can lead them to success."

"And what is 'success', Mr Hallman?"

"When I can make people follow the vision I've identified."

Dr Vella nodded and wrote something in her notebook.

"Thank you," she said and left.

Axel wanted to scream. He didn't know what day it was. He had moments of anger and moments of sadness. He tried various forms of meditation to kill time, and when that didn't work, he tried to sleep through the boredom.

And so the days passed. Axel thought a lot about his family and friends, Talk Thirteen and leadership. At times, he cursed, shouted, begged and threatened; at other times he just stared at the wall. He felt himself go mad, but not once did he turn to the camera to say he wanted to quit and go home. Despite his frustration, he found that very interesting.

Axel was lying on his back, staring at the ceiling when the door opened and Mr Nakata entered. At least that was a change.

"*Konnichiwa*, Mr Hallman," the short, grim-faced man said and sat down facing Axel. "Why you apply to Academy?"

Axel sat up without haste.

"Sir," he said almost at a whisper, "what do you want from me?"

"I want answer to my question. Why you apply?"

Axel rubbed his forehead and said the first thing that came to mind.

"It's the best Academy for anyone who wants to become a leader."

"You want to be leader?"

"Of course," Axel lied.

"Why?"

"I want to lead people. I want to make a difference in the world."

Mr Nakata hummed with obvious displeasure.

"Japanese poet Matsuo Basho once say, 'Do not seek to follow in the footsteps of the wise. Seek what they sought'." Axel had no idea what the man was talking about so he remained quiet. Mr Nakata eyed him for a few seconds and then stood up. "What you seek is not clear, Mr Hallman. You claim to be a king but yo' behave like a servant."

"What do you want from me?" Axel exclaimed, his heart fill with sour frustration.

"I want truth."

"I'm telling you the truth, damn it! I want to be a leader."

Mr Nakata shook his head. A moment later the black c closed with a heavy thud.

"But I *am* a leader," Axel yelled, and was shocked to realiset a part of him actually meant it.

When nothing happened, Axel grabbed the empty poe bowl off the table, and with all his might, he threw it againe door so it shattered in a million pieces.

"Damn you!" he roared. "I told you I'm a leader! What co you want from me?"

CHAPTER 41

In the background, Vivaldi's *The Four Seasons* played at a low volume, the gentle notes mixing pleasantly with the aroma of coffee.

"Sir?"

Smooth lowered his newspaper. Thor was standing by the door, the golden communication device in his hand. "Yes?"

"I just got some information."

The old man folded the paper and reached for his cup.

"By that look of yours, I'm guessing it's not positive information."

"I'm afraid not, sir."

Smooth frowned and then nodded towards the leather armchair that stood empty beside him. "Go on."

"It seems all the students have returned after their latest exercise," Thor said and sat down. "All but one."

"Let me guess, Mr Hallman?"

"Yes. Rumour has it he's been hospitalised for appendicitis, but at's a lie since his appendix was removed at the age of seven."

Smooth's eyes hardened. "Do we know what's happened?"

"No. We haven't been able to confirm anything –" Thor flipped communication device in his hand "– but our mole has his picions."

He read the message he'd received a minute ago. When he was ie, Smooth returned his cup to the coffee table and stood up iout haste.

'This is worrying news," he said, walking over to the window. :r a brief silence, he shoved his hands in his pocket and let out a sigh. "Let's keep this to ourselves for the moment, shall we? I : it confirmed before we inform the others."

And Mr Hallman?"

There's not much we can do, is there? He's on his own."

CHAPTER 42

It was torture. Mr Nakata had changed strategy and now, every second hour or so, he or Dr Vella entered, just to ask Axel the same bloody questions: why did he want to become a leader, did he think people would follow him, and why did he want to help people? By now, Axel realised that the Academy was trying to break him mentally, which made him all the more determined not to give up. He wondered how Thabo, Izabella, and Paul were doing.

"Why will people follow you?" Mr Nakata asked for the hundredth time.

"Because I'll show them the way," Axel replied without thinking.

"What is the way?"

"The way to the vision."

"Who decides the vision?"

"I do."

The Security and Defence teacher nodded, obviously pleased.

"And why do you want to lead others?"

"I was meant to be the seed that creates change," Axel repli without hesitation.

"What you mean by that?"

Axel was a little puzzled himself. *The seed that creates change.* W in the world had made him say that?

Mr Nakata was regarding him with noticeable curiosity, somehow Axel knew the next few words would be importan his future.

"I was meant to make a difference in the world," he said, f strangely calm when he said it. "That's why I started Talk Thi I wanted to change the future. People depend on me. I m what I was born to do."

Mr Nakata didn't say anything. He watched Axel w unreadable expression. Axel lowered his head and looked bare feet. Was he trying to fool Mr Nakata or himself, or was he being honest? He wasn't sure anymore. He'd always wanted to improve the world, but never like this. Still, here he was. Surely, that wasn't a coincidence. It had to be some kind of fate, right?

"This is my destiny," Axel whispered, as much to himself as to Mr Nakata.

The Security and Defence teacher got to his feet and left without a word. This time, Axel showed no anger. He sat on the edge of his bed feeling confused.

This was his destiny.

* * *

Professor Jackson was staring at the screen when Mr Nakata entered.

"Now that's interesting," he confessed, not taking his eyes of Axel. "Do you think he was honest?"

"*Hai.*"

Professor Jackson scratched his chin while contemplating the situation. He didn't trust Axel but, at the same time, he wasn't getting the answers he needed. Time was running out. He turned off the screen.

"All right, let him go."

There was more than one way to skin a cat, Professor Jackson thought, as he walked over to his wooden cabinet. He pulled out a bottle of scotch. One way or the other, he'd find out what was going on. He had to. He must protect the Academy no matter what.

CHAPTER 43

Nicole entered the small room and found Axel on his bed, staring at the ceiling. She felt a stab in her heart. She knew Professor Jackson was good at what he did, but that didn't mean she always approved of his methods.

"Well done, Mr Hallman," she said with as much cheerfulness as she could muster. She wasn't educated and skilled like the professors, but she could see that Axel was in dire need of some kindness and positive reinforcement. "You did it! You've passed 'Black Sunday'."

When hearing her voice, Axel turned. At first he seemed confused. Then a tiny smile spread across his weary face.

"Ms Swan." He sat up and ran a hand through his messy hair. "I...I'm glad to see you."

"That's kind of you to say, Mr Hallman. Come, let's get you back to your apartment."

"Is it over?"

The relief on his face was heartbreaking for Nicole to see.

"Yes, sir, it's over."

They left and walked side by side through one corridor after the other. Nicole kept her silence, allowing Axel to contemplate what he'd been through.

"You know where you live, don't you," she said when the reached the elevators. She pressed for the wing-shaped doors open. "Ninth floor."

Axel stared at the elevators and let out a wheezing sound.

"We're still here?"

"Yes."

"Inside the Academy?"

"Yes."

"But...the car ride?"

Nicole held up the doors. "Just a little trip around Brussels and then back again. Simple but ingenious, don't you think?"

After a moment's hesitation, he shook his head and stepped into the elevator.

"I guess." He threw a quick glance at his reflection in the large mirror and frowned. "I look like something that would crawl out of a dark alley at night." Nicole laughed and Axel's handsome face softened. "What day is it?"

"Friday."

Axel stopped flattening his hair with his hands and gave Nicole a sceptical stare.

"Friday? I've only been here six days? Jesus, it felt more than that."

Still smiling, Nicole shook her head.

"No, Mr Hallman. It wasn't just six days. You've been down here for twenty-one days."

"What?" Axel's face paled. "Three weeks!"

"Yes," Nicole replied and let go of the doors. Her contract didn't allow her to discuss Black Sunday with the students. She adjusted her suit jacket and said something she immediately regretted. "I'm very glad you made it, Mr Hallman. You're one of my favourites."

She said it as if it was the most natural thing in the world, but, true as it was, she had no right to express any opinion about a student, especially not to the student in question. Professor Jackson wouldn't be pleased.

Axel was somewhat taken aback by her comment. He stared at her as the doors began to close. Then he placed a hand between the doors, forcing them to open.

"What are you saying?" he asked. "You have more than *one* favourite?"

Nicole paused just long enough to see the playful glimmer in Axel's eyes. Then she laughed.

"No, Mr Hallman. I can't say I do."

"Good." He let go of the doors. "That means I can take it as a compliment."

"You should."

As soon as the doors closed, her phone buzzed, indicating a new text message. "I want you in my office NOW!" Nicole drew a deep breath. As expected, Professor Jackson wasn't pleased.

CHAPTER 44

TWELVE YEARS EARLIER

Sarah shook her head.

"I don't care. It is wrong."

"How can it be wrong if it makes you a better leader?" Lorena objected. "They're helping you grow, and sometimes growing is painful."

Sarah walked up to the windows covering an entire wall of her living room.

"You weren't there," she said and looked out over the Academy garden. "This had nothing to do with them helping me. They want to persuade me into accepting their theories."

Lorena cupped her hands behind her head and leaned back in the white sofa with a smile.

"This is the Academy, Sarah. It's supposed to be tough. While you were away, Professor Jackson gave Ahmed added homework as punishment for stumbling on his way out of the classroom."

"That's absurd," Sarah mumbled.

"No, as Professor Jackson explained, people make fun of leaders who trip. It happened to Gerald Ford in 1975. The amount of mockery he had to endure is ridiculous."

"How is this relevant?"

"The Academy won't do things unless it helps us become better."

"It's still wrong."

The warm sound of Lorena laughing filled the room.

"You're a rebel in disguise, aren't you?" she said.

Sarah watched the sun cast its burning gaze over the magnificent landscape outside. God she'd missed the sun.

"For four weeks they kept me locked up in a room without windows," she whispered as the dark memories returned. "Every day they came in to ask me the same three questions: Why are you here?; Why do people follow leaders?; What is power?"

"And what did you say?"

"I said that they know why I'm here, so why ask me? Regarding the reasons why people follow, I told them it's because people want to achieve something. And as to their final question, I explained that power is the ability to make individuals obey regardless of their willingness to do so."

Lorena sat up, her cheerful expression gone.

"You said that? Shit, no wonder they're pissed."

Sarah turned away from the window.

"Well, that's my opinion."

"Damn it, Sarah! They don't care about your opinion."

"They should."

Lorena put her hand on her forehead and moaned.

"They don't! I mean, Professor Jackson has said it a million times: 'Power is the capacity and willingness to act; the ability to make things happen.' Why didn't you just say that?"

"Because it's a stupid definition," Sarah snorted. "I was never powerful, but I still had the capacity, ability, and the willingness to act and save an orphanage."

Lorena shook her head and leaned over to the coffee table where a large cheese tray and a bottle of wine stood.

"You can't go on being this obstructive," she said as she grabbed her glass of wine. "You're going to get yourself in trouble."

"I'm just expressing my views. How can that be obstructive?"

"Because the Academy isn't your enemy. They're preparing us for our future. They're tough, but it's a cruel world out there, and if we're not prepared, we're going to get eaten alive."

Sarah frowned.

"I've seen children die because of malnutrition. I've met rape victims, girls who were barely teenagers, rejected by society because they became pregnant. I know cruelty. I've seen it. But you know what?" She pointed out the window. "There's more light than darkness in the world. It's just a matter of what you choose to see."

Lorena grimaced.

"I hate it when you go philosophical on me," she muttered. "It's embarrassing."

Sarah turned her back to the scenic view and crossed the dark wooden floor to one of her armchairs.

"There's cruelty in the world, but there's also compassion. Most people are kind. For every child who is left at an orphanage, there are hundreds who are embraced by a mother's loving arms."

"Your point being?"

"Why are we being trained as if entering a war? Why are we talking about people as if they're sheep? Why are we focusing on supremacy instead of collaboration? Why are we discussing strategies to win instead of strategies to make the world better?"

Lorena stared at the glass. She knows I'm right, Sarah thought. She can feel it in her heart, but will she accept it?

"You're as stubborn as they get, aren't you?" Lorena declared.

"Only when I know I'm right."

"So what are you going to do?"

"I think I must talk to Professor Jackson."

Lorena paled.

"Noooo," she said, shaking her head. "That's not a good idea."

Sarah didn't reply. She'd already made up her mind. She was going to talk to the assistant principal in the morning.

CHAPTER 45

PRESENT DAY

According to the hallway clock, it was near midnight when Axel stepped into his apartment. He found that a little odd. Why would the Academy release him at this hour?

Someone had left the lights on, so he made his way through the warmly lit hallway with tentative steps. The living room was empty. Soft music played in the background and a fire crackled in the fireplace. Next to the coffee table stood a food trolley, giving off a wonderful aromatic smell. It seemed to be begging him to explore it.

Axel hurried over. All he'd been eating for the past weeks was porridge. When he peeked under one of the silver cloches, he found a plate full of egg rolls, his favourite dish. He shoved one into his mouth, grabbed another two and headed for the shower. Starving as he was, with three weeks of dirt to get rid of, eating would have to wait a little longer.

Half an hour later, Axel sat in his armchair, a thick Academy bathrobe wrapped around him and warm slippers on his feet. He bit another piece of Belgian chocolate in half and leaned back with a satisfied sigh. He wasn't tired, just relieved that the whole ordeal was over.

To his left, the fire seemed to whisper as it worked itself through the dry firewood. Axel sipped his steaming tea and stared at the aquarium while the shark made its usual tour around the tank. Axel scowled at the animal as if the poor thing was to blame for everything that had happened.

That's when the phone rang. Axel pressed a button on his phone and Dr Vella's annoying and monotonous voice filled the living room.

"Good evening, Mr Hallman."

"What do you want?"

"Now, now. That's not very leader-like, is it?"

"I'm not in the mood for your games, doctor," he replied. "What do you want?"

"You're very rude, Mr Hallman. Of course, considering the circumstances, I'm going to ignore it."

Axel frowned. He didn't care what she thought, but he had picked up something tense and troubled in her otherwise-toneless voice.

"I have a message from Principal Cunningham," the doctor continued. "He wants you to know that, for the past few weeks, you've been engaged in an IDT: individualised training session."

Axel's eyes narrowed and, with exaggerated care, he placed his teacup on the coffee table. "What do you mean by 'individualised'? Are you saying that the Black Sunday was designed for me?"

"No," Dr Vella snorted. "Don't flatter yourself, Mr Hallman. All students have to go through Black Sunday, although they'll spend no more than twenty-four hours down there. That's why we call it Black Sunday and not Black Week."

It took Axel a few seconds to grasp the meaning of Dr Vella's words. "One day?" He choked for a second. "That's…all they did?"

"Yes."

"Why?"

"This is the Academy, Mr Hallman."

There was a pause.

"Hey! What the hell does that mean?"

"Isn't that obvious? It means that everything you do is part of your training. It's an honour. You were given three weeks of personal training."

Axel felt his frustration take over. "Are you kidding me? You locked me up for three weeks as if I was a criminal. How the hell does that make me a better leader?"

"I…I'm sorry you feel a need to question our training methods, Mr Hallman. None of the other students have."

"Well, were any of them locked in a cell for three weeks?"

"Quite frankly, I'm concerned Mr Hallman," Dr Vella declared. "Don't you trust us? Without trust, it'll be very difficult for you to continue your studies."

Axel got to his feet and stomped over to the aquarium. No, he didn't trust the Academy. Not after what he'd just experienced. Nevertheless, as the shark swam by, he began to waver. There was no denying that the EKA knew what they were doing. After all, they turned *every* student into a successful leader.

"I trust you," he mumbled.

"Good, because you need to separate the comfort of your training, or lack thereof, with the significance of it. I understand that the past three weeks were tough, but they were necessary. In addition, none of the other students has been given this much attention, so you *should* feel honoured."

So why me, Axel wondered, but he already knew the answer. "There's something fishy about Hallman," Professor Jackson had said. The Academy didn't trust him.

"Now, Mr Hallman," Dr Vella continued, "Principal Cunningham has asked me to inform you that you're not to tell *anyone* about what you've experienced. Nor will he discuss the matter with you."

"Hold on," Axel objected, "I've been gone for three weeks. What am I supposed to say to my friends? I can't just pretend like nothing's happened."

"If anyone asks, you'll tell them that you've been in hospital for appendicitis. That's what they've been told."

"My appendix was removed when I was a child."

"I know, Mr Hallman, which means you have a scar already."

"But three weeks to recover from an appendicitis operation. No one will believe that."

"Then you have to be creative, Mr Hallman," Dr Vella replied. "I have to go now. Enjoy your evening."

CHAPTER 46

Dr Vella hung up the phone and her pale eyes flashed Professor Jackson an expression that said, "Happy now?"

He gave her a little nod.

"Thank you, doctor, I believe that will do."

"You promise you'll have all this conversation erased? If Principal Cunningham finds out…"

"Don't worry. I'm a man of my word." Dr Vella pouted and didn't look convinced at all. It annoyed Professor Jackson. "I'll call Mr Nakata straightaway," he added, and, this time, the doctor nodded and turned for the door. "Oh, and on your way out, can you tell Ms Swan that I want to see her at once?"

"Yes, sir."

As the door closed behind her, Professor Jackson dropped back into his chair. Now that Axel had his instructions, it was time to deal with Nicole. What a disappointment. She should have known better than to express favouritism to a student.

Professor Jackson picked up his phone. He would have to give her an official warning. Although he wasn't proud of it, he felt a tingle of excitement thinking about it. Nicole was one of Principal Cunningham's favourites and stood under his protection. Somehow, that made it all a little more interesting. But, before he dealt with Nicole, he would call Mr Nakata as he'd promised Dr Vella. After all, he was a man of his word.

CHAPTER 47

There are those who claim that time heals all wounds, but when Axel woke up on Saturday morning, he determined that it wasn't always the case. Sometimes, time would *inflict* wounds.

He'd spent the entire night dwelling on the fact that he'd been the victim of unfair treatment, and the more he dwelled, the angrier he got. Dr Vella's argument didn't seem logical anymore and Axel was ready for war.

After a quick shower, he took the elevator to the eleventh floor, known as the Office and Administration floor. He stepped out into a waiting room that resembled a small living room with a reception desk. Warm light fell over a carpet that was so thick, one would almost need a lawn mower to cross it. There was lots of greenery and even a fire burning in a corner fireplace. On one wall hung a large TV-screen showing the Academy eagle and a golden globe slowly rotating above the text: "You are our future. You are our hope".

Axel turned from the TV screen to the reception and found a familiar face watching him.

"Good morning, Mr Hallman. How nice to see you again."

Nicole was sitting behind a computer, elegant as always. Axel smiled at her with unhidden surprise.

"Is this where you work?"

She laughed. "Yes. When I'm not needed elsewhere, you'll find me here."

It struck Axel that he didn't actually know what Nicole's tasks were.

"What *is* your job?"

"Oh, nothing fancy. I do a little bit of this and a little bit of that, depending on what the principal or assistant principal need me to do." She beamed. "Now how can I help you?"

"I'd like to talk to Principal Cunningham."

Nicole gave him a rueful shake of her head. "I'm sorry. That's not possible. He's in Portugal."

"When will he be back?"

Nicole checked her phone. "Two weeks from now, but he will only be here for a day and he's fully booked, I'm afraid." She looked up. "If you like, I can check with Mr Hennigan, Principal Cunningham's assistant. Maybe there's a possibility to squeeze you in between meetings next time the principal returns, but that's six weeks from now."

"Six weeks!"

Nicole gave him an apologetic smile. "It's the first semester with a new class. The interest in the Academy is at its peak, which means Principal Cunningham is more or less fully booked until July. Things usually slow down around then but I would assume it's a little too late for you. The assistant principal is here. Will that do?"

Axel hesitated. The wise thing would be to wait for the principal to return, but six weeks? No way! Axel wanted answers, and he wanted them now.

"Yes," he replied with a little more force than he'd intended, not that Nicole seemed to notice.

"Very well, Mr Hallman. Please follow me."

They walked down a long, dark corridor, passing several meeting rooms and offices before Nicole stopped in front of a wide, wooden door.

"Here we are." Nicole pointed to another door at the end of the corridor. "That's Principal Cunningham's office, should you ever want to see him and I'm not in." She adjusted her suit jacket. "Ready?"

Axel frowned. "Ready for what?"

Nicole knocked on the assistant principal's door. "Ready for Professor Jackson," she whispered and winked.

The door opened inward with such force, Axel could feel the suction before the professor himself appeared. He gave them an indifferent glare. "Aye?"

"Sorry, Professor, but Mr Hallman would like a word with you."

"Is that so?"

Axel stepped forward. "Yes, sir. If you don't mind."

Professor Jackson took off a pair of reading glasses and looked very much like he *did* mind. Nevertheless, he stepped aside.

"All right, come on in."

As soon as Axel entered the office, the assistant principal slammed the door shut behind him, leaving Nicole to return to her desk.

The first thing that struck Axel was the overwhelming scent of coffee. He surveyed the large office. It wasn't very bright. The windows were tinted, and the carpet was dark, as was the furniture. Three small armchairs stood positioned around a small table near the windows. Foolishly he approached them, thinking he would be offered a seat.

"No need to sit, Mr Hallman," Professor Jackson muttered. He walked around his large desk and dropped into his own wide office chair. "I have a great deal of responsibilities; things to do. Thus, time is a very limited commodity for me." He leaned forward, his eyes cold and indifferent. "Now, why are you here?"

At that instant, without any warning, Axel felt his anger wash away, leaving him with nothing but uncertainty.

"It's about Black Sunday," he began.

"Aye. Black Sunday. It's a very good exercise, wouldn't you agree?"

Axel stared at his teacher, trying to figure out whether or not he was making fun of him. "No...well, I...I don't know."

Professor Jackson leaned back in his chair, steepled his fingers and frowned. "That seems to be a common problem for you, Mr Hallman. I'm curious, what *do* you know?"

Axel tensed, absorbing the anger as it returned. "I understand I was held isolated in a small room for three weeks," he started. "Everyone else was held in a common room for a few hours."

"Aye. And?"

"I want to know why."

Professor Jackson raised his eyebrows with mock surprise. "Are you a little upset, Mr Hallman?"

"Yes. I am!"

"Then deal with it, Mr Hallman. *You're* here to become a leader, and *we're* here to make that happen. Thunderstruck, remember?"

"I beg your pardon?"

Professor Jackson snorted and stood up. "Our Leadership Allegiance! Let me hear it!"

Axel kept his head down, focusing on the man's polished shoes under the big desk. Things were not turning out as he'd expected.

"Come on, let me hear it, Mr Hallman! Let me hear you pledge allegiance to the Academy and your role as a future leader!"

Axel raised his head reluctantly. "Sir, I…"

"LET ME HEAR IT!"

Axel reared. He felt a drop of sweat trickling down his back.

"I'm the role model who leads the way," he mumbled, "People follow, and they obey. I empower and foster trust…"

It felt as if he had an invisible noose around his neck, and, with every word he uttered, it tightened. By the time he was done, he could hardly breathe.

The tight-lipped professor stood as if frozen for a good thirty seconds or so. Then he blinked.

"Come here," he hissed. "Go on! A little closer." Axel obeyed, albeit with reluctance. "You know what, Mr Hallman?" Professor Jackson whispered with venom. "That was the most pathetic thing I've ever seen. I want to shoot myself out of embarrassment. Where's the power? The honesty? You sound like a schoolboy caught fondling himself." Then without warning, the professor launched forward grabbing Axel's head between his large hands. "Now you listen to me!"

CHAPTER 48

The man sat in the corner of his dark little room. His eyes darted back and forth between the two screens while his fingers smattered against the keyboard. He was close. Any minute now…

"Access denied."

Darn. The man rubbed his face and stood up. There had to be a way. He'd been at it for weeks now, sniffing through the system like a bloodhound on a trail. It shouldn't be this hard. The system was impossible to access from outside the Academy, and, with the exception of Mr Nakata and his team, only a handful of people knew it even existed.

The man grabbed a cold beer from the fridge and returned to his desk. Mr Nakata was a paranoid chap and downright bonkers when it came to security. The system was booby-trapped to the point of absurdity. On more than one occasion, he'd been close to setting off the alarm, thinking he was on safe grounds.

He sighed and tried again.

Yawning, he pressed enter. The screens went black. Sitting in complete darkness, the man froze and held his breath as he stared at his screens. Had he stepped into a trap? He'd been tired; maybe he'd missed something?

Five seconds passed, then another five. He pushed back his chair. If he'd set off the alarm, he would have to leave immediately. There was a bag under his bed, packed with clothes and enough money to last him a week. If he survived that long, the Box might be able to save him.

The man interlocked his hands behind his neck, pressing his arms against his ears. He lacked the skills that Thor and the other spies had. There was no way he would last a week on his own. The Academy would have him dead within an hour.

Another five seconds passed, and then the screens flickered and lit up. *"Welcome to EKCOM."*

The man let out a muffled cry of relief and dropped his hands. Good Lord! He was in.

CHAPTER 49

Professor Jackson's fingers pressed hard against Axel's head, as if trying to rupture his skull. With their eyes locked onto each other, the professor began to speak with his deep-seated voice.

"I'm the role model who leads the way,
People follow, and they obey…"

He spoke with fiery passion, reading the entire Leadership Allegiance before letting go of Axel, who stumbled back.

"*Thunderstruck!*" Professor Jackson roared and stretched to his full length. "That's what it's all about. Men who spit fire when they speak; who exert power and determination; who are loved but feared; whose passion can turn anyone into a follower. *That's* what we create here!"

Axel was shocked. His cheeks burned as if the professor had slapped him, and deep within, the seething anger began to grow once more.

"Your followers must love you. Your enemies must fear you. We expect greatness, Mr Hallman, not a spoiled ungrateful little brat. Do you understand?"

"Yes, but…"

"There are no 'buts', you imbecilic! Our job is to prepare you for what's coming. *Your* job is to learn. We'll adjust your training depending on your needs and you *will* accept it, no questions asked. Or do you doubt the Academy?"

Professor Jackson said the last words as if the mere thought was absurd. Axel fought hard not to let his anger take over.

"No, sir," he replied through clenched teeth.

"Then you should know that if you were in there for three weeks, it's because you needed it."

"What did I need that the others didn't?"

"Oh, don't push it, Mr Hallman! The Academy doesn't have to justify its training methods to you. If you don't like it…"

Axel glared at the man who let the words hang. This was going nowhere; he was only getting himself into more trouble.

"I'm not quitting," he said with strained composure. "I just want to understand if I've done something wrong. How else can I improve?"

For a few seconds, Professor Jackson remained motionless. Then he dropped back into his chair with a hint of a smirk on his lips.

"Information in order to grow, you say? Well, I'll be damned. I didn't think you would play that card." He leaned back and tapped his fingertips against each other. "All right, there are two main objectives with Black Sunday." He held up his index finger. "First of all, great leaders must learn that they're never safe. There are always threats and you had better remember that or you'll end up as many other leaders in the past: dead by the hand of an unexpected enemy.

"Secondly –" Professor Jackson raised a second finger "– all great leaders face situations that will shock, scare and bewilder them. When this happens, and trust me it *will* happen, then your success depends on how well you can master your emotions. Remember, regardless of the situation, your followers will expect you to be in control of the situation. Black Sunday gives you a better understanding of how you feel and react in times of shock. From now on, all of you will work with Mr Nakata to improve your mental strength."

Professor Jackson's blue eyes narrowed.

"There's a third benefit with Black Sunday. It will test a student's willingness to become a leader. Black Sunday is a tiring exercise, and for many students it's the first time they realise what they've signed up for.

"This isn't a playground where toddlers come to play. We prepare you for the game of power. This is a game played by the biggest fish in the pond, and if you don't want this bad enough, you have to quit. If you don't, you'll get swallowed by someone bigger and meaner than you, and that would be an embarrassment to our Academy." The professor got up and walked to the door. "And *that's* why you were held longer than the rest. I need to know that you want this more than anything."

"You doubted me?" Axel asked.

"Aye, and I still do." The professor grinned and opened the door. "I have work to do and you need to head down to your class with Professor Evans."

"But..."

"No. This conversation is over. Next time you come to complain about the training, you better have a damn good reason and be far more prepared. I'll never show you this kind of patience again. You have to remember that out in the real world, people don't care about you. They don't care about how you feel or the effort you put in. What matters are results. So, if you want to graduate, you better give me results."

Axel hesitated.

"What kind of results, sir?"

"That's for you to figure out." Professor Jackson grabbed Axel by his lower arm. "And one more thing, I believe you've been told not to discuss your experience during Black Sunday, so consider this a warning: if you so much as breathe a word about this to *anyone,* me or Principal Cunningham included, you'll be expelled and I'll turn your life into a living hell. Clear?"

CHAPTER 50

TWELVE YEARS EARLIER

"The greater the leader, the greater his sacrifice," Professor Jackson barked and pointed at his door. "Take it as a compliment. Now get out!"

Sarah gave him a defiant look. She was different that way. Most people reacted like a frightened pup when he yelled at them, but not Sarah. She would stare a person straight in the eye no matter what. Professor Jackson admired that in a student, even if he found it annoying at the time. He knew what she was doing; she was trying to provoke him into continuing their conversation. It was a good strategy, but he wouldn't fall for it.

"I said, get out," he hissed. "This conversation is over."

He walked back to his desk, sat down and began shuffling papers. He could feel Sarah watching him for a few more seconds before she turned on her heels and left. Professor Jackson listened to the door close behind her. She was a wild-card. Sarah had the attitude and the brains to become great. She had the passion. Born with nothing, she'd made it all the way here. No wonder the other students disliked her. On paper she should be inferior to them all, but if she got her act together she could become one of the strongest students to ever graduate from the Academy.

Professor Jackson took off his glasses and massaged the bridge of his nose. Sarah hated him now, but he didn't mind. He did this for her. She had all the right qualities and yet she seemed determined to become a rebel. It angered him. The woman had so much potential; why throw it away on some naïve ideology? There had to be a way to change her. After all, that's what the Academy did; they turned sheep into wolves.

CHAPTER 51

PRESENT DAY

Room C wasn't very big, but it was by far one of the more interesting classrooms within the Academy. There were no windows. Instead, each wall, along with the floor and the concave ceiling, functioned as huge screens, displaying magnificent scenes from around the world.

Mr Bell frequently used the room as a means of taking the students straight into the heart of a city or culture without having to leave the Academy. By incorporating complex holograms, he provided the students with stunning and realistic environments. This way they could sit in the middle of a busy street in Beijing one day, and, the next, a small village in Papua New Guinea. The previous week, Mr Bell had taken them to a small settlement in North West Greenland, where they learnt about the culture of the Greenlandic Inuit people.

Of course, not all teachers used the room as a training tool. Some just wanted the students to experience various environments, hoping to boost their engagement. Axel assumed this was the case today. Entering the room, he found himself in a desert, near a large oasis. It was a spectacular scene.

A week had passed since he returned from Black Sunday. He was a little disappointed to find that the interest in his absence had been rather low. Not even Thabo, Paul, or Izabella seemed to care much. Everyone was preoccupied with his or her own studies.

"Good morning, leaders!" Professor Evans' joyful voice cut through the classroom as she stepped through the door, smiling as always. "Today you're up for a fun exercise. Bring your computers and come with me!"

She led her class down to the Academy basement.

"This sucks. I don't want to go down there again," Axel mumbled to Thabo as they stood packed in one of the elevators.

"Don't worry." Thabo smiled. "Whatever it is, we'll deal with it. We are leaders."

I'm doing it for Talk Thirteen, Axel thought, and steeled himself as the winged doors opened. Standing at the back he couldn't see much, but a hushed murmur told him something had baffled the other students. He and Thabo exchanged looks and craned their necks.

A few seconds later, Axel stepped out, gaping at the view in front of him. The dark, rugged corridor he'd walked through a week before was gone. Instead, he stood in a wide, cosy-lit hallway. Large, framed photographs of African animals hung on yellow-painted walls. A beige carpet covered the concrete floor, and, through the hallway, soft, soul-soothing music flowed.

A light ring told him the second elevator had arrived. Professor Evans stepped out, followed by the remaining students.

"Come on," she urged. "We have a lot to do."

"They never cease to amaze me," Izabella said, as the professor led her students through a series of short but wide hallways, each a small gallery in itself. Photos, paintings, and extraordinary statues lined the walls, making it hard to keep up with Professor Evans.

A few minutes later, they reached a door leading into a peculiar room that reminded Axel of a small wooden cabin. The walls were cladded in timber but instead of windows, there were large TV-screens showing wide-open fields and a clear-blue sky.

"I told you; they never cease to surprise me." Izabella laughed as she stepped through the door.

Professor Evans waved them in.

"Go on, have a seat." She nodded at the wooden desks lined up in neat rows. "Let me tell you about today's exercise. In there –" she pointed at a narrow door opposite the one where they had just entered "– is something we call 'the chamber'. It's a training facility. Today you'll enter it one by one. Inside, you'll find a number of mannequins holding a note with a word on it. Four of these words are related to the EKA. Your task is to identify these words as fast as possible. Once you've found them, you shall return to this room and wait for further instructions. Any questions?" No one raised a hand. "Good. Mr Hallman, why don't you start?"

Paul gave Axel a slap on the back.

"Good luck, mate."

Axel opened the door and stared into blackness.

"Step in and close the door behind you," Professor Evans instructed. "The lights will turn on once the door is closed."

Axel glanced over his shoulder. He had no doubt there was more to this exercise than just finding a few notes. He searched the professor's face for any clues but she gave nothing away.

"Go on," she said. "We don't have all day."

Axel stepped in. The door closed without making a sound, leaving Axel alone in complete darkness. He waited. Just when he began wondering if something was wrong, a light appeared in front of him. Other lights soon followed and before he knew it, he was standing in a room the size of a warehouse.

"Wow," he breathed, gawking at the wondrous scene.

He was standing on a cobblestone street that ran from one end of the Chamber to the other. There were buildings on each side of the street, a few stores, a barbershop, a bus stop, and even a real car positioned on the street. The whole scene reminded him of photo from the 1930s.

The mannequins were everywhere, dressed to resemble people going about their everyday business. Some were on the street, like the police officer appearing to stroll down the sidewalk. Others were inside the buildings, or in the process of entering or leaving one of the stores.

Leaning against the barbershop sat a mannequin dressed as a beggar, wearing ragged clothes and dirt all over its face. Nearby, three children played by the street. There were even two boys appearing to fight each other at the end of the room. The smaller of the two had beaten his much-larger opponent to the ground and stood over him with a proud expression on his face and his hands balled into fists.

Astonished, Axel began to walk down the street, marvelling at all the details. Mikael would have loved this. The man had a thing for silent films, particularly films with John Gilbert, who'd influenced Mikael to grow his ridiculous moustache.

After quick consideration, Axel decided to work from one end of the room to the other. It was an eerie feeling, moving amongst the stiff mannequins, accompanied by nothing more than the hollow sound of his shoes against the cobblestone. He picked up his speed, reading the notes attached to each mannequin's hand. Most words were such that they couldn't be connected to the Academy; words such as "Moon", "Seaweed", "Snow", "Skateboard", etc. Others were a little harder, things that one could find within the Academy; "Rug", "Restaurant", "Pool", etc.

When Axel came across a female mannequin at the bus stop, he found she had the word "Eagle" on her note. That had to be one of the words. A little later, he found the word "Brussels" on a male mannequin. It wasn't as obvious as "Eagle", but it was clear enough. The third word was in the hand of a mannequin girl playing on the street. It said "Power".

After a fair bit of searching, Axel found the fourth word, "Thunder", written on a tiny note, stuffed into the fist of the young fighter. Thunderstruck, Axel thought, as he considered the larger boy on the ground. How fitting. He shoved the note back into the plastic hand when the lights flickered and died.

The room grew black as a grave. Great, now what?

"Ms Evans!" Axel yelled. "The lights went out!"

There was a faint click above his head. Axel's heart began to pound.

"We know why you applied," a powerful female voice declared. She uttered the words without judgement, yet Axel was so startled, he reared and knocked a mannequin over. "We know the truth and we will keep it a secret if you collaborate."

Axel found his balance and froze. He didn't even breathe. He just waited, listening to the quiet, static noise that filled the silence around him.

"Who are you?" he whispered.

"In time you'll know, Mr Hallman. Meanwhile, here's something to contemplate: if you talk me into doing what you want, you call it leadership; if I talk you into doing what I want, then you call it manipulation. Tell me, what's the difference?"

There was a flickering of light, the voice vanished, and the room lit up. An instant later, the door at the end of the room flung opened and Professor Evans marched in.

"Mr Hallman! Are you all right?"

* * *

In a different part of the world, Smooth got an expected phone call.

"Yes?"

"We did it. We broke through and reached him."

"Excellent! Well done. And how did he take it?"

"Better than I expected, sir."

"Perfect. Inform the others. Let them know that as far as I'm concerned, we should proceed according to plan."

"Yes, sir."

"And Thor...make sure you're here by tomorrow morning."

"Of course, sir."

CHAPTER 52

Professor Jackson cursed at the ringing of the phone and turned away from his computer. He'd been very clear when he told Nicole that he didn't want to be disturbed. He was in the middle of grading his students' essays on business restructuring. As expected, they'd done a great job, which required him to be very creative in order to find things to criticise.

Many people disliked giving criticism but not Professor Jackson. He was of the opinion that criticism was the ticket to improvement. Know your faults and you'll be able to improve. It was as simple as that.

The phone rang once more and the professor snatched off his glasses. Glaring at the phone he was surprised to find that it wasn't Nicole who called.

"Aye?"

"We have security issue."

Professor Jackson closed his eyes. Although Mr Nakata's voice was calm as always, the fact that he'd found something he regarded as an "issue" was disturbing, *very* disturbing.

"Shit! Where are you?"

"Eagle Eye."

"All right, I'll be right down!" he barked, his Irish accent becoming more pronounced with anger.

The assistant principal stormed out of his office. With Cunningham out on business, it was up to him to run the Academy. An "issue" was troubling, and Professor Jackson didn't want anything remotely "troubling" on his watch. Shit!

He took the elevator to the bottom floor and made his way through a labyrinth of corridors until he reached a thick metal door, guarded by a woman in black uniform.

"Good afternoon, sir," she said and stepped aside.

"No, it's not," Professor Jackson muttered as he punched in a private code on his phone. The door opened and he marched into a short, sterile corridor. To his left was a double door leading to the guards' quarters, and to his right the guards' training centre. Professor Jackson stomped down the hallway to the very end, where a massive and heavily armed guard protected yet another door. The guard gave him a small nod of recognition and stepped aside.

"Good afternoon, sir."

"For you maybe," Professor Jackson growled and placing his left palm on the scanner.

"*Welcome Assistant Principal Jackson,*" a computerised voice declared, and the door opened.

The Academy's security centre, Eagle Eye, was a dark, bunker-like room, fitted with monitors everywhere. There were always three guards on duty. Their job was to be the eyes and ears of the Academy.

Mr Nakata was in the back of the room, staring at a cluster of monitors.

"What's the problem," Professor Jackson roared.

"We think maybe someone hack security system." Mr Nakata looked down at a young man sitting in front of a computer. "Mr Tilly, explain," he demanded.

"Yes, sir." The young man turned to Professor Jackson. "Ms Evans is doing an exercise with her class. She requested a visual of the Chamber for her entire session. I gave her access five minutes before class started. She logged on fifteen minutes later. Five minutes after that, the first student entered the Chamber. Everything went well for eight minutes. Then we lost connection with all cameras on that floor. For thirty seconds, we couldn't see or hear anything. Not even our back-up system worked, and that's very, very strange, sir."

Professor Jackson glared at the screen while his mind processed Mr Tilly's words.

"Could it have been caused by some mechanical or technical failure?"

"It's possible, sir, but I doubt it."

"Why?"

"Because Professor Evans called us twenty-two seconds after the system crashed and informed us that the door to the Chamber was locked. When she lost visual, she'd tried to get in to her student, but somehow the automatic lock-up system had kicked in. That shouldn't happen, sir."

"We control lock-up and lock-down," Mr Nakata added. "No one else."

Mr Tilly bobbed his head. "That's for safety reasons, sir. In fact, should our security system falter, then most of our automatic doors should *open*, not close. I've done a quick health check on our system, and I can't find anything indicating that we have a bug in our system. I need to run a few more checks, of course, but I doubt I'll find anything."

Professor Jackson couldn't believe it. It didn't make any sense.

"What are you saying, Mr Tilly? Someone hacked their way into our system? Is that even possible?"

"Anything is possible," Mr Nakata said, "but very difficult from outside."

Professor Jackson winced. "And from inside the Academy?"

"Much easier."

"I see." Professor Jackson rubbed the back of his neck. "Tell me, who was the student that got locked in when this happened?"

Mr Tilly glanced at Mr Nakata before tapping a few commands on his computer, bringing forth a blurry picture of Axel. Professor Jackson closed his eyes for a second. It might not mean anything, he thought to himself. It could be a simple coincidence. On the other hand...it might mean *everything*.

"Not a word about this to anyone," he warned. "And I mean *anyone!* That includes our Principal Cunningham, understand?"

Mr Tilly flinched.

"But, sir..."

Mr Nakata, cut him off by placing a hand on his shoulder.

"Don't question order!"

"Of course, sir," Mr Tilly faltered. "Not a word to anyone."

Professor Jackson took the elevator up one floor and marched off to the Cabin, the classroom connected to the Chamber.

"Oh, good afternoon, sir," Professor Evans began as he barged in.

Had it been a good afternoon, I wouldn't be here, Professor Jackson wanted to yell, but he held his tongue and scanned the room for Axel.

"I need to borrow Mr Hallman for a second," he snapped and gestured at the young Swede to join him.

Professor Evans was displeased, but she knew better than to challenge him.

"I want you to tell me what happened in there," he demanded, when he and Axel stood outside the Cabin a moment later.

"You already know about that, sir?"

"Just answer the damn question, Hallman!"

Axel's eyes darted towards the ceiling and back, making it clear that he was choosing his words with care. Why would he do that? Professor Jackson wondered.

"Well, sir, I was in the Chamber when the lights went out. I called for Professor Evans but she couldn't hear me. Then the lights went on again and the professor came in. She said the cameras had malfunctioned and that the door couldn't be opened for a while."

Professor Jackson tried to read the young man's face to see if he was telling the truth. "That's it, Mr Hallman?"

"Yes, sir."

"You'd tell me if something else happened, wouldn't you? I'm very concerned about your safety here."

"Oh." Axel's surprise seemed genuine. Most students were too thick-headed to realise that Professor Jackson cared about them, and Axel was no exception. "Of course, sir."

The assistant principal raised his chin and exhaled.

"Very well, Mr Hallman. You can return to your class."

On his way back to the office, Professor Jackson's cell phone rang.

"Professor, this is Carl Tilly from security. We've gone through our systems and we can't find any indication of software or hardware failure. We found a tiny bug in the audio system but that shouldn't have affected the cameras or the doors."

Professor Jackson came to a dead stop. "What did you just say?"

"Eh…"

"You found a *bug*?"

"Yes, sir, but it was tiny—"

"I don't care how small it is, you fud!" the professor barked. "A bug is a *mistake* and we don't do mistakes! You have thirty minutes to write me a full report, including an action plan! Understand?"

"Yes, sir."

"Now, tell me; were we hacked or not?"

Mr Tilly seemed to waver. "We can't find any signs of intrusion, sir. None whatsoever. *If* we were hacked, then whoever did it must have known our system in quite some detail. I just don't see how that would be possible."

"So you're telling me we *weren't* hacked?"

Mr Tilly cleared his throat. "Well…no, sir. I'm saying that we don't know."

Professor Jackson took a very deep and loud breath.

"Now you listen to me, you bleedin' muppet," he hissed. "I'm not interested in your opinion or your guesses. I have to *know* if we were hacked or not."

"But, sir, it's impossible…"

"*Nothing* is impossible," Professor Jackson shouted. "Just get me a bloody answer!"

CHAPTER 53

He felt as if he'd escaped the jaws of death. Professor Jackson was a terrifying man, especially when you had to stare him dead in the eye and lie.

With an overwhelming sense of unease, Axel watched the professor march off behind a corner and disappear. What the hell was going on? The voice in the Chamber knew the truth behind Axel's application, but Professor Jackson did not. This raised a number of questions. Who knew? How did they know, and what did they mean by "we will keep it a secret if you collaborate"? That was a threat, wasn't it? And in what way did they, whoever they were, want to collaborate?

He came no further in his pondering, as the door opened and Professor Evans peered out. She eyeballed him with unhidden distrust before glancing down the empty corridor.

"What in the world are you doing, Mr Hallman?"

"I'm sorry, ma'am," Axel mumbled sheepishly. "Professor Jackson just left."

"Then why are you standing here like a buffoon? Come on." She stepped aside, holding the door open for him. "You have work to do."

As much as it bothered him, Axel had little choice but to leave all worrying thoughts behind for the moment. He gave Professor Evans a nod and trudged back to his seat.

When the last student returned from the Chamber, Professor Evans stood up.

"All right, students. I presume you've all found the four words associated with the Academy. Please log on to Eagle Net and write down the words for me."

Eagle Net was the EKA intranet, used by both teachers and students. Each teacher had their own Eagle Net page where instructions and assignments were given and collected. Axel entered his four words.

"Well done," Professor Evans commended after a while. "All of you found the correct words. Now I'm going to ask you a series of questions and I want you to write down your answers on your computers. Hmm, let's see. First question: was the word 'Leader' found on a male or female mannequin?" The professor waited as the students typed in their answers. "Did the mannequin holding the word 'Brussels' wear a wristwatch?"

One by one, Professor Evans went through her questions. What colour was the beggar's trousers? How many "men" wore a hat? What kind of shop was furthest from the door? What serial number was written on the police officer's baton? How many female mannequins were there? She continued for almost half an hour, until she raised her head and regarded her class.

"How disappointing," Professor Evans concluded after having gone through the results. She got to her feet. "Ms Izzati had sixty-two out of a hundred and Mr Reed had fifty-nine. The rest of you had below fifty." She began to stroll down between the desks at a slow pace. "What do you think the purpose of this exercise was?"

"To test our memories," Aseem tried.

"And what does that have to do with communication, Mr Kamala?"

Aseem shrugged and Professor Evans turned to the others. "Anyone?" The students remained silent. "No? *Why* do we communicate?"

"To achieve something," Layla replied.

Professor Evans lit up.

"Exactly! For decision-makers, communication always serves a purpose. It can be anything from gaining followers or negotiating a deal. It's all about communication, and, in order to be successful, you have to adapt your communication style to the people you speak with."

With eyes unseeing, Axel flipped his phone between his fingers. What was it that the voice from the Chamber had said? "If you talk me into doing what *you* want, you call it leadership. If I talk you into doing what *I* want, then you call it..."

He looked up. "But isn't that manipulation, ma'am?"

Professor Evans stopped dead in her track. With her back to him, she stood motionless for a heartbeat. Then, nudging the purple scarf around her neck, she turned.

"What did you say?"

CHAPTER 54

"It's an interesting perspective, Mr Hallman," Professor Evans remarked, "yet I believe the definition of manipulation is something in line with; 'controlling someone to your own advantage, often using unfair or dishonest means'." She began to make her way back to her desk. "I'm not teaching you to be dishonest or unfair, but rather to analyse your target group and adjust your communication thereafter."

"But isn't that a form of manipulation?" Axel argued.

Professor Evans touched a spot behind her ear and gave it a light scratch. "Most definitely not. We all adapt our communication depending on our listener. You wouldn't use the same words, rhythm and intonation when speaking to a two-year-old child as you do to an adult, would you? And if you met a tourist who barely spoke any English, would you speak to her as you speak to me?"

"No."

"So you admit you make distinctions based on who you talk to?"

"Yes." By the way Professor Evans raised her chin, Axel assumed she thought he'd capitulated, but he wasn't done yet. The voice in the Chamber had a point. "I guess it's not manipulation if I'm trying to present my information in a clear manner, but if I try to make people think or behave against their will, then I'd say that's manipulation."

A few quiet sighs and grunts made Axel glance over his shoulder. His eyes met Julie's and she had an expression that seemed to say "why do you always have to question everything?"

"I don't think manipulation has to be a bad thing," Cordelia stated. "Sometimes it might be necessary."

Axel couldn't believe it. "You think manipulation is good?"

"I think it might be necessary at times, yes."

"I agree," said Edward. "As a business owner, I've realised that sometimes people need a little push or the world wouldn't evolve."

"That's not true," Axel snorted. "Talk Thirteen is a voluntary network and we still have thousands and thousands of followers, all willing to put in an effort for the greater good. We didn't need to manipulate anyone."

Edward shook his head. "You can't compare a network with a company. In a network, people come and go as they please, and you don't have to pay them a salary. But when you run a business, you depend on a certain number of individuals who cost you money." He pulled up his shoulders and made a face. "If I can manipulate my staff to maximise their performance and boost the revenues, then that's just part of the game."

"I thought great leaders didn't need to manipulate people," Axel said. He crossed his arms over his chest and leaned back in his chair. Sometimes he grew so tired of these self-centred, egoistic numbskulls. They thought they were better than everyone else. Why? Because the Academy had chosen them as students?

"Now, now, Mr Hallman," Professor Evans hushed. "Let's not turn to juvenile behaviour."

Before Axel could respond, Ava Taylor, a self-confident woman from New Zealand, raised her hand.

"People don't always know what they want, or what they need. In such cases, a decision-maker must show them what they want." She reached back and adjusted the ponytail holding back her thick, dark hair. "Before I came here, I led a voluntary youth group that worked with the Office of Ethnic Communities, in New Zealand. We worked hard to get youngsters interested in leadership. At first, they weren't interested. Only *after* our trainings did they realise how much they'd needed these leadership skills."

"If I may add to that, Ava," said Aseem, looking like an ostentatious prick. "It can sometimes be the other way round; people *think* they know what they want but they don't. My father is a rich and powerful film tycoon in India, known as Mr Bollywood. He says we would live on the streets in poverty, if he agreed to finance every manuscript presented to him." Aseem laughed. "It's not that people present bad scripts on purpose. They *believe* their manuscripts are good, but my father is a wise man and he's been in the film industry his whole life. He knows what will sell and what won't."

Axel began tapping the heel of his foot against the floor. "Your point being?"

"Sometimes, a leader will have to tell his followers that what they want isn't good for them. It may, in fact, ruin them. In such situations, the leader is responsible to show his followers the right path."

There was a murmur of agreement among the other students. Axel knew the smartest thing would be to just shut up, but these people were so full of crap, he felt compelled to object.

"But isn't that kind of power dangerous? What happens if leaders are wrong? Hasn't your father ever made a bad investment, for example?"

"Of course not," Aseem snarled. "He is Mr Bollywood!"

Axel held back a desire to roll his eyes. "All I'm saying is, there's a risk that a leader's ability to manipulate people will do more harm than good. Too much power can…"

Edward cut him off with a rumbling laugh. "*We* are leaders, Hallman. *We* decide what's right or what's wrong."

"I think you're missing the point, Mr Hallman," Professor Evans intervened. "This has nothing to do with power and we're not out to make people act against their will. We're trying to open their eyes. What I'm teaching you is not manipulation but the skill to make others see what you see, feel what you feel, and…"

"…do what I want them to do," Axel snarled.

Professor Evans smiled. "I was going to say; 'know what you know'. I'm trying to teach you how to give information in the best possible way. It will then be up to your followers to choose if they want to follow or not."

The professor checked at her watch. "Unfortunately, we're out of time. We'll continue with similar exercises all spring, so there will be plenty of time to practice. I'll see you all on Monday at ten."

CHAPTER 55

TWELVE YEARS EARLIER

Sarah sat in the white gazebo, surrounded by the strong scent of sweet peas and roses. From here she could admire the lush fields beyond the garden as the sun set in the east. Nearby, one of the gardeners collected her tools and headed back to the gardeners' shed behind the main building. It was called the gardeners' shed but was in fact a two-storey house, far too big to be a shed.

"It's a beautiful view, isn't it, Ms Wangai."

Sarah turned at the sudden voice and found a familiar figure rounding the gazebo in slow strides.

"Oh, good evening Mr Garner. How are you?"

The old gentleman raised his little hat and bowed. "Very well, thank you. And you?"

"Now, Mr Garner. You don't have to bow to me, you know that."

"I do, Ms Wangai, but I guess old habits die hard." The old man stopped by the entrance to the gazebo. "May I?"

"Of course."

Mr Garner entered and took a seat next to Sarah. For a while the two of them sat in silence, enjoying the view of the lush world beyond the wall.

"The staff says you haven't been at the restaurant for two weeks," Mr Garner began, keeping his eyes on the horizon. "I hope you're not dissatisfied with our service in any way."

Sarah gave him a tired glance. "Of course not, everything is fantastic. I've just chosen to eat in my apartment, that's all."

"Ah. I see." Mr Garner scratched the tip of his sharp nose. "The thing is," he said, after a while, "I've been informed that you rarely order any food to your apartment." He faced Sarah, his eyes searching her face for a reaction. "Please forgive me, Miss. I don't want to pry but...is something wrong?"

Sarah pulled her suit jacket closer around her, feeling a chill despite the warm evening.

"I'm not sure how I feel about you studying my eating habits, Mr Garner. I can't help but consider it a violation of my privacy."

Mr Garner bowed his head. "I understand, miss, but we don't keep track of the students eating habits...well, unless we find that they're gaining too much in weight." He let out a quiet chuckle and began rotating his hat by the brim. "No, I'm here because the employees care for you. A few of the servants came to me, wondering if you were ill, and so I promised I'd talk to you. They meant no harm by it. Nor do I."

Sarah reached out and touched the old man's arm. "You're a kind man, Mr Garner, but please don't worry. I'm fine."

He said nothing but she could tell that he didn't believe her.

"In that case I shall bother you no more." He stood up, brushed off his trousers and gave her a bow.

Yes, Sarah thought, as he stepped out on the stone path, old habits did die hard.

"Do you ever have doubts about it all, Mr Garner?" she asked.

The old man stopped. "Miss?"

"Do you ever wonder if maybe the Academy has misunderstood the concept of leadership?"

"That's a foolish question to ask, Ms Wangai. The Academy is never wrong and you shouldn't question your professors." He wavered a bit, then glanced over his shoulder and leaned in. "It's not my place to tell you what to think, miss, but perhaps...maybe you shouldn't..."

He shook his head and Sarah flashed him a strained smile. "Maybe I shouldn't waste my time on irrelevant philosophical thoughts?" she asked. "You know; that's exactly what Lorena keeps telling me."

Mr Garner nodded. "Well, Ms De Paz is a very clever woman," he concluded.

Then, with another bow, he left.

CHAPTER 56

PRESENT DAY

Friday evening found Axel, Paul, and Thabo sitting in the famous Delirium Café, a busy-yet-cosy pub in the centre of town. Around them, people drank, talked and laughed, the noise drowning out the funky music that played in the background. It was the perfect refuge for three young men who were desperate to socialise with people their own age without having to worry about keeping up a regal appearance.

"I told you, didn't I?" Paul slurred and then laughed as two brunettes squeezed in behind him to order drinks. "This place's a real ripper!" He raised his half-full beer mug in a cheer and emptied it. "Now if you'll excuse me..." He slammed the mug onto the bar, winked at his friends and turned to the women behind him. "Good evening, ladies. Could you do me a favour and let me pay for those drinks of yours?"

Axel sniggered. "What a Casanova."

"Yes, well, we have to be back by ten, right?" Thabo asked.

"Yeah."

"Good, then I'll have another beer. But first I need to visit the men's room."

While Thabo headed off for the restrooms, Axel turned his focus on his surroundings. Delirium Café was a beer-lover's paradise. They had such a wide variety of the golden liquor that the beer list was thick as a brick. Not unlike one of Professor Jackson's mind-numbing books, Axel thought with a grin and turned his barstool so he could take in the pleasant atmosphere of this crowded basement.

The environment was lively and rowdy. A large group of drunken men, all with a military look to them, roared and laughed under the low ceiling as they crouched around wooden beer kegs, used as tables.

Leaning against the counter, Axel beamed. It felt good to be around "normal" people for a change. For security reasons, the students had to return to the Academy before dark, unless given special permission from one of the professors. This time, Paul had approached Professor Plouffe, a man who, according to reputation, shared Paul's taste for good beer and crowded pubs. Perhaps that's why he'd been kind enough to let the three men enjoy a few hours in town.

One of the drinking soldiers slapped his friend on the arm and pointed towards the stairs. Coming down the stairs was a beautiful blonde, radiating an air of elegance. Someone let out a flirtatious whistle, which the woman tactfully ignored.

Without the slightest hesitation, she made her way towards the bar. Dressed in a grey business suit and a long black coat, she walked with confidence between staring men and jealous girlfriends, until she reached Thabo's chair and took a seat.

"Your fly's open," she said without giving Axel a second glance.

"What?" Axel's fingers flew down to his mid-region in search of the open zipper. "Ah," he said a second later when he realised he'd been fooled. "Very funny, Nicole."

She gave the bartender a wave.

"An Orval Trappist, please." Turning to Axel, she flashed him one of her stunning, dimpled smiles. "You were sitting with your legs spread like a windmill; a posture Mr Bell would disapprove of."

Axel feigned annoyance and turned to face the bar.

"I don't want to ruin your smart remarks or your perfect entrance, but you've taken someone's seat."

Nicole laughed as she paid for her ale.

"I'm sure Thabo won't mind," she said, giving Axel a little wink.

"Who said it was Thabo's chair?"

"Well, it's not yours, is it? And I can see Paul flirting with that woman over there." Nicole nodded to her right. Axel leaned over and saw Paul with a redhead a few chairs down the line. What had happened to the brunette? "That leaves Thabo, and, if I remember correctly, Orval Trappist is his favourite ale."

Axel shifted his gaze and took in Nicole's perfect profile. God must have been in a spectacular mood the day he made her: funny *and* beautiful.

He drew a deep breath, tasting the scent of her expensive perfume. Then, realising she was looking at him, turned his attention to his Coke in embarrassment.

"I assume your presence isn't a coincidence," he said.

"I'm afraid not." She accepted the ale from the bartender and placed it on the counter untouched. "Professor Evans wants a word with you."

"What? Now?"

"Yes. I've got Julien waiting for us outside."

"Piss off!"

Both Nicole and Axel turned and saw Paul swaying on his feet as he blinkingly glowered up at a brute of a man. The fellow was at least a head taller, with a shaved scalp and dark tattoos stretching across his neck and muscular arms.

"Uh-oh," said a dark voice from behind and Thabo appeared. "I'm gone for five minutes and already he's in trouble."

"I think we need to do something," Axel said and slid off his barstool.

"Bugger off!" Paul slurred and poked the large man in his chest. "You have noooo idea who I am."

"Just get him out of there," Thabo whispered.

Axel made his way towards his friend while he took in the scene. Paul was standing with his hands balled into fists. Next to him stood a woman with an anxious expression on her face as she stared up at the brute. A crowd had gathered around them, watching the events unfold with excited curiosity.

"Hey, Paul," Axel called. "We're leaving."

"Axel!" Paul yelled when he saw his friend approach. "This shithead claims I'm hitting on his girlfrie…"

Someone let out a cry and Paul went down with a right hook to his temple. Axel didn't think. He threw himself towards the brute, but just before he connected with the man, he saw movement in the corner of his eye. Shit, the brute had company. A *lot* of company!

CHAPTER 57

People were shouting and screaming. Nicole turned to Thabo.

"Time to leave, Mr Zulu," she said, keeping her voice calm and clear. "Tell Julien to start the car."

"No! I am a Zulu prince!" Thabo bellowed, and was off to help Axel.

Nicole sighed and pulled off her coat and suit jacket.

"Men and their pride," she muttered, following Thabo.

From the other end of the room came a group of hard-looking men, charging like a hoard of raging elephants, with bulging muscles and manic faces. How swell, Nicole thought.

Nicole shoved her way through the crowd. Thabo had thrown himself over the big brute in an attempt to help his friend. Paul was still out cold by the counter, being tended to by a few bystanders. From the right, the first attackers came storming towards the students when a petit woman in black pants and white blouse stepped out of nowhere and snapped the man's head back with a perfect elbow strike. The man's eyes rolled back and he dropped to the floor with a heavy crash. The second thug had little chance to react. He never saw the man in blue jeans and grey hoodie until it was too late. A quick blow to his head and he joined his friend on the floor.

Nicole made a slight right and jumped up on one of the wooden beer kegs. With a kick that Master Wú would have been proud of, she dropped one of the attackers in mid-air. She landed with a slight crouch and surprised a big fellow by kneeing him in the groin. She ducked as a third man threw a half-hearted punch towards her. Most men, even brutes, had enough decency to know it was wrong to hit women. It was a respectful trait but it also made him an easier target. Nicole blocked the man's punch without effort and slid in to give him six whirlwind blows, directly below his chest. The man let out a cry and bent forward.

"I do apologise," she said, and kneed him in the face.

Nicole turned to see the two Academy Watchers knock three more attackers to the floor with skilled efficiency. There was movement behind her. An older, big-bellied man came at her and she let her foot connect with his face with a beautiful back kick.

As he went down, Nicole considered the situation. Twelve attackers had been dealt with in less than a minute. A few of them were struggling to get up again, but none remained a threat. Her main objective now was to get students out of here.

Paul was on his knees, clasping his head with both hands. Thabo and Axel were still wresting the brute. Around them, people were chanting, for the situation had turned into something of a comical standstill. Thabo was lying across the opponent's massive legs, holding them down with all his might. Axel was on his back, *under* the big brute. He was bear-hugging the man, thereby immobilizing the brute's arms. This allowed Thabo to throw random punches or kicks at the man's torso, but because of Thabo's angle, he couldn't see what he was actually hitting.

Nicole smiled as she reached the two students. They were no fighters, that much was clear, but no one could call them cowards. She squatted and shifted her weight slightly to the right, catching a glimpse of Axel with his eyes pressed shut and a determined expression on his face. He looked cute as he struggled.

She had to wait another second or so until she saw an opening. Then, with lightning speed, Nicole smacked the brute hard on his temple, and he went limp. Well, that's that then, she thought, and stood up. It took a second or two before Thabo realised the man wasn't fighting anymore. Hesitant, he turned and regarded the man with a confused expression on his face. People were shouting and cheering.

"I got him," he wheezed and climbed off the man.

"Well done!" Nicole exclaimed, helping him to his feet.

"Did you see that, Axel?" Thabo asked and wiped his bleeding nose. "I got him."

Nicole yanked Axel off the floor.

"That was impressive, Mr Zulu, but we should leave now. We can't be here when the police arrive."

"Man! What happened?" Axel panted, staring at the chaos of moaning men around them.

"Never mind that," Nicole replied. "Please help Paul to the car. I need to get my coat."

Axel nodded and, together with Thabo, he assisted their friend towards the stairs. As soon as they turned their backs to her, Nicole made eye contact with the Watchers and nodded towards the students. The male Watcher gave her a discreet, two-finger salute of respect before he and his partner followed the students to ensure they reached the car without further incident.

Nicole walked over to her coat, got her wallet and pulled out a two hundred Euro bill.

"For your trouble," she said, handing the money to the bartender. He stared at her as if she was making a joke. "I also believe I knocked out one of your bouncers. Make sure he gets this." She handed the man a couple of more bills.

"What about your friends," the barman muttered and nodded towards the two Watchers ascending the stairs. "They knocked out the other bouncer."

Nicole laughed, hauling out her remaining bills.

"I do apologise," she said. "Heat of the moment, I guess." She buttoned her suit jacket. "I'll send someone to pay for all the damages and offer you a more reasonable compensation for your troubles." The bartender brightened a little. "Of course, if you can be a little discreet about what happened here, I'm sure my boss will increase that compensation substantially." She pulled on her coat. "Now, I must leave."

CHAPTER 58

Nicole stood under the golden eagle. She watched Dr Vella and a servant guide Paul to the elevators. A medical examination would determine whether he needed to be hospitalised or not. God, Professor Jackson would have a fit when he found out that three of his students had been in a bar fight.

"Mr Hallman," she said and looked at her wristwatch. "I'm afraid you're late for your appointment with Professor Evans. Shall we?"

He nodded and turned to Thabo with a wide grin. "We're quite a team, huh?"

Thabo touched his swollen nose and beamed.

"We certainly are. Now I'm desperate for a cold beer, a bag of chips, and an exhilarating paper on statistics. I'll see you tomorrow."

He shoved his hands in his coat pocket and strutted down towards the elevators while Axel snickered behind him.

"Did he just make a joke?" Nicole asked.

"He's full of surprises, that guy."

Nicole shook her head and motioned in the direction of the waterfall. "We must go."

She could sense his confusion as she guided him through the greenery to the little pond hidden among large trees and golden birdcages at the end of the foyer.

Professor Evans was waiting for them in one of two armchairs, holding a cup of coffee while admiring the water lilies.

"Good evening, Professor," Nicole said as they approached. "I apologise if we're a little late."

Professor Evans nodded ever so slightly, and with her cup still in her hands, she turned to Axel with a smile.

"Welcome, Mr Hallman," she said, her voice soft and friendly as she gestured towards the empty chair. "Please have a seat. Would you care for something to drink? A cup of tea, perhaps?"

"Yes, please. That would be nice."

"Wonderful. Tea it is." Professor Evans settled back, and with her eyes still on Axel, she said, "Ms Swan. Would you be so kind and get Mr Hallman a cup of tea?"

Nicole hesitated and then threw Axel a quick glance. He was considering her with his beautiful, serious eyes and, for some reason, she found herself feeling a little embarrassed.

"As you wish, Professor," she said with enough dignity to sound confident without appearing arrogant. If there was one thing the professors hated more than anything, it was an arrogant attitude from subordinates.

Walking away, her phone began to ring. Seeing who it was, she bit back a moan. "Good evening, Professor."

"You know bloody well it's not a *good* evening," Professor Jackson barked. "Get your ass to my office *now!*"

"Ye–" There was a faint click and the line went silent. Swell. The man's Irish accent had been unusually strong, which meant he was in a very foul mood, as was expected.

Nicole hurried off to the reception and found Lise behind the computer.

"Could you please do me a huge favour, Miss Davis? I need you to order down a pot of tea with chocolate biscuits for Mr Hallman. He's at the pond with Professor Evans."

"Of course, Ms Swan."

"And could you please tell him that I apologise for not delivering it myself. Professor Jackson has demanded my immediate attendance."

The young receptionist stood up and picked up a phone.

"Certainly, Ms Swan."

"That's sweet of you. I appreciate it."

When Nicole stepped into Professor Jackson's office a few minutes later, she found him sitting in his chair, arms folded across his chest and a grim expression on his face. The room was also occupied by five other individuals: Professor Plouffe; Dr Vella; Mr Nakata, and two of his subordinates, Ms Tanya Brown, master of Watchers, and Mr Eli Peretz, master of guards.

Tanya gave Nicole a slight bow of her head, a great sign of respect. Nicole returned the gesture and turned to the assistant principal. "Sir?"

"I want to know what happened," the man growled. "Professor Plouffe, you gave the three students in question leave to visit a pub after dark."

Professor Plouffe rolled back on his heels, making his pregnant-like belly wobble. "Yes, sir," he rumbled. "Mr Harris asked me if he and his friends could visit the famous Delirium Café. I didn't see any problem with that."

Professor Jackson turned to Nicole. "And Ms Swan, what happened?"

Nicole pulled off her coat and hung it over her arm. Then she told the group about the events at the pub. When she was done, Professor Jackson turned to Tanya.

"Ms Brown. You sent two Watchers to keep an eye on the students, a..." Professor Jackson picked up his glasses and studied his computer "... a Ms Emmet and Mr Kaiser, I believe?"

"That's correct, sir."

"Do they support Ms Swan's story?"

The room went silent. Nicole stared at the assistant principal as he took off his spectacles. What in the world was he doing? Did he think she was *lying*?

The master of Watchers furrowed her brows. She was in her mid-fifties and in better physical shape than most students. Her hair was white as snow and pulled back in a simple braid. She had a thin scar running down from her ear to her jaw. No one knew how she'd earned it, but it earned her respect nonetheless.

Ms Brown gave Nicole a fleeting look before taking a step forward, her hands clasped behind her back.

"Yes, sir. I've talked to them both and they..."

"Why two?" Professor Jackson interrupted.

Tanya paused. "I'm sorry?"

"Why did you send two Watchers?"

"Well, I chose two because Delirium Café is a well-known and well-respected pub, sir. The risk of something like this happening was minute."

"And yet it happened," Professor Jackson grunted. He adjusted his tie and then brushed off some imaginary lint from his suit jacket. "As I'm sure you understand, I'm very disappointed. I want to know why your people couldn't protect Mr Harris."

"I understand your disappointment, sir, but things escalated fast, and…"

"For crying out loud!" Professor Jackson roared, slamming his fist into his desk. "Mr Hallman, a bloody student, reached Mr Harris before your people did. Are you telling me our students are faster than our Watchers?"

Nicole glanced at Mr Nakata. As usual, his face was unreadable.

"Sir." Tanya's cheeks were burning red. "With all due respect, Ms Emmet and Mr Kaiser sat some distance from the students, as is required by our protection policy."

"No!" Professor Jackson snapped. "The policy states that your people should remain *unseen* by our students. It doesn't state that they should be incompetent."

Poor Tanya. This wasn't her fault, and since Mr Nakata didn't do anything, Nicole cleared her throat.

"Sir," she began with a gentle voice. Professor Jackson glared at her but she disarmed him with a smile. As long as she smiled, he wouldn't consider her a threat. "Just for the record, the Watchers saved our students today. They failed to protect Mr Harris, but the aggressor's body language was indecisive. He reacted violently without much warning."

"Are you a Watcher, Ms Swan?" Professor Jackson snorted.

"No, sir."

"Are you trained in the field of personal protection?"

"No, sir, but I know for a fact that without Ms Emmet and Mr Kaiser, twelve very aggressive men would have thrown themselves over our students and they would've been lynched."

To her surprise, the assistant principal didn't object. He just stared at her for a long time before shifting his attention to Mr Nakata.

"It's your bloody job to clean up disasters. How are you dealing with this mess? What can I tell our dear principal when I call him?"

"We have secured video from pub security cameras," Mr Nakata replied, calm as always. "People being bribed to keep silent. Some guests filmed fight, but they will erase video. I have also two people watching social media for any release of video."

"That's it?"

"*Hai.*"

"All right. You have my authorization to use any means necessary to make this bloody thing vanish. It never happened, understood?"

Mr Nakata nodded and the assistant principal moved on to Dr Vella.

"You told me you've examined Mr Harris. What's the status?"

"He has a mild concussion and will need to rest for a few days, sir. Other than that, he's fine. I also checked on Mr Zulu. I was afraid he'd broken his nose, but that's not the case. He has a few cuts and bruises, but nothing serious. I haven't been able to examine Mr Hallman yet. He's not in his apartment, but from what I could see when I met him in the foyer, he's no worse off than Mr Zulu."

Professor Jackson lowered his eyebrows, and suddenly the resemblance between him and the golden eagle in the foyer was striking. "Where *is* Mr Hallman?"

"With Professor Evans, sir," Nicole replied.

CHAPTER 59

"It was an interesting question you asked the other day," the professor said when the two of them were alone. She still held her coffee cup between her hands like a true, sophisticated lady. "The one about manipulating people. Do you remember?"

Axel nodded and his eyes wandered to the chocolate biscuits on the coffee table. He was starving and they looked devilishly delicious. As it was, he'd gained four kilos since arriving at the Academy, and needed to watch his diet, so with impressive will-power, he turned away from the plate and re-focused on Professor Evans.

"I remember, and I'm sorry if I offended you, Professor."

Professor Evans laughed.

"Who said you offended me? All you did was ask me a question." With skill, she balanced her cup on its plate with one hand while adjusting her scarf with the other. "And it's a fair question. Great leaders are powerful communicators. They know how to use all means of communication to reach deep within a person and make that individual listen. Because most non-leaders are mediocre communicators, they won't observe subtle signs in body language or react to questionable wordings. Therefore, they're more likely to be manipulated." She gave him a cunning smile. "Now, correct me if I'm wrong, Mr Hallman, but isn't that what you were trying to say earlier?"

Axel thought about it for a moment.

"Sort of. I guess I just feel that there is a lot of responsibility when one learns various communication techniques."

Professor Evans beamed.

"You are right, and 'responsibility' is a much better word than 'manipulation', if you ask me. Now let me tell you a little secret. I've taught here since the Academy started many years ago. Until today, only two other students have asked me the same question you did.

They even used the word 'manipulate'. Like you, their perspectives were challenged by their peers, and like you, they stuck to their opinion. The first time it happened, I thought the person in question would become a mediocre communicator at best. I'm sad to say she never got the opportunity to prove me wrong. But the second person did. In fact, he became the most extraordinary communicator I've ever had the pleasure of teaching. And do you know why?"

"No, ma'am."

"Because he was afraid. You see, communication *can* be manipulative if misused; in fact, it can be a devastating. This student understood that and it terrified him. As such, he decided to learn everything he could about communication, and, as history would show, that was a very wise decision on his part."

Axel grabbed his cup and, without thinking, took a sip of his tea. He pulled a face as pain shot through his lower lip, a testimony from his fight.

"Who was he, Professor?" he asked and took another sip, this time trying not to let the hot liquid touch his lip.

"I think you know already. His name was Hayato Sano."

In the pond, one of the fish splashed its tail, drawing Axel's attention. The story of Hayato Sano was well known. He got accepted to the Academy at the age of twenty-three. A year later, as part of his training, he became the CEO of Francis Security, a small global security company, about to go bankrupt. Mr Sano's challenge was to turn the company around, which he did. In twelve short months, Hayato turned an unknown company into the most advanced and successful security company in the world. It was an achievement that few thought possible, even for an EKA student.

Then two days after his graduation, Hayato Sano vanished. No one knew what happened to him. He did a number of interviews on the sixteenth of June and, on the seventeenth, he was gone.

"He was quite a remarkable man, Mr Sano," Professor Evans said, her tone low as if she was making the statement to herself alone.

She had a vacant look in her eye. Axel studied her as she fidgeted with her scarf, wondering what she was thinking. The seconds passed, and he soon found himself glancing at the plate of biscuits. Man, he was hungry.

"Who was the other student?" he asked.

Professor Evans let go of her scarf.

"Sarah Wangai."

"I've never heard of her."

"Not many people have."

"You said she didn't get the opportunity to prove you wrong. What happened?"

The professor shook her head and returned her cup to the coffee table.

"That's a story for another time, Mr Hallman." She let her eyes wander towards the ceiling. "I won't keep you any longer, but, before you go —" Her eyes dropped and locked themselves onto his. In a sudden and swift move, she reached out and grabbed him by the arm. "I want you to listen to me. Be careful. I don't mind if students challenge me. In fact, I appreciate it. It means you're paying attention. I also think that a leader must be able to see things from different perspectives and must have the courage to ask questions others won't ask." Her grip tightened and she leaned forward. "But not everyone here shares that perspective," she whispered. "There may be both teachers and students who interpret your inquiries as a form of confrontation. Whatever you do, don't get yourself enemies. This isn't an ordinary Academy. The students are not ordinary pupils and the professors are by no means ordinary teachers. Never forget that, Mr Hallman. Work hard, take the perspectives of a leader, and don't disappoint your teachers. You have no idea the forces involved here."

CHAPTER 60

The man opened the gold-plated holder with the engraved Academy logo at the front. He pulled out the business card he'd stolen from Axel's apartment and held it above the gold case. The card snapped to the lid and the case buzzed to life. The man grinned and opened it. Inside, the lid was now a screen, similar to that of a cell phone. At the bottom, a digital keyboard had appeared.

A new message was waiting for him. "*Status?*" was all it said.

"We still have access," the man typed. "I'm ready. Shall I proceed?"

It took almost ten minutes before he got a reply.

"Yes. Tuesday morning, three weeks from now."

"I'll need the sound files."

Two minutes later, the communication device buzzed. The files had arrived.

CHAPTER 61

"Today, I'm going to divide you up in pairs," Professor Evans said, pulling out a list. "Ms Taylor and Mr Reed, you'll work together. Ms Martins and Mr Zulu…"

They were in the Cabin. Axel was sitting in the back, dressed in a black training suit, chewing on an apple while balancing on the hind legs of his chair. In the weeks following his conversation with Professor Evans, he'd worked hard to keep up with the gruelling workload. He got up at around five every morning in order to complete assignments, prepare for upcoming tests, and practise in the Speechomat. During breakfast, he updated himself with the latest news until seven-thirty when classes began. The last session ended twelve hours later, after which Axel would continue his studies until midnight.

It was an exhausting process, but necessary. Axel had to do everything he could to prove himself. Of all the teachers, Professor Evans was the one he respected the most, and her warning had rattled him. If a student could get in serious trouble for asking the wrong type of questions, what would happen if the professors found out he'd lied about the events in the Chamber?

He shuddered. Not a day passed without him thinking about the incident. "We know why you applied, Mr Hallman." The mere memory made him queasy. "We will keep it a secret if you collaborate."

Axel took a big bite of the apple. Someone knew his secret and they seemed to want something in return for their silence. But what? Three weeks had passed since the incident and, so far, nothing had happened.

"So it'll be you and me, mate," Paul whispered, pulling Axel out of his thoughts. There was a hint of disappointment in his voice. "Bella's going with Thabo."

"The exercise is quite simple," Professor Evans explained. "At the far end of the Chamber is a vase with six red roses. Each team must bring me back one rose."

"What's the catch?" Edward wanted to know.

"The catch is this, Mr Reed: to reach the roses, you have to complete an obstacle course in total darkness. You'll have to collaborate. Each pair will have a 'reader' and a 'runner'. The reader will guide the runner through the course." Professor Evans looked at her students with excited eyes. "Now, who will be the readers?"

"You'll have to be the runner," Paul whispered. "You're the one who's fit as a Mallee bull."

Pulling up the sleeves of his sweater, Axel shrugged. It didn't matter to him.

"Please listen," Professor Evans said after a minute and clapped her hands. "Readers, you'll be isolated in small, soundproofed booths in the room next door. In each booth, you'll find instructions, a rough map of the obstacle course, as well as a headset connected to your partner.

"Runners, you'll communicate with your partner using a tiny microphone and two earpieces. Some of you may find the earpieces uncomfortable. As you'll notice, they block out any sound other than that of your partner. Any questions?"

"We're all doing this at the same time?" Federico asked.

"Yes, and to make things a little more interesting, the first team that returns with a red rose will win a luxurious weekend in New York next week."

Axel wrung his hands. He stood alone in a small booth within the Chamber, the microphone attached to the collar of his sweatsuit, and the earpieces firmly in his ear.

"Do you hear me?" he asked Paul while rolling his shoulders in a little warm-up.

"Clear as a bell, mate. And you?"

"Loud and clear." Axel laughed. "It's kind of creepy. It's like you're sitting inside my head."

"Cool, now listen to me. I can see you and the other runners on a digital map. You've got a door in front of you, right?"

"Yeah. I see it."

"Good. Behind it is a square room. You're supposed to go straight through it, into a long corridor, but according to this map, there's no opening between the two rooms." He paused. "Just wait a second." Axel shifted his weight from one side to the other and back again. "All right, I'm back, mate. We've also got a list of words here," he said. "It's gibberish at first glance but I reckon they'll make out the instructions somehow."

"What's the first word?"

"It says: 'In the wall of our house, hides a little grey…'."

"Mouse?"

"I guess…hold on." Paul's voice vanished again. Axel began rubbing the outside of his thighs. Man, why was he so nervous? It was just an exercise. "All right, mate," came Paul's tense voice. "Professor Evans is about to open the doors. Are you ready?"

"Yes."

"Then let's win this thing! I've always wanted to go to New York." The lights above the door faded, and the world went black. "Go," Paul yelled. "The door is open!"

Axel took off, feeling his way forward. It didn't take long before he reached the end of the first room. Running his hands over the smooth surface, he searched for an opening.

"There has to be a way in," came Paul's tensed voice. "Don't you feel anything?" Axel jumped, searching for the edge of the wall. "Come on," Paul hassled. "Thabo just got out of his room."

Axel tried to ignore the comment.

"What did you say the first words were?"

"In the wall of our house, hides…now Ava's through."

"Help me out, Paul."

"Yeah. In the wall of our house, hides a little grey…Shit! Now Federico is through!"

"Paul!" Axel stopped and took a second to think. "A little grey…" mouse? It had to be mouse. He chewed the inside of his cheek. Mice lived in small holes.

"Aseem is through," Paul barked. "You're the only one left!"

"Stop shouting." Dropping to his knees, Axel ran his hand along the edge of the floor until his fingers swept over a small round hole at the bottom of the left corner. "Wait!" He pressed a finger into the hole and a hatch opened up. "I found it!"

"Come on, mate. Hurry!"

"What's next?"

"You are in a narrow corridor. It's long, so just run!"

"And the word?"

A slight static noise brushed through his speakers, and Paul's voice vanished. Axel came to a dead stop.

"Paul?"

"Tell me, Mr Hallman; billions of dollars are invested in leadership every year. Is the world a better place because of that?"

Dreadful cold washed over him and Axel couldn't breathe.

"Who are you?" he whispered.

"Billions of dollars are invested in leadership every year," the voice repeated. "Is the world a better place because of that?"

There was a faint click.

"… the hell is wrong with you," came Paul's voice bellowing.

Axel snapped out of his coma-like state. The voice! It had been the same voice as last time, but what had she meant by…

"What the hell are you *doing?*" Paul cried. "Why the hell aren't you running?"

CHAPTER 62

"We won!" Izabella exclaimed as Axel entered the room. "Thabo and I are going to New York!"

"Congratulations," Axel managed, shaking water out of his ear.

The entire obstacle course had been a nightmare. For obvious reasons, Axel was distraught after hearing the voice, and Paul's competitive nature hadn't helped. The man had cursed, yelled, and insulted his partner until Axel, with a frustrated shout, threw his earpieces as far as he could. He tried to find the rose on his own, but he was lost in the dark without any guidance. Soon he fell into a pool of ice water. When he shortly thereafter tripped and went head first into a box filled with sand, Axel decided that he didn't care about finding the rose anymore. He crawled back through the darkness, until he'd stepped into the Cabin, angry, wet and dirty. Everyone but Paul and Professor Evans were there.

"Thabo was fantastic," Izabella continued, unable to contain her excitement. "He was a machine out there."

"You gave me good instructions," Thabo replied diplomatically.

Axel wasn't listening. His ruffled appearance brought amused sniggers from some of the others, and it angered him more than he wanted to admit.

"You look terrible," Edward jeered.

Axel gritted his teeth and pulled off his soaked sweatshirt.

"Zip it," he muttered and threw the wet clothing on the floor.

"Oh, come on." Layla giggled and eyed Axel as he took off his T-shirt. "Someone's got to be last."

"What happened out there," Izabella asked, placing a hand on Axel's naked back.

At that moment, the door burst open and Paul stormed in.

"You got us disqualified!" he yelled, pointing at Axel.

"You were being a prick," Axel snarled, kicking off his shoes. "You were supposed to help me."

"Guys," Izabella said, laughing, "don't fight."

With eyes narrowing, Paul noted her hand on Axel.

"Forget it!" he growled and steamed off to the back of the room where he slumped into a chair and stared at the desk. Once again the door opened and Professor Evans entered, grim-faced and silent. The students watched her as she made her way across the floor. Handing Axel a towel, she gave him a long look before turning to Izabella and Thabo.

"Well done. Your effort has earned you a trip to New York. Nicole will brief you on all necessary details. As for the rest of you –" she turned to her class "– while your colleagues enjoy themselves in New York, you'll write a comprehensive report on today's challenge. I want you to describe the communications strategy you used, how well you followed your strategy and what you would do differently if you had the chance. I'll post the details on Eagle Net tonight."

Annoyed, Axel began drying himself. Great. More homework. Just what he needed.

"Now, Mr Hallman and Mr Harris, I want you to stay," the professor continued. "The rest of you may leave so you can get changed for Professor Plouffe's class. As you know, he's invited a very special guest for today. Make sure your appearance is flawless."

When the last student walked out the door, Professor Evans turned to the two remaining men.

"Mr Harris," she barked with surprising force. "I'm very disappointed. I told you to help Mr Hallman through the course, not yell and curse at him. You were supposed to be his ears and eyes, not his bad consciences. Explain yourself!"

"I wanted to win, ma'am."

"And just how did your strategy work?" Professor Evans challenged, her words dripping with such glorious sarcasm, Axel had to lower his head to hide the smirk spreading across his face. "You were paying more attention to your competitors than your partner," the professor continued. "Had you focused on helping Mr Hallman instead, you might have won."

Paul raised his palms in a defensive gesture.

"I lost my head, ma'am. I admit it. I've always been competitive…"

"That's no excuse! 'I'm the role model who leads the way!' Remember? There's a reason why those words are in the Leadership Allegiance. As punishment, I want a ten-thousand-word essay by Monday, focusing on various reactions you might have gotten, had you collaborated with one of the other students."

With a moan, Paul lowered his chin, turning his attention to the floor.

"And Mr Hallman!"

"Yes, Professor?"

"Integrity and demanding respect are important parts of leadership. You can't give up simply because someone isn't paying you enough attention or giving you the respect you deserve. 'I refuse to lose or fail', as the Allegiance put it."

It was hard to hold one's head up high while standing with a naked torso, trembling with cold and embarrassment, but Axel did his best.

"Yes, ma'am."

"Next time, I expect you to react with force against anyone who shows you disrespect. You are an EKA student; act like one! Toughen up. Your followers will expect you to crush anyone who stands in your way."

"Yes, Professor."

"You too will write a ten-thousand-word essay, but your focus will be on identifying ways in which you could have gained Mr Harris's attention."

"Yes, ma'am."

"Good, now get out of here!"

Making their way to the elevators, Paul turned to Axel.

"I've got to ask; why the hell did you stop in the middle of the exercise?"

Failing to think of something clever to say, Axel shook his head.

"I'm not sure," he lied. "I just froze. Sorry."

Whether Paul believed him or not didn't matter. Axel had bigger problems to deal with. "Billions of dollars are invested in leadership every year. Is the world a better place because of that?" What kind of crazy comment was that? And what the hell was Axel supposed to do with it? It wasn't a threat or a warning. It was just a...comment.

CHAPTER 63

In a different part of the EKA building, Professor Jackson sat motionless in his large office chair. He was staring out the window, haunted by old memories. A few of the teachers had left his office after a thirty-minute discussion regarding Mr Hallman's tendency to ask irrelevant and provocative questions.

"I hate to say it, but the fellow is beginning to annoy me," Professor Plouffe had admitted, slurping his coffee with frustration. "I know he's a wild-card, but the questions he asks…Yesterday he wanted to know if leadership could pose a threat to democracy. Bah!"

"He seems uncomfortable with the idea of ruling people," Professor Williams had concurred.

As expected, Professor Evans hadn't agreed. She liked the young Swede and argued that his questions should be a sign of great potential.

"Hayato Sano was the same," she'd argued. "He challenged our perspectives and it made him the best student we've ever had."

"Ms Wangai also asked a lot of questions," Professor Plouffe had objected, "and we all know what happened to her."

Their meeting had ended with Professor Jackson promising to discuss the matter with the principal when he returned later that week. Until then…

A knock on the door interrupted his thoughts. For crying out loud! Couldn't he get five minutes alone to sort out his thoughts?

Heaving himself out of his chair, he went to open the door. He found Mr Nakata standing with his hands behind his back and the usual stone expression on his face.

"Have you found out if we were hacked or not?" Professor Jackson snapped.

Mr Nakata shook his head and entered the office uninvited.

"Not possible."

Professor Jackson slammed the door shut with fury.

"You know that's not good enough. We *must* know if our system has been breached!"

The security manager shook his head again.

"Again, not possible".

Professor Jackson tried to control his temper. God knows it wasn't easy, especially when Mr Nakata appeared so indifferent. Everyone else, except maybe Principal Cunningham, had the good sense to deflect their eyes when Professor Jackson scowled at them, but not Mr Nakata. He feared no one. And the real pisser, what truly got under the assistant principal's skin, was the fact that the man was the best in his field. If he said something was impossible, then it *was* impossible.

Seething, Professor Jackson marched back and sat down with such force, the chair squealed under his weight.

"So why are you here?" he asked.

"I show you."

Without asking for permission, the security manager waltzed in and placed his laptop on the mahogany desk. He tapped a few buttons on his keyboard and then turned the screen to the assistant principal. Professor Jackson put on his glasses and peered down.

"What am I looking at?"

"A video from Chamber today."

"Is that Mr Hallman?"

"*Hai*. He and Mr Harris work together on Professor Evans' obstacle course. Professor Evans wanted visual and audio. Listen."

Mr Nakata increased the volume on his computer and pressed play. Paul's voice shot out from the speakers.

"You're in a narrow corridor. It's long, so just run."

"And the word?"

"It says 'I once had a friend, his name was Bret. He lived alone in a sticky old…'"

Leaning in, Professor Jackson stared at the image of Axel.

"Why did Mr Hallman just stop?"

Mr Nakata made a humming sound in agreement.

"*Hai*. Why he not moving?"

"Hey man!" Paul was yelling. "Why are you stopping? Hello! Do you hear me?"

"Is it possible to get a front view of Mr Hallman?"

"No. No camera there."

"Come on, Axel! What the hell is wrong with you?"

Axel staggered, taking a step to the side as if drunk. Then he began to run. Mr Nakata stopped the video.

"I talk with Professor Evans. She believe Mr Hallman stopped to think."

"But you don't believe that?" Professor Jackson asked.

Mr Nakata backed the video a few seconds and then played it in slow motion.

"There," he said, pointing at the screen. "I think Mr Hallman talk to someone."

It was hard to see. The recording had been made with a night vision camera, filmed from above and behind Axel. Yet when Mr Nakata zoomed in, it was clear the young man's jaw was moving.

The assistant principal scratched a spot between his eyes, trying to make sense of what he saw.

"I think you're right," he said, pushing back his glasses. "But if Mr Hallman spoke, why can't we hear him?"

"Two option," Mr Nakata replied. "He make no sound, or...someone hack our system."

It was like pushing a button. Professor Jackson saw red.

"Shit!" Slamming his palms against the desk, he let out a roar. "You've told me our system is impenetrable!" he bellowed. "This is the second time you've told me our system might have been breached."

"No system impenetrable," Mr Nakata replied unruffled. "Especially from inside."

"What?" With eyes widening, Professor Jackson felt a terrifying moment when he was lost for words. "Are you saying someone from *within* the Academy hacked our system?"

"No. I say *if* someone hack our system, they did it from inside."

"So someone on your team may have hacked..."

"No!" For the first time during their conversation, Mr Nakata raised his voice, waving a finger in warning. "Never my team. Never!"

There was a fire in the man's eyes that even Professor Jackson thought best not to provoke, so he clamped his teeth together, feeling a throbbing headache begin to emerge.

"If not from your team, then who?"

"Anyone knowing our systems."

"All right, and who outside your team has such knowledge?"

"People from IT, the developers, and some analysts."

Professor Jackson took off his glasses and pinched the bridge of his nose. What a mess. As his grandmother always used to say, many a mickle makes a muckle. There had been too many incidents within a short period of time, and many of them connected to Mr Hallman. Only a fool would call that a coincidence.

"All right, we'll put a lid on this for now. Not a word to anyone, until we've sorted it out."

"Humph. The principal?"

With a flick of his hand, the professor made his point clear. "We don't know who's involved, do we? We don't even know *if* anyone's involved, so, for now, let's keep it to ourselves, even from our principal."

Mr Nakata stood quiet for a few seconds.

"Is that wise?" he finally probed, thereby breaking one of his own golden rules, to never question an order.

Such nerve! Professor Jackson's face hardened.

"Under the current circumstances, it is!"

Mr Nakata nodded, albeit with a certain reluctance. Closing his laptop, he glanced at the professor. "We have another problem. Mr Harris brother talks too much. When too much drinking, he becomes liability."

Professor Jackson sighed. Life as the assistant principal of the world's greatest academy wasn't a simple one. Great leadership demanded great sacrifices.

"I see. Then tell Ms Brown to have one of the Watchers give him an official warning."

A brief smile swept across Mr Nakata's face.

"Ah…we gave him warning yesterday."

Professor Jackson gave a confirmative nod. He hadn't expected anything less of Mr Nakata.

"Good. Then you're dismissed."

CHAPTER 64

You never know with life. Even a miserable morning could be the start of a wonderful day.

Professor Plouffe's guest was none other than the British prime minister, a very charming and humorous individual. They were in classroom E, a small, cosily lit room on the twelfth floor. It reminded Axel of a small library, with stone walls and bookshelves filled to the brim with books of all sizes and colours.

The professor and his guest were sitting in comfortable armchairs near a wide fireplace where a few logs fizzled among the flames. Axel and his fellow students sat in a semi-circle around the two men, sipping tea or coffee while nibbling on wonderful biscuits brought up from the kitchen. Axel decided that after today's catastrophic exercise, he deserved something sweet, and thus he took a bite of another chocolate biscuit.

The prime minister appeared relaxed, talking about the challenges he faced and the difficulties in leading a country. Between sips of a large espresso, he tried to answer Professor Plouffe's and the students' questions as honestly as he could. On more than one occasion he brought laughter to the room with his anecdotes.

"I remember visiting the White House for an unofficial and very sensitive business negotiation," the prime minister said. "At one point, the president's wife came by with her dog. While greeting me, the ugly little thing took a particular liking to my leg." Here the prime minister paused and smiled. "Just to clarify, I'm referring to the dog, *not* the president's wife. Come to think of it, *that* would have been an interesting experience." As expected of them, the students laughed. "Anyhow, the incident had a devastating effect on my diplomatic influence. You can't imagine how difficult it is to appear authoritarian after a Chihuahua has violated your leg. Such things are just not supposed to happen to a leader."

"Do you mean leaders have to be flawless?" Axel queried.

Behind him, a few of the students squirmed in their seats, indicating it had been a stupid question.

"No one is flawless," the prime minister replied with a shrug, "but the world expects flawlessness from us. You could say that part of my job is to *appear* flawless."

Axel nodded. That seemed to make sense.

At the end of the session, it was the prime minister's turn to ask a few questions. He was curious to know where the students came from, what their dreams were, and why they'd applied to the Academy. When he found out that Axel was from Sweden, he beamed.

"I met with your prime minister the other day," he said. "The man's a friend of mine, actually. He'll be thrilled to know that one of his countrymen has been accepted to the EKA."

"I believe he already knows," Professor Plouffe said with a grin.

The prime minister leaned back in his chair and steepled his fingers.

"Well, what a little bugger," he chortled. "He didn't say a word about it to me."

"I'm very glad to hear that, sir." Professor Plouffe laughed. "He's signed a confidentiality agreement with us."

"As have I, Professor Plouffe," the prime minister replied. "As have I." He picked up a chocolate praline and waved it at Axel before taking a bite. "And there you have another frustrating aspect of leadership, Mr Hallman. Sometimes leaders have to pretend to be less knowledgeable than we are."

Unknown to the prime minister, the statement gave Axel some piece of mind. He felt bad about having lied to Paul and Professor Jackson about the incidents in the Chamber, but as the prime minister pointed out, sometimes you have no other choice.

The guest swallowed his praline and continued. "So next time I meet your prime minister, I have to act as if I don't have a clue about you, even if *I* know *he* knows. It's all very confusing. And should he find out that I know you're here, then he'll pretend that *he* doesn't know that *I* know." The prime minister let out an infectious laugh. "We can't talk about it even if we both want to."

Professor Plouffe chuckled and leaned forward. "Not even behind closed doors," he said in a conspiratorial tone.

The prime minister laughed. "Officially? No. Unofficially? You'll never find out."

They all laughed at that.

At the end of the session, the prime minister thanked Professor Plouffe and his students.

"I'm honoured that you found my experience and knowledge worth listening to and hope this little meeting will be the beginning of a lifetime of collaboration."

Federico grinned and whispered, "I bet he does. He's just a leader as long as people vote for him. We, on the other hand, will rule the world for our entire lives. Befriending one of us will give him access to power he can only dream of."

CHAPTER 65

TWELVE YEARS EARLIER

"You've got to stop questioning everything," Lorena said, sounding remarkably troubled. "You're pissing everyone off."

Sarah bent down and smelled one of the roses. The petals were still wet after the mid-day rains and she managed to get a drop on her nose.

"What kind of world are we living in if we can't question things?" They were taking an afternoon stroll around the garden, a rare break in their otherwise busy schedules. Sarah loved this part of the premise. It was a place for reflection with its gravel paths, colourful flowerbeds, and tranquil lily ponds. "I believe that if people took their time to reflect upon things, they too might begin to ask questions."

"There's nothing wrong with asking questions," Lorena said, walking with her hands behind her back like the soldier she was. "One can even challenge the teachers once in a while. That's fine, but you're doing more than that. You're being provocative. It's as if you're determined to infuriate the professors."

"That's not my intention."

"Still, that's how you're perceived. Both by the professors and the other students, I might add."

The comment hurt, and Sarah felt her frustration grow.

"Don't you think it's strange that our professors tell us that leaders must be brave and stand up for what they believe in, but they have very little patience for students who don't share their beliefs?

Lorena gave her a worried look. "And what exactly *do* you believe?"

Sarah shrugged. "I'm not sure yet. That's why I'm asking questions." She paused, turning her face towards the sun. "But in all honesty, I'm beginning to doubt that leaders are as important as the Academy preaches."

"Jesus, Sarah!"

"Oh, please don't be upset with me. I have to be honest with you, but I would appreciate it if you don't tell anyone."

"Are you mad? They'll skin you alive if they knew what you were thinking."

They rounded a corner and came upon three gardeners pruning a hedge. The workers stopped what they were doing and bowed. Sarah eyed the woman closest to her.

"Hello, Caitlyn. I thought we agreed that you didn't have to bow to me," she said.

Blushing, the blonde woman took off her straw hat.

"Yes, Ms Wangai," she replied in a hushed tone, glancing at Lorena. "I didn't want to disrespect Ms De Paz."

Sarah laughed. "Oh, that's all right, Caitlyn; Lo's not worried about such formalities, are you, Lorena?"

To Sarah's disappointment, Lorena shifted with unease, eyes wandering in the direction of the main building.

"I think I better head back to my apartment. I still haven't completed my assignment for Professor Plouffe." She gave the gardeners a wave of her hand that made them rush back to work. Leaning closer to Sarah, she whispered, "You've got to stop this nonsense. The Academy is not your enemy. You're here so they can help you become the best of the best. I feel you're pushing them too hard. If you continue, they'll snap, and you'll end up hurt." She leaned back again, studying Sarah with serious eyes. "Promise me you'll stop."

"You wish me to stop asking questions and do as I'm told?"

"You're doing it again." Lorena sighed. "I give you some friendly advice and you make it sound as if I'm telling you to be a follower."

"And how would you like me to take it?"

Lorena's face darkened. "God, Sarah! You're hopeless!"

With great sadness in her heart, Sarah watched as Lorena marched off with long, angry strides.

CHAPTER 66

PRESENT DAY

The following evening, long after the sun had set, Axel and a few of the students were resting in the sun chairs by the pool. Above them rain splattered against the glass roof, the sound deafened by the noise of the indoor waterfall.

The large eagle, called Arthur by the staff, pushed off from his branch and flew over the four students. He made a wide circle above the trees before disappearing towards the southeast corner.

"That's it," said Izabella with a yawn, putting down the paper she'd been reading.

"Mmm," Ava mumbled. "Anything new?"

She, Thabo, and Julie were on their stomachs while skilled masseuses worked an absurd amount of oil into their tense bodies.

"No, they're still speculating," Izabella replied, lowering the back of her sun chair. "One article wrote that Principal Cunningham was seen in Brussels, but since others claim to have seen him in Tokyo, Madrid, Cairo, and New York, there is no reason to worry."

"Lucky you," Julie slurred, half asleep. "Going to New York on Thursday."

"I reckon Principal Cunningham keeps a close eye on what's being said about the Academy," Paul snapped and took a swig of his beer. "He'd be a fool if he didn't."

Izabella giggled. "Come on, Paul, let it go. You'll get to go to New York some other time."

"I wonder..." Axel began, watching the slow movement of the palm leaves above his head. "What do you think Principal Cunningham would do *if* someone found out about the location of the Academy?"

"He'd move us to a different location," Thabo said. "Why do you ask?"

"Just curious. The Academy is always a step ahead, but if someone *did* find out about the location, how would they be able to make all of this disappear?" He made a random gestured towards the surroundings. "Every box sent from here would be monitored by the press."

The others were quiet for a long time. Then Paul laughed and shook his head.

"No one will find out where we are."

The others agreed and soon their conversation turned to other things, but Axel remained quiet. He let his mind wander to matters of greater concern; things he needed to solve on his own. So far he didn't know what the voice in the Chamber wanted, but if things got ugly…

"A penny for your thoughts." Izabella laughed and gave him a gentle push. "What are you thinking?"

Axel gave her a fleeting look before turning his gaze back to the swaying leaves.

"Just thinking about something Professor Jackson said the first week we arrived; that few things are more important to humanity than good leadership."

"What about it?"

"Do you think that's true?"

There was an awkward silence, filled only by the drumming of the rain against the glass roof. He knew this was one of those questions Professor Evans had warned him not to ask, but the woman's words from the Chamber remained vivid in his mind. "…billions of dollars are invested in leadership every year. Is the world a better place because of that?" It was stupid question. The Academy wouldn't have existed if leadership trainings were useless. Yet, the statement touched something deep within Axel, something that stirred up great discomfort in his soul.

"Of course it's true," Julie chided in her thick, French accent. "Leaders have the power to change the world. Good leadership will change it for the better; bad leadership, for the worse. Why do you ask?"

"I realised I've never contemplated *how* important it is."

"My father was a powerful businessman," Izabella began. "He said leaders shape the world we live in. Without them, the world would collapse. Leaders must show their followers what needs to be done, so that the world can continue to evolve."

She got up and walked to the edge of the pool.

"He told me this when I was six. Two months later, he died of a heart attack." Izabella sat down and began to splash water with her feet. "Ever since that day, I've been determined to become a leader. I don't want to let others decide my future or the future of this world."

"I'm sorry," Axel said after a moment's silence. "I didn't know your father died when you were so young."

Peeking over her shoulder, she gave him a flirtatious smile. "Oh, don't worry about it. I hardly knew the man."

"You didn't?"

"No. He worked a lot."

Axel found Izabella's cold approach somewhat disturbing. In fact, most of his fellow students seemed oddly detached from their families and friends. There were a few exceptions. Julie, for example, often talked about her little sister, but most students seldom spoke of their families at all. They complained more about not being able to run their businesses, networks, or newspapers, than they did about being separated from their loved ones.

As if reading his mind, Thabo waved off his masseuse and rolled over onto his back with a grunt. "My father, the king, is very important to my people. They would be nothing without someone to lead them."

Axel sat up and stretched. "Well, my father calls himself a leader but he wouldn't be much without his employees, would he?"

Paul swigged down the remaining beer and smacked his lips.

"I motivate and make decisions," he began, attempting a bad imitation of Professor Jackson's, Irish accent. "I point the way and shape our visions." He beamed when the others laughed at him.

Placing the bottle by his feet he said, "What I mean is that you should ask yourself what your father's employees would be without him."

Axel hesitated and watched Arthur as he flew over the pool.

"Before I came here, I read about a company in Sweden. They're about a hundred employees yet there are no managers. The employees set their own salaries and…"

"Yeah, I've heard about that," Ava interrupted with a tone that said she was unimpressed. Waving off her masseuse as well, she got to her feet. "There are other companies like that," she continued, walking over to Izabella by the edge of the pool. "Some make a big deal about it, claiming it's a leaderless way to run a business."

"I think they call it Holacracy," Julie said.

"So isn't that interesting?" Axel tried.

Paul shook his head. "Nah. What people forget is that there's always a CEO and some informal leaders. Always! All you have to do is search a little and you'll find him."

Izabella snorted. "Or her."

"Of course," Paul said and raised his hands in a defensive gesture. "It was just a figure of speech. Anyway, you shouldn't believe everything you read, mate! No matter what some morons say, there's always someone pulling the strings. There's always a boss. Always!"

Axel thought about Talk Thirteen. When he and Peter first started the organisation, none of them had talked about management. They had just been a couple of kids wanting to make a difference. Now, in hindsight, if Paul was right, then one of them had to have been the undisclosed manager. But who? Who of the two had had more potential and a higher level of engagement? Who'd played the role of the catalyst, coming up with great ideas? Who'd taken responsibility?

Axel sighed. Hadn't they both done this? He cracked his knuckles with frustration. Why did he have to make things so complicated? None of the other students did.

CHAPTER 67

"Enough!" Paul stooped over, panting worse than a sumo wrestler on a treadmill. "Can't breathe."

Izabella made a face and glanced at the clock behind her.

"Seventeen minutes. Well, at least you're improving."

Red and sweaty, Paul dropped the ground and rolled over onto his back. "You're...evil!" he wheezed, throwing the racket aside. "You're making...me run...all over...the place."

Izabella smiled to herself as she made her way to one of the corners.

"Of course I am. That's the point of the game, isn't it?"

"I thought the point..." Paul wheezed a little louder "...was to help me...lose weight."

"And how are you going to do that if you're not moving around?" Izabella picked up a bottle of water. "Catch!" The bottle spun through the air and hit Paul right in the gut. He let out a pitiful cry. "God, you're such a baby sometimes," Izabella said with a snicker, and took a deep swig from her own bottle.

Paul lay motionless for a while. "I reckon I've lost five kilos since we first started playing, but Madame Garon wants me to drop another five before the end of this semester. How am I going to pull that off? If I see another salad, I'm going to scream."

He looked so depressed that Izabella almost felt sorry for him. The guy was struggling. The nearest thing he'd ever come to some sort of exercise was golf.

Paul hated any form of workout but loved to eat and drink. It was a rotten combination that had turned him into a freaking marshmallow. Now Madame Garon had put him on a diet with strict orders to exercise at least twice a week. That meant the kitchen wouldn't serve Paul anything unhealthy, and the EKA sports centre kept a log of all his physical activities.

Izabella sat down on the floor near her bag and leaned against the wall. By the other end of the small court, Paul lay stretched out, very much resembling a red, bloated corpse. The man needed help or he'd never lose enough weight to please the Academy.

"Let's play three times a week?" she suggested, and snorted when Paul moaned. "Well, you can always go back to the gym with Axel if you prefer. He said he'd help you."

She knew it was a mean thing to say. Few places made a fat person feel more inadequate than a gym, and many men judged their manliness based on their physical strength and appearance. For Paul, entering the gym with Axel was as cruel as placing a hippo on the racetrack with a stallion.

"Fine, let's do three days a week," Paul said. "But I'm not doing it for the reasons you think."

"Say what?"

Paul rolled over and got up on wobbly legs. "Never mind." He picked up his racket and stumbled out into the middle of the court. "Let's go. Why don't you make me run around like a headless cock for another ten minutes, so we can call it a day?"

Izabella didn't move. Paul sighed and dropped his arms to his side. "Come on, Bella. It was nothing. Let's just play."

Izabella didn't move. With Paul, that was the best strategy. Try it on Thabo and he'd just leave, Axel would ignore her, and Delilah would probably try to hit her. But Paul…he couldn't stand the silent treatment.

"Stop it," he growled. "I know what you're trying to do." He picked up the ball in defiance and whacked it hard. It struck the wall and bounced all the way back to the opposite wall, coming to a stop just in front of Izabella's feet. It was a remarkable shot for Paul, and she could tell by his expression that he was surprised himself. Still she remained quiet. "Man! You know you're bloody annoying sometimes," he muttered and took a seat next to her. When she didn't say anything, he made a point of rubbing his forehead with both hands. "Damn it. Can I trust you?"

"Of course not, you can't trust anyone."

Paul made a face, leaning his head against the wall. "Yeah, I know. Each man for himself, right?"

"Right." Izabella toyed with her racket. "I am good at keeping secrets though."

"Sure, until you decide to sell me out."

"I suppose you've got a point."

She handed him a towel, a gesture he seemed to appreciate, for he flashed her a little smile before wiping his face.

"Well, at least you're honest."

"Bah! You wouldn't believe me if I told you I could be trusted." That was a lie, of course. Izabella could fool anyone. It was a matter of knowing what made them tick, and she knew what made *Paul* tick. "Come on," she garnered, and gave him a light bump, shoulder against shoulder.

Paul pulled up his legs so he could rest his arms on his knees. "All right," he started. "What do you think about Axel?"

"What do you mean?"

"I want to know your opinion. What do you think of him?"

"That's none of your damn business."

"I'm sorry. I shouldn't have asked." Paul picked up the tiny ball and with a groan he got to his feet. "Shall we?"

She stared at him. Then a wide smirk spread across her face and she relaxed. Oh, you sly son of a bitch, she thought. If Paul thought he could trick her into dropping the subject, then he was dumber than he looked. "Fine," she said with a smirk. "I find Axel to be...different."

"In what way?"

"No, no, no. Now it's your turn. Why don't *you* like Axel?"

Paul, the moron, tried to act offended. "I've never said I didn't like him."

"Ah, cut the bullshit. You've started talking, you might as well follow through."

Paul glared at her and for a moment Izabella feared he would storm out, but then he shook his head and walked back to her.

"You're right," he grumbled and sat down again. "I don't like the guy. For one, he's annoying. Worse than a pimple on your ass."

"Oh, gross."

"He's wasting our time. We've spent hours listening to him argue with the teachers about nonsense. It gives me the shits. We're here to become rulers, not philosophers."

"I hear you, but the Academy has accepted Axel," she objected. "That means they believe in him, and the Academy is never wrong."

"Right or wrong, it doesn't matter. He's wasting our time. I've talked to a few of the others and they agree. Cordelia and Julie are even considering talking to Professor Jackson."

Izabella tightened her ponytail and sniffed. "That's the dumbest idea I've ever heard. If we can't handle a fellow student, how are we going to handle a real enemy? Professor Jackson will laugh in their faces."

Paul shook his head. "I'm not so sure about that. I have a feeling some of the teachers are growing tired of his questions as well. I'd tell him if he wasn't so bloody creepy."

"Come on. He saved your butt in that bar."

"Hey, this isn't something I'm proud of, but the guy gives me the creeps. He's calm and polite, but there's...I don't know. Maybe it's his eyes or something."

"You're such a wimp." Izabella got to her feet, annoyed that she somehow felt personally offended by Paul's comment. "Axel's a harmless little pussy cat. Now, let's play."

She walked over to her side of the court, spinning her racket in her hand. Interesting, she thought. So she wasn't the only one who'd seen it. Yes. There *was* something in Axel's eyes. Something powerful.

CHAPTER 68

It was Sunday evening when Miss Davis called from the reception. Axel, dressed in a black EKA sweatsuit, was sitting on his sofa, struggling with Professor Evans' essay.

"Good evening, Mr Hallman. I'm sorry to bother you at this hour, but your friend, Mr Mikael Andersson, left a message. He wants you to call him. It's nothing urgent, he just wanted to 'catch up', as he put it."

"Thank you Miss Davis. I'll call him."

For security reasons, friends and family had to call the EKA reception via a secret number, if they wanted to get in touch with a student. So far, Axel's parents had called a few times to ensure that their son wasn't doing anything stupid. Axel's sister had yet to make her first call but Mikael, on the other hand, called once a week just to see how his friend was doing.

Axel yawned. It was half past nine in the evening and he'd been working for more than two hours straight on his essay. It was time for a break. He was reaching out for his phone, when the doorbell rang.

Izabella stood with her legs slightly crossed and one hand on her hip. She wore a black tube skirt that snuck around her curved hips like a mermaid's tail, and a pink silk blouse, unbuttoned at the top.

"I'm back," she cooed with a coy smile and tilted her head just enough to expose her neck. "May I come in?"

She stepped forward, and the strong scent of her perfume swirled through the door.

"Of course." Axel moved to the side. "When did you return?"

"About an hour ago. I got you this." She handed him a small replica of the Statue of Liberty. "I didn't know what else to get you."

Axel grinned while turning the souvenir in his hand.

"It kind of reminds me of you when you get fired up during class."

"Oh, shut up," she giggled, placing her soft hand on his arm.

He pretended not to notice.

"Would you like something to drink?"

She smiled.

"I wouldn't mind a glass of wine."

Ten minutes later, they were sitting in the living room, snuggled in two large armchairs. On the coffee table stood a few burning candles, a bottle of wine and some mineral water. There was also an impressive cheeseboard with various cheeses, fruits and crackers, all brought up from the kitchen minutes before.

"So how was your trip," Axel asked, although he wasn't very interested.

Izabella sipped her wine while her right hand twirled a strand of hair.

"It was nice. Thabo was a real bore, though. He doesn't appreciate shopping or visiting tourist attractions. After a two-hour sightseeing tour, he concluded that New York made him feel depressed and claustrophobic. He said it reminded him of the years he spent at a boarding school outside London." She paused. "Sounds nuts if you ask me, but hey, people are different." Without taking her eyes off Axel, she brought her glass to her lips again. Her hand slid down to her cleavage, where she began toying with a gold necklace. "You know…I can't decide whether your eyes are the colour of mist or steel. I've never seen anything like it. They're almost…hypnotic."

In an attempt not to stare at her cleavage, Axel put down his glass of water and began rolling up his shirtsleeves. Was it hot in here?

"It's from my mother's side," he said with a casual shrug. "Her grandmother had grey eyes." He looked up and found she was still watching him. "Do you ever miss your family?" he asked.

She let out a little laugh.

"Sometimes, but I've accepted that from now on I'll have very little time for family and friends. I guess it's just another sacrifice."

Axel hid his frustration by turning his attention to the cheeseboard. Another sacrifice? *Please!* "The greater the leader, the greater his sacrifice," the professors kept saying, arguing that it was as inevitable as it was honourable. Axel shoved a grape into his mouth and turned to the aquarium while the sweet juice began to tickle his taste buds. Then again, maybe they were right, but if so, what kind of sacrifices would he have to make in order to graduate?

"Jaws."

Axel swallowed and turned to Izabella who was considering him with playful amusement.

"Huh?"

She leaned forward, taking a grape of her own. He struggled not to look at her breasts.

"My shark," she said. "I call him Jaws. What do you call yours?"

Axel regarded the creature in his tank.

"I haven't named him."

"You're joking? Everyone else has. Thabo calls his 'Cape' after Cape Town. Paul's is called 'Devil', which is a stupid name if you ask me. Edward has named his shark 'Tank', and I think Ava calls her shark 'Bruce'." She snickered. "Dalilah refers to her shark as 'The Little Bugger'."

Axel grinned.

"That's funny."

"You see? You have to come up with a name for yours." She flicked her hair backwards over her shoulder. "How about...Steve?"

Axel let out a laugh.

"I can't name him Steve."

"Why not?"

"It's a ridiculous name for a fish, especially a shark."

Izabella pouted her lips.

"I thought it was cute. All right, I understand. You want something more manly." She paused and bit the edge of her lower lip while she gave it some thought. "How about Arrow? He's slick as an arrow. Or maybe Killer...no Butcher...yeah, Butcher's a great name, don't you think?"

Axel winced.

"You know what, 'Steve' is fine."

Izabella giggled.

"I like sharks. They're so powerful." She got to her feet and walked her well-shaped figure over to the tank, wineglass still in her hand. "They..." She hesitated and began tracing a finger over the aquarium glass. "There's intensity in their eyes," she whispered and turned. In the warm candlelight, she watched him while her thumb and index finger began stroking the stem of her glass. "You have it too."

Her hand slipped down to her cleavage again where it found her necklace. This time, he let his eyes follow her movement until he saw the edge of her white-laced bra. For a moment, there was nothing in the world but the sound of a fire burning in the hearth, the golden light, and Izabella's inviting bosom.

He looked up as she started her way across the floor with confident steps. In one graceful flow, she placed her wine glass on the coffee table, pulled up her black skirt and straddled him. With both hands on his cheeks, she kissed him; not sensual and loving, but hard and aggressive. Overwhelmed by the rush of unexpected sexual tension, he responded. Her fingers found their way to the back of his neck and then his hair. She grabbed him, pulling his head back so she towered over him as they kissed.

Axel's hands found her waist. Sensing her hunger and determination, his grip tightened and she gasped in pleasure. She bit his lip while her hips moved back and forth in a powerful, rhythmic motion. Then her hand moved towards his manhood in a playful manner.

The touch jolted Axel back to reality, and to his shock he realised he wanted her to stop. It was madness, but he couldn't sleep with Izabella. He just couldn't and the reason was simple; he was thinking of Nicole.

Fearing how she would react, he gave her a gentle push while moving his head to the side.

"I can't..."

Izabella leaned back, her hair falling over her right shoulder.

"What?"

"I'm sorry," he whispered. "I can't do this."

She laughed, stroking her hand between his legs.

"It sure feels like you can."

He moved her hand away.

"No. I can't."

Izabella's face turned serious and her eyes lit up with a sudden wrath.

"What do you mean you can't?"

"I can't sleep with you."

Izabella gawked at him. He could see her mind trying to understand what was going on, until all of a sudden, her eyes widened.

"Are you gay?"

Axel stared at her.

"What? Hell no!"

She stood up.

"Then what's the problem? I come here for some fun and you push me away!"

"I'm sorry…"

"Screw you! You're not sorry!"

"I'm tired. I have an essay to complete by tomorrow, and frankly…I know that a lot of guys would jump at this offer, but come on, a one-night-stand would mean trouble for the both of us."

"Shit! You *are* gay!"

"No I…"

"Go to hell!"

Without another word, she stormed out of the apartment, slamming the door behind her. Axel moaned. He'd not thought it possible, but life at the Academy had become even more problematic.

CHAPTER 69

"What's wrong with Izabella?" Paul asked the following day at lunch. "Is she avoiding us?"

Axel shrugged.

"Who knows?" he muttered, shoving a large piece of a delicious chicken pie into his mouth.

Thabo gave him a funny look that said, "why do I get a feeling you *do* know the reason?" Axel ignored him by attacking his pie with silent vigour, and Thabo was smart enough not to ask any questions.

Nevertheless, in the week that followed, no one could escape the fact that Izabella was avoiding her study group. She hung out with Ava and Cordelia instead, which was fine by Axel. It wasn't his problem that she couldn't take a rejection.

Paul, the traitor, was desperate to continue his squash sessions with Izabella, and so when he figured out it was Axel she was angry with, he too began evading the Swede.

Thabo, on the other hand, remained diplomatic. Although he spent most of his time with Axel, he was careful not to take sides. His only comment about the situation was made after another one of Professor Evans more eccentric classes.

The students gathered in the Cabin late one Wednesday afternoon.

"What the heck," Edward muttered and whiffed the air as he walked into the small room. "What's that smell?"

Professor Evans beamed.

"Why don't you take a little peek, Mr Reed?" she chirped and opened the door to the Chamber.

A strong smell of hay, mud, and wet wool washed over them. Edward glanced in and his jaw dropped.

"Sheep?"

The professor stepped aside.

"Yes! There you have your followers."

"Whew! They stink!" Julie grimaced and covered her mouth and nose with her hand. "You go first," she added, giving Axel a push into the Chamber.

What he saw baffled him. The spotlights in the high ceiling were so bright, it was no different to standing outside on a sunny day. In the middle of the Chamber was a huge paddock, holding a number of sheep that grazed in peace among lush, green grass.

"I bet somewhere, a farmer is scratching his head, wondering who stole his field," Aseem joked, and, in the excitement, his Indian accent grew more pronounced.

"Come over here, please," Professor Evans said, pretending not to hear Aseem. She was standing in front of the wide gate leading into the paddock. "Today you'll be working in two teams. To succeed with the exercise, you must first herd all the sheep to that red flag over there." She pointed at a flag positioned on the right-hand side. "Once that's been done, you must separate the sheep into three groups. As you can see, each sheep has a colour painted on its side. Sheep with a red marking are to remain at the red flag. Sheep with a blue marking must be herded to the blue flag over there." She pointed straight ahead. "The remaining sheep, the ones with a green marking, have to be herded to the green flag on your left. The team that completes the task in the shortest amount of time wins."

Edward scratched his beard. "All right, so what's the prize? What do we win?"

"Honour, Mr Reed," said a scornful voice behind them. Professor Jackson strode into the Chamber with an intolerable air of smugness to him. "Or is honour not a prize worth fighting for?"

Axel glared at the man with suspicion. Now what?

Edward hesitated, probably wondering the same thing, for he had a perplexed expression on his otherwise self-assured face.

At that point, a loud and cheerful murmur reached the students. Soon, the other professors began to pour in, yakking and laughing like a group of old friends heading out for a night in Vegas. As the students watched them with growing confusion, more doors opened around the Chamber and what seemed to be an endless number of loud and jovial staff members appeared.

"What in the world is going on," Dalilah whispered.

"Welcome to The Battle of Baa." Professor Jackson grinned.

The stunned students gawked at the teachers and staff members filling the Chamber around them.

"Battle of Baa?" Edward echoed.

"Indeed, Mr Reed. Or, if you prefer, The Battle of Honour." The assistant principal chuckled. "Well, I better leave before all the good spots are taken. Good luck."

Still chuckling, and with a worrying spring in his step, he walked off. As one, the students turned to Professor Evans.

"Ah, yes," she beamed, seeing their confused faces. "The Battle of Baa is one of the most entertaining events here at the Academy. Even Principal Cunningham participates when he can. He was very disappointed that he couldn't join us today."

"Oh my God," Layla whispered as the spectators spread out around the paddock. "They're going to watch us?"

"So it seems," Thabo said, "and they're coming well prepared, I see."

He nodded towards two members of the staff who were setting up a table with drinks of various kinds; from soft drinks to bottles of whiskey.

"Please pay attention." Professor Evans clapped her hands. "I want you to organise yourself into two groups, with three men and three women in each group."

Izabella and Paul were quick to join Edward, Ava, Cordelia and Federico, leaving Axel, Thabo, and Aseem in one group with Julie, Dalilah, and Layla.

"I don't like sheep," Julie whined as she considered the paddock. "They're dumb, silly and they smell."

"No different from followers," Federico jeered.

"You'll go first," Professor Evans called, nodding towards Izabella and Paul's group. "Remember that in order to succeed you must communicate with each other."

"Piece of cake." Edward grinned as he passed Axel. "Look and learn."

Proud as a peacock among ducks, he strutted onto the field with the others in his team, reminding them it was time to prove their honour.

Five minutes later, their honour was in serious trouble. The students were running, screaming, and gesturing like mad, but all they had done was turn the paddock into a muddy soup. The sheep remained unorganised.

"Talk to one another," Professor Evans hollered. "Communicate, for God's sake! You have to work as a team."

Nearby, Axel and his teammates were clinging to the wooden fence, laughing so hard it was difficult to breath. They weren't alone. The Chamber shook under the roars of laughter and whistles. The spectators were thrilled. Professor Plouffe even raised his wine glass in a loud cheer every time a sheep outran one of the students; his big belly bounced merrily as he laughed. At one point, a sheep darted past, followed by wild-eyed Cordelia who tripped and fell face first into the mud with a high-pitched cry. This brought fierce applause from the enthusiastic crowd who began to chant, "We want more, we want more," with burning passion.

"Now that's what I call a mud-mask," Dalilah whispered with a giggle as Cordelia stood up.

"Listen, guys, I have an idea," Layla mused. "Getting all the sheep to the red flag didn't seem that hard. The difficulty appears to be splitting the group and guiding them to the different flags."

"I was thinking the same," Thabo agreed. "The sheep were calm when standing together in one group."

"Exactly," Layla nodded. "I think it'll be easier if we split the herd into their separate colours first, and then guide the different groups to their positions."

"That's a great idea!" Aseem exclaimed. "Let's do it!"

"Axel and I can guide the green sheep," Thabo suggested.

Layla rolled up her long, black hair in a simple bun and gave Aseem a tiny smile.

"Aseem and I can take the blue."

"Sounds good." Dalilah turned to Julie. "Then we'll keep the remaining sheep near the red flag."

With the plan set, the six students turned their attention back to the events in the paddock.

It took another twenty minutes for the first team to complete the exercise. By then they had the appearance of muddy scarecrows, trudging out of the paddock in shame to the sound of jeering spectators.

"All right," Dalilah said, punching Axel on the shoulder. "Ready to kick some ass?"

It wasn't easy, nor was it pretty. They had to struggle to get the sheep in place, but in the end, Axel and his team completed the exercise twice as fast as the first team. They were mocked and heckled throughout the process, but when they left the paddock fifteen minutes later, the spectators rewarded them genuine applause, and, to Axel, no sound could have been sweeter. They'd won the spectators' approval.

"Well done!" Professor Evans exclaimed, clapping her hands as they approached her. "Excellent strategy and great communication."

"Shit, Aseem." Dalilah laughed as she and Julie came squelching out of the paddock. "The way you dragged the last bugger to the pole...wow!"

Aseem wiped his forehead and gave her a nonchalant shrug. Well, nonchalant or not, he couldn't hide his pride.

"You were right, Ed," Axel scoffed as he passed Edward. "It was a piece of cake."

"All right, settle down," Professor Evans said, clapping her hands again. "Give me a minute of your time." She was struggling to make herself heard as the spectators, not unlike screaming hooligans after a game of soccer, withdrew from the Chamber. "Well done all of you," she continued. "Tomorrow we'll discuss the various communication strategies you used – or in some cases, didn't use – during the exercise. We'll also discuss how mockery and lack of focus can affect an individual's focus and communication abilities. You'll find all the details on Eagle Net."

She waved them off. Muddy and exhausted, they all trudged out of the Chamber.

"I hope Paul and Izabella learnt their lesson," Thabo whispered to Axel.

Axel pulled off his wet and cold sweatshirt. "What do you mean?"

"They're both blinded by their feelings. Izabella is mad at you because you don't love her, and Paul is mad at Izabella because she's not interested in him. It's childish. Had they been more professional, they would have been on our team and they would have won."

Baffled, Axel stared at his friend. "How do you know about Izabella's feelings for me?"

"Please. Even the sheep can see it." That was all he said about it. When Axel pressured him for more information about Paul's feelings for Izabella, he shook his head. "We mustn't gossip, Axel. We are professionals, remember?"

CHAPTER 70

Two weeks later, Thabo's point about the necessity of being professional became clear. The first class of the day was Security and Defence with Mr Nakata. Since Black Sunday, Axel's feelings for Mr Nakata and his training had been cool, to say the least.

Once they'd pledged allegiance to leadership and the Academy, Axel dropped into his chair and stared at the hologram logo above his desk. In the front of the room, Mr Nakata seemed to prepare himself for whatever sinister game he had in mind.

"Safety," he began in a low voice, tapping his right temple with his finger, "come from here. If you ready for danger, then you are more safe. If not ready, you become weak and easy victim." He dropped his hand. "Mr Harris, come here."

"Me, sir?" Paul blurted, confused.

"*Hai*. Come here."

Paul, who was sitting beside Delilah, gave her a little shrug and ambled up to Mr Nakata.

"Do you think of your safety, Mr Harris?"

Paul studied the short man.

"Eh…"

Their Security and Defence frowned.

"'Eh' is not answer, Mr Harris."

Someone giggled nervously, and Paul's face hardened.

"I think I do, sir."

The windows began to darken until the room was black as night. Then there was hesitant flicker on the wall behind Paul, and a picture appeared. A loud murmur broke out among the students.

"Oh no," Axel mumbled, "they've got cameras in our rooms!"

Paralysed, slack-jawed, and confused, Paul stared at a blurry picture of himself standing by his bed, wearing nothing but his underwear.

"You say you think of safety," Mr Nakata lectured. "We shall see if this is true."

He pressed a remote and the video began to play, showing Paul in the process of getting dressed. He was swaying his hips to some instrumental song that Axel didn't recognise, and he was...singing.

"Bella, Bella, you're so fine; I love you, will you please be mine?" Next to Mr Nakata, Paul's face drained of colour to a point near transparency. "Bella, Bella, hot and sweet; I'm gonna sweep you off your feet."

"Please, sir," Paul begged, his voice croaky and trembling. "Turn it off."

Mr Nakata pointedly ignored him, and in the video, Paul did a few obscene humping moves while buttoning his shirt. Amused, Axel glanced over his shoulder, and met Izabella's eyes in the dim light. She gave him a wrathful glare.

"It's not funny," she growled.

"Come on, it's hilarious," he mouthed back, struggling not to laugh aloud, but peering back at Thabo, he was met by a grave expression. In fact, all the other students wore solemn faces, which was very odd considering the circumstances.

"...With a bit of luck; I'll take you home so we can fu..."

"Oh dear." Thabo sighed and closed his eyes.

The video stopped and Mr Nakata turned to his class. He paused long enough to make the silence uncomfortable.

"So, did Mr Harris think safety? Is this how people imagine a leader?"

The silence was oppressive. Axel scanned around the room and, realising that no one else was saying anything, he shrugged.

"No, sir."

He looked at Paul and met an angry and disappointed face. How the hell had Thabo figured out that Paul had a crush on Izabella?

"And what happen if Mr Harris' followers saw this video?" Mr Nakata continued.

"He'd lose his credibility," Axel replied.

Paul winced and Axel felt sorry for the guy. He really did. If anyone *did* see this video, no follower would ever take Paul seriously again.

Mr Nakata nodded and turned to Paul.

"*Hai*, you have *not* been thinking safety, Mr Harris. You can return."

With his head low, Paul hurried back to his seat, where Dalilah whispered something in his ear and patted him on his shoulder.

"Ms Martins, come here."

"Oh shit," Izabella moaned from behind and got to her feet. "Not me."

"I have a feeling we will all stand up there today," Thabo said.

"You too, Mr Hallman. Come here."

Axel's heart sank. He knew what was to come. Mr Nakata started the video and Axel saw himself in his living room, watching Izabella by the aquarium.

"I love sharks," she said. "They're so powerful...They...There's intensity in their eyes...You have it too."

Axel closed his eyes. He could hear the students gasp when the kissing began. He heard his and Izabella's heavy breathing and then:

"I can't..."

"What?"

"I'm sorry. I can't do this."

"It feels like you can."

"No! I can't."

"What do you mean you can't?"

"I can't sleep with you."

"Are you gay?"

"What? Hell no!"

Mr Nakata turned off the video and the sound faded out.

"Is this how a leader should act, Ms Martins?"

Axel took a deep breath and opened his eyes. Izabella was standing next to him, her head held high.

"No, sir."

"How you think followers would react if they saw this? What would homosexuals say?"

Izabella hesitated.

"They'd be upset."

"*Hai*. And angry. So did you think safety when going to Mr Hallman?"

"No, sir."

Mr Nakata turned to Axel.

"You homosexual?"

Axel frowned.

"No."

"You think it is bad?"

"To be gay? Of course not!"

"Then why so upset with Ms Martins?"

In the light from the projector, Axel caught a glimpse of the students' unreadable faces. What were they thinking? Did they believe he was lying?

"I wasn't upset. All I did was tell her I'm not gay!"

Mr Nakata clasped his hands behind his back and approached Axel with slow, determined steps.

"If you not gay, why you not sleep with her?" he asked. "You have no girlfriend, no?"

Axel looked down at the annoying little man, feeling his anger grow.

"No, I don't have a girlfriend, and I don't see why I have to justify my decision to you."

"Oh, why justify?" There was a disturbing twinkle in Mr Nakata's eyes. "Because you want people to follow, Mr Hallman. This is strange behaviour. You, a young man, saying no to beautiful woman like Ms Martins."

"Yeah," Izabella hissed. "It makes no sense, whatsoever."

"Hey, I like Izabella, but as a friend. I don't love her."

"Why did you not tell her this?"

"I did! I told her I didn't know her well enough. I said…"

Mr Nakata looked at the screen behind him.

"This is *very* strange, Mr Hallman. I see no evidence here. Did you?" he asked his class. They all shook their heads. "See? No one saw you say this. Why do you not tell the truth, Mr Hallman?"

Axel snorted, pushing down his anger.

"You know I'm not lying. If you keep playing that clip, you'll see that I'm right. But you're not going to do that, are you?"

Mr Nakata crossed his arms over his chest.

"But there is no more clip."

"This is ridiculous. You're wasting our time, sir. I'm not going to get angry."

"So you admit. You are gay?"

Axel cleared his throat and gave the teacher a wide, strained smile.

"No, I'm not gay. Of course, I can't prove it since you're the only one with the video, but I can tell you this; if I *had* been gay, I wouldn't be ashamed of it. I might even have asked you out on a date." This brought a few giggles from the others. "Now can we please stop this nonsense?"

Mr Nakata stood motionless for a moment, his eyes on Axel. Then he bowed his head a little and backed away.

"Good, Mr Hallman," he said, turning to the class. "What is right and what is wrong makes no difference. What matters is your reaction. Enemy can use anything against you. Even truth. Never forget that." He nodded to Aseem. "Mr Kamala! Your turn."

An hour later, the last student rushed back to his seat, blushing with embarrassment. Axel felt relieved that it was all over. Next to him, Thabo sulked after having relived a conversation with his mother, the only person in the world who still had the power to make him feel childlike and frail. It had been a harmless video, but it bothered Thabo nonetheless.

"You are all angry and sad," Mr Nakata declared. "That is good. Will make you think next time. It is time you behave as rulers." He began to stroll down between the desks. "Wherever you go, you might be watched. Whatever you say, someone might listen.

Enemies do not care about truth. They care about winning. You have to be strong, powerful, and clever. If not, you'll fail."

Julie raised her hand.

"Will you remove the cameras in our apartments, sir?"

Mr Nakata shook his head.

"That is wrong question, Ms Baston. You must ask; can you live with people spying on you? No place is safe. You can trust no one. Even your closest friend can become your enemy."

Axel glanced at the others. A few months ago, he would have found Mr Nakata's comment absurd. Now he wasn't so certain.

CHAPTER 71

The young man and his father got off at Amersham underground station, the end of the Metropolitan line. The British winter offered nothing but a cold drizzle on this grey afternoon, and the two men hurried across the platform towards the exit.

"Do you think we lost them?" the young man asked with a nervous tingle in his gut.

His father made a quick scan of the platform. There were no more than a handful of other travellers, all of them preoccupied with other things. He seemed to relax.

"I do, but let's not take any chances. Come on."

They picked up their speed, hurrying towards the exit. Watchers were cunning and effective soldiers. They were fiercely loyal to the Academy and kept a keen eye on anyone or anything they considered to be a high risk. Vanishing from their radar had not been an easy task.

Thor was waiting for them as agreed, and he greeted them as old friends.

"The others are already waiting for you."

"And Cat?" the young man asked.

"She's there," Thor said with a mischievous grin. "Don't worry, lover boy."

The young man ignored the teasing and slipped into the back of the car with his bag.

Thor took them on a twenty-minute drive to their hideout cottage in Lee Commons, a small and charming village, about an hour's drive outside London. As Thor had promised, the others were already there; Smooth, his daughter Cat, and Falcon. The owners of the house and tenders of this safe haven, a lovely elderly couple named Edward and Tilly Porter, were also there but withdrew once they'd greeted their guests.

The red-bricked cottage, with its low ceilings, narrow corridors, and small windows, had a pocket-sized but cosy feel to it. The smallness, however, was an illusion. There were two floors with more rooms than would be expected.

"I took a room upstairs," Cat whispered as they hugged. "The one at the end of the corridor."

She gave him a light kiss on the cheek, filling the young man with such lustful warmth it sent a shiver of excitement through his body. She squeezed his hand and then went to greet his father.

The young man grabbed his bag and took the cramped stairs to the second floor. He chose a room a few doors down from Cat, overlooking the great garden. He couldn't wait until their late-night rendezvous, but first there were serious matters to discuss.

He took a shower, changed, and headed down. Following the smell of pizza and wine, he found the others in the intimate dining room. They were waiting for him around a long table, lit up by numerous candles. In the warm light, they all joked, laughed and chatted while soft music played in the background.

The young man smiled. It felt good to see them all gathered like this. He took a seat next to Cat and squeezed her hand under the table.

After dinner, the six individuals took their drinks to the tranquil living room. They lit a fire and, gradually, the room fell silent. Smooth picked up his glass and examined the dark colour of his scotch.

"Let us begin," he said. "As you know, Mr Hallman has been contacted. He appeared confused, but, as far as we know, he's kept the experience to himself. Nevertheless, there are a few things we need to discuss. We all know our success depends on Mr Hallman's balancing skills." The young man nodded along with the others. Their entire plan depended on Axel's ability to impress his teachers while maintaining a natural scepticism towards the EKA. "We've received some worrying news, however. Mr Hallman's scepticism, or rather his questions, are beginning to annoy the professors."

"Not unlike what happened to Ms Wangai," Falcon observed. He was sitting in an armchair, one hand resting in the palm of the other. "Am I right?"

"I believe you are." Smooth raised his glass to his lips and took a deep swig. He looked out at the others with his dark, intelligent eyes. "I've been told a few of the teachers have even contacted Professor Jackson to discuss relevant measures. They're beginning to consider Mr Hallman a trouble maker."

"In other words, *exactly* like Ms Wangai," the old man said while scratching his beard.

"So what do we do?" Cat asked.

"He needs to understand the danger he's in," the young man said.

The room fell silent, except for the crackling fire. Everyone was contemplating the precarious situation, attacking the problem from various angles.

"What if we give him another gentle push," Falcon suggested at last. "Perhaps we can encourage his scepticism while at the same time hint at the situation he's in?"

Smooth was pleased.

"Any ideas?

CHAPTER 72

In the background, fateful music played. The man stared at his screens. This was crazy. They were pushing their luck. Only a few weeks had passed since their last operation, and rumours had it that Professor Jackson had been entering the Eagle Eye on more than one occasion. Of course, that could be a coincidence, but *if* Mr Nakata and Professor Jackson suspected a breech, then completing the next assignment would be treacherous.

Rubbing his exhausted eyes, he wondered what he'd gotten himself into. Beside him lay the gold-plated communication device with the commands. For security reasons, Thor had kept the bigger plan a secret, but the instructions themselves were clear. The relevant text files had been sent. Now they were waiting for him to do his part.

They had no idea what they were asking. Programming the Speechomat wasn't a problem. The difficulty was accessing it. To manipulate the software, he had to hack into Mr Hallman's personal database protected by the ESAFE system. Getting past ESAFE was just as difficult as getting into EKCOM, which meant it was doable, but not easy. The risks were high, mainly because any changes made to the Speechomat software were traceable. There was no way around it. One could hide *who* made the changes, but never the fact that changes *had* occurred.

The man drew a deep breath, shook his hands in an attempt to release a little tension, and then he attacked the ESAFE.

CHAPTER 73

During the first couple of weeks, following Mr Nakata's dreadful class, Izabella avoided Axel. She seemed angry with him, which was absurd since she'd come on to him, and not the other way around. Paul, on the other hand, kept his distance from both Izabella and Axel. If it was because he was embarrassed or angry, Axel didn't know. Nor did he care much. It wasn't his fault that Paul had made a fool of himself.

By the third week, things started to improve. It began with Izabella who, lo and behold, apologised to Axel for her behaviour. It was by no means a heartfelt apology but, coming from her, it was impressive nonetheless.

"She must like you a great deal," Thabo later observed when Axel told him what'd happened. "I never thought Izabella would apologise to anyone."

Realising he was right, Axel swallowed his pride and made an effort to patch things up with her. It wasn't very hard. A few clever compliments and their relationship began to warm. Soon after that, Paul and Izabella buried the hatchet, and, even if things would never be what they had been, at least they could move on.

But just as life within the Academy seemed to be heading back to normal, or as normal as one could expect it to be within the EKA, something happened, something that catapulted Axel into a new state of fear and confusion.

A week after his apology to Izabella, he decided to do a little communication training in the Speechomat before going to bed. He turned on the machine and put on his 3D glasses. As he shut the door, the screen lit up and in the distance came the eagle. By now Axel was so used to the whole procedure he didn't even flinch when the bird flew right over his head. He waited for it to make its circle, but, as soon as it landed, Axel knew there was something different about this start-up.

The eagle still looked the same, but it had landed just a little bit more to the right than usual. Axel waited for the bow but instead the eagle gave off a terrifying screech, fluttered its wings, and glanced over its shoulder.

In the distance, threatening clouds began to form. The eagle turned towards the approaching storm. The temperature dropped, lightning struck, and the walls shook with the roaring thunder.

Axel grabbed the podium. What the hell...? Strong winds ripped through the Speechomat, so fierce they brought tears to his eyes. The floor started to vibrate.

The eagle screeched again and out of the nearing cloud came a tiny bird with an incredible speed. It flew right past Axel's head, followed by a powerful gust of wind. Then came another bird, and another. Soon a whole army of birds appeared. They whizzed past his head, and then, as abruptly as they had appeared, the birds vanished.

A moment of peace left the eagle shuddering under the darkening sky. Axel held his breath, waiting as he sensed there was more to come. And come, it did. In a sudden explosion, the army of birds returned. They came over his head and from the sides. The Speechomat became a confusion of wind, sound and blurring colours. Axel was standing in chaos of war, watching the small birds unleash their fury on the eagle. It lasted for no more than a few seconds, and then, when the small birds took off, the eagle was gone. Remaining was the eagle's golden crown in a puddle of blood.

Shocked, Axel stared at the macabre sight. Slowly he released his grip off the sides of the podium. The light in the Speechomat died until he stood in complete darkness, hearing nothing but the sound of his shallow breathing. As he stood there, a few golden words appeared in front of him.

"*The EKA is selling a lie.*" Axel read the words as confusion, anger, and fear filled him. Another sentence appeared. "*Who do you think is paying for it?*"

Then followed a newspaper clipping; a short article that Axel read with rising curiosity.

CHAPTER 74

"What class do we have after lunch?" Aseem asked, before shoving a large piece of sushi into his mouth with his chopsticks.

They were sitting in a secluded area of the restaurant, enjoying a delicious Asian buffet while classical music played in the background.

"That's odd," Axel said, looking at his schedule. "I have something called *IDT: Psychology*." IDT, or "Individual Training", was a training method, aimed to give the students a personalized lesson with one of their teachers. Mr Bell was a frequent user of IDT when working with the student's etiquette skills. "Why am I meeting a psychologist?"

"I guess it's your first 'emotional assessment'," Dalilah said, picking through her salad.

Like Paul, Madame Garon had put Dalilah on a strict diet, which meant no unhealthy food and limited access to alcohol. "The rest of us are having Quality Assurance with Professor Jackson."

There were a few moans around the table.

"Emotional assessment?" Paul asked, glancing at Aseem's plate with obvious envy. "Is that what Professor Jackson talked about a few weeks ago?"

"Yeah," Dalilah replied, pushing an olive aside. "But why we need to see a psychologist every semester, I don't know. It's stupid, if you ask me."

"I guess I'll know more when I meet the shrink," Axel said and turned his attention to his plate. He tucked some noodles and a tender, juicy piece of chicken into his mouth. While chewing, he considered the restaurant with its extravagant design and lavish furniture. He saw Cordelia and Julia loading their plates with food at the buffet, and behind them, a waitress walked by with a coffee pot made of gold.

The EKA is selling a lie. Who do you think is paying for it?

"How can the school afford all of this?" Axel pondered aloud.

"What, the food?" Aseem asked, while, with a distracted expression on his face, he tried to grab a pea with his chopsticks.

"No, you moron. I mean everything; this building, the gold, the cars, the pool, not to mention all the staff members. Who's paying for all of it?"

Thabo shrugged.

"The Academy has sponsors and partners."

"Well, I understand if companies want us to walk around in their clothes or use their gadgets. That's marketing, but what about all the other things? Take the gold eagle in the foyer, or the pool, for example; they must have cost a fortune to build. Why would anyone want to sponsor that? We're the only ones who see it."

The others exchanged a fleeting look and Izabella sat back, dabbing her lips with the silk napkin.

"Don't you get it? They're trying to impress *us*, Axel. We'll be very powerful one day."

"That doesn't make any sense. We don't even know who the sponsors are."

"Oh, I'm sure they'll let us know the day they'll need a favour," Izabella snorted.

Aseem set his chopsticks aside and shook his head.

"Is there a purpose to these questions or are you just curious?"

Axel cursed himself for having brought up the subject. Professor Evans had warned him; don't ask too many questions.

"Never mind," he said. "I guess it's no big deal. It was just a thought."

CHAPTER 75

As the golden wings opened on the eleventh floor, a mild whiff of cinnamon buns and apples found its way to Axel's nose. He stepped out of the elevator and into the comfy waiting room. Nicole was sitting behind her desk, beautiful as always. She lit up when she saw him.

"Hello, Mr Hallman," she said with her captivating voice. "Here again, are we?"

Axel puffed up his chest and strolled over.

"Yeah. I'm meeting a…eh…psychologist at one."

"And you're looking forward to it, I see."

"That obvious, huh?"

Nicole folded her arms on the edge of her desk and leaned forward, pushing up her breasts beneath the blue blouse. Axel struggled not to stare.

"Don't worry," she said, her dimpled smile beaming in warm light. "I believe Dr Vella's in a good mood today. I even heard her whistling a little tune on her way to her office. Rupert on the other hand…"

Axel knitted his brows.

"Hold on. Dr Vella's the psychologist?"

"Actually, she's a psychiatrist so she's also a trained medical doctor."

Axel's mind reeled back to the Speechomat incident. Of course! He remembered the article and the instructions that had followed it. "*Ask Dr Vella*". At the time, he thought it a little strange, but now it made perfect sense. Dr Vella was a shrink!

The door to the waiting room opened and the doctor in question stepped in. With one hand on the door handle and the other in the pocket of her white lab coat, she gave Axel a nod.

"Right on time, Mr Hallman. Please come with me."

"Good luck," Nicole mouthed and winked.

Axel returned the wink, feeling his mood improving. This might turn out to be a far more interesting session than he'd expected.

Dr Vella's office was bright and inviting. It wasn't as large as Professor Jackson's office but big enough to hold a set of large armchairs, a mahogany desk, a few bookshelves, and a coffee table with burning candles. There was also a couch occupied by an orange tabby cat, a massive and ugly thing that glared at Axel with devilish eyes. Yuck!

"His name is Rupert," Dr Vella explained. "He lives here on the eleventh floor."

"Is he yours?"

"God, no. I believe it was Principal Cunningham who first brought him to the Academy many years ago. Now he's simply part of the inventory, I suppose. No one likes the creature, and it's a standing joke that the Academy leaves Rupert behind whenever we move to a new location. Yet here he is," she cackled.

Axel approached the cat and it hissed at him.

"I wouldn't get any closer if I were you," Dr Vella warned. "Rupert is a little grumpy today. He bit one of the cleaners in the finger. It's the second time this week, so I suggest we let him be." She gestured towards one of the chairs. "Why don't you take a seat over there instead? Do you want some tea?" She strode over to a small table, which held a kettle, a few cups and a wooden box with various teas. "I have some Kericho Gold if you like."

"Sure."

"And you want milk in it, I believe."

"Yes, please." Axel took a seat and scanned the room. "It's a nice office you've got. Cosy."

"Thank you, but I can't take any credit for it. Our interior designer did all the work."

"The Academy has its own interior designer?"

"Certainly."

"Why doesn't that surprise me," Axel mumbled and thought about the conversation he'd just had with his friends.

The doctor watched him with arched eyebrows.

"That's an interesting comment. Would you care to elaborate?"

"No, can't say I would."

"Ah." Dr Vella handed Axel his tea and sat down. She grabbed a notebook from the coffee table and smirked. "So, do you know why you're here?"

The question made Axel cringe. Painful memories from Black Sunday flashed through his mind; the way Dr Vella had tried to crawl under his skin, finding the darkest corners of his soul. He sipped his tea. This time she wouldn't dominate him.

"I suppose you want to make sure I'm not going cuckoo."

"Are you?"

"Isn't that your job to find out?"

"It would be easier if you just told me." She paused and then let out a little laugh. "No, you're not here to be judged sane or insane, Mr Hallman. We established your sanity long before you were accepted. No, I only want to make sure you're doing okay. You're young and yet we expect you to know more about ruling people than any living king or president. That kind of pressure can be demanding to say the least, and—"

Axel wasn't listening, he was gathering courage.

"What happened to Sarah Wangai?" he blurted.

Dr Vella froze mid-sentence and her face lost all colour. "Who told you about Ms Wangai?" she demanded.

"I've read about it. In an article," he added.

"What article? Where did you find it?"

"It...it was just something I stumbled across."

"Where?" Dr Vella's eyes were hard as rock. "Where did you read it?"

It struck Axel that perhaps he should've thought this through a little better. He hadn't prepared for this kind of reaction. That was a mistake.

"Well, I don't remember," he said with a nonchalant shrug. "It was a long time ago. I might have stumbled across it at the Stockholm University library."

"I doubt it," Dr Vella said and adjusted her white lab coat. She seemed lost in thought for a second and then gave him a forced smile. "Anyway, we're not to discuss Ms Wangai."

"I read that she killed herself."

Dr Vella's smile vanished like a snowflake in a frying pan.

"She didn't! It was a terrible accident. Now let's move on, certain things are not meant to be discussed."

Axel pulled at his lip, studying the doctor. Her behaviour was interesting. Why was she so nervous? What was she hiding?

"Things that are not meant to be discussed are usually secrets," he tried, knowing he was pushing it.

"It's not a matter of keeping anything secret," Dr Vella snapped. "I just don't want to discuss this with *you*."

Axel fidgeted with an imaginary spot on his teacup. He'd already pushed Dr Vella more than he felt comfortable doing. And she was right, of course; why would she discuss these things with a student? The most logical and respectful thing to do right now was to back off.

"I've never been to a psychologist before," he said almost apologetically. "I don't feel comfortable sharing my inner thoughts with a stranger."

Dr Vella relaxed. She crossed one leg over the other, balancing her notebook over her top leg.

"That's completely natural, Mr Hallman," she replied, her voice softening.

Axel couldn't help but grin.

"I'm glad to hear that, doctor, because I'm sure there are questions *you* want to ask, that I'm not interested in answering. The way I see it, you have to meet me half way."

CHAPTER 76

Despite everything, Professor Jackson was pleased. Few things were more rewarding than seeing his students evolve. The fact that Axel was asking questions about Sarah Wangai was worrying. *Very* worrying. Yet, his attitude was decent, without a doubt an improvement. Sure, the young Swede had a long way to go before he could call himself a leader, but daring to challenge Dr Vella was a step in the right direction.

Watching his screen, he could see Dr Vella's baffled expression.

"Oh my, Mr Hallman," she blurted. "I must admit I am surprised."

Professor Jackson moaned. She hadn't seen that coming, had she? He tapped the microphone button on his headset.

"Tell you what, Dr Vella. Give Mr Hallman a little information. I'm curious to see where he's heading with this."

Just how much did Axel know, who'd given him the information, and why?

* * *

Axel watched Dr Vella with interest. She seemed bewildered by his action so he decided to push her a little further.

"So this is how I see it," he began and moistened his lips with his tongue, "the *Year of Eleven* was just a cover-up. Right? I remember my parents discussing it after the graduation ceremonies. Everyone was surprised that the Academy had only found eleven students worth training. But it wasn't eleven, was it? Sarah was the twelfth student. But she died, and you had to come up with a lie to explain why eleven students graduated instead of twelve."

Dr Vella leaned forward and pointed a trembling finger at him.

"What I'm about to tell you…" Her eyes narrowed and she lowered her voice. "What I'm about to tell you must never leave this room! Is that clear?"

Axel kept his face straight, but inside he cheered. God, he was good.

"Of course, Doctor."

"Well, then you're right. The 'Year of Eleven' is a lie. It happened before I came to the EKA. There were twelve students, one of them was Sarah Wangai, a bright, committed, and very stubborn young woman. She was born in poverty, but, by the time she was accepted, she was already running a small orphanage in Tanzania.

"Yet, despite her many skills, Ms Wangai had two clear limitations. First of all, she had difficulty dealing with the stress and pressure that comes with being a leader. The Academy may seem harsh at times but that's nothing compared to the world that awaits you, Mr Hallman. Anyone attending the Academy will be at the very top of the hierarchy, and if you intend to remain up there you must be able to deal with the stress and pressure that comes with the territory. Like I said, you're all young and the people you'll be facing will be three times as old and three times more experienced.

"Ms Wangai was also an introvert. She shunned social gatherings and had difficulty trusting people. As a result, she didn't share her burdens with anyone. No one knew how she felt and therefore no one could help her." Dr Vella reached for her cup. "So she pushed herself too far. One night, the students organised a party. Ms Wangai drank far too much alcohol and stumbled out to a balcony for air. Somehow she tripped and fell over the railing."

"The article said she committed suicide," Axel challenged.

"That's not correct. It was a terrible accident. If anyone's to blame, it's Ms Wangai and her drinking problem."

"Wait. I never read anything about her having a drinking problem."

"She did; it was her way of dealing with pressure. Had I been given a chance to talk to her, I could've helped her, but I wasn't working here at the time."

Axel was finding the idea difficult to accept.

"Are you saying that no one saw it coming?"

"No one but a psychiatrist could have foretold what would happen, Mr Hallman. That's why Professor Jackson hired me."

Axel chose not to answer and his silence seemed to trouble the doctor. She pulled on the side of her lab coat and readjusted the empty notepad in her lap.

"I probably shouldn't tell you this, but when Ms Wangai died, Professor Jackson demanded that a psychiatrist be hired. From what I've been told, Principal Cunningham said no at first."

"Why?"

"I'm not sure. What I *do* know is that the assistant principal is responsible for the application process and the choosing of our students. The principal has a veto right but will rarely use it. Perhaps Principal Cunningham was blaming Professor Jackson?"

Axel stared at Dr Vella.

"Are you telling me Professor Jackson is responsible for choosing the students?"

"Yes. You seem surprised."

"To tell you the truth, I am!" Actually, Axel felt more shocked than surprised. More than once, Professor Jackson had expressed his doubt in Axel's leadership skills. Why had he then chosen him to begin with? "I thought he didn't like me much."

Dr Vella waved a finger at him.

"Tsk-tsk. Don't judge the book by its cover, Mr Hallman. Professor Jackson cares for his students and he cares for the reputation of the Academy. He understands the game of power far better than any other teacher. I'd say even better than Principal Cunningham. He may seem stern but he merely wants what's best for you. I'm sure you've noticed, for example, that he's much more involved with his students than the principal is."

Axel's brows bent inwards in suspicion.

"You don't sound very fond of Principal Cunningham."

"Oh, no, not at all," Dr Vella replied. "He's a great man, Principal Cunningham. A great man!"

CHAPTER 77

Damn it! Professor Jackson clenched his fists, took a deep breath to control his temper, and then pressed the microphone button.

"Well done, Dr Vella," he praised, knowing how much his approval meant to her. "I believe you've given Mr Hallman something to think about. You can now move on to your intended questions."

He turned off the microphone and picked up his phone. A moment later, Mr Nakata answered and Professor Jackson wasted no time.

"The article!" he spat. "The one about Ms Wangai. You told me it was eradicated."

There was a long pause. "It was," came Mr Nakata's calm voice. "Why you ask?"

"Mr Hallman just referred to it!"

Another pause.

"What he say?"

"He said he read that Ms Wangai committed suicide."

"Impossible," Mr Nakata snorted.

"How do you know?"

"Because article was very small, printed in local newspaper in Dar es Salaam. It was interview with Ruth, the old woman working at orphanage. She say Academy had accepted Ms Wangai, but she disappeared. It never say anything about death."

Professor Jackson felt his blood boil. Shit!

On his screen, Dr Vella checked her watch. "Oh dear. Time flies, Mr Hallman. We need to move on. Why don't we start with you telling me a little bit about your relationship with your parents?" Professor Jackson closed his eyes and began to massage his temples. "I need you to do a little investigation," he whispered. "See if there are any other articles on Ms Wangai. Start with

Stockholm University library. Mr Hallman said he might have read it there."

"This is not good."

"You're damn right. Now get to work."

"*Hai.*"

"And, as always, keep it to yourself."

Professor Jackson hung up. He leaned forward, elbows on his desk and head resting in the palms of his hands. As far as he could tell, someone was feeding Axel dangerous information, and unless Mr Nakata found evidence suggesting otherwise, Professor Jackson would have to act.

CHAPTER 78

Staggering out of Dr Vella's office, Axel felt like he was leaving a battleground. It had taken all he could muster to protect himself from the doctor's snooping and prying. Certain things were too private to share with anyone, especially the Academy. Who knew when they might use it against him?

On weary legs, Axel walked out into the waiting room and found Nicole gone. She'd left behind a half-empty coffee cup and the remnants of her sweet perfume. He stood there, staring at her vacant chair, wondering what to do next. According to his schedule, he had a class with Professor Plouffe in twenty minutes.

Well, he thought and headed for the elevator. Might as well take a quick stroll around the block and clear my head.

It was a cold, sunny winter's day. Axel strolled down the sidewalk, made a right at the next corner and bumped into Mr Milton.

"Oh, sorry."

The concierge manager was standing with his phone in his hand and looked up somewhat bemused.

"Good afternoon, Mr Hallman. Out for a walk?"

"Yes, I needed some fresh air."

"I'm afraid you'll have to search elsewhere for 'fresh' air," he said, tilting his head in the direction of Avenue Louise. "I'm not too bothered though." Mr Milton held up the cigarette he was smoking, before taking a deep drag. He pocketed his phone. "How are you finding your time with us, Mr Hallman?"

Axel shoved his hands into his pockets and leaned against the wall of the building.

"It's nice. Very luxurious."

"I'm glad you appreciate it."

"It must have cost a fortune."

Mr Milton glanced out on Avenue Louise and took another drag.

"I'm sure it did, sir."

Axel nodded.

"How long have you been working for the E.K.A?" he asked.

Mr Milton gave him a forced smile.

"I'm not the one to remind you, sir, but is it wise to mention that name out here? One never knows who's listening."

Axel could have slapped himself. What the hell was wrong with him? Mr Nakata would've killed him if he found out.

"Well, I've checked and we're fine," he lied, not wanting a staff member to know he'd made such a novice mistake.

The concierge manager bowed his head.

"I'm sorry for implying otherwise, sir." He took another drag, threw the cigarette on the ground before stepping on it with his well-polished shoes. "To answer your question, Mr Hallman, I've been working here for fifteen years."

"And how do you deal with it all?"

"With what, sir?"

"The secrecy."

Mr Milton's eyes flickered between Axel and the world around them.

"One gets used to it after a while," he mumbled.

"Must get lonely at times," Axel pressed on. "Being so isolated, I mean."

"I wouldn't say so, sir. Working here is a way of life, and my colleagues are more of a family to me than the one I was born into. We may come from all over the world and be of all ages but we share the same peculiar experience and that binds us together."

"So it's always the same staff?"

"But of course! Confidentiality is everything to us. No one gets hired on a short-term basis."

Axel raised his head towards the sky in a casual manner, pretending to enjoy the little warmth that the late winter sun had to offer.

"It's quite amazing that they can keep everyone quiet. I mean with so many employees, not to mention the students, family members, and guest lecturers."

"Indeed." Mr Milton pushed back his glasses. "I'm sorry, sir, but I must return to the reception."

"Me too. Mind if I join you?" They began strolling back to the main entrance. "Fifteen years. That's a long time."

"It is."

"So you were here when Ms Wangai died?" Mr Milton flinched. Axel nearly missed it, but he saw it, and that meant he was on to something. "Were you there when she fell off the balcony?" he asked.

Mr Milton stopped short of the main entrance and shook his head.

"I'm sorry, Mr Hallman, but I'm not allowed to discuss other students with you. Not even if they've passed on. Now, if you'll excuse me…"

Mr Milton marched off and disappeared through security. There was something about Sarah Wangai's death that bothered Axel. He had a feeling Dr Vella hadn't told him the truth.

CHAPTER 79

TWELVE YEARS EARLIER

The view from up here was comforting. Sarah could see well beyond the white walls. She saw the river snake itself through the rice fields, carrying a couple of fishermen and their small boats down the gentle stream. In the distance, she glimpsed the ocean and watched it fade seamlessly into an impeccable blue sky. If she turned a little to the left, she could make out men and women in straw hats, riding overloaded bicycles on a narrow dirt road towards Hoi Ann. It was beautiful, but it wasn't home.

She drew a quivering breath and felt the faint scent of roses from the garden below. Of all the places in the Academy, this was her favourite spot.

"Ms Wangai?"

Sarah spun around. Mr Garner was standing by the short metal stairs leading down from the roof's helipad to the narrow balcony on which Sarah was standing. The old man took off his panama hat and bowed.

"I didn't mean to startle you, miss," he said, descending the steep stairs with obvious concentration. He looked so old and fragile that her instincts made her reach out to help him. He declined with a wave of his finger.

"No, thank you, my dear. I have no intention of feeling that old yet."

With a bit of effort, he made his way down on his own. They stood next to each other, admiring the garden while the sun tickled their necks and the wind tugged at their clothes. Nearby, hidden among leaves and branches, a bird sang to the world.

Sarah's eyes wandered down to the balustrade and ran her hand over its smooth surface. She knew why Mr Garner was here.

The other students considered the staff more or less invisible. To them, they were mere servants. But Sarah knew these "servants" both saw and heard far more than students and professors cared to understand. The employees talked to one another, shared information, and knew more secrets about the world within the Academy than even Principal Cunningham did.

Yes, she knew why the man was here, and she loved him for it.

"May I ask you something, Mr Garner?" she whispered.

"Certainly, miss."

"If someone held out an apple and told you it was an orange, what would you say?"

Mr Garner didn't smile or laugh; instead he gazed at the horizon, contemplating her question. "I would tell the person that I saw an apple, not an orange," he replied after a moment.

"And if ten people told you it was an orange, what would you say?"

"I'd still tell them it was an apple."

Sarah nodded. "So would I." She peered down over the railing at the stone patio several stories below. "But what if a hundred people told you it was an orange?"

The old man turned and looked at her.

"An apple is an apple, Miss."

"Yes, but a hundred people are telling you it's not."

Mr Garner pulled out a handkerchief and began dabbing his forehead. "Hmm. When you put it like that..." He readjusted his hat and tucked the handkerchief into his pocket. "I suppose I'd begin to doubt myself eventually."

Maybe it was the kindness in his voice or the genuine concern in his eyes. Perhaps it was the fact that he affirmed her own thoughts. Whatever it was, it struck something within her, and without warning, she began to cry.

"Oh my." Mr Garner placed a hand on her shoulder and she responded by embracing him, pressing her face against his chest. She felt him hesitate before he, with awkward tenderness, put his thin arms around her. "What's wrong?" he whispered. "Mr Milton said you were very upset when you entered the stairwell." She nodded. "You have to stop crying, miss," the old man continued. "You know the professors don't accept this kind of behaviour."

Sarah nodded again. She knew the others frowned upon her behaviour. Strong emotions, especially sad emotions, were unacceptable. She let go of the old man.

"I'm sorry," she said, snivelling. "I've lost my head."

"Just tell me what's wrong," Mr Garner urged. "How can I help?"

"I'm afraid you can't help me, Mr Garner."

"Let me try."

Sarah wiped her tears with the back of her hand. "You're very kind to me, but…" She couldn't make herself continue.

"Let me guess, miss. You feel that you're seeing an apple but everyone tells you it's an orange?"

Sarah let out a little laugh. "Yes."

The old man didn't return her smile. Placing his hands on the balustrade, he gazed out at the world around them, concern showing in the deep lines of his shrivelled face.

"So am I right to assume that this is connected to your questions about leadership?"

"Yes. No matter how hard I try, I fail to see what they see. What I call manipulation, they call motivation. What I call abuse of power, they call a necessity. When I see arrogance, they see pride. When I see humanity, they see weakness." Sarah shook her head. "It's hard, Mr Garner. Everyone tells me I'm wrong. They argue with me, mock and laugh at anything I say. I don't know what to think anymore. My heart knows I'm right, but my mind is questioning my sanity. "

Mr Garner closed his eyes and was quiet for a very long time. "You can't quit, Ms Wangai," he whispered at last. "You need to push on."

CHAPTER 80

PRESENT DAY

Mikael peered out the kitchen window, listening to his best friend whine about the amount of work he suffered.

"That's why I haven't called you for a while," Axel explained, his voice tired and tense. "The workload is insane. I'm studying around eighteen hours a day, including Sundays."

"Don't worry about it," Mikael said with mannered cheerfulness. "I got one of my regular visits from the Academy yesterday, and they told me you're doing well."

Axel paused.

"What visit?"

"You know, a visit from the Academy."

"No, I *don't* know. Would I ask if I did?"

Pouting, Mikael turned away from the window. He wasn't used to Axel being this edgy. Something was bothering his friend and he doubted the hefty workload was the main problem.

"I guess not."

"Yeah, well, what about these visits?" Axel continued with a mutter.

Christ. What was wrong with the guy?

"Well, every second week or so, a person from the Academy pays me a little visit to deliver a script about where you are and what you do; things I must say if someone asks me."

Axel was silent for a second.

"They give you a script?"

"Yeah. At least that's the official reason, but I think they just want to remind me to keep my mouth shut."

"Oh."

Mikael grabbed a chair and sat down. Axel didn't say anything and the awkward silence began to nibble its way under his skin.

"So anyway," Mikael said after a while, eager to continue their conversation, "I'm dating this girl. She's fantastic."

On the other end of the line, Axel cleared his throat.

"That's great, Mikael. I'm happy for you...listen; I have to go. I'll call you, all right?"

A minute later, Mikael sat in his small kitchen, staring out his window with growing concern. Axel had always been curious about Mikael's love life. Under normal circumstances, he'd pry and beg to learn more, but this time he hadn't even reacted.

CHAPTER 81

Days and weeks passed with extraordinary speed. While the trees outside Avenue Louise shifted from leafless to majestic green, Axel buried his nose in his books. He wasn't alone. By mid-April, some of the students were so exhausted they fell asleep during class. Their complaints met little sympathy from their teachers; after all, leaders couldn't stop leading because they're tired, and so the students pushed on.

They spent hours in their Speechomats and completed absurd obstacle courses. They studied military strategies, historical revolutions, and diplomatic power struggles. They had gruelling role-play negotiations; some of which went on for thirty-six hours without food, sleep, or even a break. They analysed world-affairs, business structures, and political parties.

With Mr Bell, they did voice training and practised ballroom dances. They studied art and famous painters such as Van Gogh and Monet. They learnt what colour clothing suited them the best and how to position themselves when being photographed by media. In addition to that, they also had to learn everything worth knowing about spirits and cigars.

"I don't care what your attitude towards drinking is, Mr Hallman," Mr Bell said one day, "when someone of power offers you a glass of whiskey, you will accept it with a smile on your face. Understood?"

"That makes no sense at all," Axel protested. "Whether I drink or not is my business. It affects no one but me."

"Don't be ridiculous," Mr Bell said with annoyance. "Drinking is an important part of building trust between rulers. A little alcohol will help a person to relax. It will loosen their tongue and bring out their true character. If you refuse to drink, you may be interpreted as hiding something, and no one trusts a person who refuses to let his guard down."

"There are other ways to build trust," Axel challenged.

"Indeed, and you will master *all* of them, including drinking."

Axel continued to object to the bizarre order until Mr Bell had enough and threatened to have him expelled on the spot.

"I'm not asking you to become an alcoholic," he snapped. "I'm telling you to socialize in a way that is expected of a great leader. You will do as I tell you, and that's final!"

One day in early May, Mr Nakata gave a lecture on fear. They were in Room C, which, on this particular day, resembled a deep ocean. There was nothing but blue around them. Beams of light filtered down from the surface through the slow currents.

It was a spectacular scene, and under normal circumstances, it might have encouraged an individual to search for wisdom and inner peace. Of course, peace was the last thing on Axel's mind.

Mr Nakata made his way around the classroom at a slow pace.

"Fear is weakness if not tamed," he warned. "As rulers, you must know how to handle it."

He stopped. The walls around them flickered once. Mr Nakata remained perfectly still, staring into the wall behind them. Other than the eerie underwater sound, the room was silent.

The students began to shift in their seats, glancing around the room with growing unease. Axel felt the tension build.

All of a sudden, the floor began to tremble. The ocean around them darkened, and a rumbling sound filled the room. There was movement on his right. A great white shark came at lightning speed; its jaws wide open, displaying rows and rows of knife-like teeth. As it reached the wall, it transformed into a hologram. The students gasped when the shark shot through the air, passing through Axel, Thabo, and a few other students. It reached the middle of the room and exploded into millions of tiny light particles.

An astonished silence filled the room as the hologram particles rained down over the students. Axel had stopped breathing. He didn't move for a few seconds and then, without warning, he began to laugh. He couldn't help himself, and, an instant later, the others joined him. Some even clapped their hands.

"Wow!" Edward cried. "That was awesome!"

"Do that again!" Layla yelled.

Mr Nakata clasped his hands behind his back and grinned.

"To make you strong, you now begin Face Fear Training, or F.F.T."

It was like turning off a switch. The exhilaration died, and the room fell silent.

"Uhh…What is F.F.T.?" Federico asked with obvious suspicion in his voice.

Mr Nakata's grin widened.

"A very good training."

The walls shook. This time the shark attacked from underneath their feet. Axel was close to leaping out of his seat. The great beast flew up from the floor only to disintegrate in the middle of the room.

"F.F.T. will help analyse your behaviour and prepare for enemy!" Mr Nakata continued.

"What enemy?" Axel asked.

Mr Nakata gave him a long look and turned to Julie who had raised a finger.

"*Hai?*"

"What will we do during the F.F.T.?" she asked.

Mr Nakata smiled. "It will be a surprise."

At that instance, Axel knew he'd hate the F.F.T. Mr Nakata was, after all, a man who always took his exercises to the extreme.

"Training will go on for few weeks," Mr Nakata continued. "You work alone with me. That is all I say. Now back to yesterday's discussion on guerrilla warfare…"

"This sucks," Dalilah concluded as they left the classroom an hour later. None of the others replied. They were all thinking the same.

CHAPTER 82

Axel was at the gym during their lunch break when Mr Nakata strolled in.

"Come with me," the man said.

Without a word, Axel put down the dumb-bells and followed Mr Nakata to the elevators. They rode down to the garage where Julien was waiting for them.

"Where are we going, sir?"

"Patience," Mr Nakata replied. "You will see."

They drove in silence for an hour and a half; first on back streets out of the city, and then the E40, heading east, until they came to a stop in front of a tall building.

"This is K2 Tower," Mr Nakata said with a smirk. "Fifty-two meters high."

Oh crap. Axel felt his heart begin to pound, beating hard against his chest as if begging to be released.

"Why are we here?" he asked.

At first, Mr Nakata simply looked at him. Then he did something very rare. He laughed. It was a strange and creepy sound, something between a cat coughing up a fur ball and the chuckle of a very hoarse Santa Claus.

"Oh, I know your greatest fear, Mr Hallman. Today, you bungee jump."

This is a good time to tremble, isn't it, something deep within Axel asked. He *is* talking about heights, after all.

"You look pale," Mr Nakata declared. "That is good. *Very* good. Now come. We must register."

They walked over to the entrance and were greeted by a bulky man dressed like a hippie, wearing a T-shirt that read 'Las Vegas Bungee Bunnies'. He sure didn't look like a bunny, nor did he sound like one. In a loud and annoying voice, he declared that he was their instructor, adding that before there could be any jumping, Axel had to sign a number of forms.

Regrettably, this didn't take very long, and before he knew it, Axel was standing in an elevator, heading up the tower, wearing a bright, yellow harness.

"Is this your first time?" the instructor asked, in an attempt to small talk.

"Uh-hu," Axel mumbled.

"Yeah, I could tell. There's dread in your face." Axel threw the laughing man a "please-shut-up" glare, but the instructor seemed incapable of reading it. Either that or he didn't care. "Anyway, you're lucky. The first jump is special, you know, like the first time you have sex."

"Then I should worry." Axel sighed. "My first time wasn't that great."

"All right, maybe that was a bad example," the instructor snickered. "This is *better* than losing your virginity." They exited the elevator, and walked up a narrow flight of stairs into a small room with large windows. "Okay, man. Let me just go over some stuff."

The instructor began explaining the jump in detail. Axel tried to pay attention, but he was too petrified to listen. He had to ask the man to repeat himself on several occasions.

Once the instructor had reached the end of his repertoire, he led Axel and Mr Nakata out onto the platform. Axel kept his eyes on the horizon. From here, he could see the end of the world, well, at least past an endless number of fields.

"Now I'll attach you to the rope."

The words made him drop his gaze, and, against his will, Axel looked down, out over the edge. He saw the road on his right, the buildings, and a pool far beneath his feet. Aah!

"Am I jumping into the pool?"

"Chill, man, you won't get wet."

"Then why do you have a pool there?"

"Never mind that, just keep your eyes on the horizon and jump. You'll love it, man. It'll make you feel so alive."

"Unless I die of a heart attack on the way down."

The instructor grinned. "Then at least you'll die doing something cool. Anyway, you're all set. I'll count five, four, three, two, one, jump. On jump you go…!"

"You done?" Mr Nakata interrupted.

The instructor turned to the Security and Defence teacher.

"Yeah, he's ready to jump."

Mr Nakata nodded. "Very good. Then leave us."

Axel watched the instructor frown with impressive vigour. "What?"

"Leave."

"Are you serious?"

"*Hai.*"

The instructor pulled a face that would have been comical under normal circumstances.

"I can't leave, man."

Mr Nakata clicked his tongue and reached over to pat the instructor on his arm.

"Ah, it is very easy. You take elevator down. Same as coming up. Just press button with 'G' on it."

"It's not funny, man. I have to be here for safety reasons." He turned to Axel. "This is a joke, isn't it?"

Mr Nakata folded his arms over his chest.

"No. We have special arrangement with your boss."

"Yeah…I know about the arrangement. You've booked half a day and you wanted as few staff members here as possible. I'm the only one on the compound."

"We have more agreement. You make sure the rope is safe, then you leave."

The instructor's jaw dropped.

"What…dude…I can't leave. How are you going to get him down afterwards?"

"Show me and I do it."

"Hell no! A tiny mistake and it's bye-bye to your buddy here."

Axel moaned and grabbed a metal railing for support. Mr Nakata stood quiet for a while, judging the man in front of him.

"Okay, you wait inside. Not out here. Call your boss. I tell you, we have special arrangement. When he jump, you help him down."

"Listen, dude, I don't know how you do things in China but here…"

With an aura of authority, Mr Nakata cut him off by simply taking a small step forward. "Do not insult me."

The instructor's face reddened, and with a defiant glare, he picked up his phone. The conversation that followed was loud and angry. It was in French, so Axel had no idea what the man said.

"This is mad," the instructor spat a moment later and shoved the phone into his pocket.

Axel gave a little shrug. You have no idea, he thought, and watched the instructor throw his hands in the air.

"I take no responsibility, whatsoever," the man grumbled and marched off into the building.

"I'm from Okinawa, *not* China," Mr Nakata snorted, and then, without further ado, he began interrogating Axel, asking hundreds of questions about his feelings and how they manifested themselves. Axel answered in single words, his body trembling, and his hands soaking with sweat. Around him, the world spun.

Mr Nakata fell silent and gave his student a little bow. "Good. Now jump."

With tiny, unsteady steps, Axel turned. Clinging to the railing, he looked down at the ground and stumbled back.

"Oh shit," he gasped. "It's high. I can't do it."

"Fear is only as deep as the mind allows."

"It's too high!"

"You are safe. Jump!"

"I can't. Please, I'll do anything else."

"A man who succumbs to his fears is easy to control," Mr Nakata lectured. "His behaviour, easy to predict, easy to manipulate, but man who faces fear is dangerous. No one know what he might do next."

Axel stared down. His heart was pounding with fury, rattling his ribcage like a death row prisoner behind bars.

"I can't breathe, sir," he panted. "I need air."

Mr Nakata considered the surroundings. "Up here is plenty of air, no?"

"Please! I can't do it."

"The feeling of fear is nothing compared to the feeling of failure."

They continued like this for almost two hours, until Mr Nakata spun on his heels and said, "Enough. Let's go home."

CHAPTER 83

"So did he confront Dr Vella about Sarah Wangai?" the young man asked, still ruddy and winded after their passionate rendezvous a minute ago.

They were in one of the master bedrooms at the hideout cottage in Lee Commons. A month and a half had passed since they'd last seen each other, and they had a lot of catching up to do, on both a physical and verbal level.

"I know he met with Dr Vella," Cat replied, reaching for her glass of water on the bedside table, "but I don't know what was said. I think Father's concerned, though. It seems Axel's interest in Sarah has been rather bland; not at all what we'd hoped for."

It was late and the other team members were long since asleep. Heat from the old chimney kept the bedroom warm and cosy. The young man tucked one arm under his head and stared at the ceiling.

"That's it? That's all we know?"

"No, there's more. The Academy suspects their security system has been breached, so they've made new alterations to their security system."

"So we'll breach them again."

"We can't. We don't know what changes they've made."

The young man grimaced.

"Isn't that information we can get?"

"No. No one but the EKA security team knows the set up. For now, Axel's in the hands of the Academy."

The young man felt a chill slither through his body like a cold serpent on the hunt. He rolled over onto his side. Gently he pushed Cat's copper-blonde hair away from her shoulder and let his fingers work their way down to her bare breasts.

"We have to do something," he mumbled. "There must be another way to reach him."

Cat pulled him close. "I'm sure there is. We'll know more tomorrow. Right now, I'm more concerned about Axel beginning his F.F.T. You know what…"

The young man stopped her with a kiss.

"Enough," he whispered. "No more talk about Axel." He kissed her neck. "Why don't you tell me about your book, instead? How's it coming along?"

"Mm…pretty good, actually. I should have the first draft completed by the end of this month. Do you want to read it then?"

The young man smiled and ducked underneath the duvet.

Cat giggled. "Ooo, I take that as a yes."

CHAPTER 84

TWELVE YEARS EARLIER

The automated air-conditioner hummed in a merry tone above their heads, sending cool air around the large office. Professor Jackson began tapping his pencil against the mahogany desk in a slow, rhythmic motion. He needed to talk to Mr Garner. Even with the air-conditioner on full speed, the room was far too hot for his comfort. Underneath his black suit jacket, the thin shirt clung to his back.

"Well, spit it out," he growled. "I haven't got all day."

Sarah sat in the visitor's chair, hands in her lap and a calm expression on her face. God, that annoyed him; her calm face. They were just halfway through the first semester. It was too bloody early for a student to be so confident around him.

"I'm sorry to bother you, sir," she began with her soft voice. "It's about our F.F.T."

Professor Jackson felt a drop of sweat trickling down the back of his neck.

"What about it?"

"I don't understand it. We face our fears just for the sake of facing them. I don't see how that will help me become a better leader."

"As I'm sure Mr Nakata explained, fear is a hindrance in your development. It makes you weak."

"But everyone feels fear, sir. It makes us human."

Professor Jackson put away his pencil and sighed loud enough for Sarah to hear his frustration.

"Precisely, which is why you must learn to overcome it."

"I don't understand. Do you believe leaders don't feel fear?"

For crying out loud!

"Of course they do, but they can't show it. It makes them vulnerable." Professor Jackson folded his hands in front of him. Maybe if he showed her a little more patience, she'd pay attention for once. "Listen to me. Fear is a virus. It blinds us so we see nothing but whatever we dread. It shuts down our creativity and strategizing ability. We become indecisive and begin to avoid actions that require us to face our fears. Fear is the beginning of the end, Ms Wangai. That's why your F.F.T. is a necessity."

Sarah seemed to ponder this for a while. Professor Jackson studied her tired eyes as they stared out his window. Maybe, for once, he'd gotten through to her. Then she blinked and gave him a strained smile.

"I don't think one can ever avoid being afraid," she said. "For example, it sounds to me like you're afraid of being afraid. This is a paradox, for, by forcing us to face our fears, you are trying to avoid yours."

Professor Jackson felt his anger flare and he used all his might to keep it in check. Who was she to analyse *him*?

"That's preposterous. Now, if you excuse me, I have things to do, but if you want to graduate, then you have to pass your F.F.T. It's as simple as that." He put on his glasses and turned back to the document he'd been reading. "You may leave."

Sarah didn't move. He could hear her calm breaths as he tried to read the text in front of him. A minute later, when he'd read the same sentence eight times, he threw the document on his desk and looked up.

"Why are you still here?" he barked.

Sarah still wore that pretentious smile of hers.

"I came to tell you that I can't do my F.F.T.," she said, her voice steady as always. "I can't spend an hour locked in a coffin. It is torture."

"Excuse me?"

"I'm claustrophobic, sir, but I'm not afraid to lead people. I'm sorry, but therefore I don't see the value of this exercise."

Professor Jackson became aware of a loud ringing in his ears. That was a bad sign. He could feel rage spread through his veins as his heart pumped faster and faster. How could he have failed so miserably? How, despite all her training, could this otherwise gifted student be so ignorant and arrogant? With this kind of attitude, she would never fit in with the EKA family. For the Academy's sake, as much as her own, she needed to change her mentality now.

"We decide what's valuable or not," he bellowed. "You *will* do your F.F.T. Now get out!"

CHAPTER 85

PRESENT DAY

Mr Nakata was right. The feeling of failure was bitter and repulsive. Axel had never been this disappointed with himself before. He could live with the fact that he hadn't jumped. Jumping off towers wasn't natural. What bothered him was the fact that he'd failed in front of Mr Nakata. Somehow, that felt as bad as failing an honesty test in front of God.

Thankfully, there were other students who failed their challenges that week, among them Izabella – who refused to lie down in a box filled with spiders – and Paul, who despite a protective suit, couldn't enter a burning house. Thabo was the only one among the four friends who completed his challenge on his first try.

"What did you have to do?" Axel asked when they met at the restaurant for dinner later that week.

"I prefer to keep that to myself, if you don't mind," Thabo answered.

Izabella scowled.

"Come on! We told you what *we* had to do."

"Yes, you did," Thabo said.

When it was clear he wouldn't say anything else, Izabella turned her attention to her wine.

"Fine." She shrugged. "This F.F.T. is a total waste of time anyway."

"Couldn't agree more," Paul muttered, leaning back as a waiter served him a grilled salmon fillet with salad. He glowered at his food and then glanced at Axel's plate, where a large wiener schnitzel and fried potatoes simmered in rich gravy. He made a face and sighed. "Anyway, we should be studying for our mid-term exams instead of facing our fears."

"Amen to that," Axel growled and shoved a gravy-drenched potato into his mouth. The mere thought of the mid-term exams made him shudder. Professor Jackson so kindly pointed out that all students had to pass their exams if they wanted to proceed with their studies. "How can we focus on anything until we've passed the damn F.F.T.?"

The following week, Axel got an opportunity to redeem himself. Arriving at the K2 Tower, the grey building looked nothing less than intimidating.

"It seems taller," Axel moaned while he waited for Julien to open the door for him.

"Maybe fear made you smaller."

Axel ignored the comment, took a deep breath and tried to picture himself making the jump without hesitation. This time he'd do it!

"Ah, you're back," the instructor observed. What a genius. He scowled at Mr Nakata in a pathetic attempt to look intimidating, then turned to Axel. "Want to give it another try, huh?"

Axel nodded.

"That's great, dude. You'll love it. I remember my first jump. I thought I'd die. I'd seen so many clips of people jumping to their deaths that I was scared shitless. I couldn't back out, though. My friends had already paid for the jump, so I had to do it. It was awesome. Afterwards I was high on adrenaline for hours."

"Thanks for the support," Axel mumbled, dragging his feet towards the elevator.

A few minutes later, he stood on the ledge once more. This time he'd do it, he told himself, but, in the end, it proved impossible. Two hours later, the instructor came out and helped Axel out of his harness.

"Don't worry about it, man. Bungee jumping isn't for everyone. I've seen bigger guys than you chicken out on a jump." He stood up and dusted off his pants. "Then again, I've seen small girls and boys take that leap without hesitation."

Axel glared at the instructor before he followed Mr Nakata down to the car. Julien stood leaning against the hood of the vehicle, smoking a cigarette.

"No?" the otherwise silent man asked.

Mr Nakata shook his head and that was it. They went home in complete silence.

Two days later, Izabella passed her test. She wouldn't stop talking about it. The day after that, Paul passed his. By the end of the week, every student but Axel had completed their F.F.T.

CHAPTER 86

"So did you hear about Mr Hallman?"

Nicole looked up from the file she was reading.

"Hear what?"

Mr Milton pushed up his glasses and scanned around the foyer with a glimmer of excitement in his eyes.

"He hasn't jumped."

Tired and jet lagged, Nicole watched the man. What in the world was he saying? She frowned until dread threw itself over her like an avalanche.

"He still hasn't passed his F.F.T.?"

"No. From what I hear, Mr Nakata is concerned."

Oh no.

"How concerned?"

"*Very*, I think."

"Can you be a little more specific? Has Principal Cunningham been informed?"

"No, Ms Swan." Was there a hint of worry in his voice or perhaps disappointment? Nicole couldn't tell. "Of course, if Mr Hallman doesn't complete his F.F.T. next time..." Mr Milton pushed up his glasses again and leaned forward. "We've all heard the rumours about Ms Wangai."

Nicole forced herself to turn back to the file she'd been reading. Under no circumstances would she engage in gossiping and she would *never* admit her concern for Axel. That would ruin her reputation.

Most staff members had a peculiar and somewhat ambivalent attitude towards the students. In many ways, they were proud of the youngsters and felt great respect for them. At the same time, it wasn't uncommon for members of the staff to struggle with their own subordination. Their sole profession orbited around the task of serving people who didn't give them a second glance. That sort of thing has a tendency to tick people off after a while.

Troubled by Mr Milton's comment, Nicole closed the file. Axel was different from the other students. He treated the servants with decency, which meant he greeted them with respect and thanked them for their services. It made him one of the more likable students in the eyes of the staff. Nevertheless, as a graduate, Axel would represent the Academy, which meant he had to prove himself worthy of such honour. On this *everyone* agreed, teachers and servants alike.

"I'm sure Mr Hallman will complete his F.F.T. any day now," Nicole said, her voice cold and hard.

"Of course! Of course." Mr Milton bowed his head. "I didn't mean to insinuate that he wouldn't. I simply wanted to inform you about the latest events. I thought you would want to know. After all, you have a…" he bobbed his head to his sides "…closer relationship with the students than most of us."

Nicole threw the file on the counter and gave the concierge manager a long stare.

"Indeed." She tapped the file with her finger. "I see Principal Cunningham is expected back tomorrow. Has his room and office been prepared?"

Mr Milton snorted.

"Of course."

"And Professor Plouffe's guest lecturer is coming on Friday from Singapore. He'll be staying the night with us. Is the guest suite prepared?"

"Yes, Ms Swan. It's all been arranged."

Nicole bent down and picked up her bag.

"Good. I'll be in my apartment if you need me."

CHAPTER 87

"Here again?" The instructor shook his head. "Dude, are you sure about this?"

Axel wanted to strangle the guy. Of course he didn't want to do it. It was quite obvious, wasn't it?

"Yeah, I'm giving it another try," he snarled.

And try he did. He tried so hard he almost fainted and fell over the edge. Unfortunately, Mr Nakata grabbed his harness and pulled him back just in time. That was unfortunate, because it was the closest Axel got to actually jumping.

"It would be cheating," Mr Nakata said on their way back to the car.

Axel didn't reply. He still hadn't completed his F.F.T., and once more, he'd shamed himself in front of Mr Nakata.

As the days passed, Axel grew increasingly depressed. When the other students heard about his failure, they began to make fun of him. Then Professor Jackson called him to his office to discuss the "disappointing performance". By the end of the week, Axel had reached a point where he was considering quitting. Maybe he wasn't cut out to be a leader.

"God, I hate his class," he declared to Thabo the following Monday. They were making their way to the elevators after having completed a two-hour class with Mr Nakata. "Security and Defence? Bah!"

"Is this because of the F.F.T.?"

"I don't understand the point of it. It's just torture."

Thabo shrugged, ignoring a bowing servant who, without a word, went back to polishing the floor.

"You must master your limitations," he said. "Don't let the fear control you."

"The problem is that I don't see the logic behind this bloody exercise. Okay, so I don't appreciate heights. What the hell does that have to do with leading people?"

"Try not to think so much," Thabo replied. "Just do it."

Axel snatched a leaf off a potted tree they passed.

"That's easy for you to say. You passed your damn F.F.T. on your first try."

He tore the leaf in half and dropped the pieces on the floor. He was exhaling his frustration when Nicole, elegant as always, appeared around a corner with an air of graceful sophistication.

"Ah, good afternoon gentlemen," she chirped and gave them a little bow.

"Hi," Thabo replied without much interest. He was about to continue down the hall when Axel grabbed him by the sleeve and forced him to stop.

"Wait."

"Why? Our class starts in ten minutes."

"All right, go. I'll catch up with you in a second."

Thabo muttered something inaudible before sauntering off towards the elevators. Axel and Nicole looked at each other. A moment of embarrassed silence appeared like an unwanted visitor. Axel popped his knuckles and shuffled his feet.

"So I haven't seen you in a while," he said.

Nicole smiled. "I've been away on business for a few days."

"Ah ha." Another moment of silence. Axel shoved his hands in his pants pocket. "Where'd you go?"

"I'm sorry, Mr Hallman, that's classified information, I'm afraid."

"I see." Axel shrugged as if he couldn't care less, but inside he worried. Nicole wasn't at all her usual, happy self. Was she upset with him? Or stressed? He pulled away from her gorgeous eyes. "Well...I've got to go."

Nicole stepped aside.

"Of course, Mr Hallman."

Axel hesitated. He was struggling to leave, but when he finally turned away from her, he felt her hand upon his arm.

"Good luck with your F.F.T.," she whispered. "I believe in you."

Axel felt his cheeks redden. He watched her leave in long strides and felt his heart sink to his ankles. No wonder she was acting strange; she thought he was weak.

CHAPTER 88

Despite the psychological pressure of not having jumped, Axel had little choice but to accept the fact that life within the Academy continued regardless of his troubles. The mid-term exams were approaching with gruesome speed and the teachers were quick to encourage what they called "a little friendly competition".

"Who'll get the highest score and who'll come in last?" they asked. "Who'll be the lead wolf and who'll be the black sheep?"

"I'm afraid Paul will come in last," Izabella whispered one evening when she and Axel swirled, or rather *tried* to swirl, on the dance floor, practising their Vienna waltz under the watchful eye of Mr Bell. "He hasn't been himself these past few days, and he's not studying enough. He says he's worried about his brother but won't say why."

Axel had to admit that he hadn't noticed anything, but considering the amount of problems that were stacking up around him, he had little time to care about anyone else. Nevertheless, the following day during lunch he observed a slight change in Paul's demeanour.

"These 'Case Crackers' suck," Paul whined with a pessimism that was uncharacteristic. "No wonder companies are willing to sponsor the Academy. They get to send us their crappy problems so we can work our butts off to solve them."

The dreaded "Case Crackers" were business problems, sent in by Academy sponsors every second week. The students had twenty-four hours to develop and present their solutions to Professor Jackson.

"Having a difficult case?" Izabella snickered.

"It's a bloody nightmare."

"What is it?" Axel inquired.

Paul exchanged looks with the others and poured himself another glass of beer.

"Never mind," he said.

"You know Professor Jackson wants us to solve these cases on our own," Thabo said with a low voice. "We must prove we can make decisions on our own."

"I'm not saying we should solve it for him," Axel objected. "I just thought he might want to bounce off some ideas with us. There's a difference, you know."

"Well, I don't want your help," Paul growled.

Axel shrugged. He didn't care. Putting on his most leader-like smile, he stood up and threw his used napkin on the table.

"If you don't want help, I'm not going to force you." He grabbed his suit jacket, ignoring the confused faces around the table. "Now, if you excuse me, I'm going to take a quick stroll before next class. I need to solve my own case. It's a real killer."

He walked away, wondering what the others were saying about him behind his back.

CHAPTER 89

TWELVE YEARS EARLIER

They were all staring at Principal Cunningham as he took off his small, round spectacles and rubbed his tired eyes.

Mr Garner watched him with concern. He had great respect for the man. The principal was more than ten years his junior, but displayed a knowledge and wisdom that was well beyond his years. They had known each other for seven years, yet Mr Garner had never seen the man so visibly exhausted. Perhaps the principal's life of relentless traveling, constant interviews, and endless seminars was beginning to take its toll?

"Thank you all for coming on such short notice," the principal began, looking out at the little gathering. In addition to Mr Garner, Professor Jackson was there, along with Mr Nakata and Dr Young, the chief analyst. "We have a situation," the principal continued, returning the glasses to their comfortable position on his prominent nose. "Ms Sarah Wangai has informed me that she wants to quit."

Mr Garner closed his eyes and felt his head drop forth until his chin touched his chest. You silly, silly girl, he thought. What have you done?

"I presume you've tried to convince her otherwise," Professor Jackson mumbled.

"It'll be useless," Dr Young said, wringing his hands in an anxious manner that made Mr Garner nervous. "If Ms Wangai has made up her mind, then we can't change it. We've failed."

"Don't be ridiculous, man," Professor Jackson snorted, "we never fail."

"Is there any way we can change her mind," Principal Cunningham asked. "Any way at all?"

The chief analyst ran a hand through his wild, disordered hair and shook his head.

"I'm afraid not, sir. We knew her integrity could become problematic. After all, she's a wild-card."

"We can't fail!" Professor Jackson exclaimed.

"I've done my best, but Ms Wangai is quite determined." Principal Cunningham sighed. "She wants to leave now, and we can't force her to graduate, you know that."

Professor Jackson got out of his chair and began pacing back and forth.

"The Seven will never accept it."

"I've spoken to the Seven," Principal Cunningham declared, "and we've come to an agreement." He turned to the chief analyst. "Dr Young, I want you to draft me a report, stating what you've just told me; that Ms Wangai is a woman of great integrity, whose mind can't be changed." The chief analyst bobbed his head in an anxious nod. "I also want you and your team to begin the process of finding us a psychiatrist."

"What?" Professor Jackson grimaced. "A shrink?"

"Yes. I've come to the decision that we need to evaluate our student's mental welfare during their training."

"Sir? We are supposed to evaluate our students *before* we accept them. Perhaps Ms Wangai wasn't meant to be a ruler."

Principal Cunningham's eyes hardened.

"Oh, I'm certain that if we'd reacted sooner, Ms Wangai's decision to leave us could've been avoided."

A tense silence fell over the room. Professor Jackson glared at the principal and Dr Young began fiddling with his pencil. Mr Garner dropped his eyes, wishing he was anywhere but there.

From outside the window came the faint sound of laughter, interrupting the quiet hum of the air-conditioner. The students were on break.

Principal Cunningham cleared his throat.

"Dr Young. Do you understand your task?"

"Yes, sir."

"Good, then you may leave. Let me know when your report is completed and you've found me some suitable candidates for the job as our new EKA psychiatrist."

"I will, sir."

The chief analyst got to his feet and left.

"We can't let her leave," Professor Jackson growled. "We're the Academy! We *never* fail!"

"Sit down, Professor," Principal Cunningham commanded. "What will you have me do? Force her to graduate? No. It's over."

Something died in Mr Garner's old heart when he heard those final words. Beside him, Professor Jackson stood stock-still for a few seconds.

"Sir?"

"Sit down!"

With a croaky groan, Professor Jackson slumped into his chair.

"This can't be happening," he growled. "There must be a way."

"We have our orders," the principal explained with diminishing patience, "and we'll obey them."

"But have you explained…"

"That's enough!" Principal Cunningham roared. "Now, Mr Garner, I understand that Ms Wangai trusts you."

"Yes, sir."

"Good. It's time to discuss our options."

What options, Mr Garner thought with despair.

CHAPTER 90

PRESENT DAY

Axel took off his jacket, rolled up his shirtsleeves and began strolling down the busy street. It was a beautiful May afternoon. The sun's rays tickled his pale skin, giving warmth to both his body and soul.

Hoping to escape some of the city noise and commotion, he turned his steps towards Bois de la Cambre. As he observed the people around him, his mind began to drift. These people had no idea who he was, but once he graduated…well, *if* he graduated, they'd all know and admire him. The idea tickled his ego. If he played his cards right, he'd be remembered long after he was dead. Hell, they might even name a street after him…

"Hello, Mr Hallman."

The receptionist, Miss Davis, approached with tentative steps and gave him a little bow. As always, she was dressed in her grey uniform, with the matching gold-coloured scarf. To Axel's astonishment, he felt a wave of embarrassment wash over him, as if caught with his hand in the cookie jar. Thoughts about fame and power were inappropriate. He was still a long way from graduating, especially since he had to pass his bloody F.F.T.!

Axel's reaction must have shone through, for Ms Davis eyes widened and she paled.

"Oh, I'm sorry if I startled you, sir," she blurted. "I thought perhaps…I didn't mean to…" She took a step back as if to leave and almost bumped into a passing couple. "I'm just getting Mr Milton a pack of cigarettes. I won't bother you anymore."

Axel guessed that Miss Davis, similar to himself, didn't get out very often and so he did something he'd later regret.

"I'm heading for the park," he said with his best, reassuring voice. "Do you want to join me?"

Miss Davis' eyes widened to the size of tennis balls. She glanced over her shoulder and then at her watch.

"Well...I don't think..." she stammered. "I mean..."

"Come on, I'd like a little company. If Mr Milton gets upset, just blame me."

Despite the discomfort in her eyes, Axel knew she wouldn't dare reject him, and as expected, she soon nodded.

"As you wish, sir."

They walked in silence towards the park. The young receptionist kept staring at her feet the whole time until Axel felt he was out walking a dog rather than strolling down the street with another human being.

"So, do you get out much?" he asked, desperate to find something to talk about.

"I'm afraid not, sir."

She fiddled with her scarf and then, just when he thought she'd say something else, she looked down at her feet again. Great. Axel sighed, very much regretting that he'd brought her along. Moving the suit jacket to his left hand, he began focusing on his case instead. The client was one of the most successful marketing companies in Europe. Until about six months ago, they'd never had any problems with their staff. Now all of a sudden, there were conflicts and disengaged staff. No one knew why. Axel had done a leadership audit but still couldn't figure out what was wrong. There were no new leaders and no change in leadership style. It was very odd.

"Are you all right, sir?"

Miss Davis's quiet voice pulled him back to reality.

"What? Oh...yes. I was just thinking about this case I'm working on." He noted her curious expression and it pleased him. "A company is experiencing a lot of conflict and misconduct among its employees, and I'm trying to resolve it."

"Sounds difficult."

Axel pulled back his shoulders and gave her a satisfied grin.

"Nah, most of the time these cases are simple. I just confirm there's a problem with failed leadership, give the client some advice and that's it; problem solved." He paused, realising he'd sounded a bit arrogant, and, for the second time today, he felt embarrassed. He wasn't the kind of guy who bragged. "This time, however, I'm a little confused. I can't figure out what the problem is."

Miss Davis's eyebrows dipped a little.

"So the company has a problem with their employees and not their managers?"

Axel couldn't help but laugh.

"I guess one could say that. But the managers are supposed to motivate and guide their employees, so it's still their problem."

Realising she'd said too much, Miss Davis's cheeks reddened.

"Naturally. I wasn't thinking," she murmured and stopped. "I better return to Mr Milton with his cigarettes. He'll be very upset if I don't return soon. Thank you for inviting me to join you, Mr Hallman."

She left with short, quick steps. Whatever, Axel thought, as he watched her leave. He turned and continued down the empty, dappled path. Strolling through the woods, Axel raised his gaze to the canopy. His mind began to drift again until, all of a sudden, a strong hand fell upon his shoulder.

"Keep walking," a hushed voice ordered him.

CHAPTER 91

TWELVE YEARS EARLIER

It was a nice and starlit night. The smell of grilled meat, wine, and exotic spices hung over the garden like an invisible fog. On a bench near a little pond, where swan-shaped lanterns drifted aimlessly around the black water, Sarah sat and moved her shoulders to a joyful tune. For the first time in months, she felt happy. She was going home.

Over at the stone patio, lit up by hundreds of small lanterns, the party was at its peak. The other students were dancing, drinking and laughing, unaware that she was leaving them. With the exception of Lorena, who remained a loyal friend, they wouldn't care. These days they didn't even speak to her unless they had to or wanted to scorn her.

Sarah turned her eyes to the pink ballgown she was wearing. It was the most beautiful thing she'd ever seen. It must have cost a fortune and she'd been overwhelmed when Mr Garner came to deliver it earlier that day. A gift from Principal Cunningham, he'd told her.

The principal was a kind man, not at all as stern as Professor Jackson. He'd spent weeks trying to convince her to stay; to do her F.F.T. and complete her studies. When Sarah finally convinced him of her feelings, he'd given her his blessing to leave. It would be the first in the history of the Eagle King's Academy. Tomorrow the teachers and students would be informed, and on Sunday she'd begin her journey back to Tanzania and her orphanage.

"So this is where you've been hiding." Sarah flinched at the sudden voice and found Lorena standing next to her, holding out a glass of wine. "I've been looking for you."

Sarah accepted her glass.

"And now you've found me."

Lorena sat down and took a deep gulp from her own glass.

"Ahh. Nectar of the gods." She sighed and smacked her lips. Sarah swirled the red liquid as Mr Bell had taught her and caught a scent of honey. Lorena considered her as she took a small sip. "Well? What do you think?"

"It's very nice."

"I told you." Lorena flashed Sarah a tiny smile. "Tell you what; let me grab us a bottle of this heaven in liquid form, and we'll spend the rest of the night getting pissed right here." Before Sarah could reply, Lorena was on her feet. "Don't go anywhere. I'll be right back!"

Twenty minutes later, Lorena had still not returned. Sarah sat with her now-empty glass beside her, gazing at the students on the patio. The women swirled back and forth in their fabulous dresses, while the men gave them their full attention. Sarah blinked. Maybe it was the combination of fatigue, wine and the warm night, but she was feeling a little light-headed. Leaning back, she took notice of a lantern above her head. Was it spinning?

The minutes passed and the dizziness worsened. Her eyes began to itch and she was feeling sick. Where in the world was Lorena?

More minutes passed. Sarah now sat holding her head between her hands. God, she felt ill. A moment later, she decided to lie down on the bench, hoping it would help.

"Ms Wangai?" A kind voice came through a haze. Sarah blinked, and through blurry eyes, she saw Mr Garner lean over her. She felt his hand on her shoulder. "My dear, what's wrong?"

"I don't..." She paused. Her lips and tongue were growing numb, and she was finding it difficult to speak. "Don't feel too good," she managed.

"Now, now," Mr Garner hushed. "Have you been drinking?"

"I...uhh..."

"Come, let me help you."

She felt the man's bony fingers gently grab her arm and pull her up into a sitting position. Then somehow she was on her feet. Leaning her weight on the old man, she stumbled through a narrow pathway leading around the patio.

"I...need doctor," Sarah moaned.

"Shhh," Mr Garner whispered. "Let's get you out of here before anyone sees you. It's not decent for a leader to be drunk."

"I'm...not..."

Sarah was struggling to think. It was as if her thoughts were pushing through syrup.

They reached one of the back entrances to the Academy. The door was unguarded. How odd. Where were the guards? She caught a glimpse of Mr Garner as he reached for the door. He was sweating profusely, and she could tell by his eyes that he was worried. Sarah felt herself slip out of his grip as he struggled to open the door.

It was a horrible feeling, knowing she would fall but being unable to do anything about it. That's when another pair of arms caught Sarah around her waist.

"Let me help," came a familiar voice from behind.

"Lo," Sarah slurred, and a wave of thankfulness washed over her. Lorena knew she hadn't been drinking. She would help.

"You shouldn't be here," Mr Garner said as he opened the door.

"I know," Lorena spat back. "But you clearly need my help."

Unable to object, Sarah was steered towards the nearest elevator. Her eyelids felt heavier than concrete and her legs tumbled beneath her as if they had a life of their own. At one point she became aware of Lorena who was whispering some kind of nonsense; *"I refuse to lose or fail, this is why, it's me they'll hail."* She repeated this over and over again, so quietly it was barely audible.

"That's enough, Ms De Paz," Mr Garner hissed as they pulled Sarah into the elevator. Lorena didn't reply. "You must return to the others. I'll make it from here."

Sarah sat in the corner of the elevator, her head against the wall, watching Lorena dry a tear from her eye. They watched each other as the winged doors closed, and, deep within, Sarah felt a sting of fear but it was so brief and so distant that it was lost to her.

The next thing she knew, a pair of hands grabbed her by the arms. These were strong hands. A soldier's hands, and they dragged her out of the elevator.

"There's no need for that," Mr Garner growled somewhere nearby. "We treat her with respect."

"A little late for that, isn't it?" a voice muttered, before hauling her away through a set of corridors.

Then she was outside again. A gentle breeze caressed her face, carrying with it the sounds and smells of the ongoing party.

"Do you hear me, Ms Wangai?" Mr Garner's soft voice made her pry her eyes open. She was on the roof balcony, her favourite spot behind the helipad. Beneath her, hundreds of lanterns shone among the trees. It was beautiful. Magical even.

Someone was holding her up.

"Do you hear me?" Mr Garner repeated. She stared at him, thankful that he was with her; it made her feel safe. Yet, something was wrong. There was sorrow in his eyes. Sarah had never seen him so sad and when she tried to nod, she couldn't move. "I want you to know…" Mr Garner swallowed and leaned in so that his mouth was just by her ear. She smelt his aftershave and felt his hand tremble as he held her. "Your orphanage will be taken care of," he whispered and gave her arm a light squeeze. "You are a very brave young woman, and I'm very, very sorry."

He pulled back. Sarah's legs began to buckle but a rough push forced her forward. She stumbled, let out a cry and fell over the balustrade.

Shocked faces saw her tumble towards the stone patio.

Just before she hit the ground, two words formed in her mind: *my orphanage.*

CHAPTER 92

PRESENT DAY

Axel did as he was told. He kept walking. He should be scared senseless, but he wasn't. The memory of Black Sunday remained vivid in his mind, and he couldn't help but wonder if this was another test. Regardless, it was important to remain calm and focused.

"What do you want?" he whispered.

"Have you heard of Sarah Wangai?"

Axel hesitated. All right, so the question ruled out a regular robbery.

"No," he lied, feeling a little more apprehensive.

"Now, now, Mr Hallman," the man snickered and gave Axel a push. "You disappoint me. Didn't your mother teach you not to lie?"

Axel stumbled forward. Son of a bitch! This was no way to treat an EKA student.

"Who are you?" he snapped.

"A friend."

"You don't act like a friend!"

"And you don't act like a man who's got a knife against his back." Axel felt something hard and sharp press against his spine. "Just be a good boy and keep walking, will you?"

"What do you want?"

The man kept his hand on Axel's shoulder, pushing him forward.

"I want to give you some information. You see, there's something you ought to know about Sarah Wangai," he replied. "Her death was no accident."

"I'm not following."

"The Academy killed her."

Had it not been for the knife against his back and the firm hand on his shoulder, Axel would have stopped dead in his tracks.

"Killed?" he hissed. "Why would the Academy kill her?"

"Simple; she did not conform."

"What the hell does that mean?"

"It means you need to think about it," the voice mocked. "But if I were you, I'd make damn sure I'd pass my F.F.T."

"Are you from the Academy?"

Behind him, the stranger laughed.

"If I was, you'd be in a whole lot of shit right now for tricking the Academy into thinking you wanted to become a leader in the first place. Oh yes, I know your little secret." The knife pressed harder against Axel's back. "Now my friend, you're going to continue down this path and keep your eyes on the ground. When you get back, you'll tell *no one* about our meeting. Not a single soul. If you do, you're as good as dead." The hand on Axel's shoulder released its grip. "We'll meet again."

CHAPTER 93

Professor Jackson stood with his hands in his pockets, staring out through the two-way mirror that made up the entire wall. Below, lounged around a table near the bar, sat Izabella, Paul and Thabo. They sat absorbed in their own work, all with their laptops, books and their cappuccinos close at hand. Where Axel was, he had no idea.

"So what's his excuse?" the assistant principal asked.

"He has no excuse." Mr Nakata came up and positioned himself next to the professor. "Axel blames no one but himself."

A man of honour, Professor Jackson thought with growing frustration. He turned and walked back to one of the black leather armchairs at the other end of the room.

They were in what was known as the Lounge; a cosy area nestled along the top, western wall of the restaurant. This was a place for teachers, a place where they could come to relax, drink, play some billiards or darts. There was a small but exclusive bar, tended to by staff members around the clock. There were massage chairs, large TV screens, a poker table, and even an old jukebox.

Professor Jackson seldom came here unless there was a game of soccer he'd gambled on, or, in rare cases, a student that he wanted to observe in the restaurant. On this morning, he'd woken with a peculiar desire to hold a few of his meetings here. He had no idea why, but he'd booked the room, dimmed the lights and now enjoyed a nice scotch to the tunes of the Beatles playing in the background.

"You know, I can't help but feel that Mr Hallman could make a fine leader if he just got his bloody act together," he muttered and picked up his glass where he'd left it. "There's potential in that boy. A bloody shame he's throwing it away with his bullshit questions, naïve ideologies and fear."

"Reminds me of Ms Wangai," Mr Nakata observed.

Professor Jackson winced and sipped his drink. Then, without thinking, he placed his right hand on his left forearm. Under the exclusive fabric, the scar began to itch.

"One week," he declared. "After that, if he hasn't completed his F.F.T., we'll inform Principal Cunningham." He leaned back and closed his eyes. "Crivvens. The mess we have to endure, huh?"

Mr Nakata didn't answer. He remained by the two-way mirror, staring out into the restaurant. A moment later, there was a knock on the door and Nicole entered.

"Good afternoon, gentlemen," she said with a smile. "I'm not too early, I hope."

"No. We're done." Professor Jackson pointed at a chair next to his. "Have a seat." Nicole sat down on the edge of her chair, her back straight and her endless legs held slightly to the right. He looked at them, imagining what it would be like to run his hand up those thighs. He re-focused. "How was Sydney?"

"Cold, sir. As you know, they're heading for winter."

Mr Nakata turned away from the mirror and joined the others.

"What about Mr Toby Harris?"

Nicole's smile faded. "I talked to him as requested, sir. He wasn't pleased. We've warned him twice already, but he seemed unable to comprehend the seriousness of the matter. Of course, he's eighteen years old and full of testosterone. Add to that a drinking problem, a loud mouth, and a desire to party; it's a terrible combination."

"Aye," Professor Jackson said, "but tell me something I don't know. I didn't send you to Australia to state the obvious."

Nicole bowed her head.

"Sorry, sir. Well, I decided to show Mr Harris the gravity of his behaviour by having him removed from the shabby apartment he's borrowing at the moment. I then took him to a luxurious beach house where he spent three days enjoying all the extravagance he could imagine."

Professor Jackson frowned.

"I didn't give you permission to do that, did I?"

"No, sir, but threatening the boy is obviously not working. I thought that if he got a taste of what might be if he keeps his mouth shut and lets his brother graduate, then that might motivate him to keep his silence."

"Good plan," Mr Nakata complimented. "He listen?"

"I think so," Nicole replied, pulling a strand of hair behind her ear. "We went through the agreement he's signed, I mentioned the money he'll get and he seemed eager to comply."

"I have little faith in that boy's promises," Professor Jackson snorted. "Mr Nakata, let's keep the twenty-four-hour watch on the boy. If he so much as breathes the slightest hint of what his brother is up to, let me know." He picked up his glass and nodded towards the door. "You may both leave now."

Nicole stood up.

"Yes, sir. I should let you know that Mr Milton wants to see you as soon as possible. He had something he wanted to discuss."

"Right, send him here."

CHAPTER 94

It was half past seven in the evening and Axel had been staring at Steve the Shark for more than an hour. He was trying to sort out his thoughts. The news about Sarah Wangai bothered him more than he wanted to admit. Would the world's greatest Academy kill people? No way. Absolutely not! Axel pulled at the tight skin beneath his chin. So why would the stranger lie about such a thing?

He let out a depressed, self-pitying sigh. First the events in the Chamber, then the F.F.T., and now this. Not to mention the damn mid-term exams. Life was just getting better and better.

At that point, the doorbell rang and Axel was surprised to find Professor Jackson fuming in front of him.

"Have you lost your bloody mind," the assistant principal roared. "You told a *receptionist* about your case?" He pushed Axel out of the way, nearly throwing him to the ground. He stepped in uninvited, then slammed the door behind him. "Jesus, man! The girl is a farmer's daughter, a brainless little twit who's here because her father is a friend with our dear principal! It's her first year here, and that means she's still considered a high-risk personnel."

"I didn't say anything specific, sir. I only said I was working on a case. That's it."

"It doesn't matter, you bampot! You discussed your case *outside* these walls. Do I have to remind you that you've signed numerous documents regarding confidentiality?"

Axel raised his hands in a defensive gesture, suddenly appreciating what it must feel like to be run over by a steamroller. "I'm sorry, I…"

"Sorry? A child caught lying is sorry. An employee who fails an assignment is sorry, but a leader *can't* be sorry! A leader acts and faces the consequences of his actions."

"I understand, sir."

"I doubt it, Mr Hallman. I truly doubt it!" Professor Jackson took a deep breath. "Why do you think I want you to solve your cases on your own?"

"Because as leaders we must make decisions on our own," Axel mumbled.

"Correct! Leaders are surrounded by followers who'll say and do anything to please their leaders. That's why they're *followers* and not leaders. You need to guide them, and if you don't know what to do, then everyone is lost. You're on your own, Mr Hallman and you can't trust anyone. I mean *anyone!* Not even me."

"Okay, but what do leaders do when *they* are lost?"

Professor Jackson gawped with an expression of clear confusion.

"What are you blathering about?"

"I've gone through my case and I can't find the source of my client's problem. Out of the blue, the disengagement and conflict surfaced. I've done everything you've taught us and I still can't figure out what the problem is."

"Argh! The problem is *always* inadequate leadership. If you can't see that, then you're not looking close enough. It's a matter of finding out which leader is the problem and in what way."

"Is it always that simple, sir?"

"Who said it was simple?"

"All right, let's say the global economy crumbles and people stop buying a specific product; is that still a matter of inadequate leadership?"

"What else would it be? How the company handles a faltering market is a matter of leadership, just as leadership determines how the company markets its product. Hell, whose fault is it that the economy crumbled to begin with? Everything comes down to leadership. I'm shocked you even doubt that, Mr Hallman."

Then to Axel's astonishment, Professor Jackson's eyes softened a little.

"If you can't figure out who among the managers is the problem, then find out who among them is the weakest link. Get rid of that person and give the client a few simple tips on how to motivate people. By firing a manager and giving some tips on motivation, you'll give the client a sense of direction."

"So you want me to pretend to know what the problem is?" Professor Jackson sneered.

"But you *do* know what the problem is. It is failed leadership." The professor's initial anger had subsided and he now seemed more troubled than angry. "You're not a fool, Mr Hallman, so why are you determined to act like one? It doesn't matter if you're smart or have great potential. Unless we're certain you'll make our school and our sponsors proud, we'll never let you graduate." He wagged his finger in the air. "You need to stop mucking around. Our patience is running dangerously low. You need to think well and hard about the situation you're in. The Academy never fails! Do you understand what I'm saying?"

Axel nodded. He knew a threat when he heard one, and even if he had no idea what the potential punishment would be, he knew better than to ask questions about it. Yet, when the assistant principal turned to leave, he dared one last question.

"Sir, how did you know I spoke to Miss Davis?"

The professor grinned.

"She's not very bright but at least she's honest. She told Mr Milton."

"And Mr Milton told you?"

"Aye, the same as he told me you're asking questions about the death of Sarah Wangai." Jackson's eyes narrowed, and when he spoke again, he did so in a cold whisper. "And that's what I mean about 'mucking around'. Ms Wangai's death was a tragic accident, one we're all trying to forget. You don't want to waste your time on it, Mr Hallman. You have more important things to focus on."

CHAPTER 95

In the days that followed, Axel's mood deteriorated to a new low. He was a failure and an embarrassment to the Academy. The other students pestered him with sarcastic remarks about his failed F.F.T. The teachers probably made fun of him behind his back, and he could have sworn one of the guards snickered at him the other day. He even avoided places where he might meet Nicole, terrified of what she must think of him.

It was Friday evening and soft rain fell over Brussels. Axel had locked himself in his apartment. After ordering up a pizza, he sat in one of his armchairs, practising his skills in reading micro-expressions. According to Professor Evans, this was an important part of their communication training.

"What people tell you isn't as important as what they're *not* telling you," she'd said to her class one day. "People can, and will, say anything to please you. The only thing they won't tell you is what they *don't* want you to know, which is why you'll *want* to know it. But here's the thing, people can't hide their initial reactions. If you ask them a question that they dislike or that shocks them, they'll tell you. Not with words of course, but through micro-expressions."

Under normal circumstances, Axel was pretty good at reading these subtle expressions. He'd put a keen interest in the subject, mainly for personal reasons. He was hoping to learn enough to keep his growing number of secrets and lies protected from the EKA management, yet since the beginning of his F.F.T., he was as skilled as a donkey riding a bicycle. He just couldn't do it, so he was considering giving up for the day when Thabo knocked on his door.

"I'm going for a walk," he declared. "Would you care to join me?"

Axel wasn't in the mood but there was something in Thabo's eyes that said his friend wouldn't take no for an answer.

"Sure, why not."

It was getting dark outside. The light drizzle continued to fall as the two men strolled down Avenue Louise towards the city centre. Axel kept glancing over his shoulder. Ever since the incident in Bois de la Cambre, he felt a little jittery about being outside the premises.

At one point his heart almost stopped when a tall man in a long, black coat bumped into him from behind. The man shouted a brusque apology and continued down the street, making a right onto *Rue Gachard* where he disappeared.

Thabo seemed unaware of Axel's nervousness. He walked in silence, hands deep in his pockets and his gaze on the ground in front of him.

"My people are a very proud people," Thabo began. "My family is perhaps the proudest of them all. I have 29 siblings. Many of them are older, so I can't expect to inherit the crown. Nonetheless, I'm a prince, the son of a Zulu King. Being a ruler is part of who I am, and I've known since childhood that I must never show fear or accept disrespect. I must always make my family proud. If I humiliate myself, I humiliate my family, and doing so…" He shook his head. "It is *not* acceptable."

This was the first time Thabo said anything private about his family, and Axel knew he should be honoured. It meant their friendship was evolving.

"I am not afraid of insects, rats, snakes, or lions. I fear no man and will fight anyone who challenges me. The dark doesn't bother me; neither do small places. I can stand on a ledge, hundreds of meters above the ground and I will not sweat. I don't fear death or what may come after. I fear nothing but one thing; humiliating myself or my family."

Axel looked at his friend, his proud and youthful face.

"Was that your challenge? To be humiliated?"

Thabo winced and nodded.

"I spent a whole day with Mr Nakata, facing humiliating exercises. I did everything from singing karaoke in front of a hundred laughing Belgians, to sitting in a corner begging for money." He shuddered at the memory. "I had to do many things, things I'll never talk about, but know this; no matter what Mr Nakata threw at me, I faced it with my head held high."

"To be honest, I wouldn't have expected anything less of you, Thabo," Axel said earnestly. "I wish I had half your courage."

To Axel's surprise, Thabo smiled.

"You do. You merely have to find it."

"I'm not so sure about that."

"Growing up, I spent very little time with my father; he was a busy man. But one day, when I was six years old, he took me to a neighbouring village. There was business to attend to and he let me join him.

"In this village lived a man, an odd drunkard who kept to himself and hated the company of men. He had the biggest dog I'd ever seen. It was an ugly thing, a beast that barked and growled at anyone who came too close. While my father tended to his business, I walked around the village and ran into the drunkard and his dog. When the animal saw me, it growled and barked. The drunkard was asleep under a tree, too drunk to notice. Realising I was no threat, the animal moved closer. Baring its teeth, it came closer and closer. I was afraid. I began to cry. That's when I felt a hand upon my shoulder. It was my father.

"When the dog saw him, it stopped. For a long time the two of them stared at each other. Then my father took one single step towards the dog and clapped his hands. The beast turned and ran. I'll never forget it. I was so proud and ashamed at the same time. My father, the king, had showed me how brave he was, and I had showed him nothing but weakness."

"But you were a child."

Thabo laughed.

"It makes no difference. I am a Zulu. A prince."

"Yes, but..."

"No. I mustn't be a coward. That day, on our way home, my father told me that any man who claims to be fearless is a liar. All that matters is how you deal with your fear. Then he gave me a word of advice. He said 'fear is nothing more than a simple thought'."

"A thought?"

"Yes. To deal with fear, one must learn how to put it aside. This challenge isn't about your fear of heights. It's an exercise in controlling your mind. This is what Mr Nakata wants you to learn, but you keep focusing on the jump, am I right?"

Axel nodded. "Shit, I start sweating just thinking about it!"

"That's your problem. You focus on what makes you afraid, which makes things worse. You must learn how to control your mind."

"And how do I do that?"

"By remembering that your fear is nothing more than a thought."

"Just a thought?"

"Yes. Occupy your mind with something *other* than your fear. The mind can only focus on one thought at the time, so focus on something positive."

"Like what?" Axel asked.

Thabo shrugged.

"I focus on the fact that nothing can stop me. Nothing!" He looked up at the darkening sky. "I think we should head back now. There's a storm coming this way."

CHAPTER 96

The sky roared and the man in the black coat flinched. He turned on the engine and cranked up the heat while massive raindrops smattered against the fogged-up windscreen. With some effort, he pulled off his soaked coat and threw it on the passenger seat. Outside lightning struck, accompanied by a ground-shattering rumble. God, he hated thunder, which was ironic considering his name.

Thor picked up his phone and dialled his boss. After only a ring, Smooth answered.

"Yes?"

"It's been delivered."

"Well done. Has he noticed it yet?"

"No. He was out on a walk with Mr Zulu. They just returned to the Academy."

"Then we shall see what happens."

Thor held up his cold hands in front of one of the vents. "I think Axel is genuinely troubled about his F.F.T."

"He should be."

Thor rubbed his fingers a little more, and then leaned back in his seat. After watching the rain against the window for another second or two, he closed his eyes.

"You're very quiet, Thor," Smooth observed.

"Well, you know I have my doubts about Axel. He's not strong enough. What if he doesn't jump? What if he doesn't have the guts? Are you ready to take the necessary steps to protect The Box?"

Smooth was quiet for a long time.

"Thor, what are you asking me?"

"You know what I'm asking, sir. If Axel refuses to jump, then he'll be useless to us."

Smooth let out a guttural laugh.

"You mean, am I ready to have him neutralised? My dear Thor, are you worried I'm growing soft?" He coughed and cleared his throat. "You can rest assured that I'll do whatever I have to do in order to protect The Box and its members. And I intend to do all I can to see the Academy exposed, even if time is limited."

"You didn't answer my question."

Smooth sighed. "Yes. If needed, I'll give the order. But you know as well as I do that, if Mr Hallman fails his F.F.T., we all fail."

CHAPTER 97

Cold, wet and shivering, Axel opened his front door. Despite the state he was in, he took a moment to whiff the air. There was a new scent hovering in his apartment, a scent so delightfully pungent that one could almost taste it. His body began to relax. Perhaps it was his talk with Thabo or maybe the refreshing run in the rain on the way back; either way, he felt...revitalized.

With a puddle forming on the floor beneath him, he got out of his drenched coat and hung it in the small drying cabinet built into the entryway closet. He placed his shoes at the front door so the house cleaner would polish them for him, then he pulled off his wet suit jacket.

Hold on. Puzzled, Axel leaned in and pulled out a sodden envelope from his coat pocket. It was a standard, white envelope; sealed with nothing written on it. The first questions were obvious; why was there an envelope in his pocket? Who had put it there? When had it been done and how?

For a few seconds he stood motionless, trying to get a grip on things. Then, with a quick move, he slid the envelope into the pocket of his trousers and with burning curiosity he hurried off to the main bathroom where there were no cameras to watch him.

Shivering, Axel undressed before pulling on his thick, black bathrobe. The Academy logo, embroidered in gold on the left side chest area, seemed to twinkle in the lights from the ceiling. Feeling his warmth return, Axel sat down on the edge of the bathtub with the envelope in his hand. Careful not to rip it apart, he pulled out a small, moist note and unfolded it. A single, handwritten word: Jump.

Axel stared at the note. What on earth was going on?

For the longest time, he sat paralyzed, trying to figure out what to do. Eventually, when his rear began to ache and the note had dried, he tore the damn thing apart and flushed it down the toilet.

CHAPTER 98

The day was cloudy and a little cold for the middle of June, but at least it wasn't raining. Axel and Mr Nakata were back on the platform. The instructor had his back to Mr Nakata as he attached the bungee cord to Axel's harness. The man hadn't said a single word since greeting them fifteen minutes earlier. Now he looked up at Axel with an ugly smirk on his face.

"Dude, why you doing this?"

Axel wiped his moist hands against his thighs.

"I guess I'm just stubborn."

The instructor chortled.

"You must be, for I've never seen anyone fail so many times and still return for more."

That is it, Axel thought, feeling his temper rise.

"Could you do me a favour and keep your mouth shut from now on," he said with cold composure. "It's extremely tiring to hear your bullshit when I'm trying to focus."

The instructor gawked at Axel.

"I was just…"

"I mean it. Just keep quiet."

"All right, I didn't…"

"Shhh!"

The instructor bit back the rest of his sentence and went back to work. If Axel could have seen Mr Nakata, he'd be surprised to find the man wearing a proud expression on his face. As it was, he didn't. Instead he closed his eyes, feeling his heart thumping against his ribs. No more failure, he thought. No more fear.

"Well, you're all set to jump," the instructor snapped and turned to Mr Nakata. "I'll be back in two hours to get him out of his harness."

Mr Nakata snorted.

"Don't get comfortable. This time it won't take long."

"Whatever," instructor snickered and left the platform.

Axel opened his eyes and took a deep breath.

"Mr Nakata? What will happen if I don't jump?"

"No jump, no graduation."

"Yeah, but what will happen to *me*?"

A few seconds passed without a reply. Then came a quiet, "No jump, no graduation."

Axel wiped his palms against his thighs and closed his eyes. I'm doing it for Talk Thirteen! Then with one last breath, he whispered a few comforting words; *I'm the role model who leads the way!*

He stepped off the platform and threw himself into the jaws of fear.

CHAPTER 99

TWELVE YEARS EARLIER

Professor Jackson was busy grading essays when Principal Cunningham called.

"I want you to come down to Mr Garner's apartment," the principal ordered. "Immediately!"

Professor Jackson dropped what he was doing, and a few minutes later he stepped into Mr Garner's tiny apartment. He paused by the door and took in the scene. The place was in immaculate order. It was hard to imagine that someone actually lived here.

"Close the door," the principal said. "I want you to see the consequences of our actions."

He was sitting on a stool near the wall, his fingers interlocked, and his hands resting in his lap. Professor Jackson shut the door behind him and took a reluctant step towards the principal.

"When did it happen, sir?"

"If I'm to believe Mr Nakata and his men, sometime last night. There's a note."

The principal handed Professor Jackson a tiny note. *Great leadership demands great sacrifices, but some sacrifices are too great to make*, it said in shaky, handwritten letters. The assistant principal sighed and looked up at Mr Garner, hanging by the neck in the middle of the room.

"He cared for Ms Wangai."

Principal Cunningham nodded.

"He did."

"It was the Seven," Professor Jackson mumbled. "We can't disobey the Seven. They gave us an order."

Principal Cunningham shook his head.

"There's *always* a choice, Professor. I think both Ms Wangai and Mr Garner made that very clear. You and I also had a choice but we chose to conform."

"I don't consider death a choice," Professor Jackson muttered.

"Who says death was our only choice." Principal Cunningham stood up. "I want you to organise Mr Garner's funeral. He has a niece in Cambridge. I'm sure she wants to know that her uncle has passed away from a sudden heart attack."

"Yes, sir."

"Mr Garner was also responsible for the...handling of Ms Wangai's body. Do you know if he completed his task?"

"He handed that task over to Mr Nakata two days ago," Professor Jackson explained while rubbing his temples. "You don't have to worry, sir. No one will find her body."

Principal Cunningham nodded and made his way to the door.

"I'll take it upon myself to find us a replacement for Mr Garner. Meanwhile, you keep a close eye on Ms De Paz. She was, after all, Ms Wangai's friend, and we don't want to drag any of the other students into this mess. Make sure she understands that keeping her silence will be...beneficial for her."

Professor Jackson felt the weight of the note in his hand.

"Yes, sir."

Principal Cunningham gave a sad nod and left. Then, when no one saw him, Professor Jackson hid his face in his hands.

Life at the Academy would never be the same again. The EKA had lost its innocence.

CHAPTER 100

PRESENT DAY

The thrill of having jumped was unlike any other feeling in the world. Axel felt invincible. If he put his mind to it, he could do anything he wanted. Anything! It was an amazing feeling, so powerful he still felt like he was walking on clouds when he entered the classroom the following day, whistling a little tune.

According to their schedule, the next class was communication, but instead of Professor Evans, Professor Jackson marched through the door.

"Morning," he barked and stomped over to the teacher's desk. "Professor Evans will be with you in a little while, but first I need a few minutes of your time."

"Now what?" Federico mumbled and Axel knew precisely what he meant. Life at the EKA was a life filled with sudden twists and turns. Whenever the students thought they knew what was awaiting them, the school would throw in something new, something unexpected.

The assistant principal regarded his class with the self-assured, eagle-stare that he mastered so well.

"Summer has arrived, and it's the time of year when most schools reward their students with a little break. I'm sure many of you long to go home. I regret I have to disappoint you." As usual, the man didn't look very remorseful, quite the opposite, actually. "You're not allowed to go home. There are too many risks involved."

Axel felt a sting of frustration. He *needed* a break. Just a week or so to recharge his batteries. The awkward silence of the students pressed against his eardrums, and a quick peek around the room confirmed what he'd expected; no one seemed surprised. This was, after all, the Academy.

Professor Jackson took in the students' lack of reaction with a satisfied grin. "Having said that," he continued, "we understand that you all need some rest. Therefore, we've chartered a plane, and, three weeks from now, you'll be heading for the green valleys of northern Italy. Tuscany, to be specific. We'll offer you a secluded farmhouse near the small city of Volterra. There you'll spend two weeks at your leisure, before the start of the next semester."

"Holy shit," Dalilah whispered in excitement. "I've always wanted to go to Italy."

"We'll post more information on Eagle Net this afternoon. Any questions? No?"

As if on cue, the door opened and Professor Evans entered. "Ah," she beamed. "I see Professor Jackson has told you the good news."

"I have." The assistant principal's face turned stern. "But there's one more thing I need to clarify. If you fail your mid-term exams next week, you'll remain here all summer, studying. Is that clear?"

"YES, SIR!"

Axel put on a bright smile with everyone else, but deep inside he worried. He wasn't even close to being prepared for the exams. The F.F.T. had taken up too much of his time and focus. Of course, as Professor Plouffe had pointed out many times, the great Hayato Sano had passed his mid-term exams without studying for them.

"He didn't have to," the professor had pointed out. "Mr Sano was a true leader. He knew these things by heart."

As the week progressed, Axel pondered if perhaps he too was a natural leader. After all, the world's most prestigious leadership academy had admitted him, and without any effort from his side. Moreover, he started Talk Thirteen when he was only a child. Surely, that was a sign of natural skills?

These thoughts, along with vigorous studying, gave Axel a degree of confidence. He would do well, he told himself, but on the day of his first exam, he woke up feeling sick of worry. His confidence had vanished and his mind had gone blank. The idea of breakfast was unthinkable, so he made himself a cup of tea and took his study notes with him to the living room. At the large dining table, he began to skim through his papers. Not that it helped much. His head seemed stuffed with sawdust. Nothing he read made sense.

An hour later, he wobbled into the classroom, feeling drunk on anxiety and too little sleep. He did his best not to show it, afraid to appear weak in front of the others. As it turned out, he didn't need to worry. Shortly after entering the classroom, Julie collapsed on the floor. A result of too much stress and fatigue, Dr Vella suspected, before rolling Julie out in a wheelchair for a quick medical check-up. Axel and the remaining students laughed their heads off. A *wheelchair*. Geez, even Axel thought that was embarrassing.

The doctor was right, and Julie returned twenty minutes later, pale and red-eyed, but determined to do her exam without complaints. As expected, Axel and the others mocked her savagely, but Julie held her head up high and did her best to ignore them. What else could she do?

The pressure of the exams, combined with high levels of anxiety and exhaustion, took its toll on the students. By the end of Tuesday, both Layla and Federico had fainted at their desks and were rolled out of class while the others laughed and shouted contemptuous remarks about how they were born to follow, not lead.

On Wednesday, directly before Professor Plouffe's exam on "Asian Leadership", Aseem, a nervous wreck, threw himself over a wastepaper basket and spewed worse than a fire hose. Of course, the others showed him no mercy and Aseem experienced a brutal bantering. So it continued. Cordelia developed some kind of stress rash that crept further and further up her neck as the days passed. It was disgusting and Axel couldn't look at her. Dalilah and Edward grew edgy and temperamental, while Izabella became cold-hearted and mean. No one could heckle others the way she did. Like a hen pecking seeds from the ground, she harassed the others until one of them, usually Dalilah, threw a tantrum, drawing laughter from everyone else.

The harsh attitude between the students, and the teachers' unwillingness to interfere, would have concerned Axel at the beginning of the semester. Now he knew it was all part of strengthening the students' character. After all, the students would have to fight their way to the top of the global hierarchy and fight to remain there. There were no excuses. Leaders had to deal with this kind of pressure all the time.

Everyone struggled, but Axel was determined to prove himself. He took one exam after the other, focusing on nothing else but what was next in line. He wrote his exams during the day and studied hard during the nights. He slept no more than three or four hours, yet somehow he pushed on, determined not to show any weakness.

CHAPTER 101

A week later, as the sun crawled down behind the horizon and warm winds swept through the busy streets of Brussels, students and teachers gathered in the restaurant for a ceremonial End of Term Dinner.

A nervous chatter filled the great hall, accompanied by the clinking of silverware and soft music playing in the background. On the wall behind the teachers' table, the Academy logo glowed, and below it were the words: "You are our future. You are our hope."

The meal itself was outstanding, yet Axel struggled with his appetite. He smiled, joked, and conversed with the others, but there was only one thing on his mind: the exam results.

He knew he'd done well. He'd listened to the other students discuss some of the questions, and from what he could gather, he was among the top three performers along with Thabo and Izabella. Of course, what truly mattered was who would snatch the top score. That was impossible to determine since one third of the exams were essays, graded as much on creativity and style of writing as on content.

Axel felt butterflies of steel fluttering around in his stomach. His dream, until his father crushed it, had been to become a journalist. He considered himself a decent writer, better than the other students, which made it quite plausible that he'd snatch first prize.

At last, when the burning candles on their table had reached their halfway mark, Principal Cunningham stood up. He'd lost a little weight since Axel last saw him, but other than that, he appeared to be in a fabulous mood. He gave a brief but hilarious speech, in which, with sophisticated witticism, he congratulated the students on having made it through the first six months of their training without losing their minds.

After a few minutes, when the students began to relax, the old principal fell silent. He adjusted his spectacles and picked up a gold envelope. "And now what you've all been waiting for: your results."

Without a word, he pulled out a card in the shape of the Academy logo and turned to the students. Axel held his breath, as did everyone else it seemed. The great hall was silent as a tomb. Scattered in the back stood EKA employees, staring at the principal with tensed curiosity. Under the table, Axel crossed his fingers.

"The results of the mid-term exams are as follows: The best performing student this semester gathered a total of 319 points out of a possible 350. That's an impressive score, so let me be the first to congratulate the winner...Mr Thabo Zulu!"

Cheerful applause broke out among the students. Lights flashed and hologram fireworks exploded below the ceiling. AC/DC's "Thunderstruck" began to play, and in the back, someone whistled.

Axel stared at the principal, engulfed by a new sense of disappointment that was so powerful it baffled him. He turned to the others and found them clapping with strained smiles and devious eyes.

"Well done, Thabo," Paul said, his voice drowning in the noise.

Thabo tipped his head forward in silent appreciation.

"Yes, well done," Axel whispered, his voice croaky and flat.

Izabella said nothing. She was sitting next to Axel, hands in her lap and her face calm. He was impressed until he, by chance, happened to see her small hands squeezing her napkin so hard, her knuckles were white.

"Now," Principal Cunningham said and raised his hands. The music died. "Ms Martins, you came in second, with 317 points. Also a very good result."

More applause followed. "Damn," Izabella hissed. "Just three bloody points from victory."

Axel didn't care. Aggravated, he rubbed his palms against his pants. Not first and not second? How was that possible?

"Third place goes to Mr Reed. You received 313 points. Well done. Ms Izzati and Mr Kamala, you share fourth place with 312 points each. Mr Harris, you got 310.5 points..."

Principal Cunningham continued down his list until, with unruffled arrogance, he informed everyone that Axel had received the lowest score of everyone. 283 points! It was like being slapped in the face by a wrecking ball. Axel tried to ignore the horrible feeling of humiliation, but to come in last…it was worse than being rolled out of class in one of Dr Vella's ridiculous wheelchairs.

At a nearby table, Cordelia and Julie giggled. Axel threw them a deadly glare but they just laughed. Beside him, Thabo, Izabella, and Paul exchanged looks. Axel knew what they were thinking. They were embarrassed to have him in their study group. He felt his anger bubble to the surface.

"Well, that's it, folks," the principal confirmed and peering up over the rim of his glasses. "You've all done well, but before we move on to the bar and get the mid-term party started, let's toast our winner, Mr Thabo Zulu!"

Axel stared at the glass in front of him. He was happy for Thabo but to come last…a soft hand slid up his left thigh.

"Relax," Izabella whispered while raising her glass in the air with her left hand. "We'll talk about it, but, for now, relax."

The tenderness in her voice surprised him. She ran her hand up and down his thigh. Then her lips curved into a cunning smirk and she gave him a little squeeze, dangerously close to his private parts.

Axel held his breath. A part of him was getting aroused, no doubt about it, but more than anything, he felt annoyed. What the hell was wrong with this woman? He'd just been humiliated in front of everyone!

Izabella withdrew her hand. Axel was trying to decide what to say when he noticed that, on the other side of the table, Paul was staring at him. Great. Their eyes interlocked; Paul emptied his glass and threw a pained glance at Izabella before looking away.

Axel couldn't take it anymore. Even Professor Plouffe and Professor Evans' rather amusing wiggle on the dance floor wasn't enough to improve his spirit. The others' sarcastic comments and jokes about his failure proved too much. He excused himself, blaming a bad headache, and hurried back to the elevators, leaving the party behind.

By the time he entered his apartment, the disappointment, shame and frustration seemed to smother him. He couldn't breathe.

"Shit!" he bellowed and threw his tuxedo jacket on the floor, kicking it several times and cursing as he did. Yanking off his shoes, and with impressive force, he threw them into the living room, breaking a vase of fresh roses and knocking down a pile of books from the coffee table. "Shiiiiit!"

He let out a deep moan and sunk to the floor. Exhausted as if completing an intensive workout, he leaned back against the wall and stared at the massive aquarium. What was the point of continuing now? He was a failure. A disgrace. The others would never respect him now.

Axel sat motionless for a long time until he, with great sorrow, had made up his mind. He would have to quit.

He was still sitting on the floor when his phone began to vibrate. According to an automatized calendar message, Axel had a meeting at the foyer relax area in ten minutes. Now who would want a meeting with him at this hour? On a day like this? In the foyer? All the teachers, students, and most of the servants were at the restaurant celebrating the end of the first semester.

With a bad feeling in his gut, Axel stepped out into the night-lit foyer. The evening receptionist curtsied and the guards on duty bowed their heads. Axel gave them all a quick nod as he made his way to the lily pond. No one was waiting for him when he arrived, so he strolled over to the water where he watched colourful fish swim beneath the surface.

He stood there, feeling sorry for himself. Suddenly there was movement behind him.

"Hello, Mr Hallman," said a voice so sweet, that, for the briefest of moments, his heart forgot its purpose. Despite everything, he smiled, and when she stepped up beside him, a familiar tingle dashed through his chest, stirring up emotions. She was more beautiful than ever in a sparkling, rose-gold gown, and he tried not to stare.

"Hi Nicole. What are you…"

"I only have a few minutes," she interrupted, "so you need to listen."

Nicole's directness and lack of formality wiped the smile of Axel's face in an instance. He tensed. "Okay."

"What I'm about to tell you must not be revealed to anyone. Ever! Can you promise me that?"

Mystified, and somewhat worried, Axel nodded. "I promise."

Nicole's green eyes bore deep into his.

"You're being punished," she began. There was a long pause as Axel tried to understand what she'd just said. "They didn't want you to win."

"What…? I'm confused."

"You did well, Axel. On your exams, I mean."

"What are you talking about? I got the lowest score."

"No, you didn't. You got one point below Mr Zulu."

Axel let out a laugh that sounded hollow, even to him. "Are you trying to make me feel good?"

Nicole shook her head, her expression deadly serious. "They re-marked your test. They went through your essays and stripped them of points."

Axel didn't move. "Are you saying they changed my grade so I'd come in last?"

"Yes."

"Why the hell would they do that?"

"Because they *can't* let you win. You…" Nicole spun around, eyes widening. "Did you hear that? Someone's coming." Without warning, she grabbed Axel's hand and leaned up close to his ear. "You have to conform," she whispered. "Your life depends on it!"

"I'm quitting," Axel blurted. "I've made up my mind. I…"

Nicole's face went pale. "You can't," she hissed and threw a glance over her shoulder. "You don't understand. You and Ms Wangai…" There was movement behind the greenery. "Please don't quit. There are things you need to know."

Then Nicole did something remarkable. She leaned up and gave him a kiss on the cheek; a warm, delicate kiss that triggered an explosion of wicked feelings within him.

For a split second they both stared at each other. "I...eh...wow," Axel mumbled, but Nicole wasn't listening. As if someone had pulled a mask over her face, her usual smile returned, her face relaxed and she turned with grace as a guard stepped out from behind the greenery.

"Good evening, Mr Hallman," the guard said and bowed her head. Without waiting for a reply, she turned to Nicole. "Ms Swan, Principal Cunningham wants to speak with you."

"Thank you. I'll be with him in a minute."

"No, Ms Swan. He wants you in his office immediately. He demands it."

In a dark corner of the Concert Hall balcony, the old man leaned over to his son. "I got a message for you from Smooth this morning," he whispered.

Below, the Royal Philharmonic Orchestra tackled a few gentle notes of the otherwise emphatic and majestic third movement of Beethoven's Fifth Symphony.

"What kind of message?" the young man wondered.

"You are to leave for London next Friday."

A forceful crescendo cut the old man off. Leaning back, he closed his eyes with a blissful expression on his face, letting the brilliance of Beethoven fall upon him. The young man furrowed his brows in frustration, but settled back to wait.

"You and Cat have an assignment," his father explained a minute later, when the music finally softened enough for the two of them to continue their whispering. "And it's a delicate one."

The young man shifted in his chair. He glanced around the hall, ashamed of the excitement growing in his heart. "Of course. You know I'll do whatever I have to, but, I must ask, if it's a delicate task, why aren't *you* going?"

The smile on his father's face faded and he leaned in even closer. "We have intercepted information about a simmering tension within the Academy management. It needs to be analysed."

Stunned, the young man stared at his father. "What kind of tension?"

"Sorry, Son, I can't tell you more at this point." With a discrete motion, he passed the young man an envelope. "Tickets are in there. Cat will pick you up at Amersham station at four p.m. By then she'll know the details of your task."

In the dim light, the young man accepted the envelope and slid it into the inner pocket of his jacket. With mixed feelings of nervousness and pride, he settled back in his chair as another crescendo erupted.

This was it. He was now officially part of the team that would change everything. The team that would start the revolution.

ACKNOWLEDGEMENT

We live in a world that glorifies the concept of leadership and individualism. It doesn't matter what field we look at, be it politics, business, science, arts or something else, success is often attributed to a single individual. This, of course, is rarely the case. Take the process of writing a book as an example. In its simplest form, authors offer their words and sentences to readers (or listeners) who, through their thoughts and imagination, turn these words into stories. Without readers, the story remains untold. So, with this in mind, I want to thank you for reading this book. Together we breathe life into the world of the EKA, something I couldn't have done alone.

Of course, this book is the product of many different forms of collaboration. Several remarkable and skilled people have participated in the making of this book. My wonderful wife Cindy has read the manuscript an incredible six times, each time helping me develop it further with her clever and insightful ideas. Henrik Beyer, my good friend and writer, has given me invaluable support and assistance throughout this project. The same is true for my good-hearted friend and agent-in-disguise, Anna-Liza Stojkovska, who, after reading the manuscript, has shown an extraordinary determination to get this book into the hands of those who might enjoy it. As any author will tell you, that kind of support is priceless!

My gratitude also extends to my father Ralph Monö, who continues to inspire and challenge me as a writer. He, like Christina Ross and Elisabeth Monö-Persson, are all avid readers and were therefore the perfect (though perhaps unfortunate) guinea pigs during the early stages of the manuscript. So were Adam Amberg and Anna Rex, who both have a unique ability to identify things that others tend to miss. This is a quality that they share with

Fredrik Reibäck and Håkan Ireholm, who read the final draft and returned it with superb comments.

Moreover, I've been fortunate enough to work with Shelly Stinchcomb, a phenomenal editor, whose witty, constructive and thought-provoking comments made the process of polishing this manuscript immensely educational as well as enjoyable.

I've also had the great pleasure of working with Donna Hillyer, who proofread my text and came back with suggestions on how to improve it further.

Last, but definitely not least, I want to thank my daughters, Zoey and Emmy, my mother Birgitta, sister Cecilia, parents-in-law, Kari and Ove, and everyone else who has not yet been mentioned but who has helped, inspired, challenged, and cheered me on throughout this project. You are all part of this book and for that I will be forever thankful.

Chris Monö
25th February 2017

Don't miss the second book in this series – THE BOX.

You can also visit **www.ccmono.com** for pictures, "behind the book" material, and exclusive information about the EKA.

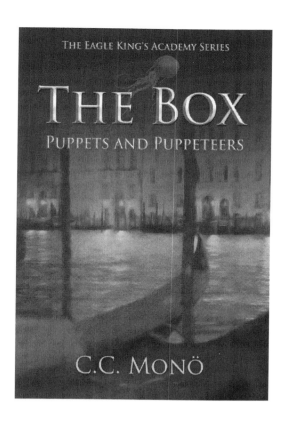

Printed in Great Britain
by Amazon